Totally Bound Publishing books by Cassie O'Brien

Single Books
The Girls' Club
From a Lady to a Maid
Ellie's Rules

FROM A LADY TO A MAID

CASSIE O'BRIEN

From a Lady to a Maid
ISBN # 978-1-83943-866-0
©Copyright Cassie O'Brien 2018
Cover Art by Cherith Vaughan ©Copyright July 2018
Interior text design by Claire Siemaszkiewicz
Totally Bound Publishing

FROM A LADY TO A MAID

Dedication

For kt-kitten

Chapter One

"Amelia. Amelia Brown. Where are you?"

I pulled my hands from the chill depths of the stone sink and wiped their numbness on the front of my pinny as I walked around the corner of the scullery into the kitchen and halted in front of the tall, bony figure of Ashton Manor's housekeeper.

"I'm here, Mrs. Price."

Mrs. Price peered at me over the top of half-glasses perched on her beak of a nose and sniffed. "Are the saucepans from lunch clean? The china from afternoon tea?"

The material of my dress cut into my armpit as I breathed in to speak. I pulled on the side seam of my bodice and eased the fabric away from my chafed skin. "Yes, Mrs. Price. I've just finished."

My movement provided some relief under my arm but tightened the material around my waist and I wriggled. Mrs. Price frowned.

"Amelia, kindly stand still when I'm talking to you. Why are you so pink in the face?"

I pulled on the front of my dress and shift to try to find a little room inside, so my chest could expand. "My clothes are too tight."

Mrs. Price looked at the stretched stitches on the side seam of my dress. "Are your laces tied at the end of their length?"

I nodded. "Yes, Mrs. Price. I can loosen them no farther."

"Yes, well...I believe it's your name-day?"

"Yes, Mrs. Price. I turned nineteen today."

"Are you sure? I wouldn't have put you at more than fourteen when I took you on as a tweenie maid last year." Mrs. Price's gaze moved down to my toes then back to my head. "Still, even I can see you've grown quite considerably since then."

"Yes, I'm sure, Mrs. Price. The day of my birth is written in the bible at home. I've grown this last year, I'm afraid."

Mrs. Price sniffed. "You can read?"

"Yes, Mrs. Price. I've had some schooling."

"Yes, well...you may have a larger dress and shifts today, as it's your name-day. Come and see me before supper. Now tidy that hair back under your cap and go and find Ellen to attend to the fires Above Stairs."

I wound a strand of my hair around my finger and tucked it under my cap. Mrs. Price walked away, her black dress rustling, and I let myself out of the kitchen door into the back yard. Cold February air wrapped itself around my body and I shivered as I trotted through damp mizzle to the sound of clunks on metal toward the glow of the oil lamp sitting on the ground by the coal shed. Ellen shoveled a last scoop into the second of two coal scuttles as I arrived.

"Ellen, you've filled mine for me. I thank you."

Ellen smiled as she put the shovel inside the coal shed and latched its door. "Well, as it's your birthday..."

I tugged on my dress and sucked in what air I could. "Mrs. Price says I may have another dress and shifts tonight. I can't wait. I can hardly breathe."

"I know. One set a year isn't enough, is it? You do know you've got to give the ones you're wearing back to Mrs. Price for the next maid who would fit them?"

"She'll be welcome to them." I winced. I gripped my scuttle handle with both hands. "Ready?"

Ellen nodded, turned down the wick of the lamp and grasped hers. I tensed my arm muscles, heaved my scuttle upward and followed her through the back yard toward the yellow glow of the oil lamp sitting on the kitchen window sill. Mrs. Price, sitting at the long, wooden table I scrubbed daily, looked up from counting a pile of linen napkins in front of her as we staggered in.

"Plenty of time before the dressing gong," she said. "Make sure you're finished and back Below Stairs when you hear it."

I followed Ellen to the green, baize-covered door that led to the flights of wooden servants' stairs that allowed us access to the upper floors of the Family's living quarters of Ashton Manor. Six flights later, I stood beside her, puffed and rested my scuttle. Ellen pushed open the green swing-hinge door that separated the realm of servant from that of Family and peeked around it.

"No sign of any of them," she said over her shoulder.

I hefted my scuttle and stepped around her onto the softness of red carpet, walked with her into a hallway of closed, polished wooden doors illuminated by whiter light from the cleaner burn of paraffin lamps suspended by chains overhead and my dress pinched me again.

"Thank the Lord. It's quicker when they're not in their bedrooms, and I could do with quick tonight," I puffed out.

Ellen stopped walking and looked me. "Your face is awfully pink. You stop here on the Bachelors' wing and just do His Lordship's. I'll run down and do the three Ladies'."

"Ellen, that's kind of you. I'll do your potty duty tomorrow morning. I'll be well by then, once I can catch my breath again."

Ellen grinned. "Fires in exchange for chamber pots? I'll take that trade anytime, I thank you. I'll meet you behind the green door on the half-landing when we've finished."

Ellen walked up the hallway toward the Ladies' bedrooms. I tapped on His Lordship's door, received no answer and opened it to find the side lamps lit, as well as the ceiling fitting. I left the door open behind me as I walked in, a signal to the room's occupant that a servant—other than his valet, Mr. Hubert—was in his room, should he return to it.

The pain shot through my ribcage as I put my scuttle down, knelt before the fire and stretched forward to rake the hot coals with the poker. My ears filled with a soft buzz and the flicker of the flames hazed before my eyes. I sat back on my heels and breathed in as deep my dress would allow when it dawned on me how close I had come to passing out face-down into the fire.

I looked over my shoulder and heard only silence from the hallway, so reached into the scooped neckline of my dress and unfastened the first few buttons of my modesty shift. My breasts billowed upward into a décolleté normally only seen on the Ladies of the house when dressed for a ball, but the cramp in my ribs eased and my vision settled. I bent forward and re-applied the poker, listening for the sound of a footstep or the dressing gong, glanced backward to pull the scuttle closer and saw a pair of male legs encased in buckskin riding breeches and soft-soled leather boots walk into the room.

I pinched my shift together as best I could with one hand, kept my back turned and carried on working the poker with the other, as if I hadn't seen a Lord enter the room, while I tried to think of a way to get my breasts decently covered again without my doing so being noticed.

"Will you be much longer?" he asked.

"My apologies, My Lord. I didn't hear the dressing gong."

"It hasn't been rung yet. I'm early."

The whisper of leather footwear on the move warned me I had no time to consider any discreet option. I weighed the idea of making a dash for the door, looked down at my chest and realized even more breast would be exposed if I jumped up to run, so decided that if I was to be discovered with more than an appropriate amount of flesh on display, it was not going to be while I was on the floor kneeling at anyone's feet.

I hung the poker alongside the other fire irons, stood and tipped the scuttle toward the flames then reached for my buttons and looked sideways at the boy, grown into a man, that I hadn't been this close to since I was seven years old. I saw no hint of recognition in his eyes, although they widened slightly as his gaze dropped to my open frontage. I recalled his attention to my face.

"If you wouldn't mind averting your eyes, My Lord."

A gleam of amusement lightened the blue of Damion's irises as he raised his gaze from my chest.

"I'd rather not. I believe I'm enjoying the view."

My heart thumped. I squared my shoulders as the servant in me sensed the offer of a quick tumble coming my way, and the woman I had been a year ago stiffened her spine and turned the offer aside in the manner I would have done then.

"Hardly befitting conduct, Sir. But as the fault is mine, enjoy away."

I put my hand on my breasts, pushed them inside my shift, refastened my buttons and picked up my scuttle.

Damion smiled. "It might have been more enjoyable if you'd permitted me to do that for you."

I didn't lower my gaze as I dipped my curtsey. "I thank you for your kind offer, Sir, but I believe I must decline. I do have a prior evening engagement that will amuse me more."

"With...?"

I stepped around him. "With the pans in the scullery that have just been used to provide your dinner."

I walked out of the room and Damion's soft laughter followed me, along with the hope that the sound of it meant the boy I had known had retained his sense of humor and Mrs. Price wouldn't be calling me to her room shortly to tell me to pack my box because of my cheek. She looked at me as I entered the kitchen.

"Ah, Amelia. Relieve yourself of your scuttle and come with me."

I put my scuttle outside the kitchen door, took a short breath in and followed her along the length of the drafty corridor to her sitting room. She walked over to a large cupboard and I let my breath escape as she opened the door to shelves of folded clothing.

"Try the dresses against yourself. Find one of better fit with enough give in the laces for farther expansion."

Mrs. Price reached in and shook creases from folded dresses and I held them against me until we found one that seemed roomy enough, along with two white cotton modesty shifts to wear beneath it.

"Let me have your old clothes back tomorrow."

"I thank you, Mrs. Price. I will."

Mrs. Price peered at me over the top of her glasses. "I didn't realize your age until you said it this morning, Amelia. It's not fitting that you're still a tweenie maid at nineteen. I have two positions vacant at the moment—laundry maid or under parlor maid. You've worked hard this year, so I will let you choose."

It took me no longer than ten seconds to make up my mind. A parlor maid's work was comprised of lighter duties than those in the laundry, but laundry maids worked mainly Below Stairs and out of the way of any visitors or house guests to Ashton Manor who might have seen me in more recent times than Damion and his family and would still recognize my face.

"I'd like the position of laundry maid, please."

Mrs. Price's eyes widened. "You're sure?"

"Yes. I thank you. It's the soap. I like to have clean hands."

Mrs. Price sniffed. "Well, if you're sure, pack your box and move out of the tweenies' bedroom and in with Molly. You may have one half-day a week to yourself without duties and an extra two guineas a year."

My heart lifted at the unexpected offer of extra salary, and I smiled. "I thank you, Mrs. Price. I like Molly. She was kind to me when I first came here, and two more guineas will be welcome."

13

Mrs. Price returned my smile. "You're a good girl, despite your tendency to laugh at odd moments, Amelia. Now run along. Staff supper will be served shortly."

I left Mrs. Price, ran to the kitchen, pressed my back against the wall for James and Bert to pass me with their hands full of jellies, blancmanges and a display of crystallized fruits to take Above Stairs for the Family's final remove and resigned myself to a last meal of pinched discomfort as the kitchen table filled for staff supper and dinner service came to an end for the Family. I sat beside Molly and pushed my bundle of new clothes under my chair.

"I can move into your bedroom with you tonight, Molly. I'm your new laundry maid."

Molly grinned at me, her smile wide but gappy from a missing eye-tooth she'd had to have pulled three months before.

"Well done, Amelia. Happy birthday. Shall I help you move your things after supper?"

"Yes, please, and my thanks, Molly. It will be lovely to share a bedroom with just you instead of being in with three others."

Mrs. Oates watched the table fill as James, Bert and Mr. Bennett returned from serving the dessert course Above Stairs, pulled a heavy copper pan from the warming oven, brought it to the table and released the savory smell of rabbit stew when she took the lid off and placed it before Mrs. Price for her to serve.

Mrs. Price sat at one end of the table, Mr. Bennett at the other, and I closed my eyes as he stood and intoned Grace. Mrs. Price ladled stew into thick pottery bowls and I dipped my spoon into one of the three hot meals a day that I now received, rather than the one sketchy offering daily that had been all my stepfather had allowed me before I'd left home and found my position at Ashton Manor.

The bell marked 'dining room' rang on the servants' board on the wall as we finished eating. Mr. Bennett stood, along with James and Bert, and they left the kitchen to clear the table and serve brandy to the men while Mrs. Oates poured boiling water into the lidded jug standing on a silver salver for the Ladies to make their tea. I looked at Mrs. Price.

"Mrs. Price, may Molly and I be excused so I may move my possessions into my new bedroom, please?"

She sniffed and inclined her head. "You may, but make sure you say the goodnight prayer yourselves if you are not to be present when Mr. Bennett says it here."

"Yes, Mrs. Price, we will," Molly and I chorused.

I let the green door swing shut behind us and Molly giggled as we ran up flights of wooden stairs. "I don't know about you, but it's not Mr. Bennett that's going to be in my prayers tonight. A kiss from James or Harry... That's what I'll be down on my knees and asking the heavens for."

I laughed and side-swiped her arm. "Molly! What about poor Fred? You were kissing him behind the stables last week."

Molly grinned. "And I'm going to kiss a few more, too, before I make up my mind who to walk out with."

I opened the door at the top of the last flight and stepped through to our servants' sleeping quarters — males and females separated left and right — in the attic space over each wing of the house. Molly picked up a nightstick from a shelf beside the door, struck a match on her Vesta box and lit the candle.

I turned left and walked over creaking bare boards with dim flickers of light to illuminate the gloom. Molly lit the way for me to carry my wooden box from the tweenies' bedroom to hers and put the candlestick on top of her own box standing beside her bed. She knelt beside it, pulled out an oil lamp from behind, lit it and blew out the candle.

"Molly, where on earth did you get that?"

She put her finger to her lips and signed for me to close the door. I pressed the door shut and she smiled.

"It's the one that Prince kicked and broke in the back yard. I found it and managed to put the pieces back together. The oil? Well, they don't notice if a little bit goes missing."

"You'll be for the high jump if they catch you."

She shrugged. "Most of us would be for the high jump if Mr. Bennett or Mrs. Price found out half of what goes on up here, but I don't worry too much. They were once at the bottom of the heap, too, and turn a blind eye if it suits them. I think that's why the butlers' and housekeepers' rooms are downstairs in the servants' hall. What they don't see, they don't have to act on."

My dress took the opportunity to bite me under my arms, and I picked up my new shift from the top of my box and laid it on my bed. "Will you unlace me, Molly? I've not enough room in this dress to reach around to my back with any ease and I can't stand much more of this."

Molly nodded and I turned my back to her. She pulled on my bow. I puffed out as she unthreaded my laces and dropped them to the floor then pulled my dress over my head and unfastened the buttons on the front of my shift. My breasts expanded forward and up. I forced my shift over my head, took my cap off with it and my hair—grown longer since I had hacked if off to shoulder-length the year before—fell halfway down my back. Molly laughed.

"Bloody hell, Amelia! Where have you been hiding those?"

I looked at my breasts, full, heavy and big enough to be out of proportion to the slimmer rest of me. "Don't. They've just got bigger and bigger these past few months. It's the food, I think. I didn't have much at home."

"Oh, I'm sorry. Could your father not find work or something?"

I pulled my new shift over my head, covered my breasts and smiled as I pictured my father as he had been before the mausoleum door had swung shut on his coffin. "No, not my father. A stepfather. A drunkard who fooled my mother and doesn't care about anyone other than himself."

"Gin, I suppose?" Molly tutted. "It's not just responsible for your mother's ruin. We had a sot in our village and his family ended up in the workhouse."

I gave a small, rueful smile as I thought of the London lifestyle that the wastrel had spent my father's money on while my mother, my sister and I stayed at home in the country, the wastrel's preference for our lack of company at our residence in Town made clear within six weeks of his marrying Mama.

"That and brandy, I think..." I pushed the memory to one side. "Still, it's better now. Look at me. I've got flesh to spare."

Molly giggled. "That you have. You'll be leading the men of the household around by their nose when they realize you've got a pair of them down your bodice."

An image of the elderly 'pig in a wig' that the wastrel had found on the marriage mart for my sister came into my mind, along with the accidental chances the prospective bridegroom had found to grope her breasts and buttocks while breathing stale breath into her ear as he made up his mind whether her young flesh was worth the price the wastrel had asked for on the marriage contract.

"If it suited me, maybe. But it will be my choice, not theirs, and any man that thinks any different will soon discover he's wrong."

I opened my box, took my thick winter shawl out of it and added it to the two thin blankets on the top of my bed.

"Amelia, you won't get the ring and the babies like that..."

"Good. I don't want either of them. You marry a man and they own you. I won't do it."

Molly pulled on the laces of her dress and stepped out of it. "But you'll end up a spinster."

I pulled back my bedcovers then tucked them around my shoulders as I lay down. "As suits me. I've got plans and they don't include being responsible for anyone but me—or being told what I may or may not do by some man, just because he's put a ring on my finger."

Molly climbed into her bed and wriggled under her blankets. "I think you might change your mind when you get one you like enough. I let Fred suck on my titties last week and it took all I had not to let his babymaker up my hole when he put his hand up my skirt."

I tucked my bedcovers tighter around my neck as a cold draft wafted over me from the gap beneath the window frame. "Well, no man is going to be putting one up mine. Well, not unless—"

"What will you do, then? Go so far and still have your fun?"

"Yes. I'll do that if it suits me. But I saw something the other day and there might be a way around the other."

"Like what?"

"Like, when His Lordship's finished with his newspaper and it comes down to us, I try to read it before it gets ripped into squares for us to use on the chamber pot."

Molly leaned up on her elbow. "You can read well enough for small print?"

"Yes. I had some schooling when things were better at home and I read an article in the newspaper about the new preventatives."

Molly snorted into her pillow. "Amelia! You didn't?"

"Yes, I did" —I plumped my pillow under my head—"and although I'd forgo the final intimacy rather than marry, still…there might be a way to have one without the other."

Molly giggled. "So, who would you do *it* with, then? If you could do *it* without getting a baby? Fred's cock felt a bit skinny and that's what sort of put me off last week, but James looks like he's got a decent package in his britches and I quite like the thought of his lips on my muff."

I lay on my back, looked out of our uncurtained window at the stars and tried to ignore the pair of amused blue eyes that floated into my mind. "Hmmm…maybe Harry. I quite like the way he can handle Prince when the horse gets a bee in his bonnet and rears up. Good shoulders, muscled flanks."

Molly grinned. "Are you talking about His Lordship's groom or his horse?"

I laughed. "His groom, although Prince is a rather stunning piece of flesh, too."

"He scares me to death. I'd walk another mile around the yard rather than go near that one when he's playing up."

I giggled at the stars. "His Lordship or his horse?"

"Both. They're both so big that it gives me a right old dose of the collywobbles to be standing too close to either of 'em." Molly sniggered and added. "Mind... The frontage of His Lordship's britches looks a good match for his mount, doesn't it?"

"Molly! We're not supposed to notice."

Footsteps creaked on the boards outside our bedroom door. Molly yawned and turned down the wick on the lamp. "That's the rest of them up, then. Night. We haven't said our prayers, but I'm still hoping for James' lips on my muff."

I smiled into my blanket. "Goodnight, Molly. Sleep well."

I turned my back to her and listened to her soft snores. A pair of blue eyes gazing at my breasts crept into my mind and my nipples hardened. My thoughts turned to a smile from full lips that might like to kiss and nibble and suck them, then to tight, well-fitted buckskin riding breeches. I slipped my fingers into the wetness between my legs and stroked the pulse of the nub hidden behind the soft folds of my sex as I imagined strong, male fingers doing it for me and sighed into my pillow as muscles contracted through my groin. I took my hand away and woke to the sound of the first bell of a new morning. Molly opened one eye as I swung my legs out of bed.

"Where are you going? That's the tweenies bell."

I shook my new dress over my shift, tightened the laces and took a deep breath in. My chest expanded with no restriction to the fullness of my breasts, so I tied the laces snug to my waist, pulled up thick, black stockings, fastened them with rag ties around my thighs and laced up my boots.

"I know, but I said I'd empty the chamber pots for Ellen, as she did extra fires for me last night. I'll see you downstairs for breakfast."

In the female washing room, I picked up the first night pot, carried it down the stairs while not breathing in through my nose and emptied it into the cesspit in the field away from the back of the house. Six trips later, I'd fulfilled my last duty as a tweenie and emptied my final chamber pot into the pit then walked to the scullery and scrubbed my hands.

Mrs. Oates stood in front of the range, stirring a pan of porridge when I walked into the servants' hall and took my place at the table. James glanced up as she set the pan on the table, smiled, got up from his chair and sat in the one beside mine.

"Good morning, Amelia. May I fill your bowl for you?"

Harry opened the door from the back yard, smiled and took the chair on my other side. "Good morning, Amelia. I find you well this morning?"

Fred walked through the green door and sat next to Harry. Molly walked through it after him. I stood and three sets of eyes flicked toward my chest then returned to my face.

"You will excuse me? I must speak with Molly."

I walked to the other end of the table, sat and muttered into her ear. "Hells bells! I know what you said but I didn't expect such an instant response."

Molly grinned and ladled porridge from the pan into two bowls. "Told you."

I spooned up my breakfast and followed Molly into the back yard and over to the stone outhouse of the laundry that sat at right angles to a row of horse loose

21

boxes. She handed me a bucket. "Sorry, Amelia. The laundry wasn't connected to the piped water when the Manor received its supply last year."

I shrugged. "I would have been more surprised if it had been, being as the installation of it was undertaken by men without the slightest notion of the processes required to get their clothes clean. Still, at least the servants' hall received a lavatory, even if it is just the one for all of us to share."

Molly smiled. "Well, we were never likely to get full bathrooms like those of the Family, were we? Such things aren't for the likes of us."

"No, Molly, they're not. I was more thinking of an extra so males and females didn't have to share or one in the attic betwixt the male and female bedrooms so the night pots and cesspit could have been dispensed with all together."

I followed Molly back and forth to the water pump in the back yard until the cauldron contained enough water for the fire to be lit beneath it. She added a block of hard, yellow soap, tipped a basket of linens and cottons into it and passed me a thick wooden baton. I pounded the contents of the cauldron with it alongside her until she nodded and picked up a pair of long wooden tongs.

"I'll get it into the rinsing sink if you go to the yard and start bringing in the clean water."

I nodded, picked up a bucket, walked into the yard and stopped to watch Harry back Damion's big, black stallion into one of the loose boxes. Prince snorted. Bonnie, Harry's own mount in the stall beside Prince's, whinnied and kicked her backboard. Harry secured Prince's halter, stepped sideways to soothe Bonnie and Prince reared to the length of his holding rope. I shook my head, walked over to the feisty stallion, put my bucket down and grabbed his head collar.

"Stop that at once, Sir, if you please."

Prince tossed his head and tried to shake off my hand. I firmed up my voice and held him tighter. "I said, at once, Sir."

Prince put his head down and I blew my breath over and up each of his nostrils. He snorted, flapped his lips and nuzzled the velvet of them onto my shoulder. I stroked his cheek and whispered into his ear. "Stop it. You make her nervous. She's not ready for you yet and you know it."

Prince snorted and chunked his teeth. I blew over his nose and kissed between his nostrils.

"You have quite a way with the beasts, Amelia," Harry said.

"I've always been able to calm them if I let them smell my breath and whisper into their ear. I don't know why."

"Horse whispering. No one knows how it works." Harry smiled. "You look very pretty this morning. The stable will be full of different mounts when the house guests arrive in a couple of days. We could take a walk over there together on Friday if you would like to see them?"

I looked at Harry, chestnut hair thick on his head, brown eyes and all his own teeth behind lips that might be worth a kiss, and smiled back at him. "Maybe I will, if my duties permit."

Harry glanced over my shoulder and straightened his face. "His Lordship..." he warned.

"What? Here in the yard?" I asked.

"He mounts here when it suits him, rather than wait at the front of the house."

I nodded, picked up my bucket, bobbed my curtsey on my way to the pump and walked quicker as my body responded with hardened nipples and a ripple through my groin to Damion's brief glance at what my new dress made more obvious than just a few unfastened buttons. I turned my back to the yard as I pumped and didn't look around again until hoofbeats sounded behind me, then took the water to the laundry. Molly rinsed the soap from the laundry and I carried more buckets of cold water back and forth until the suds were gone.

"That's the lunch bell," she said, as no more soap bubbles appeared in the water. "Let's go in. We can mangle this and get it up on the drying lines after."

A helping of mutton pie later, I passed the wet washing through the rollers of the mangle and Molly stacked it into two baskets. I followed her to a field behind the laundry, where trees and hedges provided the means to suspend rope lines to dry the washing and kept the Family's intimate items from being on public display, even when the lines were propped up with a forked wooden pole. The wind caught the skirt of my dress as we finished pegging the washing to the lines and I laughed as it lifted around my thighs.

Molly giggled. "Careful, Amelia. That was nearly your arse on show there."

I twirled, spun into the wind and smiled as it rushed between my legs and cooled my thighs. "There's no one here to see it, apart from you and me."

Molly giggled again. "I'm glad you're here and not Rosie. I don't think I laughed once when I worked with her."

I captured my skirt and pushed it toward my ankles. "As you said last night, what the eyes don't see, they can't act on. Come on. I'll race you. The last one back to the laundry has to make eyes and wink at Mr. Bennett during supper tonight."

I raced off with Molly two steps behind me but she beat me to the laundry door by more than a yard. I took my place beside her at the table at supper, smiled at Harry when he took the chair on the other side of me and muttered to her, "I'm going to do it straight after Grace."

Molly nudged my arm. "You don't have to. I won't hold you to it."

"A wager's a wager."

Mrs. Oates set a pan of beef stew in front of Mrs. Price. Mr. Bennett stood and we bowed our heads. I raised mine toward him as he intoned his Amen, summoned up a wide-eyed sneeze behind my hand and winked my eye as if clearing a little dust from it. Mrs. Price cleared her throat.

"Amelia, your handkerchief, if you please."

"Sorry, Mrs. Price."

I pulled a piece of linen out of my sleeve and rubbed it under my nostrils. Molly grinned as she passed bowls of stew on and up our side of the table. Harry offered me the breadboard. I took a slice and passed the board on to Molly.

"Did you have a nice time pegging out this afternoon?" he said.

I looked at the smile lighting his eyes. "How do you know? Where were you? There was only me and Molly in the drying yard."

Harry grinned. "You get a good view over the hedges when you're mounted, especially those that border the drying yard, if you happen to be cantering over the rise of Twenty-Acre Field on the way back from Home Farm."

I smiled and dropped my voice. "Enjoy what was on show then, did you?"

Harry leaned closer and lowered his own voice. "I certainly did, but I wasn't riding on my own, was I?"

I shrugged. "I don't suppose a flash of female leg is anything he hasn't seen before, do you?"

Harry smiled. "I wouldn't know. He's never done any lady-visiting in my company and Mr. Hubert is as tight-lipped as they come on the subject of him, but I wouldn't say he looks the type to live like a monk."

Ellen, seated on Harry's other side, leaned closer and whispered, "Don't forget Nell found Mrs. Wroithsley's chemise tucked down the side of his bedroom chair at Christmas. And last weekend when Lord and Lady Shelling came to stay...?"

Harry and I nodded.

"She's done her heir and a spare, too, and I found one silk stocking at the bottom of his bed when I changed his linen."

Molly nudged me as Mr. Bennett stood and cleared his throat.

"Ladies and gentlemen. I have an announcement to make."

He puffed out his chest. "Our house guests arrive in two days and it is my great pleasure to tell you that I have been given permission to announce His Lordship's forthcoming marriage to The Lady Elizabeth Wellingham of Sunnington Castle, who will be one of the party. The notice was placed in *The Times* newspaper today."

I swallowed a choke at the bride's name as Mr. Bennett put his hands together and the table joined in before he carried on speaking.

"I am sure we will all do our best over the following days to ensure our new Mistress will be suitably impressed with her staff. A dance will be held to celebrate the occasion on Saturday, and in honor of this special event—and providing there is no disruption to the service upstairs—we have permission to hold our own jig."

The table didn't wait for Mr. Bennett's hands and a burst of spontaneous applause rang out until he rapped his knuckles on the tabletop and we stopped.

"As I said...so long as I am satisfied that our new Mistress will be impressed with how we perform our duties here at Ashton Manor."

I whispered to Molly as the rest of the table sat straighter and moderated their voices. "What will we dance to, Molly?"

"Mr. Robinson that sees to the rose garden but doesn't live in will bring his fiddle and James is a dab hand on the spoons," she whispered back.

James leaned in on Molly's other side. "And you, Moll. You get a pretty good tune out of that washboard."

Molly's cheeks tinted pink. "Yes, well..."

"But you'll take a dance with me when we're not playing?"

Molly's cheeks turned pinker and she nodded.

Chapter Two

The house worked with more purpose over the next two days until windows and mirrors sparkled, furniture gleamed and spiders had been whisked away from the corners of guest rooms not serviced on a daily basis. I spat on my iron, watched the spittle dissolve and plunged it into the armpit of Damion's linen shirt. Molly took the shirt from me when I finished with the iron, folded it and placed it on a pile of laundry already completed.

"That's the lot. Get your cap on and we'll get it upstairs to their rooms."

I secured a cap over the pinned bun of my hair as Molly did the same. Molly held her arms out and I placed the pile of clean linens onto them then preceded her to hold doors open for her to pass through. Miss Croker took the layer of the Ladies' smalls, chemises and petticoats I passed to her at the Dowager's door and I walked ahead of Molly toward the Bachelors' rooms. She nudged my arm with her elbow as we stood outside Damion's door.

"Will you go in first if he's in there, please? Up close he makes my knees shake. There's just so much of him," she explained.

"Won't Mr. Hubert be in there this time of day?" I asked.

"I hope so. We can just hand this over at the door if he is."

I patted Molly's arm. "Don't worry. If he's in there on his own, I'll walk quick. You walk close behind me. We can be in and out in less than a minute." I knocked. Mr. Hubert didn't answer. Damion did.

"Come in."

I depressed the door handle and looked over my shoulder. "In, bob, look straight ahead, quick march to his dressing room, put the pile on the daybed, quick march back out. Ready?"

Molly nodded. I opened the door and stepped forward with Molly one pace behind me. Damion, sitting behind his desk, looked up as we bobbed in unison, turned with military precision and quick-walked to his dressing room door, eyes front. I opened it. Molly marched past me and laid her burden on the daybed. I closed the door as she took her position behind me. We'd nearly made it all the way to the bedroom door before Damion spoke.

"Wait a moment, if you please."

I turned to face the desk. Molly clutched the back of my dress and stood to the side of me, shielded by my shoulder.

"I have a message to be delivered to Bennett." Damion looked at me. "If you would wait while I write it." Then around me to Molly. "You are excused. I thank you."

Molly fled. Damion frowned at Molly's back as she sped out of the door. "Why do they do that? I was courteous and polite."

I took a deeper breath in when Damion looked at me and my nipples hardened. I hid my attraction behind my reply as Lady Henrietta and the assurance of more equal social standing. "Because you are a man of large proportions, Molly says you make her knees shake because there's just so much of you."

Damion's eyes lightened, a gleam of amusement alive in them again. "That is plain speaking. I don't make your knees shake, then?"

I permitted Henrietta to reply with a small, false sigh. "Sadly not. But do not take the blame to yourself. The gift of feminine sensibility is not mine. I'm sure I would tremble quite delightfully in your presence if it were."

Damion smiled, near-perfect white teeth to hint of sweet breath should his lips ever be near mine. I breathed in a little deeper and took my thoughts back in hand as he said, "So, in the light of that answer, may I ask a question of my own?"

"You may."

"Why did you have your shift unbuttoned if you were not seeking my attentions?"

I flicked my gaze downward, rested it on my chest then returned it to Damion's face. "Certain areas of my anatomy have expanded quite considerably of late. My clothes had become overtight. I nearly fainted when their constriction and the heat from the coals caught me. I needed to draw breath and released my buttons to allow myself to do so."

Damion's mouth twitched. "Ah... Then my apologies for my misunderstanding, and as long as we are indulging in a little plain-speaking, may I say that, poor defense though it is, as well as females running away, I do occasionally get offers I would accept."

I looked at the form and face of the man in front of me, thought of Lady Shelling's stocking and smiled. "Yes, I know you do. May I have your note? Molly will be waiting on the back stairs for me."

Damion dipped his nib, scratched it across the paper, blotted it dry then held the note out for me to take. I hesitated.

"You should seal it if it contains any information you would not like me to see."

"No, it is but a simple inquiry. You read fluently enough to be able to decipher my hand?"

I nodded and caught sight of the name of a French wine. "And also French, although not as fluently."

"You are well educated, then. Where were you schooled?"

I took the note from Damion's hand. "That, with my apologies, is where my plain speaking must end. I might find myself obliged to lie to you if you probe further and that would not sit easily on my conscience."

"Then, as you request, I will refrain from further inquiry. To force you to lie would not sit easily on mine, either."

I dipped my curtsey. "By your leave?"

Damion nodded. I walked out of his room and found Molly on the half-landing as I pushed through the green door.

"Amelia, you've been gone an age. What took so long?"

I sidestepped the content of my conversation. "It hasn't been that long. He had to write the note then let the ink dry. Let's get it to Mr. Bennett."

I began to read the note as Molly followed me down the stairs.

"You are lucky to be able to read, Amelia. What does it say?"

I read it through.

Oblige me with your reassurance that the quantity of Le Chateaux Moulin de la Rosé we have in the cellar is sufficient for Saturday.

"It's about whether they have enough of a pink wine for the dance."

Molly jumped down the stairs two at a time. "I can't wait for Saturday, can you? James has asked me to dance and we are to have half a barrel of sack sherry for us females and the men two pints of ale apiece."

"We'll have a fine time, Molly, but we've got to get through tomorrow first. There'll be a formal greeting for The Lady Elizabeth when she arrives for her first visit as 'officially betrothed', won't there?"

"Yes, but not for us. Only house servants from parlor maid upward are presentable enough to offer her their respects in the staff line-up, according to Mr. Bennett. We can peek from upstairs, though, if you want, as long as they don't see our faces through the window."

I smiled at my escape from that particular formality. "I think I'd rather watch the blood stock come into the yard, and Harry's asked me to walk with him to the stables tomorrow night, if you don't mind?"

"No. I'm quite happy to settle for James' attentions. We're going to have fun over the next few days, aren't we?" Molly said.

I laughed. "Yes, Molly, we are. We are going to laugh and dance and twirl and maybe take a kiss or two, if we wish."

"And do you?"

I dismissed black hair and blue eyes from my head and pictured thick, chestnut waves and brown eyes instead. "I think maybe I do."

I took Damion's note to Mr. Bennett in his pantry, smiled at Harry when he sat beside me at supper later, looked at his firm, work-hardened body and said 'yes' to his renewed invitation to walk to the stables after supper, once the house guests had arrived.

James brought the Family's table cover to Molly when he returned from clearing their dining table. "Lady Emma has spilt a little wine tonight, Molly. I'll light your way over if you need to take it to the laundry and get it into cold water before the stain sets?"

Molly's cheeks flushed pink as she stood. "Thank you, James. Yes, it should go in cold water directly."

Harry smiled at me and muscles tightened in my pelvis as he asked, "Will it be your turn to take the cloth over tomorrow night?"

"I could be with Molly right now if you think Prince would welcome the company?"

Harry swallowed and his eyes darkened as he got up. "I'm sure he would like to see you." I slipped through the kitchen door a few minutes after him. He offered me his arm. "Prince would be delighted to see you, but the loose boxes are closer if it was me you wanted to see."

I threaded my arm through his. "The horse boxes it is, then."

Harry shut both halves of the door behind us and I waited for him to come closer.

"Amelia, can I kiss you?" he asked.

"I was rather expecting you would."

Harry slipped his arms around my waist, pulled me closer then put his lips on mine and his tongue into my mouth. My muscles tensed as his tongue probed. I

33

returned the action, tasted and relaxed into his arms. Harry brushed his hand over my breast. My nipple hardened and he pinched.

"I dreamed of your titties when I was in my bed last night, Amelia."

Harry's words made me tingle between my legs. "Would you like to see them?"

His cock hardened against my thigh. "Yes," he breathed.

I took a step back, loosened the bow on the back of my dress, pulled my bodice over my shoulders and arms, undid the buttons on my shift to my waist and parted it. Harry stared and his gaze rippled through my groin. I cupped my breast and brushed my fingertips over my hardened nipple.

"You would like to do this, I think?"

Harry stepped closer. "I would. Very much."

I looked at the clean, swept floor. "A blanket then, if you please."

Harry took a horse blanket from its peg on the wall and laid it on the floor. I lay on it and patted the space beside me. "Come, then. You can see they're waiting for your mouth."

Harry lay beside me and fastened his lips over my breast. I murmured as he sucked. "Yes, Harry."

Harry drew the bud harder and squeezed, the hardness of his cock rubbing on the material of my dress against my thigh. I ran my fingers over the shape of his erection and the softer balls beneath it as his fierce suction wetted the lips of my sex. He rubbed his cock faster against my hand and thigh, grasped the fullness of my breasts tighter, one in each hand, tugged with his teeth then released my nipple and stilled. I stilled with him and the heat drained out of my thighs as he rolled to his side.

"I'm sorry, Amelia. I didn't last long enough for your own pleasure. It's just that I dreamed of your titties...then to be able to touch them like that..."

I smiled. "I found pleasure in your touch and would have liked more of it."

"You would lie with me again?" he asked. "I would not be unmanned with such speed the next time."

"Yes, Harry, but at the end, you won't be putting your cock inside me. You must complete your pleasure in another way. I won't risk getting with child."

Harry ran his fingertips over my breast. "To be able to touch your body and have you touch mine will be enough for me. I promise."

I sat and buttoned my shift. "I thank you. That makes me comfortable to be with you." I pulled my bodice upward. "Have you ever, though? Gone the whole way with someone?"

Harry sat up alongside me. "Just once, at the end of last summer. A parlor maid at Westergate House. I thought it was the best feeling ever at the time, but it gave me the shivers the next day when I realized what I'd done. I'm not able to provide for a wife and child yet, but I was lucky and received no word from her about any future responsibilities."

I stood and retied my dress laces. "I'm glad to hear you say that. I'm not looking for marriage or any type of walking out together, as such—just friends that touch when it suits."

Harry got up and kissed me quickly on my lips. "Friends that touch it is, then. You go on indoors. I'll go over to the stables and ensure the blood stock is settled for the night, so we don't arrive back together."

I nodded, pushed the top half of the loose box door open and peeped out. "No one in sight. Goodnight, Harry."

I opened the kitchen door and slipped inside. Mrs. Price, her workbox in front of her on the table, looked up.

"Where have you been, Amelia?"

I flicked my gaze around the room, saw no sign of Molly so crossed my fingers behind my back and fibbed. "In the laundry with Molly. We've soaped up some stains and left it to work on them overnight."

Mrs. Price smiled. "Very good, Amelia. I'm glad to see that you and Molly have taken Mr. Bennett's instructions to heart. You will enjoy yourself more on Saturday night if you have a clear conscience that your work is complete and of the standard myself and Mr. Bennett demand."

Molly stepped through the door behind me. I reached backward and pinched her hand. "Mrs. Price is pleased we've been to the laundry and are ahead of our work for when The Lady Elizabeth arrives tomorrow."

Molly held on to my hand and squeezed. "Yes, but it's made me very tired. Mrs. Price, may we be excused to take a little additional sleep to be ready for tomorrow?"

Mrs. Price inclined her head. "I'm very pleased with how well you girls are conducting yourselves when I thought you might be over-excited with the 'big event' this weekend. Yes, you may, but remember your prayers."

"Thank you, Mrs. Price. We will," we chorused.

I walked ahead of Molly at a measured pace until we pushed through the green door then planted my boot on the first step and launched myself upward. "Last one to the top has to ask Mr. Bennett to dance at the jig."

Molly's boots thumped on the stairs behind me as I pounded my way up. She caught the back of my dress as my foot stomped onto the top landing and swerved around me. I laughed. "Not again!"

Molly giggled. "Don't worry. He won't say yes. Mr. Bennett won't dance a jig."

I joined my giggles to hers at the picture that came into my mind. "Can't you just imagine it, though? Mr. Bennett lifting Mrs. Price up and swinging her around? Her skirts swirling around her bony knees while she gazes at him over the top of her spectacles?"

Molly laughed, pushed the door open, picked up a nightstick and lit it. "No, I can't. Although they've both been in service here since they were young, so mayhap they did before she grew bony and he grew somewhat larger around his middle."

"Let's keep half an eye out on Saturday to see if they give each other that knowing look when the ale and the sack go around."

Molly lit our way to our bedroom, shut the door, took the lamp from behind her box and lit it. I sat on the edge of my bed as Molly did the same and blew out the nightstick.

"So..." she said, "you were away from the kitchen at the same time as me. What were you doing?"

I took off my boots and stockings and lay on my bed. "I slipped out behind you and met Harry for a while."

"And?"

"And you first. What did you do with James?"

Molly kicked off her boots, shrugged out of her dress and hopped into bed under her covers. "Kissing and a bit of a feel over the clothes. You?"

"Kissing and my breasts. They unmanned him in about five minutes flat."

Molly giggled. "I told you they would. Are you going to – you know – let him again?"

"Yes, I am. I liked his touch and they won't come as so much of a surprise to him the next time."

Molly rolled over and bit her pillow as her shoulders shook. She peeped an eye out at me. "He shot his load? Just because he got his hands on your titties?"

"Straight into his britches."

"Oh, God! I wish I had some titties like that."

I smiled. "I didn't like it at first…when they grew so big. They're heavy and they get in the way at times, but I have to admit…I'm getting fonder of them."

Footsteps creaked on the bare boards outside our room. Molly put her hands together and raised her eyes heavenward. "Hallelujah to that, my sweet friend, and a heartfelt seven-fold amen to our hopes and prayers."

Mrs. Price's voice sounded through the door. "Goodnight and God bless." Her feet and audible sniff moved away with the barely heard, "Such good girls."

Molly grinned, leaned over the side of her bed and turned out the lamp. I laid my dress over the foot of my bed and turned my face to my pillow as I pulled my bedcovers over my shoulders, thought of kissable lips, tight breeches and the blue, blue eyes of a man that wouldn't shoot his load just from the sight of my breasts and slipped my hand between my legs.

* * * *

The sound of the tweenies bell woke me in the morning and I smiled, turned over to take another hour of sleep then rose with Molly when the bell rang a second time.

"Are you using a chamber pot in the washing room up here or waiting your turn at the water closet downstairs?" she asked.

"The water closet for me, although I'll wash here first and let the early morning pee queue die down."

I opened the lid of my box and took my towel, a tin of mint powder and my toothbrush out of it, to Molly's stare. "You clean your teeth?"

"Yes, Molly, and so should you if you don't relish having any more pulled. A toothbrush is only two pennies."

"I've got another one aching now." She sighed. "Perhaps I will."

I wagged my toothbrush at her. "The apothecary for you on your next half-day."

I walked to the washroom and found it empty as I expected, with the popularity of the water closet downstairs for needs other than washing. Cold water waited in the jug beside the wash bowl. I poured then gritted my teeth as I took off my shift, soaped my goose-bumped skin and longed for a whole tub of hot water as I rubbed dry. My shift rebuttoned, I wrapped my winter shawl around myself and walked to the bedroom to dress.

A bowl of hot porridge later, I followed Molly to the laundry and fetched my first bucket of water of the day. Molly lit the fire to heat the water and I looked at the length and depth of the rinsing sink.

"Molly, what if we heat water for ourselves when we finish our work? If we block the sluice drain in the sink, it is just about big enough to bathe in."

Molly's eyes widened as she followed my gaze to the sink. "A bath!"

"Wouldn't you like to be clean all at once instead of having to wash piecemeal, standing up? It would be lovely and warm in here if the fires have been lit for a while. We could take turns to bathe and block the door, so no one could get in and see us."

39

Molly giggled. "But we'd be bare. What if someone looked in through the window?"

"It'll steam up like it's starting to now. We could do it while everyone's busy at the front of the house welcoming The Lady Elizabeth, and if anyone did walk by, they'd think we were still in here working."

Molly laughed behind her hand. "You're on, but you've got to go first. I'm not doing it until you have."

I smiled. "Don't let the fire go out when we start the rinsing, then."

We left our bathing water to heat while we pegged out and found it starting to bubble when we got back. I took a bucket of water from the cauldron to rinse our hair, dropped soap into the residue to soften while Molly blocked the sluice drain with a large flat stone she'd found on the edge of the pegging field and we filled the sink bucket by bucket with hot water until it was half full.

"Let's do it then. Get your back against the door," I said.

Molly walked to the door and leaned her weight against it. I unlaced my dress and left it with my shift and stockings on the floor close to hand, so I could redress if anyone tried to enter. I stepped into the sink, sat with my knees up to fit its length and hot water floated over my thighs. I found a piece of softened soap, lathered my body, dipped a scoop into the bucket, poured fresh water over my hair and soaped that up, too. More scoops of hot water later, my body and hair were clean, both together, for the first time in over a year.

I stepped out of the sink, picked up a length of the flannelette we used on the ironing table, rubbed dry and redressed. "Go on then, Molly. Your turn."

Molly moved away from the door and I took her place. She stripped off, shorter than me with heavier thighs, flaxen hair, small, high breasts and pink-tipped nipples in contrast to my longer, slimmer legs, brown hair and much larger, browner-tipped breasts. She washed as quick as I had, stepped out of the sink and took the stone away. The water drained as she dried her skin and redressed. I looked at her wet hair.

"If we pin our hair, we can let it down for the wind to dry it while we get the laundry off the lines."

The wind blew through our hair as we loaded the baskets with dry laundry, and we put them inside the laundry as the dressing gong sounded inside the house. Molly glanced around the room. "Just the ironing to do tomorrow, thank goodness."

I followed her into the kitchen. Harry smiled at me and looked at the empty chair beside his. I sat.

"I thought I might have seen you this afternoon when the carriage came in."

"Molly and I had something we wanted to do while you were all busy and out of the way, but I'm looking forward to seeing the stables later."

Harry smiled. "As I'm looking forward to showing them to you."

I leaned closer as I wondered if the Below Stairs opinion would be any different from that of polite Society that I already knew. "What was she like, then? The Lady Elizabeth?"

"A tiny, little blonde thing. A bit rabbitty-toothed, if I'm honest. I'm not sure whether it was the occasion or not. She looked scared to death, but her lady's maid" — Harry grinned—"more than made up for it. I expect she'll be down for her supper when she's tidied her Lady's room. You'll see."

41

The green door opened a few minutes later and a woman walked in who was as wide as she was tall and with plenty of inches to her height. Mr. Bennett smiled and gave her a half bow.

"Miss Crinklebottom, welcome. I hope you'll be very happy with us here when The Lady Elizabeth makes Ashton Manor her permanent residence."

Miss Crinklebottom grasped Mr. Bennett's hand and shook it. "Well said, Sir. Well said. And I'm Phyliss, if you please. There's enough of me to make folk laugh without adding Crinklebottom to the joke."

Harry nudged my knee with his and caught my eye with a smile. Phyliss gave Mr. Bennett a hearty pat on his upper arm. He winced as she walked forward and said to us, "Now, here are the young ones. And who are you, my dears?"

Phyliss sat beside Molly and covered her hand with her much larger one as Molly answered, "Molly Jones, Ashton's laundry maid, Miss Phyliss."

Phyliss patted Molly's hand. "No need for the Miss, my dear. 'Phyliss' I've been all my life and 'Phyliss' I'll stay."

Harry took his hand off the table and nodded. "Harry Burton, His Lordship's groom."

"Amelia Brown, also a laundry maid. Your Lady has settled in and been made quite comfortable, Phyliss?"

"That's very kind of you to ask, my dear. Yes, indeed. My little chick has been given a lovely room beside His Lordship's mother's own and her every comfort has been provided for. Well...except that she pines for Miss Leticia, of course, but her mama, Countess Wellingham, thought it best that Lady Elizabeth should take the chance to deepen her acquaintance with her betrothed without the distraction of having to attend to the comfort of another."

Molly frowned and asked the question I already knew the answer to from reading the Society pages of the newspaper. "Who's Miss Leticia?"

"Lady Elizabeth's friend," Phyliss said. "Neither of them has a sister and they've been nearly inseparable these last few years. But still, these childhood things have to be put aside when you're grown up with marriage and the hope of children to come to consider."

Phyliss looked at Harry and continued. "But, His Lordship's groom, eh? You'll meet our own Tom tomorrow. We came ahead in the carriage and four but Tom's bringing the Countess' and Lady Elizabeth's mounts here in easy stages and should be with us in the morning."

"I'll look forward to meeting him," Harry said.

Molly smiled. "We are to have our own jig tomorrow, Phyliss, to celebrate the betrothal. Do you dance?"

Phyliss laughed a deep rumble of thunder as James approached the table and pulled out a chair. "Bless you, child. No. There's not a floor made that could withstand it, nor a man of sufficient muscle for the effort required to partner me, but I will enjoy watching you young things capering about, and you girls will like to have another young man dancing attendance on you. Our Tom is fit for the task, with a certain twinkle to his eye."

James sat, looked at Harry and neither of them smiled. Mr. Bennett stood. We bowed our heads and waited for him to say Grace. Mrs. Price dished out game stew with herb dumplings set atop it and we passed the plates around. Harry looked at me as he picked up his fork.

"Sorry, Amelia. I thought their personal mounts would be here this evening and there's not much out of the ordinary in the stables worth a visit without them. I thought some of the other house guests might have arrived today, but none are coming until tomorrow."

"I'll keep an eye out of the laundry window tomorrow and slip out and have a look at them then."

Molly nudged my knee with hers and I looked up to see Mrs. Price's gaze fix on me and Harry. I muttered at him, "I think we're going to have to be on our best behavior tonight anyway or the jig might be canceled for everyone."

Harry nodded and looked first at his plate then at Ellen sitting on his other side while I turned to Molly. "We'd best both go the laundry tonight when James brings the table cover down."

James leaned forward. "I'll still light your way over, so my doing so last night doesn't stand out. They can't make anything of that if the two of you are together."

Molly nodded. "How will you get on tomorrow, though, James? If you still have to maintain service upstairs?"

James leaned closer. "They've booked two extra footmen to circulate the trays of fizzy stuff and pink wine at the dance, so me, Fred and Bert have worked out that as the extra footmen won't expect a break, each of us can stop down here for an hour or so at a time, as long as there are still at least four of us up there in view."

James rested his knife and fork on his plate and stood as the bell rang on the servants' board. I helped Molly carry plates through to the scullery for the tweenies to wash. James brought the cloth down and handed it to me.

"It will be quicker if we both take it over," Molly said.

"I'll light your way and pump your water for you." James smiled.

Mrs. Price looked in our direction then nodded at Phyliss. "Such cooperation as you'll find between the staff here at Ashton, Phyliss. Always lending a hand to one another where they may."

Phyliss smiled. "Yes, I can see that. I've only been here a few hours, I know, but the atmosphere here at Ashton is a credit to you, Mrs. Price — harmonious and kind, from what I've noticed. Nothing here to disturb my little chick. She is of a somewhat nervous disposition…"

Mrs. Price leaned closer. "She is?"

"Well…" Phyliss said.

I pulled my attention away and followed Molly out of the kitchen door with James one pace behind us. James lit the lamp and I looked at Molly. "I've never danced a country dance. Will you explain the steps to me later?"

Molly smiled. "I'll do better than that. I'll dance them from the laundry back to the house when we've rid ourselves of the cloth, if James will oblige and partner me?"

James looked at the room lit up on the first floor of the house. "No heads in the dining room to see us. His Lordship must have removed with the Ladies. Yes, Molly. I would be delighted."

James filled our bucket at the pump and Molly giggled as I put it in the rinsing sink and added the table cover with some chips of soap. "Amelia and me had a real bath in here today, with hot water and everything."

"Molly, you never! Not all bare?" James laughed.

45

Molly grinned. "As a newborn babe, and I'm going to do it again sometime, because I liked it. Let's go and dance."

"You're such a madcap lately, Molly."

Molly grabbed my hand. "You can blame our new laundry maid. She's the one that puts all the ideas in my head."

I smiled, picked up the lamp and opened the door. James followed us out.

"I'll sit on the mounting block and watch," I said, as James and Molly stood face-to-face and clasped hands. James hummed the tune and Molly explained the steps.

"So, there will be about six couples in a line facing each other and we step to our left—one-two-three-four steps. Now I twirl under James' arm...then one-two-three-four steps back to the right and James picks me up and swings me around."

I laughed as Molly's hair loosened and flew out behind her and her skirt swirled around her knees. "Now, all but the last couple clasp hands up high and the last couple skip through the arch of hands and take their turn to lead the dance and we start again—step-one-two-three-four..."

James and Molly danced over to the kitchen door then toward me again.

"It's better with the fiddle playing," Molly said. "The music gets faster and faster and faster and the dance speeds up and up and only stops when one of the couples loses their steps. Go on, James. Give Amelia a go."

My skirt and hair flew as James put his hands on my waist, picked me up to his count of one-two-three-four, twirling and spinning, back and forth between the kitchen door and the mounting block until I laughed, breathless, after our fifth trip up and down.

"Lord, Molly. Phyliss is right! There's not a man alive that could bear the weight of lifting and spinning her through a country dance."

"But you know it well enough now?" she asked.

"Enough not to tread on anyone's toes or bring the dance to too quick an end. I thank you."

Molly smiled, glanced upward and straightened her face. "James! I thought you said he'd removed with the Ladies'?"

"What? He's in there?" James' glance followed Molly's. "Damn! I thought once he'd left the room that he'd be tucked up with his newly betrothed all night. I didn't check again when we came out of the laundry. The port and brandy are in the dining room. He must have needed a stiffener."

Molly looked at me and I bit my finger. "Don't say it, Molly."

She giggled. "I won't, but I never thought he needed any help that way myself, did you?"

"What? Dutch courage for the nerves?" James said. "Getting betrothed is a big thing, Molly, even for a Marquis. I hope we're not for the high jump, though."

Molly linked her arm through James'. I did the same on his other side and smiled.

"I don't think a little caper around the yard will be a box-packing event, James."

James pushed the kitchen door and held it open for Molly and me to walk through. Mrs. Price looked at us.

"Just in time for prayers. Take your places, please."

I took my seat beside Harry, clasped my hands and closed my eyes. I opened them at Mr. Bennett's 'amen' and Harry muttered at me, "You lot were a while."

"I've only seen a country dance and not danced at one. James and Molly showed me the steps so I may not tread on your toes or spoil the dance tomorrow."

"Tomorrow, if we can't get out tonight?" Harry asked.

Need tingled between my thighs as I looked into Harry's eyes and his irises darkened. "Prince's loose box when the dance is over," I said.

"It will be late."

I glanced toward Mr. Bennett and Mrs. Price. "Good. They'll be tired and not watching."

Mr. Bennett stood and so did the rest of the table.

"I have been reassured by your proper decorum. We will hold our jig tomorrow. Young ladies may wear their hair loose without caps, if they are not required to serve. Although, of course, any maid called to service will make sure she is properly attired to do so before she attends, and the males of the household will, as usual, always be ready for a call to action."

Molly nudged me and whispered, "Without the need for a stiffener?"

I swallowed a giggle and followed her up the stairs to bed. She pulled her bedcovers over her shoulder and blew the nightstick out. "I'm tired out tonight, what with the bath and the dancing and everything. Night, Am."

"Goodnight, Molly. Sleep well."

Chapter Three

I woke in the morning with the first bell, turned over for more sleep and followed Molly to the laundry after breakfast. Molly poked through the basket of items awaiting our attention.

"Say what you like, but for us, the start of a house visit is a good time. We're so ahead of ourselves until the guests leave and the bedding comes in. There are only smalls in here from last night."

Molly lit the fire under the cauldron but we didn't bring the water to boiling point with only lawns and fine linen to wash, along with the pre-soaked table covering. I watched the houseguests' blood stock come through the yard as we rinsed.

"I said to Harry that I'd slip over to the stables and have a look at the guests' mounts if I could. We'll have an hour or two free while this lot blows, won't we?"

"Yes, if you like. I'm going to sneak upstairs and have an hour on my bed to be ready for tonight. Let's get it on the lines."

I followed Molly to the drying field and pegged behind her. Molly ran her hands down a pair of lace-edged pantaloons that were frilled from thigh to ankle. "They're so pretty, aren't they? I wish we could wear frilly things beneath our dresses like Ladies do. I might save some pennies and buy a pair of drawers one day."

My previous experience of such items made me smile. "No, Molly, I don't wish for any. As far as I can tell, their only purpose is to make sure females can't walk, or even talk, with ease."

"But this corset... It pinches your waist in and pushes your titties up higher."

I laughed. "Yes, it does, but I think James likes your waist and your titties, along with all the rest of you, just as much without one."

"Yes, he does. But the bath thing last night... I wasn't just flirting about being bare. Now that I've had one? Well, I'd prefer it if he did, too."

"Then heat up the water and offer to slip your warm, soapy hand on or over whatever," I suggested.

Molly grinned and twirled. "Now I know what I'm going to do with my extra hour or two. James' duties are pretty light at this time of the day."

"Then I'm off to the stables. Leave the empty baskets on the step, and if the laundry looks steamy when this lot is dry, I'll unpeg the washing and leave it outside the door."

I walked in the direction of the stable block as Molly skipped off toward the kitchen. I pushed the door open when I reached it and cast my eyes over the stalls. Harry called down from the end of the block where he was saddling a gray mare.

"They've all come in at once. Have a look, although Tom and I are saddling up for His Lordship to take his betrothed and a party of the Ladies on an amble around the estate."

I looked at the mounts as I walked toward him, then at a mare waiting for her side saddle when I reached him. I stroked my hand down a dappled gray nose and the horse's dull brown eyes gazed at me. A groom, unknown to me, tightened the girth on a similarly sized chestnut at the stall opposite. He was a slim, blond man with green eyes. I guessed his identity as I walked over to the chestnut and it gazed at me with eyes that showed the same lack of spirit as those of the gray.

"You're Phyliss' Tom? I'm Amelia. I work here in the laundry."

Tom smiled and winked at me. "I am, and what do you think of our Phyliss, then?"

I smiled. "I'm looking forward to her being here after the marriage. Will you come with her?"

Tom winked again. "No, my pretty one. Unfortunately, not. My Lady's mare, Buttercup, over there with Harry, needs little attention. Both she and Blossom here are safe, quiet Ladies' mounts. You should look for me quite often, though, I think, when Countess Wellingham visits her daughter."

Prince neighed a complaint and kicked his backboard. I turned to Harry and grinned. "Prince is going out on an amble?"

Harry winced. "Don't. He could do with some calming and I haven't the time to soothe him with the mares to get ready. I've still Lady Shelling's and Miss Bathurst's to saddle."

I smiled into Harry's eyes. "That could make for an interesting ride. You will accompany them on Bonnie?"

Harry returned my smile. "I will."

"Tell me at supper?"

Harry nodded as Prince kicked again.

"Do you want me to lead him and put him in his loose box? He'll calm with a little solitary time."

"Thank you, yes. I know you can handle him and I could use the breathing space."

I walked to Prince, looped his reins, held them together close to his bit and opened the door to his stall. Prince shook his head to test the strength of my hold on him. I tightened my grip and urged him forward. Prince acquiesced and stepped out of his stall.

"Come then, Sir, and behave yourself."

I led him at a trot to the back yard then nudged him backward into his loose box with my shoulder, fastened his head collar and secured the rope to hold him. He lowered his head and snorted. I patted his neck and blew up his nostrils.

"Now, kindly remember your Society manners, Sir, and don't frighten the new mares the way you do Bonnie."

Prince flapped his lips and I kissed his nose. "Yes, all right. I agree. Those two are far too stupid to even be nervous of you."

"Your education included instruction on horse flesh, then?"

I squashed the image of my high-stepping Arabian mare Star, just as soon as she floated into my mind, bobbed my curtsey to Damion and stifled the flutter in my tummy at his closeness by picturing the double ménage-a-trois that was about to ride out. "It did."

Damion looked at my eyes. "Are you laughing at me?"

I bit my lip to suppress the temptation to do so out loud and nodded as my imagination delighted me with several potential avenues of conversation for mistress and betrothed to explore as they rode. "I am."

"Are you going to tell me why?"

I kept my imaginings of the human threesome to myself but admitted to the equine as Prince nudged my shoulder and I turned and rubbed his cheek. "A ménage-a-trois — mismatched — with no liking for the presence of the third. I've just come from the stables where I met Buttercup and Blossom."

Damion stepped alongside me and considered my reply. "Hmm... I'm not sure that's quite enough to explain the joke. How did you come to be working in service at Ashton? You were obviously not born for it."

I increased the gap between us, against my body's wish to be closer to his. "No, I wasn't, but I am now, and I find it suits me very well."

Damion brushed am imaginary fly away from Prince's face and narrowed the gap between us. "A family that suffered a reverse?"

I tilted my chin. "Yes, but if I was offered my previous station back, I wouldn't take it. I prefer the life I lead now."

"Why?" he persevered. "Why be a maid in service and not the higher calling of Governess or School Mar'm, as at least fits your education?"

I smiled as I considered my suitability to work in either role. "I wouldn't have lasted the week. I'd have been dismissed and waiting for the carrier to pick me up at the end of the drive by Thursday."

Damion's irises lightened. "Yes, I suppose so. Governesses do not twirl in the wind with their skirts raised around their thighs or dance up and down the back yard with the footmen, do they?"

I stuck my nose in the air and aped my childhood nanny's reproving voice. "Certainly not. Governesses do not possess anything quite as vulgar as legs."

Harry led Blossom into the yard, tugging on her reins to encourage her to increase the speed of her pace to more than a gentle plod, as Damion returned my smile. I widened it as I watched Harry's efforts. "I believe your social obligations call you, My Lord. Do forgive me if I prefer my bucket to what I see in store for your enjoyment today."

Damion's gaze followed mine to Blossom. "On this occasion, I believe you may be right."

I bobbed my curtsey and walked to the laundry, picked up an empty wash basket from the doorstep and walked to the drying field, then unpegged and folded each garment into it. I took the first basket back full, selected another and two more trips to the drying yard completed the task. Coal clanked on the side of a scuttle as I deposited my last load onto the doorstep and I stepped over to the coal shed.

"You're starting early tonight, Ellen."

Ellen looked up and huffed. "It's the extra guests. I'm as like as to be at it right through supper at this rate. Polly is not quick at her duties yet and unsure of her work, so can't be left alone."

I smiled at the small fourteen-year-old girl beside Ellen. "How do you like your job, Polly?"

"S'all right. 'Cept today's been 'ard."

I looked at Ellen. "Go on. Pass me a spare scuttle. I'll give you a hand. How many have you got left to do?"

Ellen smiled. "Amelia, I thank you. We've done the guest rooms on the fourth floor but we've still all of the unattached Ladies' to do, then there are four extra in the Bachelors' rooms."

I nodded, picked up a shovel, filled a scuttle and staggered after Ellen. I rested the scuttle inside the kitchen door and took a spare apron and cap from the peg. "Mrs. Price. I'm with Ellen and Polly. They have much extra to do tonight and I have a spare hour."

Mrs. Price inclined her head. Phyliss, sitting at the table beside her, looked up.

"I'll do my little chick's. She's resting on her daybed for an hour. I'll bank her fire myself when she wakes."

Ellen nodded at Phyliss as I tied my pinny and set a cap on my hair. She rested her scuttle as we reached the landing of the third floor, six flights up, and opened the green door. "At least you can breathe tonight, Amelia. I'll take the Ladies' on my own, as there are only four. If you would do the five Bachelors' with Polly?"

I nodded. "Where are they? Who have we got in?"

"The Lords Sudgley, Rossiter, Byngingham and Sir Elliott—the first three doors opposite His Lordship's and the one to the left of it."

Ellen peered around the green door. "The hallway's clear but expect some of them to be in their rooms. Family dinner's early tonight to be cleared before the local gentry arrive for the dance."

Ellen staggered off down the hallway. I hefted my scuttle and nodded at Polly.

"Knock, in. Curtsey if they're there. Over to the fire double-quick time. I'll rake and you sweep. I'll tip the coal on. Each room should take no more than ten minutes. Understand?"

Polly sniffed, wiped her hand under her nose and nodded.

"And use a handkerchief. Where's your rag?"

"S'up me sleeve."

"Use it, then. Do not wipe your nose on the back of your hand or on the sleeve of your dress up here."

I walked ahead of Polly, knocked on the first door, received no answer and opened it. A Gentleman's evening clothes lay on the bed, the wooden towel rail empty of its towel to one side of the fireplace. "He must be in the bathroom. Move it, Polly."

55

I hefted the scuttle to the fire, picked up the poker from the array of fire-irons on offer and looked at her standing beside me, breathing in through her open mouth. I knelt. She did the same beside me and I handed her the brush. I raked the embers, tipped the scuttle and tutted at her ineffective sweeps, then took the brush from her and completed the task myself. The next door along was answered by Lord Sudgley's man. Polly followed me in and made a better attempt at her sweeping. I smiled at her as the door closed behind us.

"That's better, Polly. Sweep it. Don't just tickle it."

Lord Byngingham's room was empty of his person, although his man answered the door and continued laying evening clothes on the bed as we worked. I used the last of my coal on Lord Rossiter's grate and swapped my empty scuttle for Polly's half-full one outside Damion's door as I knocked. Mr. Hubert opened the door.

"Amelia?"

I smiled. "Ellen needed a hand and I had a spare hour. A few minutes with His Lordship's fire, if you please?"

"Come along in. He's in his dressing room. I'll inform him there are staff in his room."

I walked ahead of Mr. Hubert with Polly beside me. The dressing room door opened and Damion stepped out, the top three buttons of his shirt undone, a shirt collar in his hand.

"Hubert, my collar studs if—" Damion stopped speaking as Polly and I bobbed. I fixed my gaze on the V of bare skin and a curl of black chest hair revealed by his open shirt, then gazed at his face and gave him a look of amusement of my own. Mr. Hubert flapped his hands behind us.

"My Lord, I do apologize. I had no idea you would step out. Amelia, Polly, avert your eyes at once, if you please."

Polly obliged and looked down at her feet. I didn't. Damion's lips twitched. "Do not excite yourself, Hubert. The fault is mine, I believe."

I smiled as Damion gave me my words back, knelt before the fire and applied the poker.

"But improperly attired, My Lord. I never... Well..."

Damion stepped into his dressing room. "My collar studs, if you please, Hubert."

I tipped the coal scuttle and Mr. Hubert showed us out.

"Amelia, Polly, no mention of this Below Stairs, I beg. The damage to my reputation..."

"My lips are sealed, Mr. Hubert." I smiled.

"Mention wha'?" Polly sniffed and wiped her nose along her sleeve.

Ellen waited behind the green door with her empty scuttle when I pushed through. "Is she always like this or is it just because she's got a head cold?" I asked.

"Had a head cold since the day she started." Ellen huffed.

"No wonder you can't get through your work."

"It won't bother me for too much longer. Mrs. Price says I may have the position of parlor maid when the house guests leave."

I squeezed her hand. "Well done, Ellen. I'm pleased for you."

Ellen smiled. "So am I. No more night pots for me, the same as you."

I returned my scuttle to the coal shed, washed the black grime from my hands in the scullery and saw the long, wooden table had been lifted to the far side of the room with its chairs dotted here and there about the place when I walked into the servants' hall. Three heavy-bottomed pans, along with plates, forks and spoons, sat on the table surface. Mrs. Oates, working at her range, called over.

"It's serve yourself this evening, Amelia. We're all at sixes and sevens with early dinner for the Family and the extras for the dance, let alone there's too many of us to sit to supper tonight, anyway."

I called back. "My thanks, Mrs. Oates. It all smells good, as usual."

Mrs. Oates smiled. "I've done three different pans so the visiting staff shouldn't think us too shabby."

Molly walked up behind me as I lifted the first lid and released the smell of Irish stew. "That smells good. I quite like it when it's informal like this, don't you?" she said.

I ladled lamb and potatoes onto a plate. Molly ladled beef stew and dumplings from the pot beside it onto hers and we found two chairs to sit on and eat our supper, our plates balanced on our knees. "Yes, I do. They can't keep such a close an ear out for what we're talking about spread around the room like this. How was bath time with James?"

"He wouldn't get right in it like we did but he stripped off his top half and sluiced, then I did what you said and got my soapy hand down his britches, and what with the hot water and everything, the bit I'm interested in is clean. What about Harry?"

"The stable hands soap up and sluice down beside the horse trough each night. I've never had any worries about cleanliness."

Harry walked in through the kitchen door, helped himself to supper and sat alongside me. Molly scooped up a last chunk of meat.

"I'm away to get ready for tonight. I'll see you upstairs, Am?"

"Shortly. I'll sit with Harry for a few minutes."

I turned to him as Molly walked away. "Well?"

He smiled. "Well, I have to say I think His Lordship must have allowed it because he's a far better horseman than that, but Prince spent about half an hour ambling along behind Buttercup and Blossom, trying to bite their arses but never getting quite close enough to do so, if you see what I mean."

I snorted into my stew. "And?"

"And, all the while, Lady Shelling looked like she'd quite like to bite The Lady Elizabeth. Then Lady Elizabeth said she'd become quite faint and needed to rest before tonight, and I got told to escort her and the Countess back to the Manor while His Lordship said he'd gallop the fidgets out of Prince's legs and shot off with Lady Shelling galloping after him, saying her mount needed to stretch his legs, too."

"How long until their mounts came back?"

"Lady Shelling returned before His Lordship, and all is I can say is, the Lady looked in one hell of a temper. His Lordship seemed much as normal when he returned, although he was muttering under his breath something about bloody social obligations."

I laughed. "No. Was he? I don't think Ellen's going to be finding any stockings tomorrow, then. I'll go up to Molly now, if you'll excuse me? I'll see you here later?"

Harry smiled. "I'll see you soon. Save the first dance for me?"

I nodded, took my plate to the scullery, walked upstairs and used the washing room then followed Molly down the stairs to the kitchen half an hour after I'd left it. Two barrels sat on the table, a large keg of ale with pottery mugs beside it and a half-barrel, accompanied by small, thick glass cups. Molly poured into two cups from the half-barrel and passed one to me. I swallowed a mouthful and coughed when the alcohol from the sherry hit the back of my throat.

Phyliss gave my back a hearty thump. "Easy there, girl. Easy..."

I nodded as my eyes watered, took a smaller sip, smiled at its sweet warmth and drank slowly alongside Molly as the kitchen filled. Mr. Robinson walked in through the kitchen door, smiled his crinkled smile and put his fiddle under his chin.

"Look lively, ladies. Gentlemen, take your partners for the first round."

I danced, twirled and spun with Harry, then Tom, then Fred. Molly danced with Tom, then Fred, then Harry. I fell onto a chair, breathless, and fanned my face with my hand. James joined the party and took up his spoons. Fred left it to take his place upstairs and Molly reached for her washboard to a cheer. I looked at Harry.

"I'm going to take a turn around the back yard in the fresh air for a minute or two."

Harry smiled and slipped out of the back door behind me, the moon so full and bright above us as to make a lamp unnecessary. A light breeze blew over my face as we walked away from the house. "That's better. It's hot in there, isn't it? With all of us and the visiting staff."

Harry nodded and slipped his arm around my waist. I glanced over my shoulder at the back of the house. "Let's move out of sight of the windows in case one of the Gentlemen goes into the dining room for a glass of something stronger than wine."

We walked around of the back of the loose boxes and I turned in to his arm as his other went around my waist. Harry bent his head, put his lips on mine and ran his fingers through the back of my hair as we tasted each other. I broke away as he put his hand on my breast.

"Later, Harry. We'd better get back inside before we're missed."

"Will you be able to wait up? I have the mounts and carriages to bring round for the local gentry not staying the night when the dance is over."

I stroked my fingers along his jawline and early stubble tickled the tips.

"I'm sure I will. Molly and I were so ahead of our chores that we didn't have a busy day."

Harry held out his hand. I put mine in his and we swung our arms between us as we returned to the jig. Harry opened the kitchen door and Molly skipped over with a glass cup half-full of pink wine and held it out to me.

"You missed it, Amelia, but I saved you some."

"Missed what?"

"Didn't you hear us all give a clap and a cheer a few minutes ago? His Lordship brought The Lady Elizabeth down and Mr. Bennett served this for us to give them a toast."

I took the glass and swallowed a sip. "Thank you, Molly. No, sorry. Harry and I walked well away from the windows at the back of the house, but I don't suppose we were missed in among all this crowd. How did they look?"

Molly leaned closer. "Well, not newly betrothed happy, if I'm honest—more like polite, going through the motions. She had a sort of fixed smile on her face and His Lordship? Well, he didn't even look at her and just gazed around the room."

"That's a shame, and I'm sorry for both of them then, but the peerage rarely get to marry because they've fallen in love with someone, like we do. Do they?"

"No, I suppose not. They say the Queen was lucky because Prince Albert was a love match. I just hope it doesn't make the house gloomy when they get wed."

I shrugged. "It shouldn't, as long as they don't actually hate each other. He can keep his mistress, and once she's obliged and produced an heir or two, she can go her own way, too."

Molly nudged me. "Do you think he'll be obliging with Lady Shelling tonight with his betrothed asleep just a few doors down on the other wing?"

I laughed. "I'm sure Ellen will tell us if she finds any stockings where they shouldn't be in the morning."

Harry walked over and offered me another glass of sherry from the barrel. "I'm not sure she will. James said Lady Shelling was paying quite particular attention to Lord Sudgley up there."

I swallowed the last of the rosé wine, swapped my wine glass for the one of sack and took a small drink. Tom walked over, winked and offered me a taste of his ale from his mug. "You'll dance with me again, my pretty one?"

I swallowed a sip of ale and took another of sherry as I winced at the taste. "I will, although you may keep your ale. It is far too sour for my taste."

Tom laughed and drained his mug. I finished my sherry, put the glass down then offered Tom my hand and we joined the end of dance. I collapsed on a chair and giggled when Ellen and Harry lost their steps as the dance sped up. Tom refilled my glass and passed it to me. Bert joined us, released from his duties upstairs by James.

"How is it up there?" I asked. "Not as much fun as it is down here, I'm thinking."

Bert drank his ale. "Fun it is most certainly not. The string quartet is good but the steps they dance at the moment are fiddly, and the atmosphere in the room is quite subdued."

Ellen laughed. "I would not like that. If I dance, I like the pace to be fast, even if it does mean I end it by tripping over my feet."

"It's a good job it's not any faster up there." Bert chuckled. "His Lordship is not a man built to be light on his feet. Goodness knows how it will go with him when the waltzes start up."

"How will he get on when he leads The Lady Elizabeth out?" Ellen sniggered. "She is smaller than our Queen and he must stand at least two inches over six feet. They'll never reach."

Mrs. Price clapped her hands. "A short interlude for supper has been called upstairs. Violet, Bertha, Nell... Aprons and caps on and take the salvers of fancies and dainties to the dining room, if you please. The rest of us will take a comfort break, too. Our music will resume once the Family's supper has been eaten and cleared."

Mr. Robinson laid his fiddle down and walked to the barrel to refresh himself with a pot of ale. Nell and Bertha stepped past me, holding silver trays containing morsels of chicken and asparagus set in aspic and nibbles of game pie to be eaten upstairs from fine porcelain plates with small silver forks. James and Bert followed along behind them with out-of-season strawberries from the hot house, small fingers of sponge cake and Mrs. Oates' specialty—a delicate French pastry, topped with mock cream and a slice of a hot-housed peach.

More trays moved out of the kitchen under Mrs. Price's watchful eye until she turned to Mrs. Oates and nodded. Mrs. Oates moved back and forth between our table and the kitchen and laid a platter of carved ham, a plate of cheeses, a large jar of pickled onions and a basket of warm bread rolls on it.

"A little supper for us, if any would like it," Mrs. Price announced.

"Would you?" Harry asked.

"Let's take it outside for a breath of air and have our own picnic in the back yard," Molly said.

I nodded, moved to the table alongside her and filled a roll. Tom and Harry brought their mugs of ale with them and we gathered around the mounting block and used it as an impromptu table. Harry offered me a sip from his mug and laughed when I took one and spluttered again. "How can you drink that? Molly, have you tried it?"

Tom offered his mug to Molly and she giggled when she swallowed. "It's not that bad."

Harry lifted his mug to my mouth. "Try another one. You might get to like it."

I swallowed and bit down on my cheese-filled roll. "No. It's still foul. I'm sorry."

Ellen and Polly walked out of the kitchen door and our circle expanded as they joined us. I fed Harry the last mouthful of my roll, snatched my fingers away as he tried to suck them into his mouth and brushed breadcrumbs from the front of his jacket. Polly sniffed and moved her sleeve toward her face.

"Handkerchief, Polly," Ellen and I said in unison.

Tom puffed out his chest. "What about my crumbs, then?"

I looked at Molly and she smiled at me. We moved forward together, held one of Tom's arms each and gave his front a brisk brushing until Ellen joined in with both of her hands and Tom laughed. "Enough, enough. I give in. I'm clean."

Polly stood beside us, her mouth open, and just breathed.

Mr. Robinson's fiddle sounded through the open kitchen door and I offered one arm to Molly and the other to Ellen. I glanced up as we turned and sent my silent sympathy to the silhouette in the dining room window for the boy who the last time I had shared the children's quarters with him for the month of a summer house party, had spent every available moment outdoors with his rod, his horse or his dog and gun, then I walked to the kitchen with Molly's and Ellen's hips swaying in time with mine to Mr. Robinson's tune.

Four dances and two glasses later, the kitchen clock chimed twelve and Mr. Robinson laid down his fiddle. Harry and Tom put their mugs on the table to resume their duties for carriages at twelve-thirty and Harry stopped at my side on his way to the back door.

"Later?" he asked.

I nodded and showed him my glass. "I'm going to sit on the mounting block and take a little air when I've finished this, if I can get out of the kitchen door with Mrs. Price thinking I've gone to bed."

Ellen swayed toward me and Molly. "Give me your glasses. I'll top them up with the end of the barrel. It'll be a shame to leave the last of it to go to waste."

I handed my cup to Ellen and sat with Molly until Ellen swayed back with them, full to the brim. I blinked when the room hazed a little in my eyes as she handed it to me but my vision cleared while I sipped. Phyliss helped the remaining men lift the table back into position and move the chairs into place around its edges. Mrs. Price clapped her hands at me, Ellen and Molly, still with glass cups in our hands.

"To your beds, if you please. It is now the Sabbath and time for our frivolities to come to an end."

I swallowed a last mouthful as Molly and Ellen did the same then nudged Molly's arm. "I'm going to slip into the lavatory and see if I can get out and meet Harry when Mrs. Price isn't looking."

I followed Molly to the scullery. We put our cups in the sink and said our goodnights to Mrs. Price on our way past her. Molly opened the green door and walked through it. I walked past it, opened the door to the lavatory in the corridor that led to Mrs. Price's and Mr. Bennett's rooms and locked it when I was inside.

The door rattled twice as people tried to open it and walked away to use an upstairs chamber pot when they found it engaged. Mr. Bennett's voice sounded outside it when the kitchen clock chimed the next hour.

"A most successful evening, wouldn't you agree, Mrs. Price?"

"Successful indeed, Mr. Bennett."

"Then may I tempt you to a small glass of port in my sitting room before you retire, Mable?"

"That would be delightful indeed, Bertram."

Their footsteps receded, and I counted to twenty before I released the bolt and made my way through the darkened servants' hall, trying not to trip over any of the legs of the chairs around the table as I felt my way past them. I opened the door to the back yard and took in a deep breath. Cold air filled my lungs and the yard tilted before my eyes as I stepped forward.

I clutched at the door handle until it steadied then walked to the mounting block and looked at it with one eye closed to decide which one I should sit on. I perched on cold solidness but my buttocks slipped as my shoulders wavered, so I sat on the ground and rested my back against it as the yard tilted again. I screwed my eyes shut as the loose boxes spun in front of me and found relief hovering in the form of a welcome darkness when I did, but a voice stopped me from falling into it.

"Amelia, what are you doing out here? You can't fall asleep in the back yard."

I opened an eye and smiled as two Damions settled into one. "Oh, it's you, is it? How did you come to be here? Did you enjoy your party? I did. I haven't danced at a jig before."

"Not as much as you, obviously. I saw you wobble from the dining room window when you sat on the mounting block."

I giggled as Molly's words floated into my head. "Oh, no! Did you need another stiffener like last night? And I don't wobble. I'm not a jelly, you know."

"My dining room window has been an interesting place to be this last evening or two. How many glasses did you have?"

I giggled again. "Glasses? I haven't got any. They're all still in there. Mrs. Price might lend you her eyeglasses, though, if you need some."

Damion shook both of his heads and held out his hand. "Come along. Let's get you out of here before anyone sees you on the go. Can you stand?"

I put my hand in his and my feet left the ground when my knee buckled as I got up.

"Where to hide you until you've recovered a little? I can't enter the maids' quarters and Hubert's in my room."

I rested my head against his broad shoulder as the word 'hide' buzzed in my ears. "Yes. Go somewhere safe."

67

I closed my eyes and drifted through air until I smelled paper and dust, leather bindings and man and tucked myself in tighter on Papa's lap as he sat.

"Amelia—"

I giggled at Papa's joke. "No...Henry."

"Who's Henry?"

"Don't be silly, Papa. It's me, of course."

Papa's hand stroked through the length of my hair. "Go to sleep for a while."

"Yes, Papa. He can't get me if you're here."

Papa tightened his arms around me and I nestled closer. "Who can't?"

Chapter Four

My breath bubbled through my lips as I unstuck them, my cheek against fine linen over a firm, hard chest. I opened my eyes and peered at shelves of books, a brown, deep-buttoned leather sofa, Damion's legs stretched out in front of it and my own sideways across his lap. I tried for a little saliva to moisten my mouth, glanced up into the gleam of amused blue irises and asked, "I seem to have put you to some inconvenience. Are you laughing at me?"

Damion's arm tightened around me. "I am. And I find it far from inconvenient to have you tucked tight against me like this."

I closed my eyes and relaxed in his hold. "I should really stand up and have an attack of the vapors, but you're very comfortable to sit on. What do they put in that drink that makes your mouth feel like you've been eating sand?"

"Comfortable is not normally what I hope for. How much drink did you take?"

I smiled into his chest. "My apologies. I've missed another opportunity to tremble, haven't I? Five or six or seven of the glass cups and one of your rosé wine. Oh, and some tastes of the ale. I was quite well until I stepped into the cold air and the world tipped sideways."

"Too many different drinks and cold air will do that if you're not used to them. Your fingers are near my waistcoat pocket. If you reach in, you will find some imps in it."

I dipped my fingers into his pocket and pulled out a small tin of the tiny peppermint pastilles used by Gentlemen to freshen their breath when returning to the company of Ladies after a spirit stronger than wine had been imbibed. I sat straighter and spluttered as I sucked on two of the tablets.

"Well, yes... I thank you for your kindness in offering me those, I think."

Damion patted my back. "And who do I have sitting on me at the moment? Amelia or Henry?"

I slipped off his lap and sat alongside him. "My apologies again. With the drink doing odd things to my head, I thought for a while that I was back with Papa in our library at home. Henry was Papa's pet name for me, shortened from one of my other names for my preference to ride astride where there are no other eyes to take offense at my doing so."

"Riding and French and a library and a papa," Damion said. "Why do I begin to suspect, Amelia Henry, that the surname of Brown does not belong on the end of them?"

I shrugged. "Whether it did originally, it does now. A good name is Brown, for someone desirous of leaving a name behind rather than disgrace it by their own future actions."

Damion smiled. "Disgrace it? How do you intend to do so?"

I looked at him, thought of the boy who'd only laughed at my boyish ways in the past and let a little of the truth of Henrietta out. "By working for my living, I already do so. My family's wealth is gone, dissipated by a man who fooled my mother after Papa died, but still I have an annual allowance paid to me by my godmother and could have chosen instead the more suitable occupation of genteel poverty. But I do not have to spend my allowance on living expenses if I work and can send my salary to join it. In a few years, I will have saved enough to disgrace myself completely and either start up or buy into a going concern."

"Well-enough born that to do such a thing would be considered a disgrace, then?"

"Rather too well for my future plans, I'm afraid."

The clock on the mantle chimed the strokes of the hour. "Five? I must be away. The tweenies bell rings at six and I should be where I'm meant to be by then."

I leaned toward Damion and kissed his cheek. "I do thank you, though, for coming down to me when you saw I was unsteady and for hiding me after. I would have been for the high-jump if I'd been discovered in that state by any of the upper staff. If you would let me out of the terrace door so I may avoid Bert on the chair in the hall?"

Damion pressed me close to his chest and kissed the top of my head. "Yes, you should go and take your lips away before I ask more of them than I ought."

I lifted my face, breathed in the heady scent of him and brushed my lips over his neck. "Yes, I should. Mr. Hubert is the most discreet of men, but still, this house revolves around serving you, and who you are currently bedding is soon known. I'd best take my own good advice and stay within my own station for any choice of a lover."

Damion's eyes widened to his short bark of laughter. "Did you really just say that to me?"

I smiled as I stood. "I did. And now I must bid you a good night, such of it as is left."

Damion followed me to the French windows, turned the key to unlock them and took my hand to his mouth. "But in a different time and place, you would have?"

My heart beat harder at the touch of his lips and I stroked my fingers along his jawline as he released my hand. "Oh, I think so. Don't you?"

I took my hand away to his answering smile and he opened the door to early dawn-break. I stepped over the threshold and picked up the pace of my feet as I walked away, stopping at the coal shed as I entered the back yard and marking my face and hands with daubs of black dust. The servants' hall was silent as I let myself in and ran on light feet up the stairs to my bedroom. I pressed the door shut behind me and Molly opened her eyes.

"Bloody hell, Am! Look at the state of you. Where have you been until this time? Not with Harry?"

I shook my head and loosened the laces on my dress. "No. I haven't seen him. I went out to meet him and the cold air hit me. I became dizzy and lost my bearings. I can't remember how I got there but I woke up in the coal shed about ten minutes ago."

"Am! You were lucky you didn't freeze to death."

My cheeks heated in the face of Molly's concern, so I crossed my fingers and fibbed a little more. "There are plenty of empty hessian sacks in there. I found I'd covered myself up with some."

I brushed the black dust from my face and hands with the hem of my dress, took it off and climbed into bed. "Night, Molly. Shake me hard in the morning if I don't wake with the bell, will you?"

"I will. Night, Am. I'm glad you're back safe."

* * * *

Molly's shake woke me. I used the washing room to remove any last remnants of coal dust and took a long draft of icy water from the pitcher after I cleaned my teeth. A hot bowl of porridge restored my normal good health and I smiled at Harry when he entered the kitchen and sat beside me. He didn't return my smile.

"You didn't manage to wait up for me?"

Molly leaned around me. "But she did, and when she went outside to meet you, the drink and the cold air caught her and she wandered off and fell asleep in the coal shed until the early hours. You should have seen the state of her when she got back to our bedroom. I swear the sweep's boy is cleaner!"

Harry smiled. "You did wait up. I'm sorry, Amelia. The mounts and carriages took longer to reunite with their owners than I thought. You are quite well now?"

"I am, with hot food and plenty of cold water to restore me..." I leaned closer to Harry. "But Harry...friends that touch when it suits. You don't turn up? I don't turn up? So be it. No obligation on either side."

I picked up my bowl and spoon and got up from my chair. "I'll see whether there's anything in the laundry that needs to be put to soak before church."

I left my bowl in the scullery, walked to the laundry and divided delicate lace from hardier linens into smaller baskets then walked back to the kitchen as the first peal from the church bells rang out. Mrs. Price placed a pile of linen squares on the table and clapped her hands.

"Girls, fetch your Sunday bonnets and gloves if you have them. Those that do not, cover your hair with a kerchief and keep your hands modestly clasped for prayer."

I walked up the stairs with Molly, took my bonnet and gloves from my box and put them on, threaded my arm through hers and we walked to the back yard and joined the procession of staff not on duty to wind our way down the lane for Sunday service in church.

Damion followed The Lady Elizabeth and her mama up the aisle and heads from the village peered and bobbed around each other, eager for their first sight of the soon-to-be bride. Two hours later, the vicar released us from our knees, having given his longest and windiest sermon yet in honor of her first attendance. Molly clutched my arm as a breeze with a hint of spring on it refreshed my face as we left the church.

"Oh, my. I thought I was done for there. I don't know how I kept my eyes open through that lot," she said.

I put my arm around her waist. She clasped mine and our knees bent automatically every time a Brougham carriage full of gentry passed to the side of us as we walked back to the Manor. The house wore its normal Sunday face when we returned — the Family and their guests Sabbath quiet, still to be attended to but without the bustle of a weekday. Time moved slowly until Mrs. Price released Molly and I from a pile of mending to take a breath of air on a Sunday afternoon walk.

"Remember, please, to be modest of both voice and pace and, above all, no laughing," she said.

"Yes, Mrs. Price."

James walked into the kitchen as we tied the ribbons of our Sunday bonnets under our chins. "The Ladies have decided the weather is fine enough to take a short airing in the two barouches if well wrapped up in their pelisses. I'm away to instruct Harry and Tom to prepare the carriages and the Gentlemen's mounts for them to ride alongside, if you would care to walk with me to the stables? The carriages are pretty to look at when harnessed."

Mrs. Price nodded and smiled her assent. Phyliss leaned forward.

"You permit this here?"

"Mr. Bennett and I are not inclined to place obstacles in the young people's path, so long as any, ah...prospective friendship is conducted with proper decorum."

The Lady Elizabeth's bedroom bell rang on the board and Phyliss stood. "My little chick. She must wish to change her dress for the outing in the barouche."

James offered Molly and me one arm each when he closed the kitchen door behind us. Molly and I threaded our arms through his and Molly smiled. "Proper decorum until we get out of sight it is, then."

We walked at Sunday pace through the back yard and onto the tree-lined cinder path that wound its way to the stable block. Molly looked at me as we passed out of sight of the back of the house then pulled on the ribbon of her bonnet.

"Last one to the end of the path has to goffer iron all the frills tomorrow."

She pulled her bonnet off her head and began to run. I pulled on the bow of mine and sped after her.

"Molly! Amelia!" James laughed behind us.

Molly beat me to the end of the path by several yards and grinned as she waited for me. James caught up to us and we looped our bonnet ribbons over our wrists and resumed our Sunday pace as we left the shelter of the trees and entered the stable yard. The door to the carriage block stood open, two unharnessed barouches pulled forward to await their horses in front of them and several mounts, including Prince, saddled, their reins tied to the standing post. Harry smiled as he looked up and saw us.

"I came to give you notice of the outing, but you're ahead of me, I see," James said.

"Tom received word by way of Nell being in the general vicinity when the outing was proposed," Harry said. "We're away to bring out the carriage horses, if you wanted to see them harnessed."

"I must be get back to the house. I'm still on duty." James smiled and walked away.

"Will you drive one or ride escort on Bonnie?" I asked.

"I'll drive one, Tom the other and leave William Coachman to his afternoon with his family. It's only one horse for each carriage. There's no need to be calling him from his cottage for that," Harry said and walked into the stable block.

Molly plucked her bonnet from her arm and nudged me at the sound of Damion's voice.

"Best get the fidgets out of their legs if a sedate trot beside the barouche awaits us."

I put my bonnet on my head and fastened it as Damion, Lord Byngingham and Sir Elliott approached the stables. Molly and I bobbed our curtseys as they walked past. Damion's gaze warmed on me for no more than the two seconds it took for my groin to dampen as he and Lord Byngingham acknowledged our respects with a slight tip of their heads. Sir Elliott looked at Molly, then at me, and his gaze stopped for more than a cursory glance at my chest.

He brayed as he walked on. "Fine pair of wenches there, Ashton, especially the big bubbies on the dark one. What, eh? Bend that one over the end of my bed if I find her about her duties in my room. Give her and 'em a little tickle. What, eh?"

Damion turned his head toward his guest. "Moderate your voice and language, Sir. There are no wenches here at Ashton. They are members of my household staff."

"No offense meant to yourself, Ashton. She'll probably be flattered she was even worth my notice. What, eh?"

I nudged Molly and her eyes sparked as she turned to look at me. I smiled. "Molly, dear, I do believe we have an urgent appointment in the flower garden."

Molly looked into my eyes. "We do?"

"Most certainly. I believe the hyacinths are very fine this time of year."

Molly smiled. "Yes, they are, aren't they? We must visit them at once." I walked off at slightly faster-than-the-allowed Sunday pace and Molly muttered, "What will we crush them with?"

"A couple of large stones should do it. I'll pick the leaves with the hem of my dress. You hold your pocket open for me to put them in."

"What are we going to rub it on?"

"His smalls. He hasn't got his man with him. Mr. Hubert's been laying his evening clothes out on his bed for him when he uses the bathroom. I'll go up at the dressing gong, whisk his drawers off his bed while he uses it and get them back in place before he returns to his bedroom."

"That's a brave risk, Am. I thought you'd say we'd rub it on something he sends us to launder."

"It'll be worth it if we find out from James that he's looked rather uncomfortable sitting at his dinner tonight."

Molly laughed and we walked faster, knelt to smell the hyacinth flowers in the garden and I plucked the fattest leaves from the plants and put them in Molly's pocket. Molly found two stones on our way back to the laundry and we pricked the leaves all over and pressed them between the stones to release the clear sap within. Molly found a stone outside the door with a fat dimple in its center. We decanted the liquid into it and I set it inside my upside-down bonnet. Mrs. Price looked up as we entered the kitchen.

"That was a long walk. Where is James?"

"Back on duty a good while now, Mrs. Price," Molly said. "Amelia and I took the chance to take a turn around the flower garden with the Family away on their outing. The hyacinths smell particularly beautiful this year. May we take our bonnets up and put them away before supper?"

Mrs. Price sniffed. "Very well. Yes, you may."

The dressing gong sounded as we opened the green door and stepped upward, me holding my bonnet cupped in my hands. Ellen and Polly passed us on their way down with empty scuttles in their hands.

"How was it tonight? Is Sir Elliot in his room?" I asked.

"She's getting quicker. He was but is now in the bathroom, praise the Lord. God, what a lech! He's just given my arse a right old squeeze on his way past me. Thank goodness there were two of us in his room and I wasn't on my own."

Molly and I increased the pace of our steps. I handed Molly my bonnet and opened the green door at the head of the landing. "Back in a minute..."

I tapped on Sir Elliot's door, received no answer, walked in and picked his underwear up off the bed. Back with Molly in less than a minute later, we dripped sap from the stone down the back seam of his drawers and over the seam under the crotch. I re-folded them into their original creases, passed through the green door, tapped on his door and received no answer again.

His undergarment back in its original position in less than thirty seconds, I ran back to Molly. After we returned our bonnets to our room, we sat at the kitchen table and took up a piece of linen each, stitched small stitches into parted seams and glanced at each other through lowered eyelids while we waited. James took the seat beside Molly and Mr. Bennett intoned Grace. Molly looked at James as the plates went around and asked, "How was service for you tonight, James? It ran smoothly?"

James frowned and cut his beef. "There was rather an odd atmosphere in the dining room. That Sir Elliott was getting some very cold glances from the men—" James put his meat in his mouth, chewed and swallowed. "I think maybe because he wouldn't keep still on his seat and that was disturbing the Ladies."

Molly caught my eye and smiled. "Oh dear. I wonder what was discomforting him?"

James cut another piece of meat. "I don't know, but he kept at it through every remove—lifting first one arse cheek then the other while his face became redder and redder."

I glanced at Molly and smiled at my plate. Ellen, sat on my other side, nudged my knee with hers. I tilted

79

my head to hear her. "You got the old lech? What did he do to call you to action?"

I leaned closer and spoke softly. "Thought we wenches at Ashton should be flattered to receive his attention, especially the wench with the big bubbies who was going to get bent over his bed the next time he found her in his room."

Ellen's face flushed pink. "Coarse bastard. I hate the ones who presume their advances are welcome, just because their station is so far above ours. What did you get him with?"

"Hyacinth sap on the back seam of his drawers."

Ellen smiled. "No wonder he's wriggling. I use a bit of fish oil myself, on the lining of an evening jacket in the armpits. It doesn't smell of much until it gets warm, when the Gentleman concerned sweats up a bit during the evening, then it doesn't half pong. Lord Markham hasn't visited since."

I laughed. "Well done, wench. What, eh?"

Ellen snorted and let out a giggle.

Mrs. Price looked down the length of the table and barked, "Ellen Smith. Amelia Brown. It is the Sabbath, if you please."

"Sorry, Mrs. Price," we apologized.

Mr. Bennett, James and Fred left the table to clear the Family's dessert course and Molly and I helped Ellen take the dirty crockery from our table to the scullery. James brought the cloth down.

"Sorry. Sir Elliot dropped his glass. The stain is extensive tonight. He hasn't sat with the men for port and brandy but has retired early."

I held out my hand for the cloth and stifled a yawn as the aftermath of the jig caught up with me. Molly took the cloth from James.

"I'll take it. You're tired. Sit a while and we'll go straight up to bed after prayers."

I yawned behind my hand. "I thank you, Molly. I will indeed be glad to find my bed tonight."

I sat at the table. Harry sat in Molly's vacated chair. "Sir Elliot's voice carries. I heard what he said about you from inside the stables. No wonder you and Molly didn't wait around to see the carriages. His Lordship and Lord Byngingham did not look amused."

"It happens. A Gentleman inquires because they know—as do we—that the answer isn't always no, but an occasional one will try and tumble a maid without so much as a by your leave, although most of them do not go so far as to express their opinion of our charms so openly in public."

"What do you do if one of them grabs hold of you in their bedroom?"

"It's never happened to me, but from what I've heard from others, mostly we manage to have an accident with the sharp end of our hair stick-pin on whatever bit of them we can reach as we wriggle in their grasp then get out of the room before the event can become more than an unpleasant groping." I yawned behind my hand. "My apologies, Harry. After the jig, I'm tired, but apart from the dizzy spell, I had such a happy time. You dance light on your feet and are strong enough to lift your partner with ease."

Harry smiled. "I enjoyed the dancing, too. It is a pity that we do not get to do so more often."

"You may get another chance sooner than you think, as one of the Family's personal staff. You will accompany His Lordship to his wedding. His bride's people may permit such a thing if you are not required to accompany His Lordship on his honeymoon."

"It won't be the same as at home with all of us so familiar with one another, and as to the honeymoon, I won't know until the last, will I? With only His Lordship's best man privy to the details. It will depend on whether he chooses to stay in England or follow the fashion to take train and steamer and leave these shores, although the second is what I will wish for, so I am not away from Ashton for weeks on end."

I smiled. "Then I will hope for train and steamer for you, so you may come home."

Molly opened the kitchen door as Mr. Bennett took his place at the table for our final prayer. After, I followed her up the stairs and didn't stir under my bedcovers until she shook me awake in the morning. I stretched and found the lingering aftermath of my excesses had been cured by a full night of sleep, then completed my recovery by way of a large bowl of porridge after we entered the kitchen. Mrs. Price looked at Molly and me as we ate.

"I have been considering the matter of your half-days. The laundry is at its busiest at the beginning of a week, so, Amelia, you may take your half-day on a Thursday. Molly, continue taking yours on a Friday, if you please."

My shoulders relaxed at the boon. My annual allowance being due to me, my presence was required in York during the next two weeks to take receipt of it and a half-day on a pre-determined day of the week would enable me to write to Papa's man of business with a surety of date and time when I could be there.

"I thank you, Mrs. Price," I said then nudged Molly. "My hair feels insecure this morning. I'll run back upstairs for another pin and meet you in the laundry?"

Molly spooned up another mouthful and opened her eyes wide at me. "I'll put the goffering iron on to heat for you, shall I?"

I knocked my knee on hers. "Molly, how kind. You know how I love the intricate work. I won't deprive you, though. You may keep all the satin and lace for yourself."

Mrs. Price sniffed. "Such good girls. Run along and do your duty as you know how."

I took my bowl and spoon to the scullery, ran up the stairs and sat with my back pressed against the bedroom door after I pulled my box near. I opened it and lifted out items until I came to the few essentials hidden in the bottom of it that I had brought with me from home. It included my leather stationery case that contained a slim, corked vial of ink, a nibbed pen and some vellum-crested stationery.

My note to Mr. Whistlethorpe inscribed, I added a penny stamp to the envelope, lifted out Henrietta's morning dress, tried the fit against me and found the bodice that had been so loose on me when I left home still had enough room for my enlarged chest, even if the fit would be somewhat tight. Satisfied, I folded it back into my box, sat my other possessions on top of it, pushed my box back into place and ran down the stairs to the green door that led into the Family's entrance hall.

The footman's chair was empty as I peeped around the door, so I walked to the post tray, slipped my letter into the middle of a pile of post awaiting collection then walked to the laundry, secure in the knowledge that no one had seen me do so. Molly laughed when I entered it. "So, what did you want in the bedroom, really?"

I smiled. "To write a note to someone from home, now I know on which day of the week my half-day will fall. I hope to meet with them when they visit York."

Molly's eyes moistened. "A visitor from home? How I hope they will manage it for you. It's been three years for me now and a new brother I've not yet met."

"How far away are they, Molly?" I asked.

"Bossal. Ten miles out. Too far to walk there and back in a half-day." She sighed.

"You miss them?"

"Not the living at home... There were ten of us in three rooms and never enough of anything to go around, but I'd like to catch sight of them all for an hour, especially Mother." Molly giggled. "Tho tha's be reet upskittled by I now. Reet posh as I now is."

I laughed. "That's why I didn't open my mouth much when I first came here, until I'd heard enough to be able to speak without my natural accent."

"What was it, then?" she asked.

I smiled—*even more posh*—but answered to mimic the cries of the street vendors I used to hear outside my window when in I stayed in London as a child. "Furvver souff. Mrs. Price took me on for the Season and I came north on the staff wagon when she liked my work."

Molly grinned and I picked up a bucket. "And goffering already, when we haven't even washed it, Molly? Mrs. Price must be going soft with all the romance of the wedding in the air not to notice that. I didn't tell you, did I?"

"No, what?"

I looked over my shoulder as I opened the laundry room door. "When I was hiding in the lavatory after the jig, Bertram invited Mable to his sitting room for a glass of port, and Mable responded with due appreciation."

Molly's giggle followed me out. Damion, standing in front of Prince's loose box, invited me closer with a slight tip of his head as I bobbed. I walked over to him. "My Lord?"

"Would it be possible to request a pail of water for Prince, so I may speak with you while he drinks without it seeming untoward that I do?"

I nodded, walked to the pump, half-filled the bucket and took it to the loose box. Damion opened the bottom half of the door and I put the bucket within Prince's reach and looked at him. "Something troubles you?"

"I am not perfectly acquainted with several of my house guests this weekend."

"Vouched for by a person not perfectly acquainted with your outspoken guest themself?" I ventured.

Damion nodded. "Sir Elliot found other business called him elsewhere this morning. I'll drop the hint around Town in Boodle's and White's gentlemen's clubs that he's a man inclined to step well over the boundary of polite inquiry where the maids are concerned."

I smiled. "I thought you might."

"Given his discomfort at dinner last evening, I take it you were not inclined to leave him to me to deal with?"

"No. Whatever my previous position in life, I'm a maid now and have to fit to their ways. If I'd let that offense go by without taking action, it would have been remarked on, and without apology, I'll admit to a certain satisfaction from the doing of it."

Damion smiled. "Then I'll admit to my enjoyment of it, too. He did look most devilishly uncomfortable."

I leaned forward and kissed Prince's nose. "I should get Molly her water now. By your leave?"

Damion nodded. I picked up my bucket and turned away. Molly looked up from sorting laundry into different baskets as I walked into the laundry.

"You talk to His Lordship and he talks to you? What does he say?"

I crossed my fingers in my head and trotted out a half-truth.

"Horseflesh. He's seen me with Harry, in and around the yard. It crosses the divide for a comment or two about a shared interest in the blood stock. I think maybe he realizes I would do Harry's job if females were permitted to do such a thing."

"You can ride? I think you and Harry are quite well suited, if so," Molly smiled.

"I can, although I haven't in a long while now."

"Your stepfather sold the family pony and drank the proceeds, I suppose?" She sighed.

I thought of the value of the stable the wastrel had sold, apart from such mounts as were of use to him. "Something like that."

I washed through the morning and ironed goffered tucks, pleats and frills into the Ladies' undergarments after our midday meal. I saw the embroidered mark on the seam of a peignoir that identified it as belonging to Lady Mariah Shelling and remembered the slaps Miss Mariah Fleetwood, as she was named then, had given my five-year-old leg, so I dripped the last of the hyacinth sap onto its armpit. Cap on, I carried the layers and Molly opened doors for me to pass through. Mrs. Price looked up as we entered the kitchen.

"Is that all of it? Nothing remains undone in the laundry?"

"Yes, Mrs. Price," Molly said. "Nothing remains in any of the baskets. I checked."

Mrs. Price smiled. "Good girls. I knew I could rely on you. Our guests leave us in the morning, even Lord and Lady Shelling, who were due to stay for another two days yet. I will reassure their valets and lady's maids that their Masters' and Mistresses' possessions are back in their charge."

Molly giggled as she let the green door swing shut behind me. "As long as all the stockings made it to the laundry and are not hiding at the bottom of anyone's bed, waiting to be found by Ellen when she changes the linens."

I looked over my shoulder and smiled. "The stockings are all correctly paired, but I don't believe I have the correct complement of frilly drawers for the amount of days the guests stayed."

Molly snorted. "Who's short? Not Lady Shelling again?"

"No. The insignia I'm missing is the small white dove of Mrs. Henry Carleton."

Molly laughed. "But she's not a day under forty!"

"But very well preserved."

"Pickled, more like."

"Permanently, from what I heard her lady's maid say to Miss Croker."

Molly pushed the green door open and wiped the grin off her face as she peeked around it. "All clear, but it must be nearly time for tea, so some of the Ladies might be up for a change of dress."

"Good. Their lady's maids will be, too, then. We can hand this over at the door."

Molly knocked on Damion's door and Mr. Hubert opened it.

"I'll take it. His Lordship will be up to exchange his riding gear for a day suit shortly."

Molly lifted a layer off the top of my pile, laid it on Mr. Hubert's outstretched arms and did the same with Lord Byngingham's man at his door.

"Nothing for Lord Sudgley, the unwed Ladies next, then up a floor for the married guests," Molly said.

I nodded and followed Molly along the hallway toward the Family's carpeted staircase that rose through the center of the house and made the division between the Bachelors' rooms and those of the unmarried or widowed females. Two voices sounded as we reached it.

"Oh, most certainly for the Little Season," Mrs. Henry Carleton said.

"I will send a card for our entertainment and you must call," Lady Shelling replied.

I stood still alongside Molly, our backs pressed against the wood paneling to wait for them to pass on and upward to the bedrooms of the married guests on the floor above. Lady Shelling turned her head in our direction and Molly bobbed.

"You there, girl. Is any of that mine?"

Molly nodded. "Yes, M'am."

The stairs squeaked under a heavier tread and I looked down the flight to see Damion on his way up.

"Get it to my room directly, then. I do not require to wait on your convenience."

Lady Shelling and Mrs. Carleton turned away to continue their ascent.

"Something about that other girl. Something vaguely familiar..." Lady Shelling said.

"Really? Probably some Lord's by-blow then. They do get about, don't they?" Mrs. Henry Carleton replied.

I bit on my lip and fought to keep my face straight as Damion stared after the retreating backs of yet more outspoken rudeness, then I nudged Molly and about-turned as my wayward sense of humor caught my ribs and my urge to laugh became worse. I stepped forward and Molly stepped alongside me. "Amelia, His Lordship was coming up the stairs. We didn't curtsey — and you didn't curtsey to the Ladies."

The pile of laundry on my arms shook along with my shoulders as I walked with the spring of the surface underfoot to tell me of a heavier tread behind us. "Oh dear, but he was only halfway up. I don't expect he noticed."

"You're not really some Lord's bastard daughter, are you, Am?"

"Maybe I am, Molly. Wha' der ya reckon to me chances?"

"No, sorry, Am. Tha's baint reet posh'nuff."

I laughed as Molly pushed open the green door, walked through it and I looked at her as it swung shut behind us. "Do you wish to reorganize the pile?"

She nodded, lifted the top half of the pile and we topped and tailed it between our arms, ran up the stairs and delivered clean laundry to the married guests' rooms then ran back to where we'd started, did our unwed Ladies' and returned to the kitchen for supper.

Staff left the table as supper finished, and Mr. Bennett, Bert and Fred returned Above Stairs while Ellen and Polly took up their station at the scullery sink. I walked to the kitchen dresser and picked up two copies of *The Times* set on its top. "Shall I deal with these for the pots, Mrs. Price?"

Mrs. Price inclined her head. "If you would."

I sat at the table and scanned each page before I tore it into smaller squares and left the articles that interested me as complete as I could to read in the privacy of the female washing room. I found no mention of my home in the Society pages, so had a look at the matches, hatches and dispatches as I tidied the squares into a neater pile then ran up and down the back stairs and put the sheets where they were most needed. Bert and Fred sat at the table with Harry when I returned to the kitchen. I sat alongside Ellen and listened in.

"We must get some practice in early before the match this year. We can't allow the village team to win two years in a row," Bert said.

"'Tis only March. The match isn't until the first Saturday in May," Fred countered.

"True, but we have to remove with the Family for the Little Season, so that's three weeks in April that we won't be here for our practice," Bert said.

"Depending on the date of His Lordship's marriage, I might not even get to play." Harry frowned. "But I shall practice as if I will. Bat and ball in the back field the next chance we get, lads. Mr. Bennett won't mind. You know how keen he is on the sport."

I smiled. "I'll field for you if I'm free of duties."

"And me," Ellen said.

"But you're girls," Fred objected.

"Don't be silly, Fred." Ellen laughed. "We might not be able to play in a match like you men, but even girls can toss the ball back. I used to do it all the time for my brothers."

"Well, all right then. I just hope you ain't too slow at running to fetch it in those skirts. Us men need our ball back, quick and true."

I smiled at Ellen. "Don't worry, Fred. We'll let you run after your own ball if you find us too slow or clumsy with it."

Mr. Bennett took his place at the table. "Cricket, is it? We can't have the village team getting one over on us again..."

I turned to Ellen. "How good are you with the ball?"

Ellen leaned closer. "Pretty fair. I have five brothers. You?"

"Not bad. I have no brothers, but I was ever a tomboy as a girl, and the local lads used to let me bowl for them at their practice."

Ellen glanced at Fred. "Are you going to try and take his wicket for his cheek?"

"I'm going to give it my best shot. You?"

"Any and every chance I get."

Molly slipped onto the chair beside me. James took a place beside Harry as Mrs. Price bustled up to the table.

"Mr. Bennett. The time, if you please!"

Mr. Bennett looked at the clock on the wall. "Ah, yes, Mrs. Price. My apologies, but the cricket match, you know. Fred, I believe you're on the chair in the hall tonight?"

Mr. Bennett stood as Fred left the table and the rest of us clasped our hands, eyes lowered, and waited for Mr. Bennett's 'amen' then got up and pushed our chairs under the table. I walked with Molly up the stairs, lit a nightstick and pushed the bedroom door shut behind us as she pulled the lamp from behind her box.

I blew the nightstick out as she lit it, took my boots off and sat on my bed. Molly unlaced her boots and dress and got into bed. "You haven't slipped away to meet Harry this last night or two?"

I reached into my box and took out my toothbrush and tin of powder. "No, I will not do so too often. I wouldn't wish Harry or anyone else to develop the notion that we are walking out together or are anything more than friends. Are you walking out with James now, then?"

Molly smiled. "Not quite as such yet, although neither of us will be keeping company or kissing anyone else at present, I think."

I picked up my towel. "I will ready my needle and prepare to embroider your linens at your word. You both seem very fond."

Molly tucked her bedcovers around her neck and sighed. "Yes, I believe we are. Turn the wick down when you get back from the washroom?"

I nodded. "I will. Goodnight, Molly."

I used the washroom, darkened the lamp, climbed into bed and, as I fell asleep, hoped for a future for Molly without so many births in it as to keep her and James unhappily poor.

Chapter Five

Molly yawned in the morning, watched me take my toothbrush out of my box to go the washing room and swung her legs out of bed as I returned to the bedroom to dress.

"You do that again in the morning, although you've taken no food overnight?"

"Yes, Molly. It wakes my mouth and freshens my breath."

I followed her over to the laundry after we'd broken our fast. She picked up a bucket and said, "Let's get the water on to boil. It will be a heavy load today when the beds are stripped of their linens as the guests leave, and I have to say I'll be glad to see the back of this lot, what with Sir Elliott's coarseness then Lady Shelling being so high-handed last evening and Mrs. Carleton saying what she did an' all."

"I think that maybe Sir Elliott and Mrs. Carleton are attached to the Wellinghams rather than to our Family. They've never visited before, have they?"

"No, and I hope they don't do so again, along with a hope that will include Lady Shelling if she and His Lordship are no longer intimate."

I picked up my bucket and followed Molly out of the door. "Perhaps they won't, then."

Ellen and Polly brought the first sheets and towels to us as the water came to the boil, and as Molly had foretold, their thick, cotton absorbed a great deal of water. My shoulders ached with the handling of their wettened bulk by lunchtime. We washed a second load after we'd eaten and it blew on the lines while we ironed the first and folded it over wooden racks. The steam gone from the room with the day's washing complete, we ironed some more, added it to the racks as the dinner gong sounded and left the fires banked low for the bed linens to dry completely overnight in the warmth of the laundry.

Molly rotated her shoulders as I pulled the door shut behind us.

"Two more loads tomorrow should see the worst of it done and we can catch up on the shirts, collars and smalls on Wednesday," she said.

I followed her across the back yard and stretched my arms out and up to relieve a tightness in my muscles. "Lord, I hope so. That was some work to get through. My arms are aching from the mangling of it."

I sat beside Molly at supper and neither of us found the energy to join the chatter around the table before we climbed into bed. Mrs. Price sent Polly with us in the morning to carry the dry linens into the house to be laid in the linen press with a sprinkle of dried lavender between each layer, and Molly and I washed, ironed and ached through the rest of the day. The following morning, the remainder of the linens and guest towels joined the others in the lavender-scented linen press and Molly picked through baskets of the lighter items awaiting us in the laundry.

"Nearly back to normal," she said. "Some shirts and collars and the rest is just smalls."

The laundry left to blow in the breeze, I returned to the kitchen for lunch and smiled at Ellen, sitting at the table running her fingers over the finer weave of a parlor maid's dress. I pulled a chair out from the table and sat. "Well done, Ellen. Your dress is very fine."

Ellen turned and showed me her back. "Look. I have the buttons of an Above Stairs maid and my pinny has a frill to its edge, too. I never felt so pretty in my life, even if my dress does still have to be black."

"You look it. Is Polly quick enough at her tasks now to be left to do them alone?"

"She's much better, if still a little slow. Nell and Bess will keep her up to scratch between them until Mrs. Price finds another tweenie to partner her."

"What about the cricket match? Bowling will be of risk to your dress if it fastens with buttons."

"I thought that, too. I can still throw, but only underarm."

"Call and throw the ball to me instead of back to the men if you see a chance for Fred's stumps. I'll overarm it at the wicket."

Ellen smiled. "We'll pay the bugger back for his cheek between us, to be sure."

Harry and Bert sat at the table.

"We have permission from Mr. Bennett to practice our bowling instead of sitting to lunch tomorrow," Harry said. "Will you girls be able to join us?"

"I will," I said. "It's my half-day."

Ellen nudged my knee under the table. "And mine. Mrs. Price, may we take bread and cheese over tomorrow for lunch to the men practicing their sport?"

"You may, and also some apples from the winter store. Mayhap you girls would enjoy picking some bluebells from the bank that borders the field? I would appreciate a touch of spring in a jug that stands on the table."

"Yes, Mrs. Price. Such an enjoyable task to do while the men are rushing about their business," I agreed.

Molly smiled. "It's not my half-day but I would certainly like to pick a few bluebells over the lunch hour. If I may join the cheese and bread picnic, Mrs. Price?"

Mrs. Price inclined her head. James sat at the table.

"Do you practice your cricket tomorrow, James?" Molly asked.

"If the weather is fair, I do. All the footmen can. William Coachman, not being a sporting man, has agreed to sit on the hall chair for an hour or so in gratitude of Harry not calling him from his cottage on Sunday afternoon."

"I shall hope for no rain on the morrow, then."

Lunch over, I ironed alongside Molly until it was time to put our caps on and take the clean laundry Above Stairs. "It was exciting with the jig and everything, but I'm glad to be back to normal, aren't you?" she said as we walked down the Family's hallway toward the Ladies' rooms.

I nodded and knocked at His Lordship's sister's door, received no answer from her or Miss Croker and opened it. Molly followed me in. I took The Lady Emma's layer from the top of the pile and laid it on her daybed.

"The Lady Emma will have to have her own lady's maid soon, won't she?" Molly said.

"I would think so. There'll be too many social engagements for Miss Croker to manage her and her mama together when The Lady Emma comes out, let alone that Lady Emma will wish for her own lady's maid to confirm her new stature of being officially 'out'."

Molly sighed. "I've always wondered how it must be with all the new dresses and the balls and the parties... Weeks and weeks of the Season just given over to enjoying yourself."

I smiled. "That would depend on whether it's your notion of enjoyment or not. Some debutantes are so nervous that the whole thing is just an ordeal, and the thought of their presentation to the Queen, with the managing of the court dress and the feathered headdress they will have to wear to do so, can bring on an attack of the vapors in even the most confident of them."

"You know a fair bit about it, Am?"

"A bit." I smiled as I remembered my lessons in etiquette, dancing and deportment from a time when Mama still thought my sister and I would have a Season. "Mainly from what I saw of The Lady Georgina's coming out, when I worked at the London residence last year, and the newspaper. They write reams all about the Season in them."

"Not something I will ever get to see, even secondhand, with only personal servants removing with the Family to London."

I shut Lady Emma's door behind us. "Who fills Mrs. Price's position while she's away? They won't leave those of us that stay behind without supervision, will they?"

Molly giggled. "No. I wish. The most senior maid steps into the position of under housekeeper. Last year it was Violet, and she was an absolute cow. Those of us left behind were more than thankful when His Lordship came home for a few days and Mr. Hubert took the reins back for a while."

"I did notice that His Lordship was not in residence in London for much of the Season last year."

Molly smiled. "No, His Lordship has always returned to Ashton at regular intervals during it, but I don't think he'll get away with that this year with a betrothed to attend to and Lady Emma's coming out, do you?"

I knocked on Damion's door. "I wouldn't think so. No."

Mr. Hubert opened Damion's door and held his arms out for me to lift the layer from Molly's outstretched arms and place it on his.

"Amelia, Molly, I thank you. This is very timely, considering your workload this last day or two."

Damion, sitting behind his desk, glanced up as Mr. Hubert spoke. I smiled at Mr. Hubert then over his shoulder at the warmth that flared for a brief instant in Damion's eyes as he looked at me. Mr. Hubert lowered his voice a little as he took a step back to nudge the door shut with his foot. "You are coming to watch cricket practice tomorrow?"

I nodded. "Yes. We maids are going to field for you."

Mr. Hubert continued to close the door to the sound of Damion's voice.

"Ah, Hubert, did I just hear you mention cricket?"

I walked along the hallway toward the green door with Molly. "What happens on the day of the match, Molly? Do all that can, go and watch?"

"It's like a holiday." Molly smiled. "The women from the village dress the field with flags and bunting and everyone that can turns out to cheer the teams on. Vendors make their way to us from York, and in the next field along from the pitch, there will be stalls with ribbons and bows, sweets, pies, ale and even 'Bowling for the pig'. And maids are permitted to wear their own dress if they are lucky enough to possess such a thing."

I looked at Molly and thought of her wish for a Season of new dresses. "Then, I believe it is about time we both did. I have a spare guinea saved, and if the haberdasher has plain poplin at sixpence the yard, it will buy sufficient material for us to fashion a simple panel skirt and a bodice to go with it, don't you think?"

"Amelia! You can't spend your pennies on me. You may require them yourself."

"I can and I will. Unlike you, I do not have to send most of my salary home. Let me do this, Molly. It would increase my pleasure in any new dress of my own to know that you have one, too."

Molly smiled. Her eyes sparkled. "A new dress. I've never had one. All the clothes I've ever owned have been worn by others before me."

"Then it's settled. I shall walk to the village and visit the haberdasher's when cricket practice finishes tomorrow. I may not have much of a choice, but have you a preference for color if I do?"

Molly laughed and skipped down two steps. "Pink, if they have it, please. How much I've longed for a pink dress. And you are the best friend ever and I thank you with all of my heart."

I smiled as I pushed through the green door. "You may not say so when I ask you to help set my sleeves and adjust my darts for me. I'm neat with my needle and can embroider if I must, but the finer arts of dressmaking are not mine."

Molly pulled her chair out from the table and sat. "I've not made a dress, but I've taken some apart to adjust them and know how the parts are shaped and fit. Buy a tuppenny pattern for the bodice, if they have one, though. Then we will have a choice in the style to suit the difference in our shapes. What color do you favor for your dress?"

"Blue, if they have one that is not pale — or green, as long as the shade is not mossy."

Ellen sat beside me and nudged my arm as the plates and breadboard went around and the men talked of fast balls and the prospect of wickets. She moved farther up the table after supper to listen to Fred and Mr. Hubert. Harry moved into her seat and asked, "You are in good spirits tonight? I thought you and Molly likely to fall asleep over your dinner this last night or two."

"I confess that we were. The work is heavy in the laundry after as large a house party as we have just had, but the worst is over now that the linen presses are full once more. And you, Harry? Your duties have returned to normal now that the additional blood stock has departed?"

Harry nodded. "We forked the last of their shit onto Farmer Hawes' cart this afternoon for his fields after Mr. Robinson had helped himself to a barrowload or two to spread on his roses."

"Is Prince calmer now that his rival stallions have gone?"

"Much. Now he has only his normal harem in attendance."

I smiled. "Yes, all the Ashton horses are mares, bar Prince, aren't they? Even the carriage horses."

"Prince does not react well to any competition, and His Lordship is indulgent where Prince is concerned."

I thought of Damion at thirteen and the constant companion that had always followed at his heels. "Why are there no dogs at Ashton, though? Is it not usual that at least a couple should be running around a house of this size?"

Harry leaned closer. "The old Marquis, His Lordship's father..."

A man with silvered hair, well-built but with distant, blue eyes in which a gleam of amusement had never been seen by me as a child came to mind and I nodded.

"Got to be a funny old coot toward the end. Took it into his head during his last illness that the bloodline he'd created in the hounds should die with him. He ordered the gamekeeper to shoot the pack and that included His Lordship's favorite bitch and the litter she'd just whelped. There's never been a dog, pet or otherwise, at Ashton since."

I swallowed. "Where was His Lordship that he couldn't save them?"

"I forget for what exactly, but we were out on the estate. I tell you... I ain't a squeamish man, but I'll never forget the sight when we rode into the back yard that day. All the adult dogs, each with a bullet hole between their eyes, laid out in a line, the pups of the bitches newly drowned in a line down from the female's bellies, the old Marquis strutting about counting 'em all to make sure one hadn't been missed.

His Lordship, for a big man, is a man of equable temper, but he came near to losing control that day."

I blinked against the picture in my head of rows of the dead dogs, thirty couples to the pack plus the pups, looked into Harry's troubled brown eyes and saw that whatever picture I held in my mind fell short of what must have been the reality. "I'm sorry, Harry. I can see your pain."

Harry looked at his hands resting on the table. "I don't often speak of it, but I felt I could to you. You can't tell another man stuff like that without sounding lily-livered and I knew I could tell you and you wouldn't set up a screech like a female normally would."

I smiled as he raised his head. "I think maybe you need me to hold you for a while?" The darkness left his eyes, even though the color of his irises deepened. "My need for a little fresh air will overcome me in a few minutes after you leave to settle the blood stock, I believe," I said.

Harry smiled and stood from the table. I let myself out of the kitchen door a few minutes after him, slipped into Prince's loose box and closed both halves of the door behind me. Harry stepped forward.

"Amelia..."

I walked toward to the warmth in his voice, pulled on the bow on the back of my dress, shrugged the bodice off my shoulders and unbuttoned the front of my shift as Harry put his arms around my waist. "I'm here, Harry. Would you care to unbutton your britches? I would like to see and touch you, too."

He breathed faster, unbuttoned his breeches and eased his cock out, stiff and hard. I ran my hand over the shape of it, explored with my fingers, found creases of skin at its end and eased them forward then back. His voice caught in the back of his throat.

"Amelia... Yes."

My sex dampened at his reaction. I cupped his soft balls in my other hand while I continued to cover his cockhead then expose it again. "You like, Harry? Would you like more of this while you suck on my nipples? Your fingers are welcome up my skirt, although not your cock."

Harry murmured into my neck, lifted the hem of my dress and sought the heat between my thighs with one hand, his other on my breast. He bent his head, fastened his mouth on my nipple and eased his stiffened finger into my wet center. I pushed against it as he moved it up and down but missed the throb that wanted to feel his touch. He put a second finger in and thrust his cock faster in my hand. I tilted my pelvis to urge his fingers to touch where I needed them to be and warm cream spurted over my hand as he moaned. "Oh, God..."

He panted into my neck as he removed his fingers. "That was good for you, too, this time? I was not unmanned too quickly?"

I hugged him to me, gave his shirt tail his output back and kissed his neck as I acknowledged to myself that the attraction between Harry and I shone brighter for him than for me. "Yes, Harry. You are a sweet lover and one day you will walk down a church aisle with a bride on your arm. She will be a very lucky girl indeed."

"But it will never be you?"

I cupped his face in my hands and kissed his lips. "No, it won't, my friend. Don't look for that from me. I have some family history that makes the thought of marriage so unpalatable to me that I will never attempt it. Friends always, I hope—friends that touch occasionally if we both wish it. When that special girl comes along for you, it will be with only good wishes on either side for the future happiness of the other."

Harry put his softened cock into his breeches and fastened them as I refastened my shift and dress. "I'm sorry for whatever it is that makes you pull back, but I understand. I would have always wanted you for a friend, with or without what we've shared, but for what we have, I thank you," he said.

I looked into his eyes as he smiled at me and smiled back at him as I leaned forward and kissed his cheek.

"As I will always thank you. I'll go back in."

I followed Molly up the stairs after our goodnight prayer, woke in the morning and wriggled into the pair of boy's buckskin breeches that I took from my box after I used the washing room. My dress draped over them, I walked down the stairs to find my breakfast. Ellen grinned at me as she picked up her feather duster to go Above Stairs to the morning room. Molly looked at me as we walked to the laundry.

"What's going on between you and Ellen? Something, I can tell."

I smiled. "Just that Fred's been a cheeky bugger where females are concerned over whether we can play cricket or not. Ellen and I have both tossed a ball or two when we were young, and we're planning to hit his wicket and get him run out, if we can."

Molly grinned. "Never! You think you can?"

I raised the hem of my dress and showed Molly the edge of my breeches. "Going to give it my best overarm shot, without fear of showing my arse."

"Amelia! That's boy's britches you're wearing!"

I laughed. "I know. My father always wanted a son, and I was the nearest he ever got to one. I dressed as a boy at times so I could go out and about with him."

Molly smiled. "Before you had a stepfather that got on the gin?"

"Yes, Molly, before then. But those times are gone now, and although I'll remember them always, I don't dwell on them. It's my life for the living now and I'm going to clean bowl Fred if I can."

Molly laughed. "And I will cheer loud when you do."

"Yes, I know you will. Whatever I had before my father died, everyone here at Ashton has been more of a family to me than I've known since."

"Get 'em, Am, like we would our brothers if we could."

"For all the brothers we never had or have never met, I most certainly will."

I bucketed water into the laundry, washed and pegged out then walked to the kitchen with Molly at lunchtime. Ellen smiled when we walked in through the door and lifted a basket from the table. "The men have gone on ahead. Lunch is ready to take and Mrs. Oates has given us a flagon of her ginger ale."

I looked at Mrs. Oates. "Your ginger beer? I thank you, Mrs. Oates."

"Just a little treat for you. Enjoy it and don't let the men drink it all to satisfy their thirst before you even get a taste."

"We won't, Mrs. Oates," Molly said. "I will take charge of the basket at lunchtime and make sure they do not."

Molly picked up the stoneware flagon of drink and we sauntered out of the kitchen door into air that was fresh but with a hint of the summer to come in the warmth of the breeze and the sound of a hard ball hitting a bat. I climbed over the stile into the field and took the basket from Ellen so she could do the same, and Molly followed her over. James, like the other men in the field, jacketless with his sleeves rolled up, looked over and shouted.

"Bert's just hit a boundary and you weren't here to run after it."

Ellen called back. "Well, we're here now, so you can move a little infield if you like."

I carried our lunch, and Molly the flagon, over to the trunk of the oak tree under branches full of tight, curled buds of the new season's leaves and we set them down then walked onto the field. I looked at Ellen. "Just yell 'Am' if you see a chance."

She nodded and moved farther along the green. Molly walked past her and Fred continued to bowl to Bert. Ellen, Molly and I ran for the ball whenever it came in our direction, tossed it underarm back to James or Harry for them to return to Fred until ten balls later when Bert hit his ball skyward and James jumped and took the catch.

"Out!"

Fred took the bat. Bert moved into James' position so James could take his turn to keep wicket and Harry took his turn to bowl. Mr. Hubert came onto the field, stripped off his jacket and waistcoat and rolled up his sleeves.

"Where may I best serve?"

Harry looked around the field. "To the left of Amelia, if you please, Mr. Hubert."

Mr. Hubert moved into the gap. I re-sighted the wicket and moved five paces to the left. Ellen stepped to mirror my movement and took her chance six balls later to the snatch the ball from the air and shout.

"Am!"

I stretched out my hand and wrapped my fingers around the ball as it hit my palm then half-turned, sighted the middle stump and released the ball with an overarm swing that contained every ounce of power my honed, laundry-maid muscles could give it. Fred, three strides into making his run, stared at the speed of the ball as it flew, hit his wicket with a crack and the bails fell. James laughed and gave a shout as Molly and Ellen cheered.

"Out!"

Fred looked at James and objected, "I can't be out. They're not even really playing."

Ellen hooted. "Quick and true enough for you, was it, Fred? Give in and admit it. You doubted us maids could either run or throw and we've just proved you wrong."

Fred looked at Ellen's face and smiled. "Yes, well, you shouldn't be able to do so. You're girls. You should be sitting, looking on admiringly and picking bluebells, but being as you're not, I will admit it. It was a damn fine overarm, Amelia, and I declare myself well and truly out."

Ellen walked over to Fred and chucked him under his chin. "Silly man. No sisters, I suppose. Get yourself under the tree with the basket. It's time you men ate or you'll be hungry back at your work this afternoon. Practice a little more after, if you have the time."

Fred turned to walk alongside Ellen. "You look very pretty today, Ellen, in your new dress."

James and Harry caught up with me as I followed along behind Ellen and Fred.

"Was that britches I saw when your dress tipped at the back as you threw the ball?" Harry grinned.

I smiled. "It most certainly was. There's nothing of me going on public display from a wayward skirt when I run or throw."

Bert laughed behind me. "Britches. You're wearing male trews?"

I looked over my shoulder at him. "As it has to be, being as such things don't exist in female form."

"Females can have drawers," he said.

I laughed. "Have you ever been in closer contact with a pair, other than through the eyepiece of a penny peep-show machine?"

"No, I haven't! And a penny show hasn't come my way yet, either."

"Then you'll not realize they have a wretched great split that runs back to front in the center. A pair of those would do nothing to hide anything a female might be attempting to keep from public view."

Mr. Hubert hurried up behind us. "Amelia, my dear girl... The subject matter..." He patted my shoulder and lowered his voice. "Cricket. Well, to be more precise, the opening match of the house team versus that from the village is a *big* thing and attracts attention."

I noted his quick glance at the side of the field as I dropped back to walk alongside him and directed my voice toward the hedgerow. "Oh yes, Mr. Hubert, my apologies. I understand. A person of delicate sensibilities might be offended to hear mention of anything that hints that females might have such things as legs under their skirts. Is it just females that have the vapors, do you think? Or would perhaps a male of higher sensibility be quite overset by the mention of drawers?"

"Well, Amelia... It's just that such things are not mentioned Above Stairs in polite company."

I sighed. "I know, and it's quite a problem, isn't it? How we are to return Mrs. Carleton's drawers to her is quite beyond me."

Mr. Hubert's lips tilted to a smile. "Where?"

I smiled sideways at him. "Mr. Albert Bathurst's room, on the floor beneath the bed."

Molly played housewife under the tree and handed out hunks of bread with wedges of cheese, and the flagon of ginger ale was passed around for everyone to take their share. Ellen giggled as she swallowed then hiccupped. "I wonder how she gets the bubbles in it that go right up your nose?"

Harry tossed the cricket ball from hand to hand. Fred caught it in mid-throw and threw it over Harry's head to Bert. Bert laughed as Harry lunged for it and threw it to James, who tossed it to Fred. Harry jumped up to intercept it as Fred threw the ball high in the air to loop it back to Bert and it caught in a V of crossed branches in the oak tree.

James laughed, grabbed the bottom branch of the tree and swung himself up. "I'll get it." The second branch up creaked and bowed at his weight. James climbed down. "You'll have to do it, Fred. You're the lightest."

Fred took a foothold and scrambled upward then skyward for two more branches until the next quivered under his weight and he climbed down. The men gathered around the trunk of the tree and shook it, but the ball stayed where it was.

"We've lost it, then," Harry said, "and we don't have another."

Ellen grinned as I stood. "Oh, dear. It looks like you men will have to rely on us girls again."

I looked at Harry. "Give me a foot up?"

Harry clasped his cupped hands. "I'm not sure I can manage a whole foot."

Ellen laughed and threw her apple core at him. "Harry Burton, remember I worked with Rosie."

"So, you might have, Ellen Smith, but I don't believe I had any complaints."

I placed the toe of my boot onto Harry's hands. He tensed his muscles and threw upward. I grasped the bottom branch, swung onto it and looked down at the faces looking up at mine. "Gentlemen, about turn and eyes front, if you please."

Bert laughed. "But you've got britches on."

I made a circling motion with my index finger. "Even so, I want to see a row of straight backs in front of me. Eyes front, gentlemen."

The men shuffled into line facing away from me and Mr. Hubert walked along behind and straightened them before turning his back and taking his own place. I scrambled up the branches and looked outward as I plucked the ball from its resting place, and as I'd suspected, saw Damion sitting on a raised grassy knoll in the field behind ours, high enough to see and hear us in our field but still hidden by the hedgerow from our sight at ground level.

He smiled and I sent my smile back to him, along with a brief kiss from my fingertips, before I dropped the ball into Ellen's waiting hands and climbed down. The men turned around as Ellen called Fred's name then tossed him the ball and called their thanks as they ran back onto the field. I looked at Ellen and Molly. "We'd better pick the bluebells Mrs. Price asked for."

Ellen and Molly nodded, and we took the basket to the grass bank at the side of the field with its swathe of blue flowers to snap the stems of the longest at their base until James called out. "Have you enough flowers? It's beyond time we were back at our work."

Molly turned and showed James the lunch basket. "Enough that Mrs. Price will be able to fill more than just the one jug she asked for."

We walked back to the men and turned toward the stile.

"I'll come with you to the house before I walk to the village, Molly. I'll rid myself of these britches, now that they've served their use."

"I do so hope the haberdasher's have pink. Come and find me in the laundry when you return?"

"Of, course I will, as soon as I'm back."

Fred caught up with Ellen, walking behind me and Molly. "Would you care to take a turn around the lake, Ellen? I'm off duty for another couple of hours."

"I thank you, Fred. A walk would be lovely."

I smiled at Molly and she grinned back at me. "I'll wager you that by Christmas..."

I laughed, climbed the stile and called over my shoulder as I started to run. "I'm not taking that wager. Far too short on the odds. Last one back has to pump all the water in the morning?"

"Amelia Brown, that's not fair! You've a head start and I've got the basket."

Molly planted her feet alongside mine as we reached the kitchen door. "Ha! Dead tie."

I smiled. "Take the flowers to Mrs. Price, then. You'll be in her good books for at least a day."

"I'll miss you this afternoon, Am, in the laundry on my own."

"As I shall miss you tomorrow, Molly. Have you made arrangements with James?"

Molly's cheeks flushed pink. "Well, yes. I've said I'll walk to the village with him and make my curtsey to his mother."

"Molly, you never! That's it. My embroidery needle is coming out. Would you like hearts, flowers or turtle doves?"

Molly sideswiped my arm as I opened the kitchen door. She walked in first and handed the basket to Mrs. Price. Mrs. Price smiled.

"I thank you, girls. I used to pick them myself when I was younger. These are very welcome."

Molly opened the kitchen door to return to the laundry and I ran upstairs, stripped off my breeches, tidied my hair with the comb from my box, took a guinea from my savings that I kept in the reticule bag hidden at the bottom of it and left the bedroom.

Chapter Six

The sun warmed my back as I walked down the lane in the direction of the church and village with the choice of three shops at its heart. The haberdasher's was on the corner with the general store beside it and the apothecary two doors farther on.

The bell rang as I pushed the door open and the proprietor looked up from serving a customer with a packet of pins. I spotted the poplins stacked on a shelf and walked over to look at them. The plain poplins at sixpence a yard were exactly as stated — dull — but beside them, at only three pence extra a yard, sat the colors. The proprietor bustled over as the bell rang on the exit of his customer.

"Yes, Miss. How may I be of service?"

I worked out the sum. Ten yards of each color would leave six shillings remaining for pattern, thread and buttons. "Ten yards of each of the rose pink and the midnight blue, if you please?"

"Twenty yards? Yes, most certainly, Miss. Right away."

I nodded as the bales were selected and taken to the cutting table, then leafed through the box of paper patterns until I found one with a choice of a short puff sleeve or an unadorned three-quarter sleeve and took it to the counter with two packets of the cheapest white buttons. The proprietor finished his measuring and cutting, folded the material and smiled.

"For new dresses, is it, dear?"

I smiled into the twinkle of blue eyes set beneath a bush of white eyebrows.

"It is, for myself and my friend to wear to the cricket match."

"I shall look forward to seeing what you make of them. You are in service at the Manor, dear?"

"Yes. In the laundry—and so is my friend."

"The blonde lass? I believe I've seen you together in church of a Sunday."

"Yes...Molly, and I'm Amelia."

"Then I'm pleased to make your acquaintance, Miss Amelia. John Tucker, haberdasher here in this shop for over forty years."

I smiled and looked at my pile. "A reel of thread to match each color next, I think."

"Certainly, certainly."

The cotton reels joined the pile and I did a quick reckoning. "I add that to nineteen and six, so far?"

"You are very good at your sums, dear. That is exactly correct."

I took my guinea from my pocket and looked at the calico at sixpence the yard.

"Then three yards of white calico to finish the order, if you please? I already have a petticoat but Molly does not, and the dress will look nothing without one."

John Tucker winked at me. "My last customer only wanted a quarter of a yard to hem some handkerchiefs, so you may have the rest of the yard with my compliments, so your friend may have an additional flounce under her skirt."

"Mr. Tucker, I thank you. You are very kind."

"And you are both pretty girls. It will do my establishment no harm for you to be seen wearing dresses made from goods supplied by me."

The calico measured and cut, I handed my guinea over and watched my purchases be wrapped in stiff brown paper and the parcel tied with string. Mr. Tucker handed it over the counter, followed me to the shop door and bowed me out.

"Happy sewing, Miss Amelia. It has been a pleasure to receive your business."

"And my pleasure to meet you, Mr. Tucker."

I walked away from the shop with my parcel under my arm down the lane in the direction of the Manor and saw Damion walking toward me. I paused when he reached me and offered him my hand. "My Lord. A happy coincidence that I find you here?"

Damion took mine in his, bowed over it and kissed. "Miss Brown. Such a delight and so unexpected. One might nearly believe that hedgerows have ears."

I took my hand back and, with no one to see me do so, stood on tip-toe and kissed his cheek. "You couldn't come into the field and watch the play?"

Damion smiled. "No. I could when I was younger, and play, too, but my title makes them so mindful of their manners now as to spoil the game if they see me watching. You are quick at your shopping, though. I thought I might have to pay my respects to M'father in the church yard for a time before I could happen to be in the same place as you when you walked back to Ashton."

"It is a simple matter to be quick when pink is the color wanted and what is in the parcel was the only shade of it available."

"I may walk back with you? If we cross at the stile, we can walk through the spinney without being in view of any other."

I smiled my acceptance and walked with him to the stile, handed him my parcel to hold while I climbed over it and he tucked it under his arm when he helped me down and offered me his other. I tucked my arm through it Below-Stairs style, rather than lay my hand on his forearm.

Damion asked as we walked on, "So, I hold whatever the pink is that Molly desires?"

"You do. It is material so she may fashion herself a dress to wear at the cricket match, and if it will not overset you completely to know, also the material for a flounced petticoat for her to wear beneath it. Molly is very excited at the prospect of new clothes. She is one of a large family, so all other clothes she has ever worn have been worn first by somebody else."

"You are fond of Molly?"

I nodded. "I am. We are well matched for our obligation, as younger maids, to take such liberties as we may."

"What liberties?" He smiled.

I glanced up into his smile. "Nothing dreadful. We behave with a general lack of decorum wherever we may, make silly wagers with even sillier forfeits, tease your grooms and your footmen" —I paused to flutter my eyelashes—"steal your hot water and soap and bathe naked in your laundry."

"Pardon?" He laughed.

"We bathe naked in your rinsing sink. The windows steam up when we heat our water. No one in the back yard can see that we are up to anything other than our work, and we take turns to lean our weight against the door, so it may not be opened."

"Amelia, you are indeed a shocking tease! You know I will not be able to cross the yard now without the wondering of it if the windows are steamed, do you not?"

I laughed. "I do."

Damion stopped walking as we reached the canopy of the trees of the spinney. "Sit with me for a while?"

I nodded. Damion put my parcel on the ground by a tree far enough into the spinney for us not to be seen but with enough of a view out of it that anyone approaching would be seen by us. He sat and leaned against the trunk. I sat alongside his thighs and curled my legs up beside me.

"So, is there no material in the parcel for you to have a new dress?" he asked.

"There is also some blue. Molly will not accept my gift if I do not have a new dress, too, although I do not have the same need for a flounced petticoat and will thankfully escape the stitching of one."

"Molly desires pink and frills, unlike you?"

"She does, but most of all, she desires a pair of frilly-legged drawers that are beyond her means. I have hope for her, though. Is Mrs. Carleton likely to visit again in the next six months, do you think?"

Damion grinned. "You are intending to purloin her drawers for Molly?"

I returned his smile. "I won't have to purloin anything. Intimate items found where they shouldn't be are passed to the lady's maid of the guest on their next visit. If there is no return visit in the following six months, they are placed in the ragbag and re-worked into other items. I believe the handkerchief I have up my sleeve to blow my nose on was originally" —I gave him my best attempt at wide-open, innocent eyes—"a little frilly something left behind in a certain Gentleman's bedroom by Mrs. Emmaline Wriothsley."

Damion's eyes lightened. "Whatever will you find to tease me with next?"

I wriggled a little closer. "Well, now that you come to mention it, I do have a small question that teases me, too."

Damion looked at my face. "You are about put my higher male sensibilities to the blush, are you not?"

I smiled. "I believe you are as likely to blush as I am to tremble."

"True. Ask away, then."

"So, being an unwed female, when I lived at home, I was not privy to the rules of engagement for the game of bedroom chess, but from what I've guessed since I've worked here, the pieces move around the board dependent on where the spouse is." I looked into his eyes. "I presume it is not good form to indulge in extra-maritals with someone else while your spouse is just on the other side of a connecting door?"

The gleam ignited in them to tell me I'd hit the mark.

"So, one lover trots along to the bedroom of the other." I giggled as it occurred to me. "Do any of those on their moonlit flit ever meet another doing the same in the hallway or on the stairs, do you think?"

Damion's mouth twitched. "I wouldn't know."

"No. I suppose not. The Bachelors' rooms, standing in isolation as they do, will always be the preferred choice." He snorted, a prelude to his laugh. I tapped my fingers on his arm. "Not yet. I haven't finished."

He straightened his face. "Trying."

"So, as to the Ladies' frilly things... Not that we find them so often as to be remarkable, but to me, we find them too often for casual carelessness. So, what I wish to know is... Is it part of the game for the Ladies to leave a little intimate something behind on purpose? A sign that a return match would be welcome? An opening for the continuation of the flirtation?"

Damion's lips twitched again. "As in?"

I gazed into his eyes and deepened my voice. "Oh, my dear Lady S, I seem to have found a little something of yours." I put my hand in front of my mouth in the same place a Lady's fan would be if being used to flirt, fluttered my eyelashes and trilled, "Oh, my dear Ashton. Surely not?" I widened my eyes and tapped my fingers on his arm as a Lady would with a closed fan. "I must contrive to retrieve it...perhaps some time later this evening?"

Damion let go of his laugh. "The things you say to me."

"Yes or no?"

Damion nodded through his laugh.

"I thought so," I said. "That explains it. On occasion, the item left works its way into a place where it is not discovered by the intended recipient but by us, instead. What do Gentlemen do if they do not desire any continuation of the affair?"

"If a Gentleman does not make any mention of the aforesaid mislaid property, then the subject is neither broached nor referred to by either side again."

I smiled. "Yes, I can see how the game is played now. I thank you. How very Society polite."

"And that suits you no more than frills and pink?"

"No, it doesn't. I have neither the skill nor the patience required to advance through the game step by step. Below Stairs the question is asked, albeit obliquely, and answered in the same manner, yay or nay. We live in too close quarters for it to be otherwise."

"Then, if mine own question may be asked?"

I smiled. "Of course. Plain speaking must apply either way."

"You are educated, well-born and with an allowance, yet you do not preserve yourself against the prospect of future marriage?"

"No, I don't. Whatever else my life holds, it will not be that. I have reason to dislike a woman's legal position in any such union, but I do not see why my bed should be empty because of my decision. I shall take such lovers as I please—wed or no."

Damion leaned closer and put his hands on my waist. "So, if there is a bed away from the ears and eyes of the house, will you take me?"

My heart thumped as I looked into his eyes. "I do not wish to get with child. You know how to prevent this?"

"I will not leave you with child. I have an aversion myself to adding any unwanted children to the country's population."

I leaned forward. Damion pulled me closer and I opened my mouth to his tongue—sure and searching with no hint of hesitant probing—threaded my fingers through the back of his hair and explored his mouth, warm and sweet with a small hint of imp. Damion kissed my lips as we broke apart. "The Dower House is unoccupied. Meet me in the back yard tonight when the house is settled?"

I put his hand on my breast and his fingertips found my erect nipple pressed against the fabric of my dress. He cupped my fullness, moved his thumb over and around the hard nub and my heart beat harder at the surety of his touch. I stroked my fingertips down his face.

"I'll have to find an excuse for my absence for Molly."

"Where did she believe you were on Saturday?"

"The coal shed."

Damion lifted me to sit on his lap. "How? Why?"

I curled my body against his. "I stopped at it on the way past when I left you and daubed myself with black dust. I told Molly I'd wandered off dizzy when the cold air caught me, and I remembered nothing about getting there, but that's where I'd woken up."

"You think fast."

"I was ever more boy than girl as a child and quite accomplished in explaining my untoward appearance to a disapproving eye on a return from an outing."

"Riding astride in breeches?"

I smiled. "Dressed as a boy whenever possible, although the jacket and shirt that completed the look are a little beyond my ability to fasten now."

Damion tightened his arms around me. "I can't say I'm anything but glad about that. I'll retire early this evening so the house must seek their bedchambers, too."

"I'll come down to the back yard when I hear the church clock strike twelve."

I tilted my face for another kiss then slipped off his lap. He got up, offered me his hand to rise and handed me my parcel. "Go ahead of me. I'll wait a while before I follow."

I blew a kiss over my shoulder as I walked away, then picked up the pace. Molly looked up from her ironing when I opened the door to the laundry twenty minutes later.

"Amelia, you're back! Did they have it?"

I placed the parcel on the ironing table. "They did. Do you wish to untie the string while I light a fire under the cauldron? I'm in need of a bath before tonight."

Molly clapped her hands together and smiled. "Indeed, I will. Why the urgency for a bath?"

I knelt before the kindling box, built the fire under the cauldron, struck a match on my Vesta box and apologized silently to Damion as I changed his name to his second one along.

"I met William a while ago now and saw him in the village this afternoon. I'm going to slip out and meet him after the house settles to sleep tonight."

Molly giggled. "I take it you are not referring to *our* William, then?"

I smiled as I blew to encourage the flames. "William Coachman? I believe not. The William I refer to is not in service."

Molly picked the string knot apart on the parcel, parted the paper and stared.

"Oh, Amelia… The pink is for *me*?"

"Yes, of course, and also the calico for a petticoat. Mr. Tucker has given you nearly another yard for an extra flounce. Because you're so pretty, he said."

"He never said that." Molly blushed.

I picked up the bucket and smiled as Molly picked up the paper pattern for the bodice. "He most certainly did. I'll fetch my water while you look at that."

Five trips later I tipped a last bucketful into the cauldron, swirled the water around with my hand and found it warm. Molly looked up from the pattern with the crease of a frown between her eyes. "I can see how it works, but you must read the print to me so I don't make a mistake."

"Don't worry, Molly. We will work it out between us and make sure we have the measure of it before we cut into the fabric."

I tickled the water again and added a handful of dried lavender. It started to bubble as steam rose and I picked the small scissors out of the mending basket and put them beside the sink. Molly leaned her back against the door as I filled the sink, stripped off and got into it. I wetted my hair and soaped it then held my arm up and trimmed the hair in the pit of it as close to the skin as the scissors could manage.

"Amelia, what are you doing?" Molly giggled.

"I'm trimming this. It's the hair that holds the stink if you become overwarm."

I tilted my pelvis after I'd finished trimming under my arms and looked at the thick, tight bush of curls on my mound. "And while I'm at it, I'm going to tidy the thatch."

Molly's mouth dropped open. "Amelia! You're not."

"Yes, I am. There's far too much of it. His fingers will get tangled in it before he gets anywhere near me."

I pulled up tufts and applied the scissors as Molly laughed. "This William... You really like him, then?"

I looked at a smaller, neater triangle of hair, scooped clean water from the bucket and tipped it over my head. "Yes, I do. I want him enough to risk being found away from my bed tonight, and Molly" —I stepped from the sink and picked up the flannel ironing sheet— "I've made it clear to Harry that we are only friends. This is not his business. He can have no expectation of me."

"I'm sorry. I thought you and Harry were suited."

I rubbed my body and hair with the cloth. "He's a good man, and some girl one day will be lucky indeed, but it won't be me. I like his touch but he does not heat my blood enough."

Molly stepped away from the door as I pulled my dress over my head.

"A bit like me and Fred, but James..." Molly took the stone from the drain in the sink. "I've had my eye on James for a while but wasn't sure he wanted me. But he does, and I want him, too. That makes a difference, doesn't it?"

I smiled as I laced up my boots. "I hope so. I'll let you know after tonight."

I plaited my hair wet, coiled and pinned the result on the nape of my neck without chance to let it loose to dry naturally. Molly threaded her arm through mine and we left the material on the ironing table to be cut on its wide surface, turned our backs on the pile of ironed laundry to be taken to its owners' rooms until the morning and walked to the kitchen for supper. I sat between Ellen and Molly, ate my beef stew, watched James and Fred leave with Mr. Bennett as the dining room bell rang on the board and James returned five minutes later.

"Don't prepare water for the tea tray, Mrs. Oates. His Lordship is retiring early tonight."

James offered Molly the tablecloth. She stood to take it.

"That will have to wait, Molly," Mrs. Price said. "James, put it in the scullery until the morning, if you please. Since his Lordship retires early, the house must be quiet shortly for him to catch his rest."

Mr. Bennett walked into the kitchen, took his place at the head of the table and we bowed our heads for prayers. I followed Molly up the stairs and she lit her lamp as I shut our bedroom door.

"Will you be able to stay awake?"

I lay on my bed dressed, with my boots on, and took a deeper breath in as I remembered Damion's touch on my breast. I loosened my hair so it could dry. "Yes, Molly, I think I will. Turn the lamp out, though. The moon's still over half-full and I'll have light enough."

Molly darkened the lamp and her breathing steadied, long and even, the prelude to her soft snore as the church clock struck eleven. I looked out at the stars and pictured Damion's large hand cupping the full orb on my chest, then imagined him finding the throb between my legs and easing it with experienced fingers. Finally, the church clock struck twelve.

I swung my legs out of bed, pulled on the laces of my boots, took my feet out of them, peeled off my stockings and crept down the stairs on bare feet. I didn't re-tie my laces as I put my feet back into my boots at the kitchen door and opened it. Prince snorted in front of me. I walked forward as Damion stepped out of the shadows dressed in riding boots and breeches, his shirt, collarless, open at the neck, and over it, a gabardine bad-weather riding cape rather than a jacket.

"I'll mount. Stand on the block and sit before me and the shelter of my cape will hide who I have with me."

Damion swung his leg over Prince's back. I stood on the block. He lifted me to sit sideways, tented under his cape, clicked soft with his mouth and nudged Prince with his foot to move him off. Prince walked forward. I curled my arm around Damion's waist, adjusted my body to Prince's gait and smiled.

"Oh, this is lovely. It's a while since I've been mounted."

Damion kissed the top of my head. "And have you ever been?"

I smiled into the darkness. "Been mounted by a man? No."

Damion put both reins into one hand and tucked me tighter against him with the other. "Then your first time should not involve a layer of protective shield. We should wait for your safe time."

I curved my body into his and glanced up. "You do not find that time unclean, like most men?"

Damion smiled. "No. None of the boys deflowered by Lady Georgina find it so."

"Lady Georgina?"

"Had an appetite to be a boy's first, to instruct them in ways and means. Intercourse without a preventative shield is more pleasurable and a delightfully damp and sticky business. What does it matter if there is a little pink in the mix?"

I ran my finger down the skin exposed by the open neck of his shirt and kissed where my finger stopped. "No. I suppose it doesn't matter at all. Next week, then. How young did Lady Georgina like her boys?"

"Lady Georgina didn't have a preference for an age as such, more a fine instinct for when a young man was ready to head in that direction. I was fourteen."

I smiled at the thought of how quick Damion must have grown to manhood in the year since I had seen him at age thirteen. I moved my fingers farther inside his shirt, put my lips on his chest and added the tip of my tongue.

"Are you playing with my nipple?" he breathed.

I brushed my lips over the hard nub of it and explored his chest hair a little more with my fingertips. "I believe I am. I never knew a man's nipples hardened the same as a woman's do."

"Yes, they do—along with other things, rather too early if you keep this up."

Damion moved his leg back to urge Prince into a faster trot and pulled him up at the stable at the back of the Dower House. I sprang down. Damion dismounted, secured Prince's reins to the standing post and offered me his hand. I slipped mine in his and walked with him to the garden door.

"I came over before the dressing gong and checked the condition inside, with the house being uninhabited."

I smiled as he opened the garden door. "It is cleaned and aired by us three or four times a year. You do not use it on other occasions?"

Damion lifted my chin and kissed me. "No, I don't believe I've had the need or the desire to do so before."

I breathed deeper at the touch of his lips, reached up and traced their outline. He captured my finger with his mouth and sucked on the tip. Muscles tightened in my groin and my knees promised a repeat performance of Saturday night without even so much as a sip of sack. He released my finger and offered me his hand.

"Come inside. I'll lock the door so no one can follow us in."

I put my hand back in his, stepped over the threshold onto soft carpet and toed off my untied boots as he turned the key. Damion shed his cape and picked up a lit lamp from the consul table standing to one side of the door, its wick turned low. I walked with him, my feet bare of ugly boots, through the morning room, its furniture shrouded in Holland covers.

Damion lit the way up the stairs and opened a door to a bedroom that was aglow from the flames of a fire and had heavy drapes drawn tight over the windows. I looked toward the grate, saw a residue of unburned kindling that hinted of the sticks of a boy's campfire with a slow-burn log sitting on them and walked toward it.

"You lit it?"

"Yes. Not even Hubert knows that I'm not asleep at this moment in my solitary bed."

I looked at the bed, saw a sheet on it and smiled. Damion walked behind me, moved my hair to one side and kissed my neck.

"Yes. And I also opened enough doors until I found the linen store."

I tilted my head for him to move his lips down my neck. "Then you'd better let me return the favor of your personal attention and pull your boots for you. I presume you wouldn't use a boot jack on them, even if you'd thought to bring one?"

Damion brushed his lips over my neck and laughed. "Damn. No, I didn't. I did bring a bottle of the rosé wine, though, and found glasses in the kitchen cupboard."

I smiled. "Sit, then, and give me your leg."

He sat in the armchair to the side of the fire and I knelt before him, sat back on my heels and patted my thigh. He put his leg out. I grasped his boot—toe and heel—and tensed my scuttle-lifting, laundry-pounding muscles. He looked at my grasp.

"My apologies. I should have thought and worn different footwear. They're tight. Even Hubert has a problem."

I tightened my grasp, strained and pulled. Damion's foot moved free into the wider leg of his boot. I patted my lap for his other foot.

"And with my apologies to Mr. Hubert. He is somewhat older than me, and his position is composed of lighter duties than mine."

He gave me his other leg. I grasped and pulled then sat with my legs curled beneath me on the hearth rug. He freed his leg and smiled. "I should not have doubted you after I've seen you bowl. Would you like to take a glass of wine?"

I looked at his smile, the curve of his lips, the fit of his breeches in my eye-line and shook my head. He got up and offered me his hand to rise.

"No, neither do I."

I put my hand in his and reached for him as he put his arms around me and bent his face to mine. I opened my mouth to the urge of his lips, explored his and breathed, my body pressed against his muscled hardness. He plucked on the bow of my laces. I unfastened the buttons of his shirt then stepped back as my laces loosened, took my arms out of my sleeves and my dress fell and pooled around my feet.

Damion gazed at my breasts pressed against the thinner material of my shift, and muscles tightened in my groin as he reached for the first button on it. The rise and fall of his chest increased as his gaze followed his fingers down to my waist. I eased my shift over my shoulders and the outline of his cock pushed against the tightness of his breeches. "Your shirt in exchange for my dress?" I breathed.

Damion untucked his shirt, shrugged it over his shoulders and dropped it to the floor. I gazed at his torso — the power of his shoulders, his upper arms, his forearms downy with black hair to match what ran down from his belly button and disappeared into his breeches. A need to touch and be touched tingled over my skin. I took my arms out of my shift and it slipped over my body to join my dress at my feet.

Damion breathed deeper as he gazed at my breasts with nipples erect then looked at my work-hardened waist, belly and thighs and the trimmed triangle in between my legs.

"Sweet Jesus. So beautiful..."

His gaze raced to my mound and I reached for him. "Damion —"

He scooped me into his arms and I ran my fingers through his chest hair and kissed and tasted his skin as he carried me to the bed and laid me down. I ran my hand over the hardness inside his breeches.

"I want to see and touch you, too. Take them off?"

He unbuttoned the breeches and eased them over his hips with no smalls to obscure my view. His cock sprang free, a stiff, thick pole rising from a thatch of tight black curls, standing away from his belly — not a match for his mount but more than a match for a man, with full, heavy balls hung beneath it. I reached and touched his erection as he toed his breeches off.

"Oh, yes. This is beautiful to me, too," I said.

Damion stepped closer to the reach of my hand and asked, "Not too much?"

I stroked down his length. "Nothing about you is too much for me." I cupped my breasts. "Generous enough for you?"

A vein pulsed down the length of his cock as he lay beside me, kissed my lips and filled his hands with a breast in each. "A breast that can fill my hand? Your sweet nipple waiting for my mouth? As generous as I ever hoped for." He squeezed one and fastened his mouth on it. I knotted my fingers in the back of his hair.

"Damion... Yes."

He sucked harder and squeezed the full moons of my breast then tugged on the nipple with his teeth. I grasped his hair tighter.

"Oh, please more."

He fastened his mouth on my other breast and I writhed beneath him as he pushed the fullness of each to his mouth and sucked on each apex until the mound between my legs begged for his attention, too. I moaned and reached for the thickness of his shaft.

"Damion..."

He stroked his finger through the triangle of my pubic hair and paused on the wet lips of my sex. "Oh, I think my attention is needed here — "

I whimpered. "Yes..."

He kissed his way down my body and I mewled louder as he licked my sex and explored the creases inside my mound with his tongue. I moaned as he eased one finger then another into the wet inside me and shouted out when he fastened his lips on the throb of my hidden nub and sucked while his fingers matched the rhythm of his mouth.

"Damion... Oh! Oh! Yes..."

I writhed as he lapped and more spasms throbbed through my pelvis, then I stilled, panting, as he moved up my body and paused on my breasts to squeeze and suck before he kissed my lips. I reached for his erection.

"Show me how to do that to you?"

Damion rolled onto his back. I kissed down his torso to his cockhead and found it warm and damp when I licked. I took the tip of his shaft it into my mouth and stroked my fingertips down it.

"That's it, my sweet. Take me into your mouth. You don't have to take too much... Just to where the skin moves back."

I lowered my mouth to the soft creases of skin beneath the head of his cock and sucked.

"Oh, yes... Good. Use your tongue on me but keep me away from your teeth."

I flicked my tongue over the top of his shaft as I sucked and wrapped my hand around it. Damion covered my hand with his, moved it with mine into a rhythm back and forth with a small squeeze as the creases straightened, and his breathing deepened.

"Yes, my sweet... Suck harder now."

He moved our hands faster, squeezed tighter and I increased the suction of my mouth. His stomach muscles tensed. I stroked over and under his balls with my other hand as he groaned. "Yes..." Warm cream filled the back of my mouth and he slowed the movement of our grasp.

I removed my mouth from his cock, wondering what to do with the cream, so swallowed it, licked the last drop from the slit on it to taste and found the saltiness not unpleasant to my tongue. Damion urged me upward and I moved under his arm and rested my cheek on his chest to the rapid beat of his heart as he put his arms around me.

"That was agreeable to you? You did not mislike the taste of me?"

I adjusted the weight of my breasts squashed against him. "All of it was very agreeable to me. I thank you. Do some, then?"

"Some mislike the taste of a man's seed in their mouths — others, the activity completely."

I kissed his chest. "I found pleasure in both. I think I may have to use both of my hands on the length of you to match the one of yours?"

"No. The sensation is all in the head of me and the ball sack beneath. It added to my pleasure to hear your own."

I rolled onto his chest and peeked up at him. "Oh, dear. Have I just displayed my lack of female sensibility again?"

He stroked down my back. "More delightful to me than small, brief sighs of appreciation. I thank you."

I giggled as the probability of lying still while sighing popped into my head. "Am I supposed to lie still while I sigh?"

Damion kissed the end of my nose. "I believe reclining with a due amount of posed grace and the occasional murmur of encouragement is considered a sign of true breeding in a Lady."

I let the rest of my laugh out. "It is as well I have given up on being one, then. I could no more manage that than I can stop myself laughing out loud to suit Society's comfort or pretend I do not have legs to suit its notion of respectability."

"Your open enjoyment allows expression of my own. I liked the sound of my Christian name on your lips."

I giggled as I pictured it. "What do your Society lovers sigh when in your bed? Please not... 'Oh, Ashton'?"

He smiled. "I've been called nothing but that since I came to the title except by those friends that had always used my Christian name before I inherited it."

I brushed my lips along his smoothly shaven jaw line with no downy hair and not so much as a hint of an adolescent pimple. "Below Stairs we use Christian names. I will not call a lover by his surname, peerage or no."

He stroked through the length of my hair. "To hear you use my Christian name is a pleasure to me. Few are comfortable to do so now. Even my mother and sisters call me Ashton. To others, I am My Lord or Your Lordship, and on occasions, I feel the weight of it, as if I am only the title, not a flesh-and-blood-man."

I trailed my fingertips over his shoulders and the muscle of his upper arms. "Then I will testify to the last and admit that I am comfortable to use your given name, because, before the ill fortune occurred that caused my family to pass from Society's remembrance, I did, albeit with an interval of many years now."

"You did? I do not recall a childhood Amelia."

I put my lips on his. "No. I was not Amelia then." His cock stirred against my thigh to my kiss on his mouth. I reached for his shaft and it hardened in my hand. "We can do it again?"

Damion rolled to his side. I tipped onto my back and he lay over me. "Oh, yes, Amelia Brown. I wish to taste more of you."

I mewled my pleasure as he grasped my breast and took my nipple into his mouth then breathed harder as he sucked and threaded my fingers through the back of his hair. He tugged with his teeth, moved his attention to my other breast, then between the two until I moaned his name. "Damion…"

He slid his finger through my wetness to his murmured, "You like, sweeting?"

I pushed my pelvis forward. "Oh, yes…"

He licked down my body and fastened his mouth over my throbbing sex and I moaned when he added his fingers and the waves of my final ecstasy spread through my groin as he sucked.

"Damion! Oh — Oh —"

As muscles pulsed and contracted between my legs, Damion lifted his head and asked, "I may take my pleasure between your breasts?"

"Please…" I panted.

He straddled me on his knees at my waist, grasped my breasts and pushed them close to his cock. He thrust as his hands squeezed, his eyes closed, his head tipped back. The throb between my legs extended as I watched his cockhead appear then withdraw, squashed between the valley of my breasts. I put my face forward as it emerged with cream in the split, fastened my mouth over it and sucked.

"Oh, Sweet Jesus! Amelia…"

I released his cock and swallowed. Damion moved to lie to the side of me and pulled me into his arms. I breathed in the musk of him and laid my cheek on the fast beat of his heart. He ran his fingers through the length of my hair and I tucked in closer, draped my leg over his thigh and put my arm around him. He kissed the top of my head.

"Your breasts have quenched a desire in me I have never dared ask to be satisfied before. Our nakedness is comfortable to you?"

"Very. I enjoy the feel of your skin on mine, and although I do not have a frilly anything I may leave behind me, you may take it that if I possessed such a thing, I would."

"As you may be assured that there is no corner of my room I would not search to look for it. When will you be able to slip out at night again? I leave Ashton tomorrow to spend four nights at Wisborough House. Lord Byngingham announces his own betrothal to Miss Amabelle Sutton-Hoe this weekend."

I hid my smile against his chest as he gave me the name. Amabelle—a friend who lived close enough to my family's country estate that we had met frequently during the years of my exile from Society, until my stepfather had attempted to force me to accept the wretched proposal of marriage. Then, half-starved by his orders but with a determination not to marry a man who induced in me only the desire to vomit or to permit my stepfather to refill his pockets with the price Sir Humphrey Spittlemore had offered to pay for my bloodline, I had fled my home, and had not seen her since.

"It is unequal, so a love match?"

"A Baron's daughter for a Viscount? Yes, it is. But Byng's parents are fond and gave him free choice."

"Unlike your own?"

"No. M'father and Elizabeth's arranged our marriage between them years ago. We've tried to get out of it for nearly as many years. Elizabeth is no keener on the prospect than I, but the legals on the contract are tighter than a drum. I have to marry her before I turn twenty-five in June or lose the estate to a cousin of so little brain that Ashton would go to rack and ruin in a few short years. Elizabeth will lose her dowry if she doesn't marry me."

I squeezed my arm around him. "Then I'm sorry for you, but with my apologies, even sorrier for Elizabeth, who must leave the familiarity of her home without the comfort of wishing to be with the one that offers his to her."

"As am I. I will do what I may to ease her fears, and as they mainly center around her discomfort to be alone in my company, will dispense with the farce of the honeymoon and return to Ashton immediately after the formalities have been completed."

"No honeymoon? Will that not cause comment?"

"Rather comment than inflict my presence on someone, who—in common with your friend Molly— would prefer to run away at the mere sight of me."

I lifted my head and kissed his lips. "I believe there are enough who do not. Seek me out on your return from Byng's. We can arrange when we may meet here again."

"You knew Byng, too, then, when young? If you are comfortable to use his familiar name?"

"Well enough to know that Byng does not admit to his given Christian name."

Damion smiled. "Who would?"

"Adonis! His parents might be fond, but really, what were they thinking?"

He laughed. "Euphoria after the birth of the seven girls before him, I should think."

The mantle clock chimed three times. "I should go back to the house. I have to rise and be ready for work at seven."

"You do not have to—"

I stopped Damion's words with a kiss on his lips. "Do not say it. I am here from mine own choice and fulfill my contract to work for the same reason. My self-respect depends on it. I could crumble under the weight of my family's reverse, else."

"It was that severe?"

"Yes. But Amelia Brown will move past it and it will not attach to her skirts."

Damion cupped my face in his hand. "Then, Miss Brown, I will offer no unwelcome assistance, but know, should you yourself ask for it, it will be forthcoming."

I rolled away, stood beside the bed and bobbed a curtsey. "And I thank you for it."

He smiled as I reached for my shift and he for his breeches. "Now, not only do I have to wonder about the steam on the windows, but whenever you bob in my direction, I will picture you doing so naked."

I fastened my shift and watched his cock disappear as he re-dressed. "As I will you when I do so."

Damion tightened my dress laces and picked up the lamp. I slipped my hand into his and he lit the way down the stairs and out of the Dower House. He lifted me to sit before him when he mounted Prince. I curled my arm around his waist and tucked my body close to his under the cover of his cape to a clear sky of bright stars and the more mellow light of the half-moon to light our way.

"How do you travel to Wisborough?"

"For a stay of only few days, I'll go by rail. Byng returns with Miss Sutton-Hoe and her family to celebrate the betrothal with her people at Stonely on Wednesday. I'll be back at Ashton on Tuesday. When will your safe time begin, do you think?"

"By my reckoning, Sunday or Monday. It is normally quite timely."

Damion kissed the top of my head. "The pleasure we shared tonight and the desire to be able to enter you, flesh to flesh, will not be out of my thoughts these next few days. Tuesday, if we may?"

"It will not be long out of mine, either. How is Mr. Hubert's command of the French language?"

"Nonexistent, I believe."

"Look on the table beside your bed on your return. If we may, I will leave you a message that Mr. Hubert may not decipher."

The outline of the house filled my view. "Will you set me down here, before the back yard? I can find an excuse for being found out of bed should I have to, but not if we are together."

He halted Prince. "Your kiss before you leave me?"

I lifted my face for his lips and tasted his mouth as he tasted me. He said, as we pulled apart, "I will take Prince direct to the stables. Sleep well."

I stroked my fingertips along his jawline. "And you."

I jumped from Prince's back and he nudged the horse to walk. I turned toward the back yard as they disappeared from my sight and loosened my laces in the manner of one who had thrown her dress over her head in an urgent visit to the lavatory, let myself into the kitchen with only silence to greet me, crept to the green door and walked softly up the stairs to my bed.

Chapter Seven

Molly did not stir as I pressed the bedroom door shut, took my feet out of my boots, shrugged off my dress and pulled the bedcovers up. I sighed to Damion's remembered touch as I turned my face to my pillow and Molly shook me awake — two minutes later, it seemed.

"Amelia, you sleepyhead! What time was it when you got to your bed?"

I smiled at the remembrance. "After three but before four."

"And?"

"And, yes, it was wonderful." I sat and stretched. "But with my apologies, do not trust me with any intricate work today. My head is still with him and I am like to scorch any garment too delicate for my iron."

Molly smiled. "Amelia Brown, go and do what you must with your teeth. We are due downstairs for our breakfast."

I yawned, opened my box and took out my toothbrush and mint powder. "I will…and will chastise myself for being so dizzy while I do so. Go on down. I will follow shortly."

I used the washing room, ate my porridge and followed Molly to the laundry. Molly poked through the baskets. "His Lordship's shirt, collar and handkerchief, two pairs of Ladies' drawers, three chemises, the Dowager's bloomers and some household linen. Not a great amount with no house guests and no bedding until tomorrow."

I smiled. "Good. Then leave it for me to do while you are on your half-day. Let us lay the material on the ironing table and begin the panels for our skirts."

"Amelia! We are meant to be working."

I caught Molly's eye and shrugged. She smiled. "How many yards of each have we?"

"Ten, and from the pattern, I estimate two yards apiece should be ample for the bodice and sleeves. Four panels of two-yards length will form the skirt, with the remnants from the shaping of them to cover the buttons."

Molly opened the work basket, handed me the pinking shears and tape and I measured and cut then handed her the pink thread. She looked at the sections.

"We should hem each panel all around, but with the edge the pinking shears have given this material, I do not believe we have to. We can stitch one folded edge to the other and adjust for length after."

I nodded and threaded my needle with blue, and by the time the lunch bell rang, we had three panels attached each.

"Will you be able to manage the work this afternoon?" she asked.

"It can wait. There is nothing here that is urgent. The Family have enough of everything that they will not notice the lack of what we have. I will stitch for both of us this afternoon."

Molly held up her work in progress. "It is shaping beautifully, don't you think?"

"Yes, it is, and we will both have another panel each by the end of the afternoon."

Molly smiled. "Do not mention it within James' hearing. I haven't said a word. I wish to see his face when I wear it at the cricket match."

I looked at her panels. "With the addition of a little lace, pink would be a lovely color for a wedding dress, don't you think? Are you nervous about your introduction to James' family this afternoon?"

Molly's cheeks flushed the same hue as her material. "Yes, it would and yes, I am. James' father is a skilled man—the carpenter who was entrusted with the making of the old Marquis' coffin, let alone all the ordinaries he does for real people like us."

I squeezed her hand. "Less of the ordinary, if you please. James' family should consider it their good fortune if they are given the opportunity to count you as one of their number. There is no one who will care for every one of them more than you will."

She returned the pressure of my hand. "I thank you, and yes, I will try and remember I have something to offer, too."

I smiled and let go of her hand. "Last one to the kitchen has to give Prince a big sloppy kiss."

Molly tugged on the back of my dress, pushed me to one side and ran out of the door in front of me. "There is no way I'm losing that one, Amelia Brown!"

I caught up with her at the kitchen door, ate my bowl of chicken broth alongside her and smiled when she got up from the table and walked out of the kitchen door behind James in his waistcoat of newly shined buttons. I returned to the laundry alone, set my iron on the table then ignored it in favor of my needle and stitched until Molly and I had another panel each.

I smiled when she walked into the kitchen with James in time for supper but waited to ask her how the afternoon had been for her until I'd used the washing room and closed our bedroom door behind us. She rested her back against her bedhead. I folded my dress over the foot of my bed, added my stockings then slipped under my bedcovers.

"So, how did the meeting of James' family go for you?"

She smiled then sighed. "The afternoon went very well, I think. I believe I could be on comfortable terms with them all with a little further acquaintance, but how we are to manage any more than that, I cannot see."

"Why? What is it that troubles you?"

"My family. James' family is well situated, but I do not know how my family fares. Three of my brothers should be in work by now, but I do not know if they are. My family can neither read nor write. I cannot get home or send home to ask if they could live without my pennies, and I will not leave them without, if they have a need."

I frowned as I thought. "How does your salary get home, Molly?"

"If you make your mark in Mr. Bennett's book, His Lordship's land agent, Mr. Martyn, takes the salaries to where they are needed at such times as he is in the area and finds it convenient to do so."

"Mr. Martyn? He seems a man of good humor. Would he not also take a message from you and return your family's reply?"

Molly's eyes widened to her gasp. "No, I couldn't! You can't ask Mr. Martyn to do such a thing. He is invited to eat his dinner here with the Family at least twice a year. I wouldn't dare!"

I lifted my chin. "No, but I might. I would make no request of him to tax his memory in the remembering of your question, but if I wrote it down, it would surely not be such an onerous demand on him to ask him to recite the content of a note to your mother and father."

"Oh, Amelia, would you really dare? Bertie and Stanley at least should be earning by now. If I could just know whether I may keep back more than my two shillings a week pocket money from my wages…"

"Then you will. The next time I see Mr. Martyn's roan in the back yard, I will approach and make my request."

Molly's smile widened. "Then, I thank you and will ask… Will you accompany me down the aisle in your blue as my bridesmaid, if James and I go to church?"

"I would be both honored and delighted, Molly. I thank you." I smiled. "Now, put your mind to who is good with a whittling knife. Three flounces on your petticoat will not be enough. You need some fine, thin strips of sapling stitched in to the body of it to add substance to the whole."

Molly sighed. "I'm going to be as fine as the Queen herself, I believe."

"Yes, you are. And if you wash your hair the day before you wear your dress, I will rag tie it before bed, so you may have ringlets as fine as Her Majesty's, too."

"You know the trick of it?"

I smiled as I remembered long, uncomfortable nights of rag-tied hair with sleep near impossible. "Yes, Molly, I do. And if we can purloin a sugar cube, it will ensure the ringlets will stay in place when released from the rags."

Molly slid down her bed and tucked her bedcovers over her shoulders. "Yes. Sugar and thin strips of sapling. I will turn my thoughts to the providing of both. Goodnight, Am."

I turned down the wick of the lamp and blew. "Night, Molly. Sweet dreams."

I turned to my side and thought of home as it had been when I'd had a papa, then rolled onto my back and wondered whether there would be a frilly something in Damion's bedroom in the morning as I stared out of the window at the stars. My heart thumped at the thought. I pushed it out of my head as a prospect that could be of no concern to me if I were to maintain my determination never to be dependent on another and focused instead on the phrasing of Molly's question for Mr. Martyn.

* * * *

The weekend passed with Molly and I doing as little work as possible, while escaping to the laundry at every opportunity to resume work with our needles. On Monday afternoon, I pinned the pattern for our bodices, cut the material and slipped a freshly laundered handkerchief of Damion's, along with a reel of thread and a needle, into my skirt pocket as I felt the stomach cramp of the start of my monthly flow.

Mrs. Price excused me to leave the room without due formalities for the next seven days when I whispered my condition to her. I took my chance in the female washing room after securing a pad of monthly linen in between my legs by means of a long strip of cotton to hold it in place, looped and tied around my waist, to stitch the words *Oui ce soir* at the center of Damion's handkerchief, along with a small lace rosette I'd purloined from those items awaiting the possibility of the rag bag. Refolded to hide my alteration, I slipped into Damion's bedroom on my return Below Stairs and left the handkerchief on the night table beside his bed.

The next afternoon I watched Harry drive the brougham carriage through the yard. I set down my iron and folded the Dowager's bloomers onto the pile of smalls to be taken Above Stairs. Molly looked out of the window and set her own iron down.

"That's Harry off to the station to meet His Lordship's train. What must it be like, do you think? To travel by steam at such a speed? I can't imagine it."

I smiled. "No, nor me, but I mean to one day, when I attain my majority and have saved enough. To travel to places I've only heard about is my ambition."

"What? On your own?" Molly said.

"Yes. I may have to assume the disguise of tragic widow or lone female traveling to join a husband, but I have every intention of visiting New York, a city that has captured my imagination from the reading of it."

I followed Molly out of the laundry after we'd ironed two more petticoats apiece. We made our way Above Stairs and walked along the hallway toward the

Ladies' bedrooms. The Dowager's voice floated up the Family's staircase at our approach.

"That's all very well, Ashton, but either of the Rockingham girls would have been more suitable. I know Marianna retired to the country after Rockingham's death but really... She could have stirred herself by now and brought the girls to Town for their Season. And even so... Only the next county along. He could have at least visited."

I hid a small smile at the Dowager's mention of Mama, my sister and I and paused alongside Molly, the pair of us unable to walk past the head of the staircase under the pretense of being oblivious to their presence with their voices so close.

"With my apologies, Mama. At least Byng has every prospect of being tolerably happy with his choice of wife."

"But, Ashton, Miss Sutton-Hoe or the daughter of an Earl... That the blue blood of our rank shouldn't mingle with that of the lower orders aside...just think on the Rockingham dowry that's gone a-begging. What a waste."

Molly and I bobbed as they rounded the head of the stairs. I glanced into Damion's eyes and saw the brief flare of desire when he looked at me. He and his mama separated and walked left and right of the staircase. We waited for them to pass out of sight before walking after the Dowager. Molly nudged my arm. "Am, I think he just looked at you — you know — a bit fond?"

I diverted Molly's observation with a shrug. "No, not unless I've suddenly grown four legs and a tail."

Molly chuckled. "Or maybe he caught sight of you, thought of your interest in the stables then remembered Lady Shelling. I looked at her sideways when she was looking down her nose at us and there is something quite horsey about her face."

"Yowl, Molly. Sheath your claws" —I nudged her arm — "although I did drip the last of the hyacinth sap onto her nightie."

Molly grinned and I smiled. We straightened our faces at the Dowager's door, passed Miss Croker the clean smalls and returned to the laundry.

"Molly, I feel a little sticky. I believe I will feel better for a bath."

Molly's mouth opened, closed, then opened again. "You can't do that during your flow, Amelia. Washing—let alone bathing—is dangerous when you are open to let the flow out. You must surely know that?"

I picked up a bucket. "You think? Shall we discover the truth of the matter? If I'm dead by morning, I will thank you to remember that I do not like the heavy smell of a lily for my coffin top."

I brought a bucket of water from the pump and lit the fire under the cauldron before I fetched the second. Molly bit her finger as I tipped the fourth bucket in. "Amelia, really, you shouldn't."

I smiled. "Molly, what do you think will happen to me for a little soap and hot water? They are both cleansing agents and cannot harm me. I intend to slip out and meet William tonight and desire to be clean."

Molly put her hand over her mouth. "You're not intending to…? Not in your flow?"

I bucketed lavender-scented hot water to the sink and found a piece of soap as I stepped in. "Yes, Molly, I am. The worst day is over, and I am safe not to get with child for the next few. William is not squeamish over such matters and neither am I."

"Amelia!"

"My apology if it disturbs you, Molly. I would not wish you to go against your inclination, but put your mind to such matters if you and James do not wish to gather more children than you can afford. William will use a preventative when I'm not safe. I've never seen one but will tell you whether they are of any use when I have."

Molly giggled. "No! Will he really?"

I stepped out of the sink, dried my skin, secured a clean pad between my legs and redressed. "He won't be entering me without one at any other time."

Molly blushed and looked at her feet. "Tell me when you know? I like James rather too well and do not wish to end up like Mother."

I plaited my hair wet, secured it in a coil on the nape of my neck and offered Molly my arm. "I most certainly will. Supper?"

Molly linked her arm through mine and sighed. "Oh, yes. I haven't set eyes on my James this half-a-day."

I sat at the table and couldn't concentrate on the chatter as I wondered whether Damion had found my message and whether he would be waiting for me in the back yard, until Bert returned from clearing the Family's dessert course.

"No tea tray, Mrs. Oates. His Lordship is fatigued from his travels and is retiring early tonight."

Fred entered the kitchen with the table cover in his hands.

"In the scullery, if you please," Mrs. Price said.

Mr. Bennett took his place at the table. We intoned his amen and I followed Molly up the stairs, used the washing room to clean my teeth, lay on my bed and waited. The church clock chimed twelve.

I tiptoed down the stairs, opened the kitchen door to the back yard and Damion moved out of Prince's loose box, caped, his shirt open and collarless but him wearing evening trousers and house shoes. He lifted me to sit before him after he mounted. I put my arms around him under his cape and pressed close. He clicked Prince into a walk, held his reins with one hand, held me to him with the other and kissed the top of my head.

"A delightful message to leave for me. I thank you. I have my frilly something locked in my desk drawer where no other fingers, bar mine, ever stray."

I kissed the skin in the V of his shirt. "I'm sure Mrs. Carleton will not miss one small rosette."

"Or Molly. You could pass the item to her on the morrow, if you wish, with my assurance that Mrs. Carleton will not visiting in the next six months – or indeed again."

"Vouched for by someone else, as was Sir Elliot?"

"Another acquaintance of the Wellinghams, and I have to say I've never hosted such an uncomfortable weekend as that one. I loathe dancing, cut a laughable figure when I do, and with guests to blush for and an outrageous request to turn down, my discomfort was assured."

I hid my smile behind the shelter of his cape. "I did hear the Lady was in one hell of a temper. What did she request of you, a man soon to join the ranks of the married? Shall I take a guess at 'official mistress' with an 'official allowance' to accompany the position?"

Damion tipped my chin and looked into my eyes. "So, a witch with second sight, a gypsy with a crystal ball or was there something she recognized in your face?"

I reached up and stroked his cheek. "Something, although I have no second sight as to what, as she hasn't seen me in more than a dozen years. But she attached herself to my sister for a year or so before Mama worked her out and cut the acquaintance."

"I'll admit I didn't have the measure of her until that weekend."

"Who does with that type? All sweetness and delight until they have your affection, then the demands start. Was she there at the weekend or had Byng given the Shellings the cut in line with you?"

"Yes, he has. So, no, she wasn't."

I smiled. "Shame. You could have seen whether she looked rather uncomfortably itchy."

Damion grinned. "You didn't."

"I most certainly did. Damn woman gave my five-year-old leg such a slapping for leaving my hoop and stick on the floor for her to trip over that it was near two weeks before her hand marks faded."

"And that's why you wouldn't give her your curtsey? I heard Molly's rebuke to you for the lack of it."

"It doesn't concern me whom I have to bob my respects to now that I didn't before, but there are a few persons I will refuse to do so to and without apology. She's one of them."

Damion squeezed his arm around me and pulled Prince up at the back of the Dower House. "I should stable him so he's not in view."

I jumped from Prince's back. "I'll fasten his head collar, if you like."

Damion dismounted, backed Prince into his stall, unbuckled his girth straps and lifted the saddle while I swapped reins and bridle for a head collar and secured the holding rope. Damion offered me his hand. I put mine in his and we walked to the garden door. He shed his cape, me my boots and we walked upstairs by the light of the lamp to the bedroom. I looked at the bed as Damion set the lamp on the night table beside it to supplement the light of a fresh-burning log.

"Perhaps an extra sheet folded beneath if you have located the store of them. My virgin blood added to that of my flow may be a little more than pink, I think."

Damion walked closer. "Yes…but first."

He reached for me. I met his lips and roamed my hands over the contours of his back as we kissed. Damion breathed into my ear as we broke apart. "The linen press is on the landing. I'll bring us an extra sheet."

I loosened my laces, looked at the nightstand beside the bed and took the chance to open the drawer and drop my soiled monthly linen into it. Then I took off my dress and lay on the bed in my shift as Damion returned and handed me a folded sheet. I laid it beneath me and undid one of my shift buttons for each one he unbuttoned on his shirt. He dropped his shirt to the floor. I slipped my shift over my shoulders and took it off as he released his cock from his trousers. I gazed at his muscled torso, his erection standing away from his belly, and he gazed at me, my nipples hard, my breasts moving as I breathed faster in anticipation of his touch. "So beautiful… That you will let me look on you naked while you look at me…" he breathed.

"The sight of you naked heats my blood, as does the desire."

Damion lay beside me and kissed my mouth as he cupped my breast and squeezed. I stroked his back, his buttocks, his balls and shaft while we kissed, and I whispered into his ear as our lips parted. "More, please."

Damion kissed my neck then my shoulder and fastened his mouth on my nipple. I arched my back and pushed my breast forward. He squeezed the full mounds of my breasts as he sucked on first one nipple then the other, to my moan.

"Oh, yes."

I wrapped my hand around his shaft and the anticipation built between my legs as I felt the length and thickness of his cock. He shifted his weight to his knees and lay over me. "I want you, sweeting. You're sure?"

I parted my legs. "Yes."

Damion stroked and divided my wetness then eased his cockhead inside me, his shaft entering inch by inch, stretching and filling me. I breathed deeper at a sensation more intense than any I'd experienced before, lifted my hips to meet his and squeaked at the snap and sharp stab of pain as he whispered softly by my ear, "Amelia...yes." He stilled. "Do you need me to withdraw, my sweet?"

The pain was gone in an instant, and I kissed his lips. "No. Please, don't. You feel wonderful inside me. I want more of you—all of you." He pushed his cock forward and I responded to my body's demand and tilted my pelvis until my hips met his.

Damion gazed into my eyes. "You have all of me now." He rocked his cock inside me. "You like this?"

I raised my hips and breathed deeper as his hardness rubbed against my wet softness. "I do, very much." He eased his cock forward then back and the sensitive nub hidden beneath my mound throbbed and demanded more. "Yes, Damion, more..."

He moved faster. I lifted my hips as he breathed into my ear. "Yes. That's it. Move against me."

I tightened my hold around his back, wrapped my legs around his thighs and ground my pelvis against his, panting, my eyes closed. The friction built as his cock hit deep inside me. He squeezed my breast, pinched and tugged on my nipple, and the throb exploded in crescendos through my groin and into my thighs. "Oh... Oh, Damion, yes..."

My muscles tightened and I writhed on his cock as wave after wave of their contraction raced through my pelvis. He thrust again and again, then once more and groaned, "Amelia..."

I stilled, breathing hard. Damion quieted above me, panting as hard as I was. He eased his cock out and rolled to his side with me captured in his arms. I draped my leg over his thigh and my arm over his chest as he ran his fingers through my hair and kissed my lips.

"I've thought of nothing but being here in this bed with you these last few days. To be your first and to enjoy your pleasure has fulfilled every wish of my imagining."

I sighed as muscles all over me relaxed. "Your touch delights me. I fear that Molly found me not a little distracted this weekend."

"As must have Miss Sutton-Hoe, me. I was a sadly inattentive guest."

I smiled as I pictured it. "I don't suppose Amabelle noticed. She'll only have had eyes for Byng. She's been nuts about him for years."

"You are familiar with her, too, then? Why don't I remember you? I should, shouldn't I?"

I caressed my fingers over Damion's chest as my instinct warned me. *Admit to Henrietta before the not doing of it becomes more deliberate deceit than avoidance to a man you have no reason to doubt.* "Does it tease you?" I asked. "I have reason to hide it, but I will tell you my birth name if you wish — if you will still think of me as Amelia once you know it?"

Damion stroked through my hair and down my back. "How could you be other than Amelia to me now?"

I took a deeper breath in. "Then, I will say it." I rolled onto his chest and looked into his eyes. "We inhabited the same children's quarters at summerhouse parties of sufficient length for us to accompany our parents when we were young. The last time we were together, you were thirteen and I was a grubby seven-year-old with a general absence of front teeth, who hated her dolly, climbed trees and always wanted to be doing what the boys were doing."

I saw remembrance dawn in his eyes at my description of myself.

"And yes, your mama named me this afternoon."

The gleam lit Damion's eyes to his short bark of laughter. "You are telling me I have the daughter of an Earl working in my laundry, are you not?"

I bit the end of his nose. "She's very good at her job."

He smacked my rear. "So, admit it, Henrietta Rockingham. You left those big, fat spiders in my bed, didn't you?"

I squealed then laughed. "Of course...and Byng's centipedes."

"Why?" he asked.

I bit his nose again. "Because when you two went off with your rods and I wanted to go too, then Nanny said I mayn't because I was too young and a girl, you and Byng only laughed."

Damion smiled. "The girl whose only use for her dolly was to throw it for the dogs to fetch. I never heard your name shortened to Henry, though, or saw you in breeches."

"No. That was only with Papa and only between ourselves. Mama did not encourage it."

Damion tilted my chin, the crease of a frown between his eyes. "And the Rockingham fortune is gone? I've not heard so much as hint of it being so around Town."

I smoothed the crease away with my fingertip. "No, but you will. Townley had nearly run through the funds by the time I left home. It won't stay long-hidden when the family silver starts appearing in auction rooms to feed his addictions."

"Townley? The same Townley that inherited a fortune? The tenant that rents your London residence because your mama prefers to live retired in the country?"

I smiled a small smile. "And best known for the size of his gambling wagers, I believe, and, unfortunately, not a tenant—my stepfather. Everything we had belongs to him now."

Damion's eyes widened. "It's the Rockingham funds he's spending? How on earth did that come about?" He kissed my lips. "No, don't tell me now. I'll fetch the washcloth. Sit with me and take a glass of wine?"

I nodded.

"Lie still, my sweet. I'll bring the cloth to you."

Damion lifted a washbowl from the hearth, set it on the night table beside the bed and asked. "You have a linen?"

"In the pocket of my dress."

Damion laid my dress over the foot of the bed, took the linen from its pocket, wrung out the wash cloth and wiped my thighs in between my legs, rolled my linen to a cigar shape, eased it up inside of me and kissed my lips at my squeak of surprise. "Another something an unwed virgin is not privy to."

I wriggled my hips and sat, found the linen blockage not uncomfortable, so that I could move with my normal ease without an embarrassment of bloodied linen wedged in between my legs, and smiled. "This is very comfortable. I thank you."

Damion looked up from wiping the pink of me from his cock. "If you tie thread around it and leave the length of thread outside of you, it will ease its retrieval."

I put my feet to the floor, picked up my shift and put it on as Damion fastened his trousers and added his shirt without buttoning it, then poured wine into two glasses. "The wine is rather warmer than it ought to be."

I took the glass he offered me and took a small drink. "It still tastes somewhat better than the sour ale the men were drinking on the night of your party."

Damion sat in the large, over-stuffed armchair to the side of the fire and patted his lap. I set my glass alongside his on the side table and joined him. He put his arm around my back.

"Tell me, then, how Townley managed to capture a fortune which I would have presumed was protected and guarded."

I picked up my glass and sipped. "Well, there you have it. It wasn't. With an unbroken line of male heirs until me and Julianna, the estate was fee simple."

His eyes widened. "An Earldom with no entail or deed of settlement?"

I drank again and shook my head. "No. An entail had not been needed thus far. When Papa died as suddenly as he did, the deed drawn up to protect the estate from being entirely subsumed to her new husband if Mama remarried was discovered unsigned in his desk. Papa's man of business advised Mama to keep the matter close while he drew up fresh documents, but Mama found she couldn't bear to be at home without Papa and removed to the Sherringhams' for an extended visit, where she met Townley."

"All concern and sweet delight that he managed to persuade her to confide the fact of the matter to him?" Damion offered.

I nodded. "Mama returned home to us after four months, married to him by special license. The marriage was not made public, as her widowhood was not even eight months gone. He showed his true colors as soon as he assumed control over our affairs — removed to Town, left us in the country for the sake of Mama's health and the spending began. Mama has never recovered from the shame of the catastrophe she has caused, so gray and worn that you would not recognize her now if you saw her."

"And there was no legal redress? No intervention possible to recover at least your portions from Townley when his extravagance became known?"

"No. Papa's man of business searched every avenue. For a male, even underage, the recourse is there, but for a household of mere females? Short of murdering any or all of us, he may do with us what he will and still be in the right of it, as a male."

"No wonder you have an aversion to the legal position of females when they marry. You seem remarkably unbitter about the whole, though. I'm not sure I could be so."

I sipped with a small shrug. "I've had some time to become accustomed to my reduced circumstances and have decided never to put myself in the way of having a decision forced on me against my free will by marrying, while the law in regard to a wife is as it is. But as to the rest? I can sit and mourn what I have lost or accept that it has happened and make the most of that which remains to me."

Damion put his glass on the table and tucked me closer. "Brave, though."

"Not really." I smiled. "I have an excess of energy unsuited to the requirement of being a Lady, along with the comfort of an allowance that ensures that I do not have to work for my living should I decide not to do so. I have freedom now from the restrictions I found so irksome before. I wouldn't willingly return to being The Lady Henrietta."

"Is there nothing you miss of being her?"

The image of Star floated before my eyes. "My Arabian mare, Star. A high-stepping beauty sold to a good home, though, so I have no worries for her. But apart from that..." I leaned forward, bit Damion's chin then kissed it better. "Perhaps the taking of tea and polite tittle tattle — and maybe Society's habit of talking around a subject for so many minutes that one could scream and possibly the changing of an outfit at least four times a day while wearing undergarments of such restriction that there is no breath remaining with which to do so."

Damion laughed. "Then may we add every spindle-legged morning room chair that threatens to collapse under the weight of a man and the sadist who invented the waltz?"

I set my glass on the table and circled Damion's nipple with my fingertip. "And perhaps all to do with lying still and sighing?"

Damion tipped my chin and kissed my lips. I straddled him, my knees on either side of his thighs. "Perhaps I could ride you this time?"

Damion's irises darkened as his cock hardened. "I wish you would."

I traced my finger down his chest and unfastened the top button on his trousers. He reached for my shift buttons and slipped them out of their holes as I released his fly. I unplugged the blockage and dropped it to the floor as he eased his trousers down and off. I parted my shift, raised my hips, grasped his cock and teased it through the wetness in between my legs. Damion's head tipped back as his eyes closed. I opened myself with my fingers, eased down the length of his shaft and rocked to his soft moan. "Yes, sweeting. Take me..."

I rocked faster and gripped his shoulders as he grasped my hips. His cock rubbed inside me. I closed my eyes and bounced, panting. He tightened his hands and urged me on. I ground my pelvis against his on each downward movement and the sensation built. Damion's muscles tensed under my hands. I grasped my breast and offered my nipple to his lips. He sucked it in, bit its hard nub and I stiffened as waves of muscle contractions pulsed through my groin.

"Oh, sweet Jesus!" he cried out.

"Damion. Oh...yes." I stilled, whimpering.

He pressed me close to his chest, breathing hard. "My sweet, how you enjoy me."

I relaxed, my arms around his neck, his around my back and breathed in slightly overwarm man, along with the scent from a cologne or soap. "Mmm...cedar."

He kissed the top of my head and breathed in. "Clean laundry. Fresh sheets on the bed."

I smiled. "Eau de carbolic soap and dried lavender, although come the summer, it will be eau de carbolic and rose when Mr. Robinson deadheads any flower that dares to put a petal out of place."

Damion kissed my shoulder. "A perfect rose, sought after but rarely possessed by any but me at this moment."

I lifted my head and kissed his chin. "Are you trying to put my sensibilities to the blush? I haven't any, as you know."

He cupped my face and kissed my lips. "No. Only false affectation is absent, I believe."

My cheeks heated and I turned my face to his shoulder. "Your next virgin may delight you just as well, although she appears shy."

Damion held me tighter. "If that prospect is my future wife, she will be staying so."

I raised my head. "You will not make the attempt to provide an heir?"

His lips tilted to a half-smile. "Let alone that Elizabeth and I find ourselves mutually unattracted, I would no more send Prince to cover a ten-hand Shetland pony and expect a happy outcome of the birth of any foal. If that is what our fathers intended, they should have waited to see the form of us both when grown. I will look after Ashton while I may, but after that, Ashton had better hope my cousin sires offspring with more brains than he has."

I stroked his cheek. "Then I'm sorry, but with my apologies again, more so for Elizabeth. You may go your own way but without providing an heir. She may not."

"I sometimes wonder if she already does. In purely feminine company, Elizabeth is relaxed but stiffens when a man approaches, and she and Letty are particularly affectionate to one another."

I looked into Damion's eyes and saw the gleam. "You think her and Letty's closeness may be intimate? The thought does not offend you?"

He smiled. "I have no wish to be privy to Elizabeth's private life, so it cannot offend. Public courtesies aside, she may live her life as she sees fit, with no interference from me. She returns to Ashton soon to select rooms for her personal apartment. I will try and direct her choice to the floor above Mama as the more private." The mantle clock chimed four. "I must get you back to the house to catch some sleep before your duties. You have free time on Thursday you would share with me?"

"I do and would, but I am committed to visit York. Henry has to take receipt of her annual allowance."

"And how will Henry travel there?"

I smiled. "Amelia's legs are quite capable of walking. It is only five miles each way."

"There is a gamekeeper's hide on the edge of the copse a mile out of Ashton. I will leave one of the hacking mounts tied there for your use. What time is your appointment?"

My smile widened at the thought. "I should not put to you so much trouble, should I? But I will, with my thanks for the pleasure of being able to ride again. Mr.

Whistlethorpe uses an office at Pugh, McGrew and Cuthbert when in the north. I've arranged to be there at two."

"Not altogether altruistic, my sweet. If it speeds your transit to and from York, I may yet be able to steal an hour of your time."

I kissed his cheek. "No theft involved. What leisure time I have is freely given to you."

He pulled me closer and deepened our kiss. I pressed my breasts closer to the tickle of his chest hair and he patted my rear as we pulled our lips away.

"Bed for you or I'm like to have a laundry maid falling asleep over her work tomorrow. The clock has just chimed another half hour."

I slipped off his lap, reached for the washcloth and applied it to my thighs, rinsed it then handed it to him as I replaced my linen blockage. He adjusted his clothing and picked up the washbowl. "I'll empty this in the bathroom."

I tightened my laces and looked at the bed. "I'll take the sheet."

I folded the sheet in on itself while he was gone and tucked my linen from the drawer inside it. Damion picked up the lamp on his return. I slipped my hand in his and he lit our way down the stairs.

Prince snorted his impatience as Damion replaced the horse's saddle and I his bridle and reins. Damion mounted with me before him, urged Prince into a walk then kicked his leg back for a faster trot. He pulled up within sight of the house. I lifted my face for his kiss and sprang down from Prince's back.

I detoured to the laundry on my way to the house and hid the sheet beneath other laundry awaiting our attention in the morning then loosened my laces and made my way up to bed. I woke with the first bell in the morning and drowsed until the second, remembering Damion's touch on and in my body.

Chapter Eight

I followed Molly over to the laundry after breakfast, picked up a bucket and began my trips back and forth to the pump, and as I filled my last bucket, Mr. Martyn, on his roan, trotted into the back yard. I sped back to the laundry. "Molly, Mr. Martyn's here. I'll slip into the house and write your note. Lay The Lady Emma's peignoir over my arm. I'll take it Above Stairs as my excuse."

Molly draped the robe over my forearm. "You have the wording of it?"

I nodded. "Your wish that your note finds your family in good health, then your desire to put some money aside for your future if they no longer have need of all of your salary."

"Yes, I thank you," Molly said. "I just hope Mr. Martyn will not think my asking a cheek and will agree to take it."

"He would have to be a hard-hearted man not to do so, and I do not get that impression of him." I said as I opened the laundry door.

I carried Lady Emma's garment up to her room then detoured up another floor to one of the vacant guest bedrooms. Ashton Manor-crested stationery sat in the room's desk drawer, ink and a nibbed pen in the standdish on its top. I tore the crested top from a sheet of writing paper, wrote Molly's inquiry on the remainder and folded it into my pocket when the ink dried. I walked into the back yard not a moment too soon, as Mr. Martyn stood ready to re-mount his roan.

I looked in his direction and caught his eye with a small smile then walked closer and bobbed my curtsey when I reached him. He looked at my face before his eyes glanced in the direction of my chest. I pretended not to notice that they had when they returned to my face.

"You wish to speak to me, little maid?" He smiled.

"If it would not inconvenience you greatly, Sir, I have come to beg a small favor on behalf of my friend? She is too shy to ask it for herself."

Mr. Martyn considered the matter. "Hmmm... So, she sent her pretty friend to ask it instead?"

"That it is kind of you, Sir, but I believe most would say Molly Jones is a pretty girl herself."

"That she is," Mr. Martyn agreed, "although maybe that would depend on a man's preference for dark over fair."

I bobbed another brief curtsey to acknowledge the compliment. "Mayhap it would."

"So, little maid, what service may I render Molly Jones?"

I took the note from my pocket. "If the next time you deliver her salary to her family in Bossal, you would read the question written on this out loud to her mother and father? The answer to be returned would not be much more than a simple yes or no."

Mr. Martyn took my note and read it. "Well-formed script written by a practiced hand. Yours, little maid?"

I nodded. Mr. Martyn took a pocket book out of his jacket and leafed through it. "I will be visiting Bossal two sennight hence. I do not take your salary home to your family, I believe?"

"No. My salary is my own."

"Hmmm...interesting. Yes. You had best give me your name for the return of any answer."

"Amelia Brown, as it please you." I bobbed.

"That it does," Mr. Martyn smiled. "I will seek you out with an answer when I have it."

"You are very kind, Sir," I said. "I will look for you on your return."

I walked to laundry and puffed out as I closed the door behind me. Molly jiggled between one foot then the other. "He took it. I saw him. Has he said he will bring back an answer?"

I nodded. "He will after his visit to Bossal two weeks from now, but I think I've just invited an unlooked-for complication into my life."

Molly put her hand over her mouth. "What? Mr. Martyn? What did he say?"

"Enough to make his interest clear. Still, I have some time to decide how to turn it aside without causing offense."

"But would you want to?" she asked. "He's not yet thirty, comfortably situated and not married. He may be looking for a wife."

"My views on marriage aside" — I smiled — "I very much doubt whether that is what will be on offer. Comfortably situated men do not marry laundry maids. They offer to set them up in a little cottage somewhere with an allowance and suitable provision made for any little bastards that happen along the way."

"True," Molly agreed. "Although, to be fair to him, a lot of girls would jump at the chance if it was all written up and properly done."

"Not this one. Is the washing clean enough for rinsing?"

Molly nodded. I picked up my bucket and made my trips back and forth to the pump until the lunch gong sounded then walked with Molly to the kitchen to eat. Harry walked in as the plates were served and sat on the empty chair between Ellen and Mr. Hubert.

"Just in time," he said. "His Lordship took a fancy to visit York this morning." He leaned around Ellen and winked. Ellen and I leaned closer to hear him. "I don't know for who, if he and Lady S have ceased their involvement, but I had to hold the horses outside of one of those apothecaries that sells fancy, smelly stuff."

"Perhaps a gift for his betrothed?" Ellen whispered. "Mrs. Price told us this morning to pay particular attention to some of the guest rooms, as she will visit Ashton again shortly."

Harry and I nodded then returned to eating our lunch while I wondered whether it was one of those apothecaries from which, with a certain nod, a Gentleman could purchase preventative necessaries. I walked to the laundry with Molly after lunch and smelled it as soon as she pushed open the door — the heady scent of roses. Molly found the source of the perfume first—a bar of fine pink soap sitting beside the rinsing sink, a perfect rose carved in high-relief on its top. Molly held it close to her face and breathed in.

"Oh, Amelia, have you ever seen such a thing? Who could have left it here? It's beautiful…" She stopped speaking and looked at the half-smile on my face as I gazed at my frilly something. "It's for you from your William, isn't it?"

"It's for both of us to use, I believe." I smiled. "But let me warm a knife and take the rose from the top. That is for me to keep."

I warmed a knife in the fire and separated my rose from the block beneath it. Molly picked up the bar and sniffed. "Your William must be a man of means if he can afford such a thing, let alone that he must have paid someone to deliver it if he does not work here."

"I suppose so." I nodded. "Shall we use it tomorrow? I should like to smell of roses when I meet my visitor from home in York."

"Your visitor has really come?" Molly said. "Who is it? Can I know?"

"A long-standing acquaintance of my father who tried his best to look out for my interests after he died."

"Oh," she said. "Elderly, then. Never mind. A face from home must always be welcome for the news they bring."

I picked a shirt out of the rinsing sink and took it to the mangle. "I hope so. Shall we get the washing pegged out?"

Molly nodded, and we mangled then pegged to the lines and took our chance while the washing blew dry to set some stitches in the bodices of our dresses. She held hers up. "Just the sleeves to be set in place now."

I handed her a packet of buttons. "Put these and some offcuts of the material in your pocket. If we plead tiredness to Mrs. Price this evening and ask to be excused, we could get the buttons covered and ready to be attached."

She nodded and filled her pocket as I did the same and added my soap rose. We brought the washing in from the lines and, immediately after supper, begged to be excused and ran upstairs to our bedroom to complete the fiddly task of covering plain white buttons to match the material of our dresses. Molly lined hers up on the box beside her bed and fell asleep gazing at them while I took my rose from my pocket, smelled it and fell asleep looking at it sitting on the top of my own box.

I woke with the first bell in the morning, my body aquiver with the thought of riding again, then dozed to the second in remembering the pleasure I had shared with Damion. Molly asked as we sat for our breakfast, "What time do you meet your father's friend in York?"

I left out the fact that I would now be riding. "I allowed two hours to walk the five miles, so two o'clock."

Mrs. Price looked at me. "You have a visitor from home, Amelia?"

"Yes, Mrs. Price. A long-standing acquaintance of my late father."

"Elderly?"

"Yes, Mrs. Price. Quite silver-haired now, compared to when I was a child."

"Then you must not rush your return to Ashton if your company is wanted and you are invited to stay for your supper. The elderly must receive all consideration due to them for the attaining of their years."

I smiled as I tried to picture Mr. Whistlethorpe patting my hand and inviting me to stay for supper in the manner of a fond uncle but found I could only imagine him reaching for his smelling salts at the notion of such a major breach of social etiquette. "I thank you, Mrs. Price. I will do so, if invited."

I walked with Molly to the laundry and picked up a bucket. "Let's bathe first or I will have to make my way to York with wet hair."

"Bring the water in, then," Molly agreed. "I will begin work with the iron while it heats."

I did so and ironed alongside Molly until the water bubbled and the windows steamed then filled the sink and lathered sweet rose soap over my body and through my hair. Molly swapped places with me, did the same and we left our hair unpinned to dry while we worked. I picked up the brown paper and string wrapping from our haberdasher's parcel and took them with me when the lunch bell sounded, and I ran upstairs to prepare for my visit to York.

The bedroom door shut behind me, I took Henrietta's clothes from my box and added my reticule containing the salary I'd saved to them then slipped one of the matched pair of Lady's pistols that Papa had made for my hand into the side pocket of my skirt for my guineas' protection. My comb completed the pile and I made a tidy parcel of it all with the brown paper and string then put on my bonnet and gloves, ran down the stairs and let myself out into the back yard.

Prince snorted inside his loose box as I walked past it and gave me notice that Damion was most likely watching for my departure from an upper window. I walked on and heard a soft whinny in the copse to the side of me just after the church clock had chimed the next half-hour. I crossed at the stile and saw, tied to a tree, the dappled gray mare with a lightning-shaped marking between her eyes that Harry had named to me as Storm. I walked closer, took her bridle into my hand and blew up her nostrils. "Hello, lovely girl. You are mine today, I think."

Storm bowed her head. I kissed her nose, breathed in, scented no sign of a spring-awakened cycle to push Prince beyond the boundary of a competitive ride and whispered to her, "He will have seen me leave Ashton and will not be long behind. We will not win. Are we to acquiesce or show him our tail?"

Storm snickered and nuzzled my shoulder. "Good girl. But first I must change from Amelia into Henrietta."

I ducked into the gamekeeper's hide and exchanged my maid's dress for Henrietta's sculpted mulberry silk town dress, added my flounced petticoat, plaited and looped strands at the front of my hair and secured them into the whirl of a bun on the top of my head. My bonnet tied tight under my chin, gloves on and with the drawstrings of my reticule containing my pistol and guineas looped around my wrist, I found a convenient tree trunk and swung onto Storm's side-saddle. A crop was tucked into it. I picked it up and set her to walk then trot around the clearing. Damion trotted Prince into the clearing after our third go-around.

My heart beat harder at the sight of him and raced on as I trotted Storm closer with thoughts of his giving chase. I moved my leg back under cover of my skirt and flicked my crop on Storm's rear to ask for her canter. Storm responded and stretched her legs. I urged her to greater speed with my crop and we sped out of the clearing to Damion's amused shout.

"She's got a head start, Prince. Get after her."

I tightened my leg around the floating pommel, sat upright with my shoulder held back for a jump made side-saddle as we approached the edge of the field and Storm cleared the first hedge. I kicked her on to Damion's call behind me.

"'Ware rabbit holes, my sweet."

My heart pounded at the speed of Storm's gallop and the sound of Prince's hoofbeats behind us. We cleared the next two hedgerows in the lead but Prince's legs stretched ahead of us after the fourth. I slowed Storm. Damion pulled up Prince and walked him closer as I smiled. "That was delightful. I thank you."

"You are certainly a fearless rider," he said. "You retain no qualms, given what happened to your father?"

"No. Papa's accident was mere chance. A covey of pheasants broke cover under Bess' hooves at full gallop and he went over her neck as she stumbled."

"And Bess?" Damion asked.

"Old, fat and cropping the grass in the home paddock the last time I saw her. For all that the accident was not her fault, none of us could bear to ride her after."

"No, I don't suppose you could." Damion lifted his watch from his waistcoat pocket. "It is not quite half after one."

I nodded and turned Storm alongside Prince at a pace of no more than a fast walk with ample time to cover the last mile to York.

"You will accept my escort into York?" Damion asked. "Unchaperoned and without a groom, it will cause you less notice, even with my face being known around the town."

"Yes, I thank you. My face is not familiar there, and with gloves to disguise my lack of a wedding ring, it will not be untoward for me to be with you. Can I request that you do not greet me by the name I use now when Mr. Whistlethorpe bows me out? He prefers not to know it or the address at which I may be found."

"Of course, but why so?"

"Mr. Whistlethorpe is a man to whom subterfuge is a difficult matter. What he has no knowledge of, he can deny with perfect honesty if he is ever questioned as to my whereabouts."

We trotted under the stone arch of the city gates and along the High Street until I spotted the gold lettering on the window of the office I sought. Damion dismounted, called a boy to hold the horses then assisted my dismount. I smiled my thanks. "My business should not take so very long. I will not keep you loitering here for many minutes, I think."

I stepped to the office and the door opened to my ring on its bell by a clerk who escorted me into Mr. Whistlethorpe's presence. He smiled, rose from his chair and bowed over my offered hand. "Lady Henrietta… A joy to see you again. I find you well?"

I inclined my head to acknowledge his greeting and sat stiffly upright on the edge of the chair in front of his desk. "And you, Sir. You are very kind. I find myself in excellent health. I thank you."

"I may offer you refreshment, My Lady?"

"No. I thank you. I find myself regrettably short of time."

Mr. Whistlethorpe sat and pushed a sheet of paper toward my side of his desk. "Then if you would sign and confirm that you have not entered into a contract of marriage this last year?"

I took the sheet and read.

I acknowledge that I, The Lady Henrietta Qwendolina Amelia Rockingham, remain a spinster and entitled to my annual allowance of the sum of one-hundred-and-fifty pounds.

I signed and passed the sheet back to Mr. Whistlethorpe, who signed his own signature as witness beneath mine.

"You still wish to entrust receipt of these funds to my care, My Lady?"

I opened my reticule and placed on the desk the thirteen guineas I'd saved from my salary. "If you would be so kind, and, also, if you would add the remaining guineas of my year's salary to my fund."

Mr. Whistlethorpe sighed. "Much as it grieves me to criticize my betters, I still don't know what possessed your mama to marry that man in such a fashion. I never thought I'd live to see the day when you would be reduced to having only an allowance from your godmother, intended to purchase a few frivolities for the Season, and a few guineas saved, as your annual income."

I smiled. "At least Townley couldn't spend a personal behest, and it still remains to me, although I have some sympathy for Lady Sarah's estate. Such are my marriage prospects now that it will end up paying my allowance for many more years than Lady Sarah envisioned, I'm afraid."

"The Duchess of Mayville would have been more than happy to do so. She was very fond of you and your sister, and your allowance is all that stands between you and penury."

"Have you any news of Lady Julianna?"

Mr. Whistlethorpe shook his head. "No, I haven't seen your sister since her allowance ceased on the day she married. Your mama's condition remains much the same—no better, but no worse."

I nodded and got up from my chair. Mr. Whistlethorpe rose from his. "I thank you for your kindness in caring for my funds, Sir. I know it grieves you to see me reduced like this, but with my allowance and salary saved, I hope in a few years to be more comfortably situated."

"And perhaps there may be a husband who will value your other qualities and not look for a dowry," he ventured.

I smiled with a brief shake of my head. "With my mama and Lady Julianna's example, you must not look for that for me. I will not marry."

"Such a shame, My Lady. Such a shame."

Mr. Whistlethorpe walked ahead of me and opened the office door then repeated the action at the street. I offered him my hand. He took it and bent his bow over it. "Goodbye, My Lady, and my good wishes for your continued health until we meet again next year."

I smiled and inclined my head. Mr. Whistlethorpe did not let go of my hand. "There is something else, Sir?" I asked.

"I keep alert for any whisper that concerns your estate and family, My Lady. Townley did not totally believe your sister's mourning clothes and is still alert for any sign of you. He now counts Lord Walden of Kendall as one of his acquaintances and may come north on a house visit to the Walden estate, so I have heard."

I took my hand away. "I'll heed your warning, Mr. Whistlethorpe, and I thank you for it. Be assured that I will take care."

I stepped away and saw the question in Damion's eyes, although he didn't speak until he'd tossed a coin to the boy who held the horse's heads and assisted my re-mount. We turned our horses to walk side by side down the High Street and he asked, "Townley believes you dead? He would be of danger to you if he discovers otherwise?"

I shook my skirt to cover my feet and hide the fact that I wore sturdy lace-up work boots rather than the elegant, side-buttoned pair of a Lady, as I asked, "What do you know of Townley?"

"Not a great deal," Damion admitted. "He is of a generation above me and not part of my set. That said, I've occasionally come across him in Town, and apart from his over-fondness for brandy and gambling, I've not seen or heard anything worse of him than that he has those two vices."

We passed under the arch of the City Gate and urged the horses to a faster pace, but one that still allowed for conversation.

"We thought that way at first," I said. "When control of our finances passed to him and he removed to London, we stayed at home in the country and received news of his exploits from visitors passing through the county and the Society pages of the newspaper. Townley only returned to us at Gosmouth for short visits — maybe once or twice a year — until the funds began to run low. Then he began to return more frequently, and if his public face is that of a good-natured, charming reprobate, in private, he is a deeply unpleasant man and one whose demands I have every intention of avoiding until I attain my majority at twenty-one and he loses all authority over my person."

"What does he wish of you?" Damion asked.

"Not just of me but of Julianna, too. There are no funds remaining for our dowries, but with our bloodline still holding value, Townley has found two bridegrooms willing to pay him a price for our marriage contracts. You will not have heard of it because even Townley retains enough sense not to leave himself open to public ridicule by posting notice of the event in the newspaper, but Julianna is now the wife of Sir Paul Proudfoot."

Damion coughed then spluttered. "Sir Paul? What does he want with a wife as young as Julianna? He has heirs from his first wife, is already a member of the peerage, is large to the point of being immobile and not a day less than seventy. He's surely not still capable of..."

I shook my head and interrupted. "What does any of that matter? Sir Paul is rich and willingly handed over twenty thousand pounds for the privilege of marrying Julianna. As to the other? No, he is not capable of intercourse — but he is a connoisseur of beauty and has a marble pedestal in his private room on which Julianna must pose naked at his command for his pleasure."

Damion turned his face away. "That is disgusting. Most Gentlemen are not so base."

"Of course, they are not" — I smiled — "but a few are, and your command over us in such instances is disproportionate and wrong. If I manage to attain my majority unhindered, Lady Henrietta will re-emerge, and you will find her standing on her soapbox in Hyde

Park protesting the matter alongside the best of the 'shouters' at Poet's Corner."

Damion turned his face back toward me. "I think I may join you."

The gamekeeper's hide came in sight. I halted Storm, looped her reins and jumped down as Damion dismounted. He secured Prince's reins to a branch, took Storm's from me, tied her and offered me his hand. I put my hand in his. He pulled me close, bent his head for my kiss and the brim of my bonnet hit his nose as I tilted my face. I laughed as he winced, untied its ribbons and released my hair to fall loose down my back as I took it off then lifted my chin to receive his kiss. "Two bridegrooms, you said?" he asked as we broke apart.

I sat on the grass and smiled ruefully as Damion sat beside me. "Oh, yes. For twenty-five thousand, the even more lovely Sir Humphrey Spittlemore."

Damion's face whitened. "No, not him. He is black-balled at most Gentleman's clubs in Town. His vices are disgusting and well-known. No wonder you fled to Ashton."

I smiled. "Not quite to Ashton but certainly to London. I presented Amelia Brown and her excellent references from Lady Henrietta at a domestic agency. Mrs. Price sought additional staff for the Season, mistook my age for younger than I was because I was so thin and employed me as a tweenie maid. I came North when she liked my work well enough to offer me a permanent position at Ashton."

"Thin? How so, my sweet?"

I intertwined my fingers with Damion's and looked at the pink health of both of our hands as I pictured the wizened digits I'd possessed a year ago.

"When I refused to countenance Spittlemore's offer, Townley thought to deal with my resistance as he had with Julianna. He confined me to my room and reduced my food intake to barely enough to sustain me, but he didn't know my true nature well enough to realize that I am missing a certain feminine something that normally ensures male willpower wins. I waited him out until I was thin enough for the ivy outside my window to take my weight, threw what of my possessions I thought might be of use out of it, wrapped in my shawl, then followed them down and made my way to London, dressed as a boy. I bought what I needed to appear as a serving girl in need of work when I arrived there."

Damion raised my hand and kissed. "London is some distance from your estate in Hampshire. How did you travel?"

"There are plenty of carters delivering their goods willing to offer a lift to a grubby urchin making his way home to visit his sick mother. I managed to see Julianna on my way through Sussex and she was shocked enough by my ill-appearance to agree to pretend to have heard a whisper that I'd fled the country and died abroad of a fever. And even if Townley discovers otherwise, I don't believe he would think to look for me amid the ranks of the serving class."

"He would have no reason to suspect you might be at Ashton?"

"No, none at all. It was by random chance that I came to Ashton and there is no obvious connection for him to find. My only risk of exposure would be for my face to be recognized in my new position, but I have been out of Society for such a length of time that there are few that could match my adult face to the child they knew."

Damion wrapped his arms around me. "Chance or not, I am nothing but happy that you are here."

I relaxed into his kiss and pressed close, my arms around his neck. I kissed his cheek after our lips parted. "And I thank you for my beautiful frilly something. I separated the rose from the bar and have it on my box beside my bed."

Damion nuzzled his lips into my hair. "I believe I will shortly be concerned that the Dower House may becoming damp and require that the furnace be lit and maintained to provide some warmth. The key to the garden door will be on the lintel, should you wish to make use of the hot water that will then be on tap in its bathroom."

I held him closer. "Mayhap I will sometime, if you would join me in the activity?"

He breathed deeper. "I should like that very much. Do you have an hour at which you must be back today?"

I smiled. "I am not expected back until later this evening, in lieu of my maybe eating supper with my elderly visitor from home."

Damion tilted my chin. "Then may we ride to the Dower House?"

"I'd best not ride any closer to the Manor in daylight. If you take the horses on ahead, I'll change my dress and meet you there."

"I mislike riding while you must walk, but I will go and unlock the Dower House," he said. "If I'm not within when you arrive, I will be delivering Storm to her stable and will not be long behind you."

I stood and ducked into the gamekeeper's hide as Damion mounted Prince and took Storm's reins in hand to lead her home. I changed, replaced my pistol into my skirt pocket and re-wrapped Henrietta's clothes. The Dower House standing a half-mile farther on than Ashton, the church clock chimed five as I let myself in through the garden door. I called Damion's name and received no answer, so hid my boots and stockings behind the floor-length curtain, placed my parcel on the consul table and looked around the morning room.

The upright pianoforte standing on the back wall caught my eye and I sat on its stool, lifted the lid and ran my unpracticed fingers over the keys to see whether I could still find the notes. The instrument was not badly tuned, so I played the remembered tune to *Cherry Ripe* and *Come Into the Garden, Maud,* until fresh air wafted into the room and I turned to see Damion close and lock the garden door.

"Very prettily played." He smiled.

Muscles tightened through my stomach and groin as I gazed at him with the privacy the locking of the door allowed. I got up, walked closer and saw a picnic basket in his hand. "You brought supper with you?"

"I do occasionally take a picnic with me if I take my rods out of an evening."

He put the basket down as I reached for his waistcoat and unfastened the buttons on it. "And do you often go fishing in a three-piece suit?"

Damion threaded his fingers through the back of my hair as I loosened his cravat and released the buttons of his shirt. "I fear your impatience in the hours spent changing from one dress code to another is becoming infectious."

I tilted my head for his lips on my neck as he plucked on the bow on the back of my dress, his hardened cock pressing against my thigh. I stroked the erection straining at the front of his trousers, stepped back and took off my dress. "Remove them, then?"

"Here? In the morning room?" he breathed.

I unfastened the buttons on my shift. "Yes, here."

I eased my shift over my shoulders and it slid to the floor. Damion's chest rose and fell faster as he stripped off his clothes and stood before me, naked, his cock stiff. My skin heated at the intensity of his gaze as I drank in the muscled size of him, along with the thickness of his shaft. I wrapped my arms around him, my nipples hard as I pressed my breasts against his warm skin, his erection pulsing on my belly, the mound between my legs wet from the wanting of him. "I've wished for nothing more than to be naked in your arms since the last time I was."

Damion caressed my shoulders, down my back and around my buttocks. "As I have you. I wanted nothing more than to pull you from Storm's back this afternoon and discover whether Henry has the same aversion to underclothes as Amelia does."

The thought of his strong hands doing so quivered down my spine. "Mmmm...alfresco ravishing."

Damion tightened his arms around me. "And you would like that? To be ravished by me?"

I breathed harder. "Yes, I would." I rubbed my mound against his thighs. "I want you."

He breathed into my ear. "As I want to feel your sweet, wet warmth on my cock."

Damion grasped under my rear and lifted. I clasped my legs around his thighs and he stepped us to the chaise lounge. I released my linen and parted my legs when he rested me on it. He eased his cockhead inside me and I writhed as he filled me, tilted my hips for his shaft to rub on my sensitive ache and moaned when his cock hit the spot. He kissed my neck then my shoulder as he thrust. I pressed my fingers into his back and moved my hips in rhythm with his, panting, and he moved faster. I grasped the rounded smoothness of his rear, pumped my pelvis and my orgasm raced free as he pushed my breast to his mouth, sucked and tugged on my nipple. "Oh, oh... Yes."

Damion thrust again and again and groaned, "Amelia..."

I stilled, my chest heaving as he stroked through my hair. "Beautiful, my sweet. To feel your body move against mine, your breast in my hand, your nipple in my mouth..."

I nuzzled my lips on his neck. "I adore your touch and the feel of your cock pleasuring me." We lay quiet, entwined in each other's arms until a certain need caught me and I leaned up on my elbow. "I need to visit the lavatory."

I put my feet to the floor, picked up my clothes and took my now lightly stained linen with me as I ran upstairs to relieve myself then wash using the cold water on tap, if not yet the hot. Damion redressed in his trousers and shirt, used the room after me and brought the picnic basket over to where I sat with my legs curled up beside me on the hearth rug when he returned. "Do you wish to eat here or at the table?"

I patted the rug. "Here. It is a picnic we are having, after all."

Damion put the basket in front of me, sat and opened it. I looked inside and giggled as I saw a bottle of champagne wrapped in a towel containing ice, pâté de foie gras, a raised pie, soft French cheese, white bread and out-of-season fruit from the hothouse. "And this is the picnic you take with you when fishing, is it?"

Damion released the cork from the bottle and smiled as he passed me a glass of bubbling wine. "Just about every time I do so, while wearing Town dress without my tackle and rods, which, to date, has been not at all."

I sipped from my glass. "Then I thank you for thinking of it and for the delightful contents of the basket."

Damion pinched the side of my buttock. "That is too formal a reply. Feed me, wench. I'm starving."

I hiccupped as the bubbles from the wine attacked my nose, blinked then stuttered. "What, eh? If you take the plates from the basket, I will cut the pie."

Damion smiled at our shared joke and released plates and cutlery from the leather straps holding them in place in the lid of the basket while I spread a checked cloth on the hearth rug and lifted out the food. I cut him half the pie, took a slice of the pâté with cheese and bread for myself and laid the same again on his plate.

"Will your mama move here, into the Dower House, when Elizabeth becomes Mistress of the Manor?"

Damion sliced a cucumber for us to share. "No, Mama will stay in Town, chaperoning Emma, and after the Season, they will remove to Georgina and Montfont's estate for an extended stay. She has made no mention of wishing to live here, and I have seen no sign that she and Elizabeth are not in accord over the running of the household. I think Mama would like to indulge herself with less responsibility while still enjoying the comfort of the Manor but would be happy to step back up to the mark should Elizabeth require her assistance."

I smiled as I spread pâté onto my bread. "I'm glad that is so. It will be more comfortable for you if there is no jostling for position between them."

Damion cut into his pie. "There are certain things that, as a wife, Mama could not control for her children, but where she may, her actions always promote our best interests."

"Unlike mine?"

"Could she not have done more to protect you and Julianna?"

I sipped a little wine. "No. Mama is a woman of proper female sensibility. She promised to 'obey' before God, and although not without tears and much hand-wringing, would not break that vow by any act of defiance."

"Not a stance you favor?"

I shook my head. "No. The legal position aside... To me, Townley made his marriage vows with the intent to deceive, every word of them a deliberate and conscious lie. I would have considered myself free of the restraint of mine to him when I discovered the truth of that."

Damion speared a piece of pie on the tines of his fork. "As would I, although I am about to do the same thing, I suppose. Certain of the vows I will make before the altar, I have no intention of honoring. *'With my body, I thee worship'*, will certainly not be taking place."

I swallowed my mouthful. "I think that could be excused and even trumped by the vow 'to cherish'. Being as your abstinence from 'body worshiping' is due to your concern for what may happen to Elizabeth and child if you do."

"*Wilt thou love her?*" he quoted from the marriage service. "I don't."

I sipped my wine and dismissed that notion with an airy flick of my hand. "Oh, that one is easy — brotherly love, the kindness of one person to another. Your care for Elizabeth's well-being pockets that one straight into the bag."

Damion snorted. "You play billiards?"

"Strangely enough, I do," I said. "Papa had a cue, reduced in size, made for my seventh birthday and taught me the game, although I had to stand on a stool to play him and kneel on the table to reach a ball in its center."

Damion took my hand to his mouth and kissed. "So, for my final offense, your opinion on *'forsaking all other'*? I have no intention of complying with that edict, either."

I stroked along his jawline as he released my hand and considered the wording of the vow as I ate a little more pâté. "Tricky...but you could mispronounce the words. 'Fortsaking all other' and 'keep bone-ly unto her', if spoken smoothly without undue hesitation, would make nonsense of the rest."

Damion let go of his laugh. "So it would. I shall practice every day so that particular pronunciation rolls off my tongue with ease."

I giggled as I pictured him doing so. "I would give the game away with an unmaidenly grin if I had to do it, I think. When is the deed to be done?"

"At the end of the Little Season, the Tuesday after Easter Day."

"At Sunnington?"

"Yes. And as soon as is politely possible, I will come home. I will not play the happy bridegroom at my wedding breakfast or linger at it for any longer than civility demands." He refilled our glasses, dipped a strawberry in his and held it to my lips. "I could face the dreaded deed in better spirits if it was you that would be in my bed on my wedding night."

The warmth of his gaze tingled over my skin and my heart responded with a quick double-tap at the thought of the unsought, mismatched marriage he faced and of him spending such a night alone, so I said, "Yes. When the house recovers from the surprise of your unexpected arrival home on that night, I will risk coming to your bedroom."

His irises lightened. "Then the rest of the day is as nothing."

I smiled and ate my strawberry. "How does Elizabeth feel about her lack of a honeymoon? The same as you or are you staying with tradition and not informing her of your plans until after the ceremony?"

"Nothing to do with tradition, but I do not know. Elizabeth will not speak with me above mere commonplace and excuses herself from my company if I attempt anything more. She will answer any inquiry I make of her by way of a note or letter, but the subject of our wedding night and honeymoon is not one I care to commit to permanent record in writing. I will make another attempt to engage her in private conversation when she returns to Ashton to select her rooms on Monday."

"Oh, dear. That shy?"

"Most certainly, in mixed company. There is no rail line between Ashton and Sunnington as yet, and the five hours it will take to return here, cooped up in the carriage with each other, is not a journey I am contemplating with much relish."

"Is Letty to be bridesmaid?"

Damion nodded. "Elizabeth has had some conversation with Mama on the subject of the dresses for her bridesmaids. Lemon, to match her bouquet, I have been informed, as the carnation of my buttonhole must also be, apparently."

"Very nice." I smiled. "But therein could lie your salvation. It is not untoward for a bridesmaid to accompany her bride on the honeymoon. Send word to Elizabeth that you would be happy for this to be so, and I would hazard a guess that you will have Letty in the carriage as a third. Then, as there are no travel arrangements for your best man to go ahead of you and sooth, you can put him in the carriage for a fourth."

The gleam lit Damion's eyes and he hooted. "Byng will surely wish to kill me for asking it of him, but yes… I will oblige him to do so and pen a line to Elizabeth to assure her of her bridesmaid's welcome, should she wish for her company."

I laughed, altered my sideways position onto my other leg and the handgrip of my pistol dug into the soft flesh of my outer thigh, to my unladylike expletive. "Ow! Damn!" I shifted my weight, retrieved it from my pocket and laid it to one side.

Damion's eyes widened. "You are armed?"

"Yes," I admitted. "I had no prior knowledge of your accompaniment when I set out today and had my year's salary with me to entrust to Mr. Whistlethorpe's care."

Damion eyed the barrel of my weapon. "Mama has a small, silver muff pistol, but yours is a revolver?"

"If you will not inform on me to Mr. Colt," I requested. "Yes, it is. Papa sent to America and purchased a pair of his revolvers for himself then had our gunsmith replicate the design and make a matched pair small enough to fit my hand."

Damion picked up my pistol and broke it open. "My hunting guns are double-barreled but my pistols, single shot. This fires five?"

"It does. I don't carry it with me as a rule, but with Mr. Whistlethorpe's warning in mind, there will one in my pocket as of today, if I'm away from the protection of the house."

"Because of Townley?"

I nodded. "The law entitles him to use any force he deems necessary to compel me to return home to Gosmouth. I will not be complying with his demand that I do so."

"You could stay within sight of the Manor?" Damion suggested, the crease of a frown between his eyes.

"I do not leave its boundaries so very often," I reassured him. "Today was the first time I've done so since I arrived here. It would be but a mere chance for me to come across Townley. The pistol is a comfort to me, but I have no real expectation of having to use it."

Damion closed the barrel and examined the finger guard. "I couldn't fire it. My finger is too large."

"The last gift I received from Papa," I said. "For my ninth birthday…and, happily, my adult hand has not managed to outgrow them."

"I am glad you have them, though I would wish for there to be no need for you to use them."

"I've escaped notice for over a year. In somewhat less than two more, I'll be free of him." I looked out of the French doors to see dusk descending as I took another strawberry from the basket. "I must return to the servants' hall soon before darkness settles to make it implausible that I walked back from York."

Damion cut into a peach and offered me the slice from the fruit knife. "Elizabeth arrives on Monday and we depart for the Little Season on Friday. Will you gift me your half-day so we may meet here again before I leave?"

I took the peach. "With hot water on tap?"

Damion smiled and cut another slice from the peach. "Miss Brown, what are you suggesting?"

I ate my peach and batted my eyelashes. "I believe I'm asking if you would like to smell of rose?"

"Or...? Being as I bought a whole bouquet."

I laughed, tapped his arm and trilled. "Goodness, Sir. You never! I shall await my next flower, not without a little trembling."

Damion's smiled widened to his laughed, disbelieving. "Oh, you will, will you?"

"To be sure... If I can remember my lessons on how to do so, but either way, *oui. La semaine prochaine.*" I looked out of the French door to deepening darkness and not enough moonlight to warrant any further excuse. "But for now, I must run back to the kitchen while there is still enough light."

"*Si vous le devez, ma rose.* I will pack away our basket and leave enough interval before your return and mine."

I leaned forward for Damion's kiss, got up when our lips parted, replaced my stockings and boots at the door and picked up my parcel. I blew a kiss over my shoulder as I closed the garden door and opened the kitchen one, red-faced from running, my stomach gurgling a protest over the exertion while full of rich food and wine, to the sound of Mr. Bennett's 'amen'. Mrs. Price opened her eyes and looked at me.

"I'm glad to see you, Amelia. I was beginning to worry."

I fanned my hot cheeks with my hand. "My apologies, Mrs. Price, but a five-mile march…"

"Yes, well…as long as you left the old gentleman happy?"

I thought of Mr. Whistlethorpe's concern and my reassurance to him that all would finish well for me in the end and gabbled, "As happy as is in my power to provide."

Mrs. Price inclined her head. "Very well. I presume you have eaten?"

"Yes, Mrs. Price. A share of a pie," I said, omitting the remainder of my supper.

Mrs. Price looked at the empty chair beside Molly. "Join the table then and assist in the passing of the breadboard and plates."

I did as requested and my stomach emitted another grumble as a small fizzy burp rose to my lips, which I hid behind my hand as I sat.

"Lordy-lor, Am," Molly muttered. "What on earth was in that pie?" I caught her eye and smiled. She grinned and nudged my knee with hers. "Tell me later?"

I nodded, took the breadboard from Ellen and passed it to her. The plate of braised beef with onion and carrots that I handed to her next invoked more protests from my well-fed belly, to Molly's raised eyebrows and her snort. I tried to ignore the bubbling in my stomach while the table ate, but the pressure inside me rose and I sighed my imminent relief as Mr. Bennett spoke our goodnight prayer. I ran up the back stairs with Molly one sniggering step behind me and let out a loud, gassy belch when I sat on my bed and she lit the lamp.

"Amelia!" she squealed, laying back onto her bed and laughing. "Holy cow! What have you eaten?"

A second belch burst from my mouth and I put my hand in front of my face and laughed with her. "I think it more that I stayed longer than I should have then had to run back to Ashton with a belly full of food and wine."

"I take it you did not eat supper with your elderly visitor, then?"

"No. I received his news then ate my supper with William."

"An expensive gift of soap and now supper with wine." Molly giggled. She waggled the ring finger of her left hand. "He seems fond, maybe enough for you to change your mind?"

I shook my head with a laugh. "Dismiss that notion. He is contracted in marriage to another."

"Damn!" she snorted.

"As suits me." I smiled. "I wish you and everyone of like mind a life of happiness after you exchange your vows, but a promise to 'obey' is not one that will ever be coming out of my mouth."

"I don't think it's meant like that, Am." She smiled. "It's just so's a husband can make a decision on behalf of both, should he need to."

I opened my box and took my toothbrush, powder and towel out of it. "Then the words of the marriage service should be altered. 'Wilt thou love, honor and commit to act upon such decisions as have been discussed and agreed between thee?' should be asked of both."

"Am!" she hooted. "Like the church would change a holy service that's been used for hundreds of years!"

"Probably not." I shrugged as I stood and reached for the door handle. "Which only reinforces my belief that I want nothing to do with the union."

I used the washing room and saw Molly's cheek resting on her pillow, a half-smile on her face when I returned.

"Goodnight, Molly."

"Night, Am," she mumbled. "I'm going to look so pretty on the day of the cricket match that he will not be able to hold the question back for any longer, will he?"

I hopped into bed, pulled my blankets up around my shoulders and smiled. "Prettier than the Queen, for all her riches, has ever been in her life. And do not forget Mr. Tucker gave you an extra yard of calico for your petticoat because he thought so, too, and Mr. Martyn named you a very pretty girl. With their admiration and you appearing before James' eyes dressed as you will be... How will he not?"

I turned the lamp out to her soft sigh. "I just want him to be mine and me to be his."

"Then my hope is that it will be so..."

Chapter Nine

Four days later, The Lady Elizabeth and her mama arrived, their traveling carriage loaded with trunks as the first of Lady Elizabeth's personal possessions arrived at Ashton.

"The Lady Elizabeth has selected a set of rooms on the floor above our Ladies' for her personal use, while His Lordship has decided to retain his current rooms," Mrs. Price informed us as we sat to lunch. "An additional set of connecting doors will be added to form Lady Elizabeth's private suite while the Family is in London for the Little Season. Violet, in my absence, you will supervise the preparation of the rooms when the builder and the carpenter depart. Molly... Amelia... You will take the opportunity to refresh the soft furnishings. I expect to see the rooms prepared according to my instruction and sweet of odor on my return from the London residence."

"May we inspect the rooms in advance?" Molly asked. "I should like to examine the fabrics that will be under our care."

"You may," Mrs. Price replied. "Report back to me if you envision any difficulty."

I followed Molly Above Stairs after lunch and saw three bedroom doors standing open. The Lady Elizabeth and her mama were standing in the middle of one of them discussing the placement of sitting room furniture. Molly and I bobbed.

"If it would not inconvenience you, M'am, My Lady. We have come to inspect the curtains and fabrics for the refreshing of them," Molly said.

The Countess inclined her head then looked at her daughter. "Are you replacing any of the soft furnishings?"

Lady Elizabeth smiled at her mama. "No, I believe not. The furniture I have selected for my sitting room will look well in here against the gold brocade of the curtains, and the damask in the bedrooms is pretty enough."

I followed Molly over to the heavy floor-to-ceiling curtains at the windows. She lifted the hem and examined the fabric as Lady Elizabeth continued to chatter and smile. "The cream of the chaise lounge will offset the gold nicely, do you not think, Mama? And the pale blue embroidered French chairs from the morning room with the round table inlaid with mother of pearl that…"

The smile left her face as Damion entered the room with two men holding tape measures and notebooks, the leaded pencil of their trades tucked behind the ear of each. Molly pinched my arm and flicked her gaze at the back of the curtain. I nodded. We bobbed and stepped into the window embrasure behind the drapes.

"Madam… My Lady… You are finding the rooms to your satisfaction?" Damion asked. "These gentlemen are here to take their measurements for the fitting of the connecting doors."

Molly plucked at the curtain, looked at condition of the protective lining and mouthed at me. "James' father."

"I like them very well. I thank you," Lady Elizabeth replied in a dull monotone, "but I find myself fatigued. You will excuse me? I am in need of rest."

"Yes. Forgive us. It is the excitement of it all, Ashton," her mama offered.

"Then, please," Damion said. "Do not let me detain you."

The rustle of their skirts faded after a few seconds. Molly leaned close to my ear. "Let's go and return later."

I nodded. We stepped from behind the curtain, bobbed and exited the room. "Lordy-lor. She is somewhat less than fond," Molly said as we pushed through the green door. "I've never heard the tone of a voice change so quick."

"As long as all remains civil." I shrugged.

Molly and I returned to the rooms the following day to take a further inspection. Molly parted the curtain from its lining. "We can remove and launder the lining but for the brocade of these and damask of the others, we can do no more than sprinkle bicarbonate powder onto the fabric to eliminate any odor and apply a soft brush to remove the residue."

I looked at the length then at the gathered fullness of the curtain. "Thank the Lord for that. They would weigh a ton wet."

"I shall still exaggerate the task" — Molly grinned — "so Mrs. Price doesn't devise any further time-filling duties for us to complete while she is away."

I smiled my appreciation of her plan as we walked out of the room, straightened my face to bob my curtsey alongside her as Lady Elizabeth and her mama walked down the hallway toward us, turned away in the direction of the green door and saw Damion and his mama approaching. Damion caught my eye over the top of his mama's head for a moment as Molly and I bobbed our respects for a second time, then pressed our backs against the wood paneling for them to walk past us, Molly clutching the back of my dress. She let go as I gazed after Damion's broad-shouldered rear view.

"Scoot, quick, before one of them thinks of an errand for us to run."

We quick-walked away and Molly said as I pushed through the green door, "I'll stop by and beef up the work required to Mrs. Price, if she is in the kitchen."

I returned to the laundry alone, looked up when the door opened minutes later and smiled as Phyliss entered, an evening gown draped over her arm. "Would you inspect this stain on my Lady's gown? It has so far defeated my efforts to remove it."

I took the pale green gown from her, laid it on the ironing table and looked at several spots of red turned blueish-mauve from Phyliss' attempts to remove a stain that had been caused by the spillage of a little wine or the juice of a berry. "What have you tried?"

"Sponging, then lemon juice and after that, a paste of soda."

I nodded. "Then salt is all that is left. If the stain is re-animated, an application of salt may draw the purple color from the material."

"I've not used the method. May I leave the gown with you for your attempt? My little chick is particularly fond of this dress and wished to wear it tonight if the removal of the stain may be managed."

"I will attempt it," I offered, "although with no surety of success, I'm afraid."

"And with no fault to you, if you cannot." Phyliss smiled. "The gown is ruined anyway without your intervention. If you succeed, would you bring it up?"

I nodded, walked to the shelf and lifted down a pot of coarse-ground salt as Phyliss let herself out of the laundry. I applied the salt—damp, but not wet—and Molly inspected the work in progress when she returned.

"This must be a favored dress if Phyliss has sought our help. Given how possessive valets and lady's maids are over the clothing in their care, apart from the linens and smalls they allow us to launder."

I nodded. "She said as much—and that her Lady wishes to wear it tonight."

I looked at the gown again an hour later and found the stain had lifted somewhat, so blotted it with a damp cloth, added fresh salt and two more applications removed it.

"If you take it Above Stairs, I will fetch the frillies from the drying lines," Molly said.

I nodded, walked to Lady Elizabeth's room and her voice bade me, "Enter."

I opened the door, bobbed in the direction of the fireside chair where she sat reading a novel, took her gown to her dressing room and laid it on the daybed. Her voice halted me as I walked to the bedroom door.

"I'm an observant person—possibly unnaturally so. I've seen how his eyes warm if he catches sight of you about your duties. You are his mistress, are you not?"

The hair on the back of my neck prickled and I turned to face her. "If you believe that to be so, it is not a question you should be addressing to me."

Elizabeth looked at me over the top of her book with a tremble to her hands that belied the calmer tone of her voice. "Possibly not. But I wished you to know that you will not find me objecting, if it is so. If you are in his bed, he will not be in mine."

I noted the shake of the book, along with a look in her gray eyes that reminded me of Bonnie's when Prince was near, and I answered her statement rather than turn it away as I had been intending. "Then I will advise you, without confirming or denying such matters. Address your concerns to your future husband. You may discover your bed is not a place he is ever intending to be."

I opened the door.

"Wait," she said. "You mean it? It is so?"

I looked over my shoulder. "Broach the subject. He will be your husband, not mine. He doesn't bite, you know." I thought of Damion's mouth on my body as I stepped into the hallway. *Well, not unless you wish him to.*

I pondered what Damion had told me while I ate my supper, about Lady Elizabeth's discomfort around men and the nervous fear I had seen in her eyes, along with a stature so small that most males towered over her, and I was not altogether surprised when the laundry room door opened the following afternoon and she stepped in. She inclined her head in Molly's direction. "You are excused for the present. I thank you."

Molly set her iron down with a glance at me, bobbed her curtsey and walked out of the laundry, shutting the door behind her. I noted the shake of Lady Elizabeth's hands as she did so, swallowed the comment I had been intending about her lack of discretion in approaching me in such a fashion and asked, "You wish something of me, My Lady?"

"Yes," she said, her voice calm against the betrayal of her hands, "a boon you have no reason to grant, but I have tried to voice my concern to him and cannot find the words."

"Why?" I objected, as I pictured Damion's good-natured smile. "He is the most considerate of men."

"Possibly, but I have a history..."

I smiled at the echoing chord her words struck in me. "Then speak plain, tell me of it and what you wish from me."

She swallowed and nodded. "I witnessed something once, when I was but four. My nanny was fond of a nip or two of rum in her night-time cocoa and I couldn't wake her. I set off in search of my mother. I knew of no reason why I should not. The bedroom door was imperfectly closed. I pushed it open" — she shuddered — "and saw in the mirror, a naked body covered in hair where we have none, a great, ugly protrusion sticking out of the front of him and a look on his face that was just...so, so...greedy."

"Your father?" I asked.

Elizabeth nodded as the shake of her hands worsened. "I could never look at him afterward without seeing him in the same hideous state and found myself uncomfortable near all males. My discomfort turned to fear as I grew to womanhood and realized that whatever was happening in the bedroom that night is a fate that awaits me also. Please, your reassurance if it is not so?"

"But your father knew something was amiss? Your dowry is extensive?" I probed, while I decided whether or not to provide it.

She nodded again. "By the time I reached fourteen, he decided he would have to take action if he was ever to see me settled and he let the size of my dowry be known. Ashton's father was one of many who took the bait and he was the highest-ranked prospect. The paperwork was drawn up and signed between them with neither Ashton nor I informed of it until it was fait accompli."

I met her eyes and made my decision when I saw nervous hope within. "I should not speak on his behalf. I have no right to do so. But as I believe he will understand why I did and that I mean no ill of my interference between husband and wife, I will. Damion will not consummate your marriage. He believes any child you may conceive from him would be too large for you to bear without loss of life."

Elizabeth stared. "He will not? He has truly considered my well-being rather than his own base instincts and need to provide an heir?"

"As I have said, he is a considerate man."

"Then I will thank you for admitting me into your confidence. I believe I could be easier in his company with this knowledge to comfort me."

I inclined my head and made an end to the subject. "That is not my business. I will inform Molly that with my face known to you from my delivery of your gown to your room, you wished to discuss your private requirements for the provision of your monthly linen with me."

Elizabeth's eyes widened at her dismissal. "You are a very assured for a laundry maid. More so, I begin to think, than just for reason of being his mistress."

I stiffened at the dependency the word 'mistress' implied to me but bit back a retort with the realization that my doing so might lead her to question my origins further and, instead, bobbed my curtsey. "But a laundry maid is what I am, My Lady."

Elizabeth inclined her head to acknowledge my return to subservience. "As you will." She turned and left.

Molly opened the door a few minutes later, a puzzled frown creasing her face. "Well, that was odd. What did she want?"

"To discuss her monthly arrangements with a face familiar to her from when I took her gown to her room."

"Why didn't she send Phyliss to inquire?"

"I have no idea." I shrugged. "But the gentry are a law unto themselves and have some very odd ways at times."

"True," Molly acknowledged. "The old Marquis took to inviting his horse to dinner in his last year, so I heard. William Coachman said they had terrible trouble persuading it to mount the stairs to the dining room."

I snorted as I pictured it. "And removing its manure from the carpets?"

She laughed. "It had a shit-sack tethered under its tail, I believe. Let's go and eat our own blessedly shit-free supper."

I sat beside her at the table and Harry took the seat to my other side. She turned to talk to James after Mr.

Bennett intoned Grace and Harry emitted a soft cough to attract my attention.

"Um, Amelia," he said, "Mr. Tucker that owns the shop in the village has a... um..."

I looked at the slight flush staining his cheeks. "A granddaughter, a niece, a goddaughter?"

"A granddaughter... Um, Daisy."

"I'm happy for you, Harry." I smiled then teased, "But which cricket team will she support?"

"With the wedding taking place the week before the match, I will have to wait and see if I am at home to play — or traveling the country on His Lordship's honeymoon." He smiled. "But it will answer a question for me one way or the other if I am."

Knowing that Harry would be home, but not able to offer him the reassurance that he would be, I made no answer and just returned his smile.

Molly turned toward us. "James has just told me you will get to ride the railway on Friday, Harry."

"Yes," he said, the smile leaving his face. "If the journey is made in the carriage and four, His Lordship must sit inside it with his betrothed being present, rather than ride beside the vehicle on Prince, as is his normal preference. Such restriction does not suit his active nature, so a Pullman rail carriage has been reserved for the Family and a second class 'ordinary' for the staff."

"Traveling by rail does not excite you?" Molly asked.

"Not much." Harry frowned. "I will admit that a journey from York to London in a little under four hours rather than the usual four days is causing me a little apprehension. We will travel a whole seventy miles every hour when eight miles in an hour, mounted, is what I'm used to."

"And me," James added as the breadboard went around. "I've not ridden in any conveyance other than the staff wagon, and that does not even travel eight miles in an hour."

I exchanged a smile with Molly as I said, "It will be adventure and you will return triumphant to recount to all of us left behind how it was for you. Word and the wonder of your doing so will be the talk of the cricket match, I'm sure."

The frown left Harry's face. "Yes. Whether I am here for the game or not, there won't be many that will have done so. The event will still be worthy to relate, even by the time I return home."

James sat straighter. "It will be something to tell that my father has not done before me."

I passed plates of braised pig cheek on to Molly until my own came to rest in front of me and I dipped bread into the thick, rich gravy. Phyliss, sitting across the table from me, looked up from her plate. "We were at opposite ends of the table yesterday evening, Amelia. I didn't find an opportunity to relay to you that my little chick was delighted to receive her gown from you after your efforts. She wore it to sit at her dinner."

"It is kind of you to say so," I said.

"This is a kindly house. I believe my Lady will be comfortable here after the wedding." Phyliss smiled.

"We will do our best to make it so," Mrs. Price said from the end of the table. "For if the first Lady of the house is content, it lightens the load for us all."

"Yes," Miss Crocker agreed, sitting two places farther along from Mrs. Price. "Forgive me for the saying of it, but the Lady I served in my youth had a very critical eye indeed and the atmosphere in that household was a sour one, unlike here at Ashton."

"No forgiveness is required, Miss Croker." Mr. Bennett smiled down the table. "You did not name the Lady concerned and only complement the tone set by our Family with your observation."

The bell rang on the board. Mr. Bennett stood and James, along with Bert, followed him from the kitchen. Bert offered me the cloth when he returned. "There is barely a mark been made on it tonight."

I took it from him.

"Then it can stay in the scullery overnight and we will deal with it in the morning," Molly said.

I glanced at her. She caught my eye and said, "I am tired tonight. Are you, Amelia?"

"Now that you mention it, Molly, I believe I am. From what we have calculated today, we should catch our rest so as to be ready to face the size of the task ahead."

"Yes. Well" — Mrs. Price sniffed — "you are excused to go to your beds if you promise to say the goodnight prayer yourselves."

"Yes, Mrs. Price," we chorused.

I walked through the green door and Molly chased me up the stairs to the attic. I lit the nightstick, blew it out when she lit the lamp after shutting our bedroom door and perched on the side of my bed. "I believe, from your look, you were excusing yourself from someone other than Mrs. Price?"

Molly sat on the side of her bed facing me. "Yes, also from James. I have been doing some thinking today. I wish him to come to the point, but why should he when I am so eagerly available?"

I thought of Harry and guessed. "Because he is a careful man and cannot provide for a wife and child?"

Molly lifted her chin. "I do not expect that of him yet. I know that will take at least a year of saving our pennies, if not two, but I wish his assurance that it is the future footing on which we stand. An evening or two of me being unaccountably unavailable, coupled with three weeks apart, will have him throwing caution to the wind, I hope."

I lifted the lid on my box and took my toothbrush out of it. "Could you not just pose the question to him, instead?"

"Amelia!" she squealed. "The woman pose the question to the man? The very idea! No, I could not."

"I don't see why not," I said as I walked toward the bedroom door, "if you know he is as fond of you as you are of him."

Molly's giggles followed me out. "You have the strangest of notions at times, you know."

I smiled over my shoulder. "I believe I do."

I used the washing room, saw Molly had turned the wick of the lamp down when I returned and slipped under my bedcovers to her murmur.

"James will speak soon. I'm sure of it. Night, Am."

I turned to my side. "Of course, he will. Sleep well, Molly."

I looked at the stars and contemplated the difference between a Below- and Above-Stairs marriage proposal. One desired, for at least initial attraction. The other, more usually, the final handshake to seal a negotiated business proposition, and I smiled a sleepy half-smile as my eyelids closed on the thought that from my own choice, I was free of the angst of either.

* * * *

I woke to thoughts of Damion and the Dower House, worked through the morning then walked into the kitchen with Molly at lunchtime to hear Ellen's words to Nell.

"Another picnic basket, Mrs. Oates told me. And it is not to share with his betrothed. She is sitting to her luncheon with her mama and our Ladies."

"Too many females and only one man. I expect he's scooted rather than face their chittering. I would," Fred muttered.

"Well, from what I heard of the basket's contents, it's for sharing with a Lady, if not her. And what do you mean about chittering? I thought you liked my *chittering*?" Ellen scolded.

"Oh, I meant no offense," Fred spluttered. "It's just that when there are too many of you, it can be overwhelming for a man."

Ellen glanced up, saw me listening and grinned. "What can you do with him? One of seven brothers and not a single sister to teach him anything at all."

I laughed, ran up the back stairs, placed my pistol in my pocket and tidied my hair then slipped out of the kitchen door without notice while the table concentrated on its lunch. I completed the walk to the Dower House in the mid-spring warmth before the church clock had struck the half-hour and I felt above the lintel of the garden door until my fingertips touched a key.

I put the key into the hole on the other side after I unlocked, hid my boots with my stockings stuffed in them behind the curtain, then walked up the stairs to the bathroom, opened the door and breathed in summer freesia. The bar of soap, pale yellow in color, sat atop a pile of folded towels placed on a small cane-topped chair beside the bath, the flower already separated from the main bar. I turned the tap, found the water hot then took my flower to the bedroom flooded with bright daytime sunshine and set it on the night table beside the bed.

The garden door rattled. I put my hand over the shape in my pocket, walked to the head of the stairs and looked down. Damion gazed at me to the faster beat of my heart, smiled and stepped upward. I wrapped my arms around his neck when he reached me and pressed my body tight to his as his tongue searched my mouth, his cock hardening against me.

"It is as well you work in the laundry," he murmured as our lips parted. "If your duties allowed me to catch sight of you more frequently, the game would be up, I believe."

I held him tighter. "I'm allowed to lower my gaze so my want of you is not seen, but yours to me has been noticed."

"By whom?"

I fingered the erection pushing against the front of his trousers. "Later? This first?"

Damion nuzzled my neck and flicked his tongue, warm and soft, over the skin under my ear. "Always."

Shivers raced down my spine at his touch. I put my hand in his, led him to bathroom, turned on the faucet and put the bung over the drain then loosened the laces on the back of my dress and watched him toe off his shoes, hang his suit jacket on the hook on the back of the door, unbutton the fly of his trousers and release his thick, hard cock. I pushed my dress over my shoulders, then it and my shift downward and stepped out of them as Damion shed the remainder of his clothes. I gazed at him to the gush of hot water as he stared at me. He stepped into the bath. I climbed in after him and sat in the V of his legs, leaned against his chest and sighed at the feel of his skin on mine, his balls and cock pressing into my back and the luxury of the hot water rising to my chest. He dipped the soap into the water, lathered his hands and soaped my shoulders. My nipples hardened. He murmured his appreciation as he moved the bar over the full globes of my breasts. "Beautiful. Did they really expand quite suddenly?"

I relaxed into his soft, slippery massage. "They did. Mrs. Oates' cooking restored my previous shape, but my breasts didn't get the message that I had done so and carried on fattening themselves."

Damion circled my nipple with his thumb. I mewled with pleasure to his sigh. "I'm really rather happy about that." He kissed my shoulder and slid the soap around my breasts then under the water and over my belly to my thighs. I took the bar from him as his soapy fingers stroked my mound. I turned belly-down and lay over him. "I believe it is your turn to smell of freesia."

He smiled and I lathered his shoulders then each muscled arm and through the damp curls of his chest hair, his cock digging into my belly. The rise and fall of his chest increased as I soaped down his stomach and into the dark curls of his pubic hair. I released the bar and stroked his shaft. "You have a preventative?"

"Yes," he breathed, "in my jacket pocket."

I kissed his chest, flipped belly-up, slid down the tub and soaped my wetted hair. Damion ran his fingers through its length to release the soap when I dipped my head under the water. I squeezed the excess from it then climbed out of the tub, wrapped a towel around my body and another around my hair. Damion stepped over the side of the bath and wrapped a towel around his waist. I took the one from my head, rubbed my hair with it, did the same to Damion's chest then stroked the erection tenting the front of his towel as I dropped both of mine to the floor and looked into his eyes. "I am going to hazard that the etiquette of this should be that you don the preventative in your dressing room while I recline and adjust my pose and draperies to show off my best assets in the bedroom?"

I watched the telltale gleam appear in his eyes and he untucked his towel to join mine on the floor.

"Do not hide it from me. I wish to understand what they are."

He kissed the top of my head and removed a slender box from his jacket pocket that could have contained gloves, if they were half-size to fit a child. I put my hand in his and we walked to the bedroom. I sat on the bed, swung my legs up and rested my back against the bedhead and Damion sat alongside me and lifted the lid of the box to reveal five opaque finger shapes. I looked at his cock then back into the box. "Um... Are they not a little small?"

"They are a thin layer of vulcanized rubber," he said. "They stretch and fit tightly where the old-fashioned alternative was formed of animal intestine and had to be softened in warm water then applied to shrink as it dried, with not always a perfect result."

"Clever. I wonder if Mr. Goodyear ever envisioned his invention being put to this use when he patented the process." I plucked one from the box. "Show me?"

Damion took the shield from my hand, pinched the end, rolled it over his cock as I would a stocking up my

211

leg and it became thinner and more translucent as he filled it.

I stroked over and down the length of his shaft. "But there is a loss of sensation for you?"

He breathed deeper. "Not so very much."

I straddled his legs, lowered my head and licked around and under his balls. "But not here?"

His breath hitched. "No."

I sucked his ball sac, raised my head and squashed my breasts against his crotch. "And this?"

His eyes closed to his soft moan and my sex wettened to the tightening of muscles in my groin. I raised my hips, eased his cockhead in, sank down his length and moaned as I found no loss of sensation. He grasped my hips. I clutched his upper arms, rocked on his shaft and ground down to feel him deeper, as the throb of my hidden nub demanded more.

He squeezed my buttocks and rasped, "Yes. Move on me."

I rocked faster and the ache built. I dug my fingertips into his arms as sweet pleasure exploded through my mound to his groan as he grasped my breasts and squeezed. "Amelia…"

I whimpered as the waves of my climax pulsated through my groin and I wrapped my arms around his neck, panting as he put his arms around my back and held me to his chest, his heart pumping against my breast. I sighed as my breathing slowed. "I felt no less pleasure with your cock shielded inside me. What do you do with it now?"

Damion kissed my neck. "To feel you, warm and wet on me, would be my preferred choice, but the difference is negligible compared to the consequence of not using one. I will now send it down the lavatory."

I eased away from his cock. He rolled the rubber off it, knotted it above the cream-filled bubble at its end and swung his legs off the bed. "I brought luncheon with me. Have you a preference for where we shall leave our crumbs today?"

"So I heard." I smiled and patted the mattress. "Here, with this sunshine brightening the room...if you would bring my shift?"

Damion smiled. "Yes. Then I would know more of who has noticed what."

He left the bedroom and reappeared minutes later dressed in his trousers and shirt with the picnic basket in one hand and my shift in the other. I shrugged my garment over my head as he placed the basket between us, sat and swung his legs up, his back resting against the bedhead. I folded my legs beneath me and looked at the picnic basket with a smile.

"Show me the contents so I may see what gave notice Below Stairs that you are sharing your luncheon with a female other than the one that is eating hers with your mama and sister?"

Damion lifted the lid. "They have no notion that it is you?"

I peeked in and snorted as I saw an iced towel wrapped around a bottle of the rosé wine, delicate fingers of cucumber sandwich, glazed portions of roasted duck, quail eggs boiled in their shells and steamed-to-soft asparagus. "No. Such things are not for sharing with servants. They look to the prospect of a Lady within easy riding distance who has so far escaped their notice."

"Damn, nosy bunch." Damion smiled and took the bottle and corkscrew from the basket. He poured wine

213

into two glasses after releasing the cork and handed me one. "So, if not them, whose notice have we attracted?"

I set my glass on the night table, released the plates from the lid of the basket, put two portions of duck on Damion's plate, picked up a quail egg and removed the shell. "Elizabeth. She asked me yesterday if I was your mistress and gave me her reassurance that she had no objection to my being so."

"Pardon?" Damion spluttered into his wine. "She believes it to be so and acknowledged the possibility to your face?"

I plucked a sandwich from the basket. "She did."

"And what reply did you give her for the suggestion of it?"

I picked up my glass and sipped. "I had intended to turn it aside until I looked at her to do so..." I paused to find the words and swallowed a little more wine.

"And?" he prompted.

"And there was something in her stance, a look in her eyes, the way her hands shook, that gave me pause. So, I advised her, without denying or confirming whether we are intimate or not, that if she had any concerns, they should be addressed to you, not to me."

"She has not done so."

"No. She sought me in the laundry today and told me she had tried to but had not managed to summon the words, then she admitted as to the why."

Damion set his glass on the night table and placed asparagus on my plate. "Now this I would like to know."

I put the peeled egg on his. "As a young child, she witnessed her father naked, fully erect, at the height of his passion. She was but four and it frightened her."

"Ah…I begin to understand," Damion said. "And as a gently bred female, she could have sought no explanation nor received any reassurance for the why and how?"

"None. The subject is taboo for unwed females of our station. To skate even near the edge of it is enough to have one's mouth washed out with soap and water."

"As was yours?" Damion grinned.

"Of course" — I smiled — "although not for the mention of that. Julianna and I had free run of the library after Papa died and found his copy of *Becklard's Physiological Mysteries* hidden behind some tomes of a more improving nature."

"Amelia!" Damion snorted. "And you read it?"

"We did" — I laughed — "although not until our teenage years when we were old enough to be curious over 'The Great Secret'. I believe Amabelle and I only had to revive Julianna from her swoon two or three times each."

"Byng's fiancée?"

I nodded. "Her mama and mine are particular friends, and we were often in each other's company before I left home."

"She will be a visitor to Ashton from time to time now that she and Byng are betrothed."

I nodded. "Given the closed ranks of our social circle, there has always been a chance that there would be a visitor to Ashton that could recognize me, but my work in the laundry does not bring me Above Stairs very often and I will find good reason not to do so for the length of her stay."

"She would not give you away should she catch sight of you, though?"

"Not intentionally, but she has a particularly close bond with her mama. I would have to oblige her to withhold a confidence she would normally share, and she would feel deceitful for the doing of it. I will not ask it of her."

"The devil take Townley!" Damion swore.

I picked up a sandwich. "In a little over eighteen months it will not matter who recognizes me or where. Society may look down their noses at me for falling so low, but I will thumb mine back at them."

Damion cut some slices of duck and put them on my plate. "Those that do are not worthy of your notice in the first place. How did you leave matters with Elizabeth?"

I chewed and swallowed pink tender meat coated with a sticky plum sauce. "Oh, this is good, and with my apologies if I should not have done so, but I told her of your planned abstinence and the reason behind it, then made an end to the subject and excused myself from any further involvement in the matter."

"You have only my thanks for speaking on my behalf." Damion smiled. "From what you have relayed, I don't think she would have ever confided the heart of the matter to me or allowed me to broach the topic for myself. I will hope that with her fear soothed and Letty's acceptance of the invitation to accompany her to Ashton after the wedding, she will go on more comfortably now."

I ate some more duck. "She sits beside you at dinner?"

Damion nodded. "I sit at the head of the table with Elizabeth to one side and her mama on my other to ensure I do not get to eat my dinner to any enjoyment of the conversation."

I smiled. "At staff meals, conversation is not restricted to only the person on each side of one and may pass across and up and down the table, but that aside, if you make an inquiry of Elizabeth at dinner tonight on a matter she would normally brush away, the manner of her reply may provide your answer."

"Being as our conversation is usually at an end once we have exchanged pleasantries on the weather of the day, my choice is plentiful," Damion said. "What would you suggest?"

I peeled another egg and put it on Damion's plate while I ate an asparagus spear and drank some wine. "Letty," I said. "Offer her another layer of reassurance – your pleasure that Letty has accepted her invitation, your happiness should Letty's visit to Ashton prove to be an extended one."

Damion ate his eggs then some duck. "And if I do not receive my usual tepid answer, perhaps my suggestion that she and Letty arrange such visits and excursions as please them without reference to me, burdened as I am with matters that require my attention pertaining to the estate."

I smiled my agreement and finished my meat and asparagus then sipped my wine while Damion ate the remainder of the sandwiches and repacked the basket. He set it on the floor. "At what time must you return?"

"After you, but before staff supper. I have no duties until the morning, but it would attract notice for me to be absent from the offer of a hot meal without good reason."

Damion looked at mantle clock. "As it would me, if I do not sit for dinner on Elizabeth's last evening at Ashton as my betrothed."

I followed his gaze to the clock and saw our late luncheon had left the hands at half-the-hour after four, reckoned the time forward for more than the hour it would take Damion to redress, return Prince to the stables and be in his room for when the dressing gong sounded. "You should return. I will tidy the bathroom."

Damion pulled me into his arms. "I know, much as I would wish not to do so. On any other occasion, I would have excused myself—"

I cut his words off with a kiss. "You cannot, which I know as well as you."

Damion stroked the side of my face as our lips parted and he swung his legs off the bed. I did the same and brushed crumbs from the sheet as he walked to the bathroom and returned fully clothed with my dress in his hand. I took it from him and gave him a parting kiss. "Safe travels tomorrow."

Damion pressed me to his chest. "I will wish for the next three weeks to pass with speed, although I fear they will drag their heels and take their time in going."

I looked up, smiled into his eyes and teased. "I expect your mantlepiece in Town is already groaning under the weight of gilded, embossed cards you have received. You'll be caught in such a mad, giddy social whirl that you'll barely have time to breathe."

"Which I shall enjoy as much as would you," Damion retorted. "The completion of this wedding business and Emma's coming out will find me refusing to set foot in Town for the foreseeable future for anything other than matters of business."

I laughed and said, "Damion William Debucy Ashton, go and do what you must, and I will meet you in your bed in a little over three weeks."

Damion smiled and bent his head for a final kiss then picked up the picnic basket and left the bedroom while I replaced my dress. I slipped my soap freesia into my skirt pocket after I tidied the bathroom and folded the towels over the rail to dry, then replaced my stockings and boots in the morning room and walked to the Manor, picking bluebells on my way to replace those that had wilted in Mrs. Price's jug.

She smiled as I let myself into the kitchen and held out two large bunches of flowers. "Well, there is no need to ask how you spent your afternoon. I thank you, Amelia. These are most welcome, even if I will only be able to enjoy them until tomorrow."

"They would keep during travel, I think," I said, "if a piece of damp flannel was wrapped around the stems."

"Yes." Mrs. Price nodded. "A lovely notion. I will take some of them with me to brighten the London kitchen."

Molly nudged my knee with hers as I sat beside her at the table and she murmured, "Well done, Am. Another mark in her 'good book' for us."

I smiled and passed her the breadboard without taking any for myself, but I did manage to eat most of my portion of cottage pie with the thought that there would be nothing else on offer until the morning.

The kitchen remained busy after the brandy and tea tray had been served. Staff removing to London but not in possession of their own traveling case of thick cardboard were handed an empty hessian sack to fill with such possessions as they needed to take with them. For the next two hours, all those leaving Ashton in the morning passed back and forth as they packed and placed their baggage in the corridor, ready to be loaded onto the staff wagon that would take them to the train station in the morning.

Mr. Bennett didn't say our goodnight prayer until long after midnight, and there were many yawns from those who had completed a full day of work before their additional activity, as we trooped up to bed. Molly didn't light the lamp, given the lateness of the hour, but whispered as she climbed into bed and extinguished the candle, "Another evening without giving James so much as a kiss because it was so busy. I just hope it will make him miss me as much as I'm going to miss him."

"I expect it will." I smiled and turned to my side to feel the rub of my shift against my sensitized nipples to remind me where Damion's mouth and fingers had been, and I fell asleep with my smile still on my lips.

Chapter Ten

I looked out of the laundry room window the following morning and watched Harry drive the staff wagon through the yard just after nine o'clock and William Coachman the Family's traveling carriage shortly before ten.

"That's all of them off, then," Molly said.

I nodded. "What will you do with your half-day with James away?"

"Before I started walking out with him, I would go to the village and spend my pocket money, but I can't be frittering it on toffee and buns when I am supposed to be saving, so perhaps I will begin to stitch my petticoat."

I looked in the laundry baskets and thought of the quantity of vigilant eyes that had just departed Ashton. "There is nothing much to be done until the tweenies strip the beds and bring us the linens and towels. Thread your needle. I will go and pick a novel from the library and read to you while you stitch."

Molly put her hand over her mouth. "Amelia! You can't steal His Lordship's books."

"It is a loan, not a theft," I said. "The book will be returned to its place on the shelf with no detriment to its value just because I turned the pages and read the words out loud."

"I've never heard a story," Molly said, "other than what the vicar reads to us from the Bible on a Sunday."

"Then I will return shortly." I smiled.

I ran to the house, slipped into the library and found the books arranged in alphabetical order as I hoped, rather than by subject and category, so selected volume one of Miss Austen's *Pride and Prejudice* as a happy option, rather than one of the more despairing Brontë tales. I returned to laundry then sat on the floor with my back against the wall, opened the book and spoke the opening line. "It is a truth universally acknowledged, that a single man in possession of a good fortune must be in want of a wife..."

"Like Mr. Martyn?" Molly nodded as she plied her needle.

"However little known the feelings or views of such a man may be on his first entering the neighborhood..."

"Ooooh...not like Mr. Martyn then. He is already here."

I read on and Mr. Bennett entered the scene.

"*Our* Mr. Bennett?" Molly gasped.

"No," I said, laughing, "just a product of the author's imagination. Writers of stories need to name their characters in a manner that is plausible to us when we read their book."

"Oh... Yes."

I read on and Molly giggled as I altered my voice to suit each character's speech lines as I read them, and between us, the 'great skive' began, with Violet more relaxed in her role of under housekeeper the second time around, so as to give Molly and me the opportunity to do the smallest amount of work possible each day and allow me to read aloud while she stitched and gathered her petticoat's flounces until my first half-day arrived and we walked to the servants' hall for lunch.

I took my seat beside her and passed plates around until my portion of tripe and onions came to rest in front of me. "I need to stretch my legs. I will take a little time to visit the paddocks after lunch before Miss Bennett ventures into Derby."

"She will encounter Mr. Darcy there, won't she?"

"We shall see." I smiled. "But I will not leave you hanging for too long."

I walked out of the kitchen as knives and forks were rested on plates, walked to the stables and saw one of the stable lads standing in the middle of the paddock with Prince's head collar in his hand. Fenced off, in the next paddock along, the mares milled around, two of them pointing their rears toward Prince while lifting and twitching their tails. I leaned against the railed fence and watched.

The stable lad held out his hand and stalked toward Prince. "Come 'ere or you'll not get yer ride."

Prince stood still until the lad was close then bared his teeth, bucked and backed off with a contemptuous snort. The lad noticed me and walked to the fence. "I don' know what's up with 'im. 'E will suffer none of us to catch 'im this last day or two."

I looked at the mares and knew the cause. "Show me the bribes you have in your pocket and I will catch him for you." The lad smirked, but Prince's ears pricked up at the sound of my voice. I held my hand out. "I advise you to wipe that look from your face before I box your ears."

The lad blushed and put his hand in his pocket. "Um…yes…sorry."

He pulled from his pocket a not-quite-moldy crust of bread, half a sugar cube and the end of a carrot. I selected the carrot as the freshest and stepped forward with it hidden in my held-out hand with Prince's head collar behind my back in the other. "Come and meet me, Sir, or you will not get my gift."

Prince stepped one pace forward for every one of mine toward him as I whispered endearments for his ears only, until we were close. I turned my fist and opened it. He took the carrot and munched as I slipped his head collar on, fastened it then walked him to the cross-bar gate. "If he will not suffer you to catch him, he will not allow you to ride him. Saddle him and I will do so."

"'E won't take a side-saddle."

"Did I ask for one?" I said. "Get him saddled."

The lad grinned. "Are you the one 'arry says Prince likes? I'm Stanley, if yous is."

Prince nudged my shoulder. I stroked his cheek. "Let us discover whether that is so. Saddle him. I will return shortly."

I ran to the house, replaced my stockings with my breeches, returned to the stables and saw Prince tied to the standing post while Stanley waited to the side of it.

"It ain't my fault if 'e tosses yer," he said and offered me a crop.

I took it, walked to Prince and put my lips on the side of his head. "They are out of your reach. Shall we run it off for a while?"

Prince flapped his lips. I led him to the mounting block and swung my leg over his back to Stanley's round-eyed stare as my dress rode up to expose breeches rather than a stocking-clad leg. I nudged Prince to walk then to trot as we cleared the stable yard and faster into canter as we reached open ground. Mr. Martyn's voice sounded to the side of me as Prince's hooves sped up.

"Little maid? Don't! You'll never hold him."

I did not look toward the sound of his voice and acted as if I hadn't heard it, shortened my reins, moved my leg back and gave Prince permission to gallop. The hedgerow approached. I tilted forward, body lined low over his neck to jump riding astride, and my heart sang at the muscled power between my legs and the height at which he cleared it. I galloped and jumped him until the sheen of sweat on his coat began to steam, slowed him to canter then returned to the stable yard.

Stanley hovered beside the standing post. Mr. Martyn, his arms folded across his chest, stood beside him. I walked Prince twice around the yard then approached Stanley and dismounted. "Rub him down. I will return tomorrow for his ride if he is still proving awkward."

Stanley grasped Prince's reins and said to Mr. Martyn, "As I said, Sir. An' meaning no offense like, but 'arry said she can 'andle Prince an' 'e won't let none of us near 'im at the moment."

"Very well," Mr. Martyn huffed.

I looked at him as Stanley led Prince away. "If my riding him caused you concern, Sir, my apologies. But my affinity with him is known to Lord Ashton and I thought he would maybe prefer Prince to be ridden by whomever he will allow on his back rather than have his health suffer due to a lack of exercise."

"Yes, I agree, but even so, I believe it would be more suitable for me to take the obligation to myself for tomorrow."

"As you will, Sir," I acquiesced and bobbed with thoughts of Molly in mind. "May I inquire whether Bossal has been within your remit as yet?"

"It has, little maid," Mr. Martyn said, "and the reply I bring is that two of her brothers are in work, and if she could continue to send five shillings a month for the maintenance of the baby, they are willing for her to keep the remaining twenty-five to herself."

I returned his smile. "That is the best news, Sir. I will return to the laundry and tell her."

Mr. Martyn turned his footsteps alongside mine. "I also have business at the house. You are happy in your position here?"

I nodded and gave him a hint that hearth and home was not what I was looking for. "I am and would not wish to exchange it for any other until such a time as I am able to leave for America."

"America? You intend to join the ranks of the immigrants and make a new life there?"

"As to that, I'm not perfectly sure, but it is my intention to travel to New York and see if the city matches the reports written of it."

"You are an adventuress?"

"Maybe," I said, "but I will not know the truth of that until I attempt one."

"You do not desire the comfort of secure settlement?"

I looked into his eyes and gave him the heart of the matter. "I do not, any more than Prince will let you mount him tomorrow. If that be the case, you may call on me again."

His eyes widened. "Tread carefully, little maid. Your words challenge my authority and that I will not permit."

I considered the matter and saw a way to secure my ride. "A challenge? Or perhaps you would prefer to take my words as a wager? I do not believe Prince will allow you near him. You may name the forfeit I must pay if you manage to catch him without resorting to the use of a lasso. I win the wager if you fail but I manage to call him to me."

Mr. Martyn's irises darkened as he glanced at my breasts then my face. "Little maid, do you not know what you have just offered by way of your open-ended forfeit?"

I shrugged my lack of concern with a small smile as we arrived at the laundry room door. "I do, Sir, as I also believe I will not have to pay it out or that you would demand anything a gentleman should not, if I have to do so."

Mr. Martyn's face brightened to his laugh. "Clever girl. And what will be your reward should the result of the wager be in your favor?"

I turned the door handle. "That if I call Prince to me and secure his head collar, you will not take him from me but allow my ride."

Mr. Martyn agreed with a nod of his head and held out his hand. "Very well."

I clasped it and shook to seal our bargain then opened the door and stepped inside. Molly hopped between one foot and the other as I shut it. "That was Mr. Martyn. What did he say?"

I smiled. "That if you will continue to send five shillings a month home for the youngest, the rest of your salary is yours to keep."

Molly squealed. "They only need five shillings a month? Oh, how I wish James were here so I could tell him."

"The news will not spoil for the keeping of it."

"True," Molly acknowledged. "And now may we return to Derby?"

I sat on the floor, opened the book and began to read of Pemberley.

* * * *

The following day, I put my breeches on beneath my dress and Molly and I treated ourselves to a rose-scented bath apiece before I began to read. The laundry room door opened as the church clock chimed eleven, so I hid the book beneath my skirt and plucked a handkerchief I was supposedly hemming from the workbasket.

Stanley walked in. "'E says, can yer come?"

I replaced my sewing into the basket and added the book. "I'm needed at the stables, Molly. I'll be back when I can."

I followed Stanley to the stable yard and saw Prince standing in his paddock and the mares behind the fence in theirs. I walked through the field containing his equine harem, looked at those with their rears facing him and selected the most actively twitching tail. The gray mare's flanks quivered as I stepped near, and I took a moment to soothe her then passed my hand along her back and allowed my sleeve to brush against the lips of her sex as her tail flicked to one side. I saw enough wettened spots on the dark material to satisfy me as I walked on.

I looked at Mr. Martyn as I climbed through the rails of Prince's paddock. He held the horse's head collar out to me. "He is a bad-tempered brute today."

"'E wouldn't even come 'alf-way near for the carrot or the sugar. Though Mr. Martyn's still 'as 'alf the apple 'e brought with 'im if yous needs it," Stanley added.

"No," I said. "His temper must be worsening by the day. They will not now suffice." I took the head collar then walked around Prince in a wide circle, feeling for the breeze to be on my back and stopped still as I found it to call him. "Come here, Sir."

His ears twitched as his nostrils flared but he took a pace toward me. I held my arm out, my hand empty, my bribe invisible to the eye but threading its way through the air to his nostrils. "I said, come here, Sir. You know you wish to."

I stepped closer and Prince edged toward me with a snort and a curl of his lip for every pace he took. He tested my shoulder with a firm butt of his head when he reached me but, expecting it, I stood firm and slipped his head collar on, to Stanley's hoot.

"'e only bleeding well fancies 'er!"

I pulled on Prince's leading rope and walked him to the gate. "No, Stanley, he does not. What takes his fancy is the gray mare. She is spring ready and I have the scent of her season on my sleeve."

Mr. Martyn shook his head when I reached him. "Clever, I knew. Devious, I did not."

"Or you could name it good horse-craft?" I suggested.

"That I will, little maid." He smiled. "The result of the wager is yours. Enjoy your ride."

"I thank you," I said then called to Stanley, "Saddle him, if you please."

I rode Prince out across country with the road to York to the side of me and felt for my pocket as I halted him on the rise of a meadow when I saw a hansom cab on the York road, heading toward the Manor. The carriage stopped, the driver pulling hard on the reins. I put my hand on the pistol in my pocket and positioned my leg ready to kick Prince on. The door swung open and my breath caught as Damion's tall figure stepped out.

He spoke to the driver as I wiped the silly grin off my face and trotted Prince to the stile in the hedgerow. The carriage moved on, found an off-cut and turned back toward York as he approached the stile. "Miss Brown, have you purloined my horse?"

I laughed, took my feet from the stirrups and slid forward on the saddle. "I believe I have. Would you care to repossess him?"

Damion climbed over the stile, put his foot in the stirrup and swung his leg over Prince's back. I leaned against him, relinquished the reins to his hand and tilted my head for his kiss on my neck.

"The express rail service between London and York, at four hours, I have found to be a wonderful thing," he breathed. "Urgent business has called me home overnight."

My skin tingled with anticipation. "How urgent?"

He kicked Prince on and pressed me closer as he tightened his hold around his waist. "Very."

My sex wettened at the feel of his arm around me and the firmness of his body behind mine. "We are not headed in the direction of the Dower House?"

"Given the daylight, the near hour it takes for you to walk there from the spinney is an hour too long. Another house, out of view of the Manor, has an occupant engaged elsewhere at this time."

I held the front of saddle, relaxed against him and he kissed my neck, his crotch pressing into the small of my back. He pulled Prince up at an ivy-covered, four-square, more than substantial cottage, swung off his back, secured the reins and offered me his hands for my dismount. I sprang from the saddle to his hands around my waist but instead of standing me on my feet, he threw me over his shoulder to my squeal, smacked my rear, marched to the front door, pushed it open and carried me inside. "Ravishing time, my wench."

He threw his hat onto the hall table and I giggled as he carried me up the stairs. "Are wenches about to ravished meant to be wearing breeches?" He smacked my rear again. "They will not be shortly."

Anticipation flooded me as he opened a bedroom door, dropped me onto the bed, flicked up my skirt, tugged my breeches down and plunged his face between my legs with a soft moan. I curled my fingers through the back of his hair as he lapped and nibbled. "Damion, yes…"

I loosened my dress laces, plucked open the buttons on my shift and mewled as he sucked the creases of my thighs, licked my split and the plumpness of my pubic mound. He moved up my body, tugged my dress and shift over my shoulders and exposed my breasts. I fumbled with his trousers and unbuttoned his fly as he squeezed then fastened his mouth on my nipple. I writhed beneath his hard suck and the pressure of his hands. "Please, now…"

"Yes, now," he rasped, took the box from his pocket, rolled a rubber down his shaft and plunged his cock into me to my moan.

"Please… Don't hold back."

He again thrust his length into me and bit my neck. "You like, sweeting?" The brief nip of pain from his teeth tingled through my sex.

"God! Yes."

He pinned my shoulders and worked his cock in and out of me as I panted beneath him, my fingers digging into his jacketed back until I felt the delicious tightening in my sex and writhed beneath him as waves of sensation reverberated through my groin. I ground against his pelvis to extend my pleasure. He tensed and groaned deep in his chest to my panted sigh. "Oh, Damion…"

I stilled, relaxed the grip of my fingers then put my arms inside his jacket and held him to me.

Damion kissed my neck then my shoulder. "Beautiful."

I lay still until I caught my breath then asked, "And whose bed are we currently dirtying, having not got around to taking our boots off?"

Damion rolled to his side and I moved under his arm as he removed the rubber and knotted it. "Mine. I had the cottage refurbished at a time when I needed to stay close to the Manor but also had a need for an occasional night's respite away from it."

I stroked the side of his face. "During your father's last illness?"

"You've heard tell of it?"

"Some, but most particularly the loss of your hounds."

Damion's lips tilted to the ghost of a half-smile. "It was a difficult time. To see M'father so reduced from what he was before. Mama removed with Georgina and Emma to Town to save them the distress of witnessing his decline. I stayed at Ashton to manage the estate, but it was largely by good will, without true authority, and if I was not immediately on hand to intervene, his orders were carried out."

"And that is why you no longer have a dog at your heels?"

He nodded. "I find I cannot look into the trusting eyes of a hound now without seeing the dead, vacant stares of the pack he culled."

I put my arm over him and tucked in close against his body, finding words of sympathy inadequate for a hurt I had not experienced and could only imagine. Damion held me tighter and we lay quiet for a time until he kissed the top of my head. "But on occasions, he would sink deep in his cups to insensibility and I could escape here for an evening of normality and a night of relaxed sleep."

I began to have an inkling as to whom the absent occupant of the cottage was. "To stay in the care of a woman, fond, but with a certain no-nonsense manner?"

"Of course." He smiled.

"Where is she?" I laughed.

"In the interests of the coterie to which they all belong, at the Tinnion's. Nanny Jenner broke her ankle and Nanny Prout has removed to Devon to hold the fort while she is splinted and immobile. What became of your Nanny Elliott?"

"There was no chance of a pension for loyal retainers who were of no use to Townley, but Nanny Elliott was younger than most and moved to Wales to give service to the Butes."

I looked at the mantle clock time as it chimed the hour. "They will begin to worry at the stables if Prince is not returned soon."

Damion adjusted his trousers. "I will dispose of the preventative and take you back."

I pulled my breeches up from my ankles and rebuttoned my shift. "The yard lads will accept Prince's return with you on his back rather than me with no more than a shrug of a shoulder, but Mr. Martyn may be waiting with them for my return. If so, would you say you saw me, repossessed Prince and sent me about my business?"

"Mr. Martyn? Why would he be at the stables?"

I tightened my laces, put my feet to the floor and walked to the door. "I visited the paddocks yesterday and found Prince refusing his exercise. He has not allowed the lads to halter him these past few days, so I did it then took him for his ride. Mr. Martyn saw me on his back and expressed his doubts over the 'fitness' of my being there."

Damion followed me out, stopped at the lavatory then we walked down the stairs. "Prince is high-spirited but not normally disagreeable. How did you persuade Mr. Martyn of your suitability to ride him?"

"Mr. Martyn thought to take the responsibility of Prince's exercise to himself, so I made him a wager and won the ride."

Damion replaced his hat and opened the front door for me pass through. "You enticed Mr. Martyn into accepting a wager? I have never known him to be a betting man."

I stepped over the threshold. "Well, he accepted mine. I wagered him he would not be able to catch Prince without resorting to a lasso but that I could. He failed. I didn't. Knowing nothing of me, though, he doubts my ability to hold Prince and may be waiting at the stables for his safe return."

Damion clasped his hands to assist my re-mount then put his foot in the stirrup, swung up behind me and kissed my neck. "I will offer reassurance of my confidence in your ability to exercise Prince, should there be a need. Meet me later? Invitations I cannot avoid arrive by the day. I must return to London tomorrow and will be without opportunity to come home again before the wedding."

I leaned against him and tilted my head to give him more of my skin to kiss. "Yes. The house is somewhat less than vigilant with you all away."

He nudged Prince to walk and nibbled under my ear. "Oh, is it?"

"Most certainly." I smiled. "I have not only purloined your horse but also the volumes of Miss Austen's *Pride and Prejudice* from your library, which I read out loud to Molly each day."

Damion laughed. "You are welcome to her. I prefer Thackery or Trollope to Miss Austen's unlikely romances. That two of the improvident Miss Bennetts should land husbands of wealth and position such as Bingley and Darcy is so improbable as to make the story a piece of nonsense to me."

"I agree. Such a happy resolution as to be near a fairy tale." I smiled. "But I picked it for Molly. Miss Austen does not hide meaning behind clever words. The reasoning of the characters is made plain, which suits someone who has never heard a story of fiction before."

Prince trotted up to the spinney. I turned my face for Damion's kiss then sprang down from Prince's back and rubbed his cheek. "Behave yourself, Sir. I'm sure your relief will not be long coming, now that your Master is home."

"His relief?"

I looked into Damion's eyes and tried not to grin. "You left no instruction regarding any mare who became spring-ready during your absence, I believe?"

His irises lightened. "Ah... No, I believe that matter may have escaped my attention."

"So, the stable lads have neither brought them to him to cover nor removed them from his range." I laughed. "There they stand, just out of his reach, twitching their rears at him, moving their tails aside to tempt him and his bad temper has increased by the day."

Damion grinned and patted Prince's neck. "My poor boy. I shall sort your comfort when we arrive home. Until midnight in the back yard?"

I nodded, blew Damion a kiss and walked on through the spinney as he turned Prince to circle around it. Molly looked up as I opened the laundry room door. "You've been gone an age."

"I know. I rode Prince out to calm him when Mr. Martyn could not and encountered His Lordship, so handed his mount over then walked back."

"He caught you riding his horse?" Molly squealed. "Oh, holy cow! Are you for the high jump?"

I shook my head. "No. I had Mr. Martyn's permission to ride. Shall we walk to the servants' hall and discover whether our help is needed with the unexpectedness of his arrival?"

Molly nodded, followed me out of the door and we found Violet and Mrs. Oates' cook maid, Lilly, sat at the table turning the pages of the pen and ink drawings in a menu catalogue. Violet pointed at the page. "Look, fish. We have fish in the larder, do we not?"

"Yes. But not as is suitable for Above Stairs." Lilly frowned. "They are salted sprats that I'm to prepare for staff supper on Good Friday. Drat Mr. Herbert for not being with him. I can't design a menu and its removes. I cook what I am told to. That is all."

I sniffed the savory aroma floating on the air and asked, "What are we having? It smells good enough to be sent up to the dining room."

"I can't serve him that," Lilly said. "It is but rabbit casserole tucked beneath a bed of sage and onion stuffing."

"I don't see why you shouldn't," I said. "If you pretty it up with a clever choice of serving platter and present several sides to accompany it, each in a silver chaffing dish."

Lilly sat straighter. "Yes... Yes, I begin to see it. Violet, what do you think?"

"I agree." Violet nodded. "Served fancy, it will be acceptable. What about his final remove?"

Lilly looked at me with a hopeful expression.

"If there are any of Mrs. Oates' sponge fingers in the tin, those with hothouse fruits and a side of a jug of warm vanilla custard?" I suggested.

"Yes." She smiled. "I will soak the fruit in sherry and sugar. But is a trifle enough? There should be more items placed on the table for a final remove than just a bowl and a jug."

I thought of Damion dining in solitary splendor and found no reason to resist. "Then perhaps another jug with cream, should the custard not be to his taste, the silver-topped sugar shaker in case he finds the fruit not sweet enough, bonbons on a silver plate, a selection of delicacies he could add to the trifle to suit his taste — shavings of chocolate, sweetened dried coconut and some of the sugared rose petals Mrs. Oates serves to decorate a cake."

Violet smiled. "Yes… If each item is served in a bowl with a small silver spoon, I think the table will look very well indeed. I will go to the hothouse and select what is ripe. Lilly, if you would make a start on the rest?"

Lilly closed the menu book and stood from the table. "Procure a helping of the asparagus and also of green peas if there are sufficient ripened pods, if you please? A fricassee of potato fried with bacon can complete a trio of sides."

"A sugared rose petal." Molly sighed. "I wonder how such a thing would taste?"

Violet pushed her chair away from the table with the hint of a wink. "We shall find out when Lilly twists open the lid of the jar. One petal each for just us four."

"Oooh," Molly said, "is there any help we can give to deserve our treat?"

"If I pass you the serving dishes, would you line them up, ready to be filled?" Lilly said.

We followed her to the kitchen at the side of the servants' hall, helped where we could, and at seven o'clock, watched the savories leave the kitchen on trays carried by Ellen and Bess, with Violet accompanying them to open doors, lift the food onto the table and remove the warming covers from the dishes. They returned fifteen minutes later.

"He was only reading a book sat to table." Ellen giggled. "Although, he laid it down as we walked in."

Ellen and Bess began to lay the place settings for staff supper and Violet said, "Molly... Amelia... Your assistance with the final remove, if you please."

Lilly waited around the corner of the kitchen, out of sight of the table with the jar of rose petals in her hand, and we gathered around her as she unscrewed the lid then took one petal each to taste. I bit the tip from mine. It dissolved on my tongue, leaving no taste of rose but an overwhelming sweetness. Molly put the whole of hers into her mouth and closed her eyes with a sigh. I offered her the remainder of mine when she licked a last grain of sugar from her lips and opened her eyes. "It suits your sweet tooth more than mine." She took it with a grin and sucked until it was gone.

Lilly shook petals into a silver bowl, replaced the lid and picked up another screw-capped jar. "Sweetened coconut. Perhaps a pinch each to try, Violet?"

Violet nodded. Lilly unscrewed the lid and I found my pinch more palatable for the exotic taste of the coconut, despite the presence of the sugar. Lilly shook the jar over a last empty silver bowl. "I did hear mention from Mrs. Oates that some cooks now serve soft fruits with a dash of vinegar, but whether white or brown? I do not know."

"We will offer him both," Violet said. "If they are not to his taste, he won't add them, but the cut glass of the bottles will add to the presentation of the whole."

I watched the trays move out of the kitchen when the dining room bell rang on the board then took my place beside Molly at a table only half-full with the staff away at the London residence. Lilly put our pan of rabbit in front of Violet for her to serve as she, Ellen and

Bess took their places after putting the dishes from the first remove in the scullery. Violet spoke Grace and said to Lilly as she filled our plates, "The final remove was well received, I think. I'm sure he nearly smiled as we placed everything in front of him."

Lilly passed the breadboard on. "Good. There will be no comment made that might come to Mrs. Oates' ears that the meal we offered was unsatisfactory."

The bell rang on the board as our table was cleared of dirty crockery for Polly and Nell to wash in the scullery. Violet, Ellen and Bess left the kitchen and Violet beamed at Lilly when they returned. "The dessert went down very well, I think. He ate all of it, every single scrap. Well, except for the vinegar and the sweetened rose..."

"But he must be intending to nibble on the petals during the evening, for he would not allow us to remove the bowl," Ellen added.

I smiled while wishing to giggle as I wondered what he'd done with it all, sure as I was that whole jugs of cream and custard, along with the sickly contents of the silver bowls, were not currently sitting in his stomach.

I followed Molly up to bed once the kitchen was tidied and she sighed as she set the nightstick on her box and sat on her bed. "A whole bowl full of sugared petals. Can you imagine such a thing?"

I took my toothbrush, powder and towel out of my box. "I can imagine my stomach being sick if I ate a whole bowlful, and I'm sure the Misses Bennett would not do so, due to the tooth rot they would suffer if they did, which would spoil their chances of gaining a husband."

"Yes, I must be careful. James has all of his teeth."

"Have you ever had the chance to eat your fill of something sweet?"

Molly shook her head and I said, "Then, on the day of the cricket match I'm going to buy the biggest portion of homemade fudge I can afford, so you may satisfy your craving."

"Amelia! You can't spend more pennies on me."

"I can and I will, as I will also promise you that once you have eaten as much fudge as you wish, your craving for sweetness will settle to the enjoyment of just an occasional treat."

I soaped and dried my body in the washing room and saw Molly with eyes closed, tucked under her bedcovers when I returned. "A pink dress and James and fudge. I think I will dream of that tonight."

I blew out the nightstick, took my boots off, slipped under my covers still dressed and crossed my fingers against my fib. "I'm sure you will, although I will admit, my stomach feels a little unsettled, so if you see my bed empty in the night, it will be because I've had to run to the lavatory. Goodnight, Molly."

"Night, Am."

I released my stockings under my bedcovers, took them off and waited for the church clock to strike twelve, then, with my boots in my hand, crept from the bedroom, down the back stairs to the kitchen and out into the yard. Damion stepped out of the shadows and mounted Prince. I stood on the mounting block. He scooped me to sit side-saddle before him and I hid my smile in the shelter of his cape. "I believe dessert was to your taste?"

Damion tucked me tighter against him and laughed. "How I kept a straight face as they unloaded the trays, I do not know. I have never seen such a bizarre selection laid on a table but recognized your hand in the matter when the rose petals appeared."

I giggled. "What did you do with it all? And do not pretend you ate it."

"The chocolate and coconut I added to the soil of the potted palm. The rest I tipped into the largest trumpet of the silver epergne, excepting my petals, which are now in an emptied collar stud jar sat alongside my frilly something in my desk drawer."

I laughed. "I will empty and clean the epergne tomorrow."

"I enjoyed the rabbit, though. I haven't had it served that way for years."

"I thought you might. It wasn't until I started work here that I realized that nursery food is the same meal that is served at staff supper—something that can be prepared and left to its own devices in a side oven while the cook prepares the more intricate dishes to be offered in the dining room."

Damion pulled up Prince at the Dower House, dismounted and secured his reins as I jumped down. Between us, we unsaddled and stabled him then Damion let us in. I took my feet out of my boots as Damion locked the door, shed his cape then toed off his shoes and left them behind the curtain alongside my boots. I put my hand in his and he grasped the lamp in his other and lit our way upstairs.

I walked to the window and pulled the curtains shut against any flickers of light that might give notice to our presence as Damion set the lamp down on the table beside the bed. I plucked on my laces and walked closer to his smile as I said, "Shall we disrobe a little more this time?"

He unbuttoned his shirt then the fly of his trousers. "Naked is ever my preference."

I pushed my loosened dress over my shoulders and released the buttons of my shift. "And mine."

Damion shrugged his shirt over his shoulders and took his arms out of its sleeves as I pushed my dress and shift over mine to expose my breasts. He gazed at the twin peaks standing proud and licked his lower lip then eased his trousers down and off. I pushed my shift and dress toward the floor and gazed at the width of his shoulders, his muscled torso, the power of his thighs and his cock erect above his balls surrounded by a nest of tight, black curls. He stepped closer. "Jesus, Amelia. What it does to me when you gaze at me as if you could eat me up."

I sank to my knees in front of him and licked the length of his cock. "Because I could." I grasped his shaft, fastened my mouth over the end of it and sucked to his sharp intake of breath then squeezed my hand back and forth as he'd shown me. The muscles tightened between my legs as he threaded his fingers through the back of my hair to accompany his small inarticulate moans of pleasure.

I tasted a drop of salt on my tongue and sucked harder as his abdominal muscles tensed to his groan and his cream filled my mouth. I put my hand between my legs, rubbed and released my own pleasure, sharpened by his enjoyment of that I had given to him. I released his cock and swallowed the taste of him with a soft moan. Damion dropped to his knees and put his arms around me. "That you will do that for me and enjoy it, too…"

I pulled him closer. "My pleasure increases when you like what I do."

Damion took my hand and we walked to the bed. I lay beside him in his arm, curled my body against his and brushed my lips through his chest hair as he stroked down my back. "I would that I did not have to return to Town."

I smiled and kissed his nipple. "As I wish you did not have to, either. Has Elizabeth been any easier in your company?"

"Somewhat, if still a little stilted in her conversation, but she now speaks with me sufficiently to soothe my dread that I may have been made an exhibition of at the wedding."

"You thought to be embarrassed?"

"I did. I had contemplated her trembling and being so overwrought by the occasion as to attract comment, along with the prospect of my outright humiliation if she fainted and had to be revived."

"She would have been itching until next Christmas if she damn well had." I huffed.

Damion snorted with a grin. "Amelia!"

I tucked in tighter and rubbed my cheek against his chest with a smile. He held me closer and I caressed his shoulders and down his torso while he stroked my back until my eyelids fluttered. I lifted my head with a small yawn. Damion kissed my lips and patted my rear. "Redress, wench. I had best take you back before we fall asleep and are found missing from our beds come the morning."

I smiled, put my feet to the floor and dressed as Damion did the same then lit the way down the stairs. We reclaimed our footwear and he locked the door behind us and placed the key above it on the lintel. Then, with Prince re-saddled and bridled, I mounted sideways before him with my arm around his waist. I smiled as he nudged the horse off into a walk.

"What did you decide about Prince's equine temptresses?"

Damion kissed the top my head. "I have a fancy to breed a Derby winner from him if I can find a suitable filly. Winney and Tess are nice mares but neither is a suitable prospect, so they have been moved three fields farther on from his reach and will be taken to Home Farm to be covered tomorrow by their stallion."

I patted Prince's neck. "Shame."

Damion pulled Prince up before the back yard and I turned for his parting kiss then slipped off the horse's back and kissed my fingertips to him as I walked away. Molly did not stir as I let myself in to our bedroom and toed off my boots, so I got into bed without caring that the rest of me was still dressed and slept for what remained of the night.

* * * *

I followed Molly to the shortly to be Lady Ashton's rooms after breakfast and we detached the linings from the curtains and washed them. I found half an hour while they blew on the line to empty the contents of the epergne down the lavatory then rinse and replace it. The next day we ironed the linings, the day after, re-attached them to the curtains and, the day after that, opened the windows wide to allow fresh air to blow through the rooms while teasing any dust from the fabrics with a soft horse-hair brush.

Molly smiled as she shut the door behind us. "A dish of dried lavender in each room before Mrs. Price returns will finish it."

245

I nodded, followed her to the laundry and, with Prince settled beyond any excuse of mine to interfere, spent the days until Easter adding the finishing touches to my dress and completing the reading of the Miss Bennetts' story.

Molly clasped my waist and I hers as we walked down the lane to church on Easter Sunday to her smile. "I can't believe Easter is finally here. When do you think everyone will return?"

I considered the matter and thought of the distance between London and Sunnington. "Most probably tomorrow. The wedding party will need at least a day's grace to arrive in a timely fashion for the event, I should think. The staff can return to Ashton once they depart."

Molly squeezed my waist. "I will hope for tomorrow, so I may see my James, with my hope that he has missed me as I have him."

I squeezed back. "Surely so."

Molly's excitement mounted during the day and I woke twice in the night to her restless turning back and forth in her bed. We did not even pretend to work in the morning but smuggled our dresses and her petticoat up to our bedroom and draped them with their skirts spread out over the stiff back and unforgiving seat of our room's only chair then returned to the laundry, heated water and took a rose-scented bath apiece. The staff wagon rumbled into back yard midway through the afternoon.

Molly rushed to the window and looked at the those climbing down from it then opened the door and gazed out. James' expression when he caught sight of her left no room for doubt as to how matters stood with him. The back yard busy with staff passing back and forth between kitchen and the wagon, he walked closer without notice and I slipped out of the laundry as Molly grabbed his hand, pulled him inside and shut the door.

I walked into the kitchen to see Mrs. Price and Mrs. Oates surveying their domain while Violet and Lilly hovered, awaiting their verdict.

"Yes. Clean and tidy in so far as I can see," Mrs. Price sniffed.

Mrs. Oates walked to the range. "No grease or spills, Lilly. I am pleased."

"There is a pan of stew ready to be heated against the possibility of the return of the staff today," Lilly said.

"Very well," Mrs. Price said then looked at Violet and me. "The task I set you is complete?"

"Yes, Mrs. Price," we said.

"I shall be inspecting the rooms most particularly tomorrow. Where is Molly, Amelia?"

"Tidying the laundry and re-stacking the soap bars and unguents," I fibbed.

"Then you may make yourself useful and assist in the laying of the table for supper."

The servants' hall resumed its more lively but controlled atmosphere with Mr. Bennett and Mrs. Price back at the helm. Molly took her place beside me at the table after the bell rang the notes of staff supper and nudged my knee with hers, a little pink in the face. I passed her the breadboard and leaned closer to hear her breathless whisper. "I'm going to do what you did and hide in the lavatory tonight. I've said I'll meet James in the laundry when the house is quiet. That is why he sat farther up the table, so we do not attract the notice of Mrs. Price or Mr. Bennett."

I nudged her arm, passed her a dish of stew and we ate our supper listening to the hum of conversation as the marvels and terrors of those that had traveled by steam engine passed around the table. I walked through the green door as Molly walked on past it after Mr. Bennett intoned his amen and pulled my bedcovers over my shoulder with a smile at the remembrance of my more-than-tipsy state that had led to me sleeping on Damion's lap, held tight in his arms, on the night that I had walked past the green door myself. I turned my cheek to the pillow and pictured him holding me close then lay on my back, gazed out at the stars and let the imagery of him doing so flow through my mind while my skin warmed at the thought that he would do so again tomorrow. Molly opened the bedroom door a little after the church clock chimed two and, still awake, I struck a match on my Vesta and lit the nightstick. "So?"

She giggled and twirled around the room. "So, as much as I still can't wait to wear it, it didn't take a pink dress after all."

I smiled at the delight on her face. "I'm happy for you."

Molly reached into her pocket and pulled out a small, red-velvet bag. "Look, Am. He bought this for me in London—a token of his love." She tipped the contents into her hand and I saw a fine silver chain with a silver, heart-shaped charm dangling from it. "I shall wear it only for best, of course," she added.

My smile widened as I looked. "It's perfect—a gift bought for no special occasion other than that he considered the happiness you would feel to receive it."

Molly dropped her necklace back into its bag. "And when we were talking, he said, '*When we are wed*'."

I laughed. "Molly Jones, get into your bed or you will be fit for nothing in the morning!" She giggled, put her treasure on the top of her box, loosened her laces and placed her dress over the foot of her bed then hopped in under the covers as I blew out the flame of the nightstick.

"Night, Am."

"Goodnight, Molly. Sleep well."

Chapter Eleven

I woke in the morning to the chimes of the second rising bell and used the washing room in the comfort of it warmed by nearly summer air rather than the icy conditions of earlier in the year that had made the task so unpleasant a chore.

Our breakfast porridge eaten, Mrs. Price beckoned us. "My inspection of the staff bed linens at the London residence resulted in at least a dozen sheets in need of side to middling. You will find them in a hamper in the laundry. Begin work on them immediately, if you please."

Molly lifted the lid of the hamper when we arrived at the laundry. "Oh, well, it might have been worse. The last time all of the Family were away, to leave little work for the laundry, she made me and Rosie wash every blanket in the house, even those from guest rooms that hadn't been used that year."

I opened the work basket and took out the scissors as Molly unfolded a sheet and laid it on the ironing table. I cut it from end to end through its worn, over-used center, while Molly threaded her needle. I handed her the two pieces of the sheet to be re-assembled by the stitching of the unworn sides together, edge to edge, then cut the next sheet for myself and began to stitch.

"I wonder what is happening at Sunnington while we sit here sewing?" Molly said.

I thought back to my sister's less-than-happy wedding day. "Well, the groom is not supposed to catch sight of his bride before they meet at the altar, so maybe they will be taking breakfast in their rooms."

"Then maybe her hair will be dressed while she sits before her mirror wearing a beautiful satin wrap?" Molly guessed with a smile.

"I would think so." I nodded. "And afterward, Phyliss will fasten her into many layers of undergarments, which will take some time."

"While her bridesmaids giggle and flutter around?"

I smiled. "From what we have observed, I'm not sure there will much in the way of fluttering and giggling to be had at Sunnington today."

"True." Molly laughed. "Although there will be on my wedding day if I get to marry James."

I wagged my finger at her. "*When...*"

She laughed louder and we stitched on, but I found her speculation of the event taking place at Sunnington had taken root in my head. I plied my needle and moved the fictional wedding day on with every hour the church clock chimed, until the lunch bell rang. I followed Molly to the kitchen and saw both hands of the wall-clock standing at twelve.

A picture of Damion's tall, well-built figure standing before the altar immaculately attired in his tailed morning suit and about to make life-long promises of love and commitment to his bride, bounced into my mind. I pushed it away, pulled my chair out from under the table and sat but found the subject was not to be avoided with the comments that were running around the kitchen.

"What time is the service? Midday, isn't it?"

"Will she be fashionably late?"

"She must be at the church door by now. I wonder what her wedding dress looks like? Will she wear a veil like the Queen? Or a bonnet?"

"She is very small and not properly pretty, but brides always look beautiful on their wedding day, don't they?"

"I expect His Lordship looks particularly fine today."

Mrs. Price smiled indulgently as the table filled. Mr. Bennett stood behind his chair and cleared his throat.

"Ladies and gentlemen, in honor of the great occasion currently taking place at Sunnington" — he looked over his shoulder and beckoned. James and Bert walked in from the scullery, each holding a tray filled with glasses of bubbling wine — "His Lordship has ordered a glass of champagne to be served to us all."

James and Bert circled the table and put a glass beside each of us then took their own seats. I looked at mine and my heart gave an unruly thud for the memory of the last time I had drunk it. I took my thoughts back in hand against such silly, frilly thinking, picked up my glass and joined the rest of the table in Mr. Bennett's toast. "To the happy couple."

Speculation calmed while lunch was served and eaten but started again as the table was cleared.

"They must be eating their wedding breakfast by now. How many tiers to the wedding cake, do you think?"

"What about the honeymoon? How many weeks will they stay away?"

I looked at the clock and my discomfort eased when I saw that the service must be complete to the echo of the words in my head, *It is done.* Mrs. Price sent Polly to fetch Molly and I during the afternoon and we accompanied her to the new Lady Ashton's suite, where she inspected our work and pronounced herself satisfied.

"Yes, I am pleased. The addition of a bowl of dried lavender in each of the rooms will keep them smelling sweet until Her Ladyship returns from her honeymoon. You may finish work for the day and take your ease in the kitchen until supper."

"Thank you, Mrs. Price," we chorused, then followed her to the kitchen and saw Violet, Lilly, Ellen and Bess sitting at the table with a cup of water and milk cocoa each and a plate of 'Parkin' cake squares to share.

"A treat for our preparation of Lady Ashton's rooms, Mrs. Price said." Violet smiled.

"Yes, indeed," Mrs. Oates said, putting two cups of cocoa on the table for Molly and me. "And for Lilly, for rising to the challenge in the provision of His Lordship's dinner."

I took a sugar cube and put in my pocket rather than into my cocoa then listened to more talk of the wedding as we ate our cake. My heart thumped again, but this time in the pleasurable anticipation of Damion being on his way home and of my joining him in his bed. Staff drifted into the kitchen, free of duties earlier than usual with no Family in the house to serve, and supper was placed on the table an hour in advance of when we normally ate. The commotion started just after eight as a horn being blown sounded the imminent arrival of a carriage at the front of the house. Mr. Bennett placed his knife and fork on his plate, stood and straightened his jacket. "James... Bert... With me, if you please. We have visitors arriving."

Mrs. Price looked at Mr. Bennett. "I can't imagine who would be turning up like this on His Lordship's wedding day. Anyone well enough acquainted with him as to be visiting here should be at Sunnington."

Mr. Bennett led the way through the green door and Bert ran into the kitchen five minutes later. "Mrs. Price. Mr. Bennett says there is no honeymoon. His Lordship has only gone and brought her straight to Ashton. Fred, you're to come with me to carry in their luggage. James is gone Above Stairs to light the lamps."

Mrs. Price stiffened. "Well, that's caught us short and no mistake. Violet... Ellen... Polly... Bess... Caps and pinnys on, if you please. There can be no formal greeting for the bride as there should be, but we must be ready if our services are required."

Mr. Bennett walked into the kitchen. "The tea tray for our new Mistress and her bridesmaid to her apartment, if you please, Mrs. Price, with a plate of Mrs. Oates' sponge fingers or whatever she has on hand. His Lordship requires no refreshment other than the brandy decanter and has retired to play billiards with Lord Byngingham."

Mrs. Price peered over the top of her half-glasses, her mouth a round O and stood from the table as Harry came through the green door and joined it. "Mr. Hubert, Phyliss and Lord Byngingham's valet Mr.

Tyler are two hours behind us in a Wellingham barouche and pair driven by Tom. Is there any supper left that we may have?"

Mrs. Oates followed Mrs. Price toward her cooking range and store cupboards. "Well, goodness! I wasn't expecting this. Our supper is finished but I have some eggs and will fry you all some potatoes."

The questions and comments began as Mrs. Price and Mrs. Oates walked away.

"How come you are home already, Harry?"

"No honeymoon. Isn't that odd?"

"Oh, she must be disappointed! I expect she had a whole new wardrobe made to wear on her honeymoon."

Mr. Bennett walked into the kitchen and rapped his knuckles on the table. "Ladies and gentlemen, cease to chatter, if you please. It is not our place to question the choices of our betters. It is unseemly."

The table quietened and left Harry to eat his supper. Mr. Hubert, Phyliss, Tom and Mr. Tyler ate theirs to stilted conversation when the arrived with the subject the table ached to discuss declared taboo. Tom and Harry left through the back door for the stables as the others walked through the green door to attend their respective Masters and Mistresses after they ate, and I followed Molly up the back stairs to bed after Mr. Bennett had intoned Grace.

"Well, I knew they weren't fond, but I can't say I expected that," she said as she pulled her blankets over her shoulder. "I thought the gentry would at least pretend to be so for a while."

"Maybe not" — I shrugged as I dropped the sugar cube needed to set her hair into my box — "if there is no point to it."

I listened to Molly's snores until the church clock chimed twelve then put my feet out of bed and wrapped my shawl over my shift. The house held an atmosphere of sleeping-quiet as I padded on bare feet down the back stairs and through the green door. Damion lay in his bed with a side lamp lit as I slipped into his room. I turned the key and dropped my shawl as he smiled and lifted the bedcovers. I unbuttoned my shift as I walked toward him, took it off as I reached the bed and moved into the warmth of his arms. He pressed me close. I kissed his cheek, his cock hard against my thigh. "It's over now. Your duty is done."

Damion kissed my neck, his breath soft under my ear. "I spoke the words and wished it different. Of equal station, it could have been us."

I threaded my fingers through the back of his hair and held him to me. "I can no more go back and alter the fact that Papa died to leave Townley in his place any more than you can erase your father's signature on your marriage contract." I trailed my fingertips through his chest hair, down his belly to his cock and caressed the length of his shaft. "But still, here we are, naked in bed."

Damion moved his lips to mine. "Yes. This, at least, is not denied to us."

I opened my mouth to his tongue and deepened our kiss as he traced over the contours of my body. I cupped his balls, squeezed gently and stroked over and around the firm domes of his buttocks with my other hand. He squeezed my breast and fastened his mouth on my nipple. I moaned my pleasure and ran the edges of my fingernails from his balls down the inside of each thigh then up through the creases to each side of his groin and over his pubic mound to the increased rise and fall of his chest.

He released my nipple and sucked the other, erect and begging for his mouth. I grasped his shaft under his cockhead and moved the creases back and forth as he'd shown me, with small mewls to his hard suck on my breast and him exploring my wet sex. My skin heated. My groin pulsed and I writhed, threaded my fingers through the back of his hair and sighed as the sensation threatened to overwhelm me. "Damion...please."

He released my breast, kissed then bit the tender skin under my ear. "Let me hear what you want of me?"

I whimpered louder at the brief nip of pain that ricocheted through my mound and panted. "Your cock...inside me."

He reached out, plucked a preventative from the box on the night table and kissed my neck. "Yes, my sweet. I'm going to take you now."

I panted harder as he rolled the rubber on, parted my legs as he lay over me and moaned as he eased his cock in, inch by delicious inch. I wrapped my legs around his thighs as his groin met mine and rocked against him. He pulled back then plunged his shaft deep inside me. I slammed my pelvis against his with an inarticulate cry as his cock hit the spot, dug my fingers into his back and matched his thrusts with the movement of my hips until the throb reached its peak and waves of contracting muscles spread through me to my wail, "Damion..."

He stiffened and his thrusts shortened to his groaned, "Sweet Jesus! So beautiful."

I wrapped my arms around his neck and held him, my chest heaving with his breath hot and fast in my ear, and neither of us moved until our heart rates steadied. He eased out of me, removed and knotted the rubber, deposited it on the nightstand and we lay on our sides, wrapped in each other arms, our heads on the pillow facing each other.

I stroked my fingers down his cheek and along his jawline. "How was the day?"

He captured my hand, took it to his mouth and kissed. "Not pleasant, but not as dreadful of that of my previous imaginings, with Elizabeth now easier in my company."

I caressed his shoulder. "She was composed?"

"Perfectly, to the point where I would say she enjoyed the day."

"I expect she did," I smiled, "safe in the knowledge that with you for her husband, what she dreaded will not come to pass, along with your permission to live her life according to her own design."

Damion kissed my lips. "I hope she will, and to promote that notion, I wrote to Coutts this evening and instructed them to deposit the monies of her dowry into her personal account and not into the Ashton accounts that are mine."

"That will raise some eyebrows."

"I married Elizabeth to keep Ashton. It is not sitting well with me that I will turn a profit from doing so. I have revenue enough to follow my own choice in the matter."

The mantle clock chimed half after one. Damion picked up his pocket watch out of its case laying on the night table. "At which hour should I set it to repeat?"

"Half-an-hour after five should see the back stairs still empty before the tweenies rise at six."

Damion fiddled with the dial and I smiled as I noticed a pink rose, its stem shortened and bound, sitting on the night table. "That does not look so very much like a lemon carnation."

Damion set the watch back into its case, turned down the lamp and pulled the bedcovers over us. "A small mutiny, I know, but I preferred my own choice of emblem to wear on my chest today." I tucked in closer, breathed him in and sighed at the feel of his arms around me and the warmth on his skin on mine. He kissed my hair and stroked down my back, his fingers soft and soothing, until my eyelids fluttered closed and I knew no more until the tinkling chimes of his watch woke me.

I nuzzled into his neck and enjoyed the unaccustomed feel of waking held in strong arms, then kissed his lips as he stirred. "Stay asleep. I must slip away now." I put my feet to the floor and picked up my shift to his sleepy smile, slipped it on and, with my shawl wrapped around me, unlocked the door and peeked around it. The hallway was empty of any but myself, so I closed it behind me and sped through the green door. Molly opened an eye as I shut our bedroom door behind me and yawned. "Night pot?"

I nodded, climbed into bed and fell asleep until the ring of the second bell, then refreshed my body in the washing room and followed Molly to the laundry after a large bowl of porridge. She poked through a new hamper when we arrived. "His Lordship's shirt and cravat. Lord Byngingham's shirt, cravat and singlet. Two pairs of Ladies' drawers and their stockings."

I picked up the bucket. "We'll only need a pail or two, then."

Molly nodded, picked kindling from the box and began to build the fire. I propped the door open with the stone we used to bathe in the rinsing sink to allow in the early summer air and walked to the pump. Prince and Byng's mount, Roxy, stood in their respective loose boxes. I greeted them with a kiss between their nostrils apiece as I walked back to the laundry with the water, and Byng's voice sounded in the back yard a few minutes later. "Well, you're remarkably chipper this morning for a man who spent his wedding night alone."

I heard no reply from Damion but presumed Byng must have noted some telltale sign on his face when he snorted. "You were not alone at all, were you? Your mystery lady was with you."

Molly gazed at me round-eyed as Byng added, "Damn, it! You've never held back so with me before. Why will you not admit to her name?"

"My Lady has her own reasons for not desiring her name to be known."

"Definitely a Lady, then?"

"Every beautiful inch..."

Hoofbeats sounded and I did not have to hide my smile at Damion's compliment in the face of Molly's giggles. "They must not have noticed the door is ajar. Who do you think it can be? Ellen racked her brain when he ordered the second picnic basket but could not come up with the name of a Lady within possible riding distance of Ashton."

"I would not like to hazard a guess" — I smiled — "not being from these parts."

"Nell did suggest Lady Brockley, as she has been widowed for just over the year, but she is even older that Mrs. Henry Carleton, so I am not so sure."

I let my laugh out as I thought of Lady Brockley in Damion's bed—strict, upright and barking orders at near fifty, as her younger self had done to me as a child. "Well, maybe…"

* * * *

The following afternoon I began Pemberley's conclusion to Molly's lazy stitching but hid it under my skirt and reached for the work basket as the laundry room door opened and Mr. Hubert stepped in.

"Amelia… Your advice, if you please? We have had a careless guest in the library. His Lordship selected a volume and found the cover stained and also some pages inside. May I request you view it and determine whether an ingredient used to remove a stain from fabric may also be used on paper?"

I nodded and set a stitch in the same bedsheet I had been repairing all week. "Lemon and sunlight may help if the printed words are not badly stained. Do you wish to leave the volume on the table in the library? I could view it after I finish my work here."

Mr. Hubert fixed his eyes on mine. "I believe *immediately* would be more convenient."

I laid the sheet over the book and stood at his pointed request. "Perhaps the remedy should be applied without delay."

I smiled at Molly, closed the laundry room door behind myself and Mr. Hubert then looked at him. "And?"

Mr. Hubert's brow creased to a frown. "And His Lordship has a visitor with him. He sent James from the hall chair to summon me and asked that with whatever subterfuge necessary, I was to find and abstract you without due notice then bring you to the library."

I turned my feet away from the kitchen door and toward the side of the house. "The terrace door, then. How does the visitor appear?"

"A tall man, silver-haired. Very thin and so neat in his dress so as to suggest to me a man of precise habits."

I frowned as I recognized Mr. Whistlethorpe's description and considered what reason could have persuaded him to seek me out. Mr. Hubert opened the French doors from the terrace into the library. I stepped behind him to allow the precedence his superior household position demanded then followed him in. Mr. Whistlethorpe, seated before Damion at the desk, looked at Mr. Hubert then behind him and jumped to his feet. He gave me his bow as Damion stood.

"My Lady, you are actually here? I only thought to inquire of your direction from Lord Ashton after recognizing him when he spoke with you in York. I find you well, My Lady?"

I held out my hand and he bent his respects over it. "You do, Sir, although a little perplexed to see you here. Only a matter of urgency could have caused you to seek me, I presume?"

Mr. Whistlethorpe released my hand. "Indeed, yes. And my apologies, My Lady. I had thought to discover your whereabouts without breaching your incognito."

I glanced at Mr. Hubert's rigid expression. "Do not overly concern yourself, Sir. Lord Ashton is familiar with my history, although poor Mr. Hubert looks in need of the smelling salts."

Mr. Whistlethorpe patted his waistcoat pocket to locate the small bottle he kept in it for the use of Ladies of suitable sensibility when delivering unwelcome news. "Yes, yes, of course. I have them to hand."

Damion's mouth twitched as he looked at me. "Do not fret yourself, Sir. I believe Lady Henrietta was not being entirely serious." He turned toward Mr. Hubert. "You are excused, Hubert. I rely on your normal discretion. Outside of these walls, The Lady Henrietta remains Amelia, as she has always been at Ashton."

Mr. Hubert squared his shoulders to his half-bow. "As you command, My Lord."

I sat on the edge of the seat of the chair before the desk, my head erect, my spine straight.

"Do you wish to be private?" Damion asked me.

"No. I would tell you the content of this conversation afterward, anyway."

Damion nodded and took his seat. Mr. Whistlethorpe sat on the chair next to mine, removed his handkerchief from his pocket and dabbed his upper lip. "My Lady, forgive me for appearing here suddenly without due notice, but I could not allow your first news of Townley's latest disgrace to be from the reading of it in a newspaper. It is a subject inappropriate for you — gently bred and unwed — but I believe I must speak of it."

I nodded my encouragement. "Then do so, Sir. My present circumstances have accustomed me somewhat to the inappropriate, you will find."

Mr. Whistlethorpe's cheeks reddened. "Yes. Well..." He took a deep breath, swallowed and cleared his throat. "Yes... Well... It is my unfortunate duty to have to inform you that Townley has turned Gosmouth House into a...a...um...a... A house of assignation."

"Your pardon. Do you mean a *brothel*?" I said.

Mr. Whistlethorpe mopped his brow and looked at Damion. "Ah...ah...um."

I looked at the perspiration beading his upper lip and relieved his suffering. "Tell Lord Ashton in my place, if you wish, Sir. If you turn my chair, I will present you only with my back." I stood and Mr. Whistlethorpe adjusted my chair.

"So, a brothel?" Damion asked.

"More a private members' club for paying guests, My Lord, run along the lines of the old Hellfire Club, I believe."

"Good Lord!" Damion coughed.

"Exactly," Mr. Whistlethorpe said. "From whispers I have heard of the entertainment on offer, the gossip columns will be unable to resist writing extensively of the scandal. The first rumors of it have already appeared in the press and have become the talk of the Town this last sennight."

"A guest has been indiscreet in his cups? There is illegal activity involved?"

"Yes to both circumstances, I fear." Mr. Whistlethorpe sighed. "Word has got out that not all that is on offer to those Gentlemen invited involves the participation of courtesans plying their trade."

"Where is Mama?" I asked the sofa in front of me.

"Removed to the Dower House these three months past."

"Safe from all but the scandal of it, then."

"The scandal will further sap her spirits, I fear. She remains very low."

My face heated and I gave a small shrug of my shoulders. "That is a small cross to bear, considering it was by her actions that we come to be in this situation."

"My Lady!" Mr. Whistlethorpe spluttered.

I turned on my chair. "If I sound a harsh or undutiful daughter, I will not apologize, Sir. Mama could have done more to prevent the worst of Townley's excesses when they first came to light. They have only become more inexcusable with each passing year, due to her failure to do so."

"But her duty to him as her husband prevents—"

"Her duty to Townley be damned!" I interjected to the further flush of my face. "She had a duty to protect and care for her children, a duty not to allow the name and memory of the husband who fathered them to be besmirched by the one who replaced him when he proved himself to be untrustworthy."

Mr. Whistlethorpe considered my words and my temper calmed somewhat as he said, "Yes, I believe I agree with you, My Lady, although the law of the land does not."

I stood and offered him my hand. "Unfortunately not, Sir. But that aside, I do thank you for bringing me warning of the scandal before it breaks. It would indeed have been a shock to have come upon the detail of it unexpectedly in the newspaper."

Mr. Whistlethorpe stood and bent his bow over it as Damion rose. I inclined my head as my hand was released. "Until we meet again when my allowance is due, Sir."

I walked toward the terrace door. Damion followed me and lifted my hand to his lips as he opened it. "We will speak more of this on your half-day tomorrow?"

I nodded as his kiss whispered over my knuckles and his tilted smile followed me out.

I walked along the terrace in the direction of the laundry and was not surprised to see Mr. Hubert standing at its end, his frown still furrowing his brow. He stepped alongside me. "I do not understand how this has come to pass. If you are *the* Lady Henrietta, your father must be a Duke, an Earl or a Viscount. The daughters of men of such rank do not work. It is unthinkable."

"But there you have encompassed it without knowing so, Mr. Hubert. You speak of my father in the present tense when it should be the past. He died near ten years ago and my family's wealth is gone, my mother diddled out of all we possessed by a plausible rogue. I have the same need now to work for my living as everyone here, and I do not admit to my birth name as I would not find employment as The Lady Henrietta."

Mr. Hubert's frown deepened. "But that only adds to my confusion. Of any of those ranks, you are of the same station as His Lordship. You stand on familiar terms. Surely you could just request his support?"

I stopped walking, lifted my chin, fixed my eyes on his and gave him a double-barreled blast of Lady Henrietta. "And just what is it about me, *Sir*, that lends you to think that I would *beg* on another's charity when—for what is only the swallowing of a little false pride—I can do for myself?"

The frown left his brow and the question his eyes. "Ah, yes. There speaks the nobility. I understand it now."

I smiled and continued to walk. "I thank you for it, Mr. Hubert, and offer my apologies for my earlier ill-bred remark. The Lady Henrietta has had a rather wretched time of it and Amelia Brown conceals her loss behind the odd flippant remark that should not have been directed toward someone who has never been anything but kind and is undeserving of it."

Mr. Hubert smiled. "That you admit your error only proves your superior breeding. Your hurt is severe and the stance you have adopted to deal with the consequences will only excite my admiration."

We arrived at the laundry room door. "I will tell Molly the book was ruined beyond saving."

Mr. Hubert pressed my hand and gave me his half-bow. "Be assured of my discretion. I will see you at supper, Amelia."

I stepped inside the laundry, closed the door and picked up the book from the sewing basket. "The volume in the library is ruined. Shall we return to Darcy's resolution for Lydia and Wickham?"

I read while the laundry blew dry then Molly and I heated up the irons, pressed the creases away and took it Above Stairs. I gave Byng's shirt, collar and smalls to Mr. Tyler at his door then to Mr. Hubert, Damion's shirt, collar and cravat with a notable absence of 'smalls'. I hid my smile that I had never seen Damion's cock obscured by any garment other than his breeches or his trousers as we walked up a floor to Lady Ashton's suite and I composed my face as Molly knocked on her sitting room door and her voice bade us, "Enter."

"M'am," Molly said as we bobbed in the direction of her and Letty sat holding hands, side by side, on the chaise lounge.

Elizabeth waved an airy hand at Molly. "In my dressing room, if you please."

Molly walked through the door of it. Elizabeth looked at me, smiled and inclined her head. "It was as you said. I offer you my thanks for the reassurance of it being so."

I inclined mine to acknowledge her compliment. "If you found your ease, I am glad."

Molly stepped out of the dressing room and nudged my arm as we walked toward the green door. "Well, that explains why he sought comfort elsewhere on the wedding night. How unfortunate that the date they picked matched the course of her flow."

I smiled and didn't correct her illusion that Elizabeth was referring to my provision of her monthly linens as we walked down the back stairs and listened in to talk of the forthcoming match when we sat to the table.

"Well, you're home now, Harry. You should captain the team," Fred said.

"No, Mr. Hubert is the senior man."

"No, Harry," Mr. Hubert replied. "You have an eye for the game. Leave me in my place lower down the order, if you please, and take to yourself a task I would perform with less skill."

"Well...if you're sure?" Harry said as the breadboard was passed around and Mr. Hubert nodded.

"We could take a walk together around the stalls during the interval when the game breaks, if you would like to, Molly? And Mother has said she would be delighted if we joined the family picnic for our lunch," James said.

"I thank you, James. Yes, that would be lovely." Molly smiled.

I nudged Molly's knee with mine at James' public acknowledgment of their relationship and followed her up the back stairs after Grace. She put the nightstick on her box and jumped into bed after loosening her laces and removing her working dress. "I will be doubly glad to have my pink dress and my petticoat to wear on the day of the cricket match now. James' family will see that I'm not some poor dab of a female that possesses no clothes of her own and that my best friend has her own dress, too."

I took my toothbrush and towel from my box. "We shall look very fine so as to leave a good impression, I'm sure."

Molly's eyes were closed when I returned from the washroom, so I extinguished the candle and slipped under my bedcovers, finally with the leisure to be able to turn my thoughts to what Mr. Whistlethorpe had told me was happening at Gosmouth. I searched my memory for any spark of recognition, heard or read, of The Hellfire Club but found nothing, although the name alone hinted to me of liaisons more sinister than those which took place in a brothel, especially as I pictured Mr. Whistlethorpe's stuttering blushes and Damion's coughed, '*Good God!*'. I determined to purloin any copies of the newspaper sitting on the dresser in the morning and take them to the laundry to study the Society pages with a thoroughness I could not normally manage when reading them in the servants' hall or washroom while I waited to be able to speak to Damion on the matter.

* * * *

The following morning dawned bright and sunny with not a cloud in the sky to give promise that the fair weather would stay over the next few days and not disturb the match. There were four copies of the newspaper sitting on the dresser when I walked into the kitchen and I picked them up with a smile toward Mrs. Price when I finished my porridge. "We are a little short in our washrooms with no papers being delivered while the Family was away. I could divide the sheets into squares while the water heats in the laundry?"

"I would appreciate it," she said.

Molly snorted as I shut the kitchen door behind us. "As will everyone else."

I laid the newspapers on the ironing table, picked up the earliest edition and turned to the gossip columns in the Society pages as Molly looked through the contents of the linen baskets. The bold print of the lead column gave me the headline that Mr. Whistlethorpe had known would attract my attention—*A Sweet Little Songbird Sings of a House Party held in the Southern County of 'H' at the Estate of 'G'.*

I pushed the paper aside, reached for the next edition and read, *A masquerade of unusual 'entertainment', trills our little bird,* then opened the next to see *The delighted encouragement of the joy on offer must surely have been heard in 'S' and 'D', the counties to each side of 'H'.*

I folded the newspaper and didn't open the last copy as I faced the fact that if Townley hadn't completely ruined us by the spending of our fortune, his latest activities would surely destroy any shred of reputation left to us when more hints dropped into the gossip columns, and Gosmouth, along with the Rockingham name, began to be guessed. A shiver ran down my spine as the new consequences of my face being recognized at Ashton occurred to me, but I managed to push them aside as Molly said, "Were you looking for something in the paper, Am?"

I began to tear the sheets into quarters. "Not really. I just thought there may have been mention of the wedding in them, but there isn't."

Molly built the fire under the cauldron and fetched the water while I finished providing squares for the night pots, then we worked through the morning until my half-day began with the chimes of the lunch bell and I said, "I need fresh air more than lunch."

Molly closed the door behind us. "I will see you at supper, then."

I walked out of the back yard and made my way through fields and over stiles until I arrived at the Dower House. The garden door was locked and the key in its place over the lintel, so I let myself in, walked upstairs and ran hot water into the bath. The garden door remained unrattled by Damion's entrance by the time the tub filled, so I placed my pistol under a towel on the chair beside the tub, stripped off and stepped in. The door stayed silent while I bathed and once clean and scented with freesia, I pulled the bung from the drain, dried myself and redressed, then walked to the bedroom to look for a note or a sign from Damion that he may have had to excuse himself.

The bedroom held nothing out of place, so I ran the ivory comb I found on the dressing table through my towel-dried hair and heard the squeak of the garden door as I reached into my pocket for a hair pin. I ignored the pin but put my hand on the pistol beside it then withdrew it to the sound of foot-tread on the stairs and Damion calling my name.

I walked toward the bedroom door as he stepped through and put my arms around his neck to his around my back. "I thought you may have given up on me. I was waylaid by the vicar calling to offer me his felicitations and hopes for my long and fruitful union, preferably in the form of many additional prayers and blessings at Sunday service this week. Needless to say, I turned his proposition aside."

I tilted my face for Damion's kiss then asked, "Was he offended?"

"More disappointed at the loss of opportunity to display his oratory skills, I think."

I smiled. "He does rather enjoy the sound of his own voice."

"A good man but the most dreadful old windbag," Damion agreed. "I only took him to oblige M'uncle and have never ceased to regret that I didn't gift him the living attached to the hunting lodge in Scotland."

I giggled and Damion tipped my chin. "I am not in bad odor with you for my sharing of your secret with Hubert, then?"

I stroked the side of his face. "Of course not." He smiled and pressed me closer. "I will admit it gave me some qualms as to whether to admit to your presence at Ashton or to offer to be the bearer of a message from him for you to meet him at a different time and place. Then I considered what you had told me of his cautious nature and realized he would not have come here unless he considered the matter was of such import as should not be delayed."

"I read some back copies of the newspaper this morning and Mr. Whistlethorpe is correct. It will not be long before the venue of these 'entertainments' is guessed and linked to the Rockingham name."

Damion removed his jacket and hung it over the back of the bedroom chair. "I will admit I have avoided the Society pages of late, having no wish to come across the description of my wedding." He sat in the armchair before the unlit fire and patted his lap.

I sat, curved my body against his to his arm around my back and asked, "So, The Hellfire Club? Was it as its name suggests?"

"Rumors of black magic and satanic rituals were never proved, although from letters that were made public after its founder Sir Francis Dashwood died, parodies of religious ceremonies did take place. The members styled themselves The Knights of St. Francis, referred to each other as monks and met several times a year in a series of caves under St. Francis' house at High Wycombe."

"And the entertainment?"

"Each member was invited to attend the meeting accompanied by a 'lady' of cheerful and lively disposition to provide entertainment for all and who were also encouraged to make 'select' parties to entertain each other during the intervals between drinking and feasting."

I closed my eyes and the picture built. "So, a drunken orgy with all those invited willing participants, even if they were being paid for services rendered, but Townley has taken the notion one step further?"

Damion tucked me in closer. "I'm sorry, my sweet, but from Mr. Whistlethorpe's reaction, I fear the worst. There are more men of extreme tastes than just Sir Humphrey. If Townley is receiving enough money to satisfy his addictions, he must be catering to their desires."

I shivered as I pictured the foul breath, bloodshot eyes and bodily stink of my prospective bridegroom, who obviously still believed bathing should be only an annual activity. "I do not know what his actual vices are, just that his person turns my stomach to the point where I believe that he must also be in possession of some revolting habits."

Damion held me closer. "It has never been proven, as no victim has ever been persuaded to give testimony as to what they suffered at his hands, but it is known around the clubs that degradation and pain are his lusts."

I shuddered. "I suspected it. Townley invited him to Gosmouth to inspect the 'goods on offer' and his every glance in my direction was lascivious, but with a coldness to his eyes to warn me that he was also a cruel man. Poor Papa. That such men should be infesting his home and attaching to his name..."

"I had a little more conversation with Mr. Whistlethorpe after you left us. He will send word to me here if he receives the slightest whisper that Townley has departed Town northward bound, rather than south. Townley will not take you from Ashton."

I swallowed at the thought of Damion's respected name being linked to the filth of mine if Townley did so and knew the action I must take if such a thing became a possibility. "No, he will not find me here."

I cuddled in closer and urged Damion's face toward mine for his kiss. He opened his mouth to my tongue then stood with me in his arms and walked us to the bed. I gazed as he unbuttoned his shirt to expose his torso, eased open my laces and pushed my dress down over my shoulders then released my shift to bare my breasts. My nipples hardened as he stripped off his trousers and plunged his face into the valley between them. I pushed their fullness against his cheeks to his murmur of appreciation then knotted my fingers through the back of his hair as he sucked and squeezed on my orbs, whimpering as he nibbled and bit each hardened nub. I reached for his cock. He pushed my dress and shift down and off, and I straddled him above his thighs when my legs were free of it. His irises darkened as I took his hands, held them above his head and dangled my breast just out of reach of his lips. He tried to suck my nipple into his mouth. I pulled back and teased his lips with it then lifted my hips and tickled his cockhead with the wet lips of my sex. He groaned, tipped me onto my back, pinioned my hands and fastened his mouth over my breast. I mewled my pleasure as he sucked and tugged with his teeth on first one then the other. He bit my neck and rasped as I writhed. "You want me?"

"Yes. Now," I answered.

He released my hands, reached to the nightstand for a preventative, rolled it down his shaft then eased open my sex and plunged his cock in up to the hilt. I bucked beneath him as he filled me. "Damion, yes..."

He captured my hands and pinned them above my head to his bite on my shoulder then my neck as he thrust into me. I wrapped my legs around his thighs and lifted my pelvis to meet his as he pummeled my sex with his cock. The sensation built until I cried out the joy of my release. He let go of my hands, squeezed the flesh of my breasts in his and pumped out his own final pleasure with a low groan.

We stilled, panting, and did not move until we'd recovered. Damion moved first, his breath warm in my ear before he rolled away. "Beautiful, my sweet."

I lay in his arm. "As are you." I draped my leg over his thigh with my arm across his chest and he kissed the top of my head.

"Byng solicited an invitation from me for Miss Sutton-Hoe to join us this morning, although he could give me no prior knowledge as to exactly when she will arrive. She travels under chaperonage of Lady Cheshire, who is passing through the county on her way home, so is dependent on that Lady's convenience as to how many nights they will be on the road to make the journey here."

"Amabelle's arrival will not pass without notice," I said. "I have my excuses prepared to avoid entering any part of the house where she could catch sight of me. How many nights will she stay?"

"I cannot think her visit will be any shorter than three weeks, having journeyed so far to reach us." Damion frowned. "It is dependent on whether Elizabeth has any arrangements in place that would cut short her chaperoning Miss Sutton-Hoe while she is here. I will make the inquiry of her at dinner."

I smoothed his frown away. "I'm sure Molly will oblige me if I suggest she services the Ladies' rooms while I attend the Bachelor rooms where Amabelle will not be. As to the rest, I do not expect to come across her in the back yard, although I will check it is empty of her presence before I enter it. But I will have to forgo leaving servants' hall on my half-day while she is here."

"Damn!" Damion swore. "Byng caught me unawares with his request. I would have found good reason to turn it aside, else."

I smiled and kissed his chest. "I would not have you snub Byng or have Amabelle feel the slight of an invitation wished for but not received. I will meet you in the back yard on Thursday night though, if you wish it?"

Damion put his face down for my kiss. "Always."

I stroked his cheek as we broke apart. "Midnight on any Thursday that she is here it is, then." I drowsed for a while in the enjoyment of his body touching mine until the mantle clock struck five and I stirred.

"You are going to dispatch me to dress for dinner when I would rather lie here with you?" he asked.

I kissed his cheek with a smile. "Yes, while I am going to walk to the cricket field and view the stalls being assembled so I have a half-day activity I can admit to at staff supper tonight."

Damion swung his feet to the floor and began to redress while I did the same and asked, "Do you have houseguests staying to watch the cricket match this weekend?"

"Not as such, other than Byng, although the neighboring gentry will be entertained to lunch and tea in the marquee on the field."

"Lady Brockley?" I inquired with raised eyebrows.

"Oh, good God! They can't be thinking that?" Damion snorted with a laugh.

I tightened my dress laces and giggled. "Well, now that Mrs. Carleton has proved herself to be 'game', no female of the upper order is considered out of bounds."

"But I'm not yet twenty-five and she is over fifty, let alone hatchet-faced!"

I laughed. "Perhaps you'd better to pay your attentions to someone a little younger on Saturday and restore your reputation."

"No." Damion smiled. "If they are prepared to focus their attention on her as a prospect rather than you, she will do. I shall be incredibly polite to her at the match. Go on ahead of me if you're walking to the field."

I lifted my face for Damion's parting kiss, laced my boots at the garden door and quick-walked to the field of play when I let myself out. A glance around showed the bunting in place and I took note of the colors and positioning of it before watching three of the under-gardeners hammering the wooden pegs on the end of the guy ropes of the marquee into the ground before I walked back to the Manor.

Chapter Twelve

Staff supper was alive with talk of the match and I was able to give a good account of how I'd managed to waste my half-day in watching the proceedings at the field before those sitting around the table departed for bed. The following morning, I finally finished the stitching of my first bedsheet and put it with the two Molly had completed while I read to her then found a torn pillowcase in the rag bag after lunch and tore strips from it to use on Molly's hair while she took her half-day with James.

Molly and James returned and joined the table in time for supper and she nudged my arm. "We did the same as you and walked to the field. The stalls are in place in the one beside it now and we saw several tinkers spreading their cloaks to sleep under the stars tonight with their trays of wares."

I smiled at her excitement and followed her up the back stairs at Mr. Bennett's 'amen'. She lit the nightstick and pulled her lamp from behind it while I took the cotton ribbons from my pocket along with the jar lid from the bicarbonate powder. "Do not blow the candle out when you light the lamp," I said. "The sugar will dissolve best in warm water. We can heat it in this."

Molly nodded and lit the lamp. I put a little water in the lid when I used the washing room then held it over the candle and watched the sugar melt as the water warmed. Molly held the lid, sat on the side of her bed while I dipped the end of the comb in it and passed it through her hair, then twisted hair around a rag and wound the tail of the rag back up around the hair and knotted it. I turned down the lamp, blew out the candle and got into bed. Molly patted her rags with a smile as she pulled her bedcovers over her shoulder.

I woke in the morning to early summer sunshine filling the room and saw Molly awake, looking at the red velvet bag on the top of her box. She smiled as I yawned and stretched. "The dawn woke me when the room lightened around five. I couldn't return to sleep after."

I put my feet to the floor and took my toothbrush from my box. "Shall I run to the kitchen and beg us a slice from the tweenies breakfast so we do not have to release your rags until you are dressed?"

Molly nodded so I put my toothbrush on the lid of my box, threw my black dress on over my head and slipped my feet into my boots. "I'll use the washing room after, then."

Just the tweenies occupied the kitchen with no sign of Mrs. Oates as I walked in through the green door, and they only yawned as I took two thick doorsteps of bread from their board, smeared each with a little beef dripping from the pot and returned with it to our bedroom. I handed Molly her slice and we sat on the edge of our beds to eat.

"The match begins at eleven, but the field will fill before then," Molly said. "We should make our way there directly when we are ready, so Mrs. Price does not find us an errand to run to disturb our enjoying ourselves for the rest of the day."

I swallowed my mouthful and looked at the pink soap on the top of my box. "I will take the bar to the washing room when I clean my teeth and put the scent of rose on my skin."

"Oh, yes," Molly smiled. "As will I, then."

I used the washroom then lent Molly my towel so she didn't have to use her shift to dry her skin and took the chance to transfer my pistol from the pocket of my work dress into the one of my blue skirt while she was gone. She sat on the side of her bed in her dry shift when she returned. I took up my comb and released the first rag. A long curl, slightly stiff with sugar to hold it, sprang free as I unwound it and I smiled as I released the rest. "They have set very well. I do not believe they will lose their shape today."

Molly patted her stiffened hair with a sigh. I gathered her curls into one hand, combed the front and sides of her hair back from her face with the other then twisted the whole into a top knot with curls falling downward from it and secured the result with the hair pins she passed to me. She sighed again when she felt the result tentatively with her fingertips. "I think my bonnet may spoil them."

"Then do not wear it and I will not wear mine. Not all maids possess one. We have no obligation to do so if we are not frightened of gaining a freckle or two on our faces from not being shaded from the sun."

"Well, I will not mind at all." Molly smiled. "I have several already and would prefer to gain more rather than spoil the arrangement of my hair."

I combed mine, secured it into a low bun then opened my box and lifted out my petticoat to Molly's look.

"You possess one, too?"

I stepped into it and tightened the drawstring around my waist. "I took some things that were mine alone when I left home — my britches, my petticoat and my shawl, along with my bonnet and gloves."

Molly stepped into her own petticoat and tightened the waist. "As would I have done. They are very fine. Your father must have been at least a tenant farmer to have afforded such things."

I thought of the wardrobe in my dressing room at Gosmouth that had contained an over-sufficiency of such garments and shrugged. "Whatever he was, he isn't now. There is but me and a few things left over from that time. Now, lift your arms above your head so I may pass your skirt over them and settle it over your petticoat."

Molly did as I asked, and I threw her skirt over her arms then fastened the button at her waist and tweaked it to flutter over the stiffened lines of her petticoat. Mine, made full by many more flounces than Molly's and with no sapling hoop, I bundled between my legs and released it as I stepped into my skirt then smiled as Molly rocked her hips so that her skirt swirled and swayed around her legs. I passed her bodice to her. "When you sit, tilt your hoop up at the back and keep your weight from it. If you do not, the front of your skirt will rise and display your muff for all to see."

"Amelia!" she cried.

"Try it. Sit on the side of your bed with your weight on your hoop." I smiled.

She hooted when she did so and I joined my laugh to hers as the front of her skirt flipped up and exposed her thighs and the hair of her sex. "Now, do it again, but this time tilt your hoop so you do not sit on it."

Molly giggled then repeated the action with more care, and the front of her skirt stayed in place. I nodded and fastened the buttons on the front of my bodice with its plain elbow-length sleeves, in contrast to the puffed sleeve of Molly's, as she put her heart-shaped charm around her neck and did up the clasp. Then, with the weight of my pistol resting comfortably against my leg, I took half-a-crown from my reticule, dropped it into my other pocket and offered Molly my arm. The church clock chimed ten as she threaded hers through mine and said. "Holy cow, Am! Where did the time go? I thought we would be ready by nine at the latest."

I opened the door. "It all takes a while."

I followed Molly down the back stairs and we found the servants' hall empty as we entered it. I opened the door to the back yard and Molly clasped my waist as we stepped through it. I clasped hers and we sauntered to the field of play. I took in the scene as we arrived. The caned and wicker chairs that normally graced the lawns of Ashton were sitting in front of the marquee and to its left, the supporters of the house team. On its other — those cheering on the team from the village.

Molly's eyes roamed over the field and settled on the house team practicing their batting shots. James looked up and his smile lit his face as he saw Molly. I nudged her arm. "Lovestruck, for sure."

She smiled, and we walked toward where Ellen and Polly sat gaping at us.

"Molly... Amelia... Where did you get those from?" Ellen asked as we arrived.

"We stitched them ourselves," Molly said, passing her hand over the pink fabric of her skirt, "from material Amelia bought from Mr. Tucker."

I glanced toward the marquee, took a look at the gentry gathered before it and relaxed as I saw no new faces to disturb me. Mrs. Price and Mr. Bennett circulated, directing two maids and two footmen from the agency to serve lemonade to the Ladies and porter to the Gentlemen, the Family not yet having arrived for the eleven o'clock start. Our team ran toward us and James smiled at Molly. "We won the toss and will bat first."

I looked at Harry. "Is Daisy here?"

"Her father has a stall to sell ribbons and the like, so she must serve this morning. I would introduce her to you if you will take a walk with me when the game breaks for lunch?"

"I should like that." I smiled. A buzz rippled through the throng. I looked over Harry's shoulder to see several nudges and pinches pass between the village supporters, which told me that Damion's lack of a honeymoon had caused as much speculation there as it had at the house, as they caught sight of his bride, although what they made of the fact that she was arm-in-arm with Letty while Damion and Byng followed along behind them, I couldn't overhear. The church clock chimed the hour as they took their places in the middle of the front row of chairs.

Our men lined up in their batting order and sat behind the rope boundary. James and Bert walked onto the field and the village men took up their fielding positions as the vicar, belonging to neither village nor house, took his place dressed in a white umpire's coat. Molly and I sat with Ellen and Polly and play commenced with Harry still in possession of his bat at the one o'clock lunch break while Bert had been bowled out for a duck and Fred for twenty, for Stanley to take his place.

Violet, in the role of under housekeeper with Mrs. Price on duty, opened a large hamper and passed out meat and potato pasties with wedges of cheese as the gentry retired into the marquee to eat poached salmon and salad in the proper fashion, sitting to table with a knife and fork. Molly and James left us to find his family and Harry sat beside me and offered a drink from the flagon of watered cider he had just refreshed himself from. I drank a mouthful and passed it on to Bert and Ellen as Harry brushed the crumbs from his front and looked at me. "Shall we?"

I stood, and he offered me his arm as Polly said, "Oh, where are you going?"

Harry offered her his other. "To the stalls. Come with us if you wish."

"Oooh, yes, please." Polly smiled without so much as the hint of a dropped vowel or 'h'. "I have a sixpence from my pocket money and wish to buy a ribbon for my hair with it."

We passed in front of the marquee, averted our faces toward the field so as not to be thought to be gawping at our 'betters' while they ate, and climbed over the stile between the two fields to hear the buzz of good-natured chatter and vendors calling out their wares. Harry led us toward a girl with pretty auburn hair and a pale green dress standing behind a stall. She smiled when she saw Harry, her eyes as liquid brown and kind as were his. I smiled at Mr. Tucker standing beside her and he bowed his head toward us then offered Harry his hand. He looked at my dress after they shook.

"I see you have made a fine job of sewing your dress with my material, Miss Amelia. I saw your friend Molly a few minutes ago and the both of you look as fine as sixpence."

"I thank you, Mr. Tucker." I smiled. "This is Polly, who wishes a ribbon for her hair."

Daisy offered Polly a tray. "They are but two pennies each."

Polly moved her finger through the bright colors. "Oh, it is difficult to choose. I have always wanted a red ribbon, but the blue is pretty, too."

"If you have threepence" — Mr. Tucker smiled — "you may have both for that price."

Polly grinned, offered Daisy her silver sixpence and received a bronzed threepenny piece and her two ribbons for it in exchange. Mr. Tucker looked at Harry. "Our Daisy here will be free of her duties after the lunch break when her cousin Sally arrives to take her place to serve this afternoon, if you happened to be wondering."

"Grandpa!" Daisy blushed.

Mr. Tucker patted her hand. "There's no need to be missish, my pet. When your young man asked Father for permission to walk out with you — properly, as he should — Mother said you were agreeable to the suggestion."

"I will still be at the wicket." Harry flushed.

I looked at Daisy. "Perhaps you would like to come and sit with we maids and watch Harry play?"

"A very good notion, Miss Amelia." Mr. Tucker beamed.

Harry's eyes did not leave Daisy's face as he waited for her answer.

"I thank you and yes, that would be very agreeable."

"Can we visit the sweetie stall next?" Polly asked. "I still have three whole pennies to spend."

Harry smiled at Daisy, offered us his arms and we walked away in search of Polly's sweeties and Molly's fudge. I looked at Harry and asked, "Question answered?"

He smiled. "Yes, Daisy has two brothers playing for the village but has chosen to sit with the house."

Polly selected a sugar mouse with a string tail, two halfpenny lollies and a licorice stick when we arrived at the stall, which she was handed in a small paper bag, while I ordered five portions of fudge at sixpence-the-quarter and received my pound and a quarter of fudge in a much larger one. Harry grinned as I took possession of it. "You must have purchased nearly half his stock of the stuff."

I smiled. "It is for Molly, to cure her sweet tooth."

"You are going to feed her all of that?"

"As much of it as she wishes to eat."

Harry laughed. "You'd best have a chamber pot standing by."

I handed him the bag of fudge and climbed the stile. He and Polly followed me over. "I certainly will. I aim to remove one from the washroom before anyone pees in it tonight."

Harry gave me my bag and was still laughing as we walked past the marquee, all arm in arm, with Polly's giggles joining his noise to Lady Brockley's bark. "How coarse! Ashton, you really should take your servants in hand."

"The sound of happiness will never be unpleasant to me, Madam," Damion replied.

"Well, it wouldn't happen on my watch," she harrumphed.

"I can imagine any number of things that probably do not happen on your watch, Madam…" I heard to my silent giggle as we passed out of earshot.

Daisy joined us as play resumed and I introduced her to Molly and Ellen. Harry managed two single runs and one boundary before a wild shot made with intent to impress resulted in a shout of 'out' and he left the field to sit next to Daisy. At three o'clock, Mr. Hubert entered the field to a round of applause, the last man left to bat for the house, and I noticed William Coachman, blowing hard, puff onto the outer edge of the field ten minutes later. I knew the cause when he spoke to Mr. Bennett and Mr. Bennett walked over to Damion and Byng and Byng's face creased into a smile. I pinched my cheeks to redden them then looked at Molly. "I must run back to the Manor for a while. This fudge is melting in the heat, as am I."

I stopped at Violet's side on my way and asked her to excuse me to Mrs. Price for my feeling unwell due to too much sun without the protection of a bonnet, then skirted the fields in the lee of the hedgerows and took a longer path to the Manor that allowed me to enter the back yard from the direction of the stables and out of view of any Above Stairs rooms, bar the out-of-hours dining room.

The servants' hall was silent, apart from the tick of the clock as I let myself in through the back door. I ran up to my bedroom, put the fudge on Molly's box, removed my dress and petticoat and lay on the bed in my shift. The hours passed slowly, but as I could not risk being found doing anything other than lying quiet and ill on my bed, I counted the minutes until I heard the creak of bare floorboards in the early gloom of dusk to warn of another person in the attic. I slapped and pinched my cheeks and neck over and over until the door opened to reveal Mrs. Price.

"You are unwell, Amelia?" she asked.

"My apologies, Mrs. Price. I believe I have had too much sun."

She walked closer and studied my face. "Well, goodness. Yes, indeed. Have you vomited?"

"Yes, Mrs. Price. I am sorry."

"I will give Molly a bottle of calamine lotion and a pitcher of cold water. Dab the lotion on the affected areas and drink at least four large cups. I will look in on you again in the morning but send Molly to fetch me if your symptoms become any worse."

My face flushed to add to my self-inflicted redness in the face of her concern. "I am sure I will feel well soon if I just lie still for a while."

"We will see." She sniffed and left the room.

The door opened again an hour later. Molly stepped in with a nightstick in one hand and a pitcher of water in the other. I made no movement but let out a poorly sigh, with a need to still be ill enough come the morning to be able to avoid appearing in church.

"Oh, Amelia, I didn't realize you felt this unwell."

I put my hand over my eyes against the brightness of the candle and asked faintly, "Did we win?"

Molly put the nightstick down on her box but didn't light the lamp. "We did, and it was James that took their final wicket. Bowling like he'd seen you do, he said. How everyone on our side cheered!"

I could not keep the smile from my face. "I am glad but sorry I feel unwell. The fudge I promised you is on your box."

"I will save it until you are better." Molly smiled. "I have the bottle of calamine in one pocket and your cup in the other."

Molly shook the bottle, tipped it onto a clean rag, dabbed my face and neck and I felt the relief on my reddened skin, no matter that the sun hadn't caused it. She poured me a cup of cold water after and I swallowed it thankfully, having not taken a drink since the watered cider. She topped up my cup and I set it on my box as she twirled in her floating pink skirt then released the button at its waist.

"This has been the most special day of my life, so far. I felt truly beautiful and I thank you for it."

"Then no matter what else, I am content." I smiled.

Molly draped her finery over the bedroom chair, put her necklace on her box and yawned as she blew out the candle. "Night, Am. I hope you feel better in the morning."

"Goodnight, Molly. I am glad you enjoyed your day."

Molly emitted small puffs of slumber as I gazed out of the darkened window at the stars, and, not tired enough to sleep, tossed and turned throughout the night as if I had the fever of my pretended illness. I pinched my face and neck again as dawn filled the room and Mrs. Price opened the door at the ring of the tweenies bell. Heavy-eyed with a lack of sleep, I looked at her.

"Hmmm." She sniffed. "No church for you this morning. I will send up some lemon-barley water."

Molly poured me some water before she left the room to find her breakfast and returned a little later with a jug smelling of lemon and two dark, dry biscuits on a plate. "Mrs. Price says, if you can manage to nibble on them, they contain charcoal that will stop you feeling nauseous."

The back of my eyes burned to unshed tears over the kindness of those at Ashton, but I swallowed them down as I remembered Papa's words — '*Only silly, frilly girls cry over matters that cannot be mended by their doing so. Stand tall, Henry. Wet eyes will not heal a scraped knee, or indeed anything at all*' — and thanked her instead. Molly took her bonnet and gloves from her box and left the room to attend church.

I sat straighter, having achieved my goal to avoid Amabelle at church, ate the biscuits with two chunks of fudge to ease my hunger pangs and drank the lemon water as I considered what excuse I could give to avoid Sunday service if she was still at Ashton the following week. Mrs. Price opened the door when the church clock had rung out two more hours. "You appear a little better?"

"I do feel better, Mrs. Price," I said. "I believe I could dress and make my way downstairs shortly."

"Bide a while," she said. "Get dressed and come down if you feel you can manage a little supper later."

I nodded, turned my cheek to my pillow as my restless night caught up with me and didn't wake until the dressing gong sounded, then dressed and made my way to the servants' hall. I took my place beside Molly and listened to the chatter as the table filled and the finest moments of the match were retold. My plate of mutton and dumplings came to rest in front of me and I ate only half, hungry as I was for the full portion, with the thought that persons who had been sick should display a loss of appetite. I then stayed quiet from the conversation passing around the table until Mr. Bennett said Grace and released us to find our beds.

* * * *

I woke in the morning and knew my normal complexion had returned when the burn from my slaps and pinches had gone, swung my legs out of bed then went with Molly to eat my breakfast and received more kindness that I did not deserve by way of various compliments on my return to good health.

Molly peered at me as we entered the laundry and she picked up the bucket. "I will fetch the water today. You still look a little pale." It made me feel more ashamed for my deceit, but still, I didn't object and let her do it so as to be able to stay out of sight indoors. I looked at the pile of laundry after we finished our work and crossed my fingers for Molly's preference to avoid Damion as I said, "There is not so very much to be taken Above Stairs. If you wish to service our Ladies, I could deliver Lord Byngingham's and His Lordship's to their rooms?"

Molly smiled her agreement and I divided the clean laundry into two smaller piles with a puff of relief that I would not need to act on my secondary plan to take a tumble and injure a limb to provide my excuse not to accompany her Above Stairs. Molly walked on down the hallway and I tapped on Damion's door to his answer of, "Come in."

I opened his door, stepped in and saw no sign of Mr. Hubert as I took his shirts to his dressing room. Damion followed me. "I saw you leave the field on Saturday. You managed to avoid church?"

"I feigned illness and feel quite dreadful for it. Everyone has been so kind."

Damion kissed the top of my head. "Do not. A little misplaced kindness does not matter, compared to the alternative."

I placed his shirts on his daybed. "I will hope their sympathy does not run thin when I hurt my leg so as not to be to walk there next week."

Damion frowned. "Meaning no offense to Miss Sutton-Hoe, but I will be glad to see her safely away from here. Church next Sunday will be the last one of her stay. Elizabeth has accepted an invitation to visit Letty's family and she departs in their company the following Wednesday."

I smiled my relief and blew him a brief kiss as I left the room with Byng's laundry. Molly walked toward me as I raised my hand to tap on his door, but before I did so, it began to open. I prepared to bob or hold out the laundry, dependent on whether it was Byng or Mr. Tyler that opened it, and instead came face-to-face with Amabelle when the aperture widened.

She gasped as she looked at my face. "Henrietta? You are here?"

I froze and tried for an excuse but came up with nothing as Molly reached me and Amabelle called over her shoulder. "Byng! Byng! Come and see. Henrietta is not dead after all."

Molly stiffened beside me and my heart tightened at the completeness of my exposure as I said, "Amabelle, lower your voice, you goose. What are you doing in Byng's bedroom before you are wed?"

Her cheeks flushed a little. "I had a private matter I wished to discuss."

Byng arrived behind her. "Good grief! So it is. Forgive my not recognizing you on any previous occasion, Henrietta, but you have changed somewhat since we last met."

Amabelle looked at my cap then down the length of me. "Why are you dressed like that?"

Damion's door opened. He walked out his room and stood behind me. Byng looked at him over the top of my head. "This is the name you withhold from me?"

"By My Lady's request."

Molly clutched the side of my dress. I felt a tremble run through her, took in her whitened face and pinched nostrils and thrust Byng's laundry at Amabelle. "That aside...a chair for my poor Molly before her knees give way, if you please."

I supported her into Byng's room and he pulled forward the chair from behind the desk. She protested as I walked her toward it. "No. No, Am. I mustn't, not in front of the gentry." I pressed her shoulder, urged her down then kneeled before her and patted her hand. "Just for a minute, Molly, until you catch your breath."

Amabelle looked at the laundry I'd pushed into her hands. "You are working here, Henrietta? In service? Please, say it isn't so." I didn't answer, with my cap and dress to do so for me, and she looked at Damion. "My Lord? You know about this? And you allow it?"

Damion looked at me and smiled. "Do you know of an instance when The Lady Henrietta was persuaded to do anything she wasn't half-inclined to do already, for I cannot imagine one."

I answered the smile in his eyes with the same from my own as a heavy weight dropped into the pit of my stomach at the thought of the action I must now take and I said. "If you would offer Amabelle and Byng my explanation, I will take Molly to our room and attend to her there."

I held my hand out, helped Molly to stand then clasped her waist. "Come along. Through the green door and back to where we belong."

She leaned on me and I walked her out of the door. "So, are you some Lord's bastard daughter then, Am?"

"No, Molly. I'm some dead Lord's daughter and the bastard is the stepfather that has taken everything we had."

We made our way up the back stairs and I sat her on the side of her bed. "You've disguised it well, Am. I wouldn't have guessed."

I sat on the side of my bed. "Do not think badly of me for hiding it from you. I have good reason for doing so."

"He is your William?"

"His second name along," I admitted with a small smile. "And now I must leave him and everyone here. Word of my whereabouts will not be long in making their way to my stepfather's ears now that I have been recognized. He will come for me and I must not be here when he does."

"Why?" Molly asked.

"There is a price on my marriage contract he would like to collect from a man I have no intention of marrying. He can take me by force until I am twenty-one and I will take the steps that I must not to allow that to happen." I opened my box. "I can only take with me what I can carry. May I leave the remainder with you until I'm able to return for it?"

"You will come back?" She sniffed.

"One day. At least for a visit, I promise."

Molly pulled her rag out of her sleeve and blew her nose as I took out of my box the same items I had deemed necessary when I'd left home — excepting my boy-sized shirt and jacket — and put them on the shawl on my bed. I opened my stationery folder and used the lid of my box as a surface to write on.

D,

With the consequences of Amabelle discovering me today, I think you will be not be surprised to receive this.

Townley will come for me, and given the current interest he is exciting in the press, my resistance to him if he finds me at Ashton cannot but result in further scandal that will link your name to the stench of mine. I will not allow that to happen and have left Ashton to circumvent the possibility of it doing so.

With fair wind and good fortune, I still hope to mount my soapbox. Until then?

A.

I let the ink dry as I addressed an envelope then sealed my note inside it, took another sheet, tore the crest from it and wrote to Mrs. Price.

Forgive my leaving your employ without due notice to yourself but bad news received has necessitated my departure from Ashton without delay. My working dress I will return by post. If you would, keep the arrears of my salary currently owing in payment for my retaining my shifts?

My apology for the hasty manner of my note but the matter to be resolved is urgent,

Amelia Brown

I folded the page, wrote Mrs. Price's name on it and placed it on my pillow. "Say not a word until I am missed this evening, then wonder if I have been taken poorly again and come up here in search of me. You can find my note and give it to Mrs. Price with no consequences to yourself."

Molly nodded and I offered her my sealed envelope. "If this could find its way onto the post tray in the hall in the morning?" She nodded again and put it deep in her pocket. I added my stationery folio to the pile on my bed, folded my shawl over it and made a tidy parcel of the lot with the haberdasher's string then stripped the sheet from my bed and rolled it untidily around my package until it looked like a bundle of linen on its way to the laundry.

Molly followed me out of the bedroom and down the back stairs, and I paused before I pushed open the green door. "Eyes front. We are just going about our normal business."

I breathed out as I closed the kitchen door behind us. "Head for the drying yard." We walked on and I unrolled the sheet from my package and handed it to Molly when we were concealed behind its tall hedges. "I will push through the gap in the corner and skirt the fields in the lee of the hedgerows."

Molly's eyes filled with tears as she looked at the sheet. "I'll miss you, Am."

I squeezed her hand. "As I will you and all here at Ashton. But be brave for me, Molly? If you are seen with tears in your eyes, they will want to know why."

I let go of her hand and gave her a smile I was not feeling myself. "It's not forever, just for a while."

I waved at her one last time before I pushed through the hedge and began to consider my options as I walked. The salary accumulated in my reticule since I had seen Mr. Whistlethorpe in March amounted to three guineas, two half-crowns, a sixpence and seven pennies, but I had a dress to purchase, and if I was no longer able to obtain lifts for free dressed as a boy, I knew the remainder would not allow me to travel far. I thought of writing to Mr. Whistlethorpe to withdraw some funds, but the hard work completed to earn them left me reluctant to do so.

The road to York came into view ahead of me, so I headed for the stile, climbed over it and thought on the possibility of finding paid work in the city as I walked, and the longer I thought on it, the more the idea appealed to me as a double-bluff for Townley. For if he did not find me at Ashton, he would surely expect me to have fled farther than just a few miles down the road to York.

A piece of good fortune fell to me when I reached the outskirts of the city with the spire of the York Minster ahead of me and the Dog and Duck posting inn to my right. A paper notice stuck to the inside of a front window caught my eye and I read, *Help Wanted. Apply around the back.*

The door to the kitchen was open against the heat so I tapped on it and peeped inside. A maid standing before the sink up to her elbows in sudsy water looked me up and down and said, "Yes?"

"I read the advertisement in the front window...for help wanted?"

The maid shouted above the noise of the kitchen. "Mrs. Bunting. Thas a lass at door what says she's read yer paper."

A plump lady bustled toward me and I bobbed in her direction. "Read it, you say? Repeat the wording of it to me, then?"

I did so. "Very well," she said, "and can you reckon your numbers?"

"Yes, m'arm." I nodded.

"The eight times table to twelve? The measurement of weight?"

I duly parroted the multiples of the table followed by the ounces and pounds in a stone and she beckoned me in. "Bring yourself inside."

I walked in her wake toward a large cooking range with a scrubbed wooden table standing in front of it. "These are the bread ovens and I require a baker of bread. It is a precise art with no room for error in the measuring of quantities or timings. Have you ever baked any?"

"No, m'arm, although I have watched the process many times, and if you would demonstrate your preferred method but once, I believe it would not beyond me to do so."

The lady looked at me and nodded. "I am Mrs. Bunting, the head cook here at the Dog and Duck. We are a busy posting inn and serve near two hundred meals a day. Our food is served on bread trenchers for customers of the public bar. For patrons paying an extra shilling to eat their meal from a plate in the dining room, fine white bread is also required. Our guests need to be served quickly while a change of horses is made. I will give you a trial. Return here at five tomorrow morning if you still wish to be considered for the position."

I bobbed my curtsey at my dismissal. "I thank you, Mrs. Bunting, and I will."

I left the inn, walked farther into York and turned down the first street I saw where the appearance of the houses in it spoke to me of clean and tidy respectability. I found what I sought halfway along its length by the statue of the Virgin Mary sitting in the window and the lettering painted on the inside of it.

Mrs. Pratt's Boarding House for Ladies of Biblical Virtue.

I rang the bell and cast my eyes downward modestly as it opened. "I wish to inquire if you have a room for rent?"

The lady sniffed in a manner that so reminded me of Mrs. Price that I nearly smiled. "Thas be confirmed? Thas attends church?"

"Yes, M'arm."

"This be a respectable house. I allows no male callers over the threshold."

"As I hoped by the wording of your window."

The lady sniffed again. "A garret is available at five shillings the fortnight, as it suits thee?"

I nodded. She widened the front door to allow me in and I followed her up several flights of stairs to a small half-landing with a door cut on an angle to fit the slope of the roof to each side. She unlatched the one on the right and nodded at the one on the left. "Thas Mrs. Grey's room, a widow of small income."

I followed her into a room not dissimilar to the one I'd shared with Molly, with an iron bedstead under the slope of the eaves, a fireplace with a trivet and pan set in its grate, a small, round table accompanied by a single upright chair, a wooden shelf with hooks beneath it and a wooden storage box.

"The po's under the bed. Kindling and a bucket of coal each day be sixpence the week, should thas need it."

"I would—and will take the room, if you please? I have the shillings to pay in advance."

"Then thas had best tell me yous name. I is Mrs. Pratt, as be named on the window."

"Amelia Brown, as it please you." I bobbed and released the string of my shawl. I dug around inside it without displaying the contents until I located my reticule, and a farther wriggle of my fingers found a half-crown then a sixpence, which I offered to my new landlady.

Mrs. Pratt took the coins. "Then thas rent is due of a Tuesday. The front door be bolted at ten of an evening."

She left the room, shutting the door behind her. I gave it closer inspection and found the mattress to be filled with straw—not feathers—but clean, with no sign of any small bug that may like to bite me in the night. Inside the storage box, I found a pottery washbowl and jug, lifted them onto the table and replaced them with my shawl-wrapped possessions then tapped the floor in search of a loose board. I found what I sought to one side of the fireplace, but without the means to release it, I put my reticule in one pocket, my pistol in the other and ventured out.

A right turn then two more to the left brought me what I hoped for—a row of shops, respectable, but not displaying any goods to attract a person of fashion. In the first shop I bought a tin plate, candles, a knife, fork and spoon, in the second, a bed sheet and in the third, a brown dress of shapeless wonder and a large mop cap. My last purchase was a hot meat pie, which I took with my parcels back to my room to see a small bucket of coal and kindling sitting outside it.

I took the fuel inside my room, ate my pie then set to work with my knife, pried up the floorboard, stowed everything to do with Henrietta to one side of the joist then emptied the contents of the bucket on the other. The night watchman rang his bell and called the hour of ten as I tucked my sheet over the mattress and added my shawl. I removed my boots, stockings and dress and crawled beneath it. My eyelids closed in an instant but opened as the night watchman called, 'all is well' at three then stayed that way with the unfamiliar crunch of straw beneath me and my thoughts of all those I had left behind at Ashton.

Chapter Thirteen

I gave up any attempt to return to sleep when the watchman called four, dressed in my brown dress and watched the May dawn-break lighten the sky as I walked to the Dog and Duck with my black dress under my arm, wrapped in the brown paper from my shopping and addressed to Mrs. Price. Mrs. Bunting looked at me as I entered the kitchen. "I was not sure you would be here."

"With my apologies, why?"

Her face creased into a smile. "You would not believe how many try to pull the wool over my eyes over the reading and the reckoning. Those that have cheated know they will be found out and do not turn up again. Take a pinny. I will bake the first loaves then we shall see how you do."

I watched her and noted the quantities of the ingredients with the method she used to form the bread then found my laundry-pounding muscles were ideally suited to the kneading of dough. My first batch of loaves were coarse bread for the trenchers. Mrs. Bunting patted the bottom of each as I set them aside to cool, nodded her approval then showed me her method for the baking of finer white bread. My loaves, when fresh out of the oven, returned the smile to her face.

"Yes, you have the touch. You'll do. The wages are seven shillings a week. You may take your meals while on duty. Sunday is our quietest day and you may take the day if you have baked sufficient loaves of a Saturday."

I nodded my acceptance then baked, glowing with heat from the hot ovens for the rest of the day. The kitchen was a hive of activity as stews and cutlets were ladled onto thick bread trenchers and sent to the public bar or dished onto plates and dispatched to the dining room with white bread, thinly sliced and buttered. I ate my two allotted meals and pulled two trays of coarse bread to one of fine white out of the oven after I'd eaten my second meal.

"Very good." Mrs. Bunting nodded. "You are excused until the morning."

I left the kitchen, posted my parcel and returned to Mrs. Pratt's with my mop cap pulled low and one hand on my pistol. The following day, I completed my duties without supervision and began to settle into the routine of my self-imposed exile from Ashton. The inn was busy enough to divert my mind from dwelling on my time there, but at night in my rustling, crunchy bed, I longed for the feel of Damion's arms around me and the pleasure of his cock inside my sex.

Winter set in and my position as part of a large staff in a well-run country house provided the comparison to the misery of making my way to and from the Dog and Duck each day, with ice and snow thick underfoot and the wind finding gaps in my shawl to leave me chilled to the bone. I soon discovered that even with the addition of the surplus fuel I'd gathered under the floor board, the fire in my room did not throw out enough heat to warm me after my walk back to Mrs. Pratt's, and I shivered under my shawl until Christmas, then gave in and spent half a guinea on another bedcover of eiderdown.

The New Year arrived and the celebratory atmosphere in the tavern did not cheer me as I pictured the high spirits of the Below Stairs New Year staff lunch and the games played after it. My mind drifted toward Ashton as I settled to sleep that night, and I sighed at the thought that if I'd been there, I might have ended the year and started the next in bed with Damion. The bleak words 'out of sight, out of mind' came to me and I tossed and turned for the remainder of the night with my imaginings of who was in Damion's bed if it wasn't me.

* * * *

January and February crawled past, and I struggled as heavy rain replaced the snow, creating an everlasting fight to keep myself and my clothes dry and reasonably clean. It was not until the first week of March, when I felt the first hint of spring in the air as I returned to Mrs. Pratt's after my Sunday visit to the public bath house, that my spirits lifted with thoughts of being another year closer to my majority and of it being time to write to Mr. Whistlethorpe.

The following morning I sought out Mrs. Bunting and requested leave of absence on the Thursday two weeks hence.

"You may." She nodded. "Of all the staff here, you are the one that asked no boon of me over Christmas or the New Year."

I smiled my first genuine smile in months and wrote to Mr. Whistlethorpe when I returned to Mrs. Pratt's, while squashing a small, frilly spark of hope that Damion would remember the Thursday of the third week of March last year. The day arrived, and with my longing to see him refusing to be extinguished, even if for just this one day of the year, I walked to the public bath house and paid a penny for my towel and another for my sliver of soap. Back in my room just after twelve, I dressed as Henrietta and my heart thumped while I searched the street as I walked, hoping for the sight of the dark hair of a man taller than most.

My heart steadied when I arrived at Mr. Whistlethorpe's office without seeing any such thing, and I completed the formalities for my allowance but could only pass him five guineas to add to my fund with the additional living costs I had paid from my salary.

He looked at the small pile. "My visit to Ashton was not the reason for your leaving it, I hope?"

"It was not, Sir," I reassured him. "My face was recognized by a visitor two weeks later. May I inquire how come it is that you know that I am no longer situated there?"

"Lord Ashton visited my office in London several months gone now to request to be informed if I received word of your whereabouts. It grieved me to refuse what he sought, but as I explained, 'If The Lady Henrietta wished you to have this information, you would. I do not know it and it would not be my place to give it if I did.'"

"And for that, I thank you, Sir. I did not wish to leave Ashton, but the scandal of my name being linked to it for the fact of Townley discovering me there gave me little choice."

Mr. Whistlethorpe's eyes slid toward his desk at my words.

"But you have agreed to provide Lord Ashton with some information, Sir?" I guessed.

Mr. Whistlethorpe met my gaze again. "My apologies, My Lady. He is a persuasive man, and I agreed that if you changed the venue of this meeting, I would inform him that you had done so, but not as to where it would then be held."

My heart lifted to my smile. "A persuasive man he certainly is, Sir, and no apology is needed."

I stood from my chair. Mr. Whistlethorpe bowed me out of the street door and I looked left and right above the heads of the people up and down the road before I turned in the direction of Mrs. Pratt's. My hope lasted until I turned in to the street that contained her house and I squared my shoulders at the thought that with the passage of the months that had gone by, the want of me must have faded into Damion's past.

I let myself into my room, blinked away the tears and refused to let them fall while I exchanged Henrietta's silk dress for my working one of brown. A commotion sounded outside my room as I lifted the floorboard to hide my morning dress, so I walked out to the landing and looked over the loops of the bannister to see Mrs. Pratt attempting to push the door shut on a large male shoe that was preventing her from doing so.

"But, my good lady, I haven't come to visit," Damion said.

"I telled thee, Sir. This be a respectable house."

My heart threatened to burst out of my chest at the sound of his voice and I could not prevent my mad grin as I called out, "I'm up here."

The front door opened wide, whether Mrs. Pratt wished it to or not, and Damion's smile widened as he fixed his eyes on my face. He thrust his hat into Mrs. Pratt's hands and took the stairs two at a time. "Townley came but months ago now."

I flung my arms around his neck as he reached me. He swung me off my feet then put his lips on mine. I threaded my fingers through the back of his hair and closed my eyes to deepen our kiss as Mrs. Pratt's voice screeched up the stairs to recall me to my senses.

"Dinna I just tell thee? This be a respectable house..."

I moved my lips away and Damion held me to his chest. "I left him no shadow of doubt of the fate that awaits him if he dares set foot on my land again. Will you please come home?"

I pressed closer and nuzzled into his neck as every fiber of my being answered, along with my voice. "Yes. Please, take me home."

Damion kissed the top of my head. "Gather your things. Hubert waits outside with the carriage."

I walked into my room, scooped the contents of the space beneath the floorboard onto my shawl and folded it into a parcel. The rest I left. Damion tucked my belongings under one arm and offered me his other. "My Lady?"

I laid my hand on his forearm. "My Lord."

We walked down the stairs and Damion glanced at my dress. "Where did you obtain that garment, my sweet? It is truly revolting."

I looked at my shapeless gown. "Yes, but rather suitable if you are working in a tavern."

"A tavern? Yes, of course." He smiled. "Why I have searched any more respectable place of employment for you these past few months, I can't imagine." He retrieved his hat from Mrs. Pratt as we reached the end of the bottom flight.

"I thank you, Mrs. Pratt, for my room," I said. "If I leave under a cloud, I offer you my apology but would beg a last favor and ask you to give Mrs. Grey everything I've left in my room."

"Thas kind of you, and I will, but as I told thee, this be a respectable house an' not for females what thinks nothin' o' kissin' a nob in public."

Mrs. Pratt closed the front door behind us with a snap. I looked at the roadside, saw a hired, plain carriage with its window curtains closed, a boy holding the horse's head and Mr. Hubert perched on the box.

"I thought the Ashton crest might attract notice, as might I," Damion said. "Hubert sat in the coffee house opposite Mr. Whistlethorpe's office then followed you to Mrs. Pratt's while I waited in the carriage, out of sight."

I smiled toward the box as Damion opened the carriage door. "Mr. Hubert, I am very happy to see you."

Mr. Hubert returned my smile. "And I you. We have been a little out of sorts at Ashton these last months without you with us."

I climbed into the carriage as Damion held the door. "Perhaps we should stop at the Dog and Duck and inform them I will not be returning to work."

Damion swung into the carriage, shut the door and threw his hat onto the other seat as he reached for me. "Bugger the Dog and Duck."

I met his lips with mine as he pulled me close, his tongue hot and hungry in my mouth, and returned all my need of him with my own. I put my hand inside his jacket and plucked at the buttons of his waistcoat to unfasten them, then those of his shirt in my desire to touch his skin as he roved the contours of my body over my dress. I found his warm torso as he squeezed my breast, whimpered, tugged the skirt of my dress upward and kissed him harder. Damion slid his hand over my bare thigh as I slipped mine past the waistband of his trousers and toward the erection straining inside them.

I could not reach what I sought, so I withdrew my hand with a small moan, unfastened the buttons of his fly and released the length of his smooth, thick shaft to my caress as he sought the warm wetness between my legs. I parted them and he stroked through my sex as I moved his foreskin over his cockhead and back, both of us lubricated and ready. My skin heated to his touch as my center throbbed its need to feel his cock inside me and I moaned. "Oh God, I want you."

"Take me then," he breathed. "I have no shield but will say when I am close so you may withdraw."

I didn't hesitate but straddled his thighs, eased his cockhead inside me and moaned as I sank down the length his shaft and rocked to the motion of the carriage, my mouth pressed into his neck to muffle my mewls of pleasure. Damion grasped my buttocks under my skirt, his voice low in his throat. "How I've wanted you every day of these last months."

I rocked faster, my flesh feverish as his shaft rubbed. Damion grasped my rear harder and I ground down as I bounced, panting. Muscles tightened in my groin and I moved faster, the apex of my climax building. "Withdraw, my sweet," he murmured.

My muscles contracted around his cock and I tipped over the point of no return, to my wail. "I can't..." Wave upon wave of sensation pulsed out from my sex, spreading through my pelvis and into my thighs to his answering low groan.

"No. No more can I."

I stilled, panting into his neck. "Oh Lord, Damion! What have we done? A babe is not always the end result, is it?"

He held me to him, breathing hard. "No, sweeting. Couples that desire one would not have the difficulty some do to conceive if that were so. How far through your month are you?"

"About twelve days have passed since it."

He clasped me tighter. "Then we should be safe enough. The four days before a woman's flow pose the most chance of producing a child, according to Doctor Beckland, I believe." He tilted my chin. "But should there be a babe, I will have the paperwork drawn up to legitimize our child."

"You would want the child?"

Damion kissed my lips. "A child given to me by the woman that holds my heart? The woman who I would have wished to be my wife? A baby born of our union would be nothing but a joy to me."

My face heated and I buried my face in his shoulder. "I have not been used to being very much loved by anyone these last years."

Damion kissed the top of my head. "I know, but you will be. Do you not love me, too?"

Memories rushed through my mind at speed — of the boy who put up with me tagging along, who invented stories of ghosts or pirates for me, who laughed at my own boyish ways and the man who delighted me for more than the pleasure he gave to my body. "Yes, I do. I always have."

"Then whatever the outcome, all will be well."

The rhythm of the carriage changed with the sound of hooves and wheels on gravel. I eased off Damion's cock and we smiled into each other's eyes as we rearranged our clothing.

"The Dower House for being more private tonight?"

I smiled as the carriage halted and Damion picked up my shawl and opened the door. He climbed out and offered me his hand. "Return the carriage to the ostler's, if you please, Hubert. And also stop by the Dog and Duck Inn and inform them Amelia will not be returning to work there, if you would be so good?"

Mr. Hubert nodded. "I will be delighted to do so. And your hat, My Lord?"

"Is not required. See it back into my room, if you will?"

Mr. Hubert bowed his head. "As you wish, My Lord. I will return to the Dower House at nine of the clock tomorrow for your instructions."

Damion offered me his hand as the carriage drove away and opened the garden door into the morning room, where I saw no sign of Holland covers but a fire burning bright in the grate and smelled a savory aroma. Damion put my shawl parcel on the consul table and locked the door. "I requested the room be prepared and supper left in the warming oven in the hope of finding you today. Shall we take a glass of wine before we eat?"

I nodded my acceptance. Damion took a bottle and glasses from a cupboard, poured then placed them and the bottle on a side table and sat. I perched myself on his lap, curled my body against his and tilted my face for a kiss. He held me close and we kissed until we ran out of breath. I stroked the side of his face. "Tell me what occurred with Townley?"

He handed me my wine and took a sip of his own. "Mr. Whistlethorpe wrote that Townley was on his way north, not a month after you left, and he arrived at Ashton within three days of that. He was shown to Elizabeth's sitting room with me being occupied on estate matters with Mr. Martyn, but Bennett stopped by the library and told me of her visitor, so I joined her to find him inquiring as to his missing daughter who might be working as a maid and showing her a miniature of your likeness."

I drank my wine. "Mama must have given it to him, then, for there is only one and that was painted for her around the time of my sixteenth birthday. Elizabeth must have recognized me from seeing it?"

"She did." Damion nodded. "But to her credit, she made no reaction other than to excuse herself on the grounds of not having been living at Ashton for long enough to be familiar with all of its staff and she passed the portrait to me. I did not deny your employment here and I was about to inform him exactly what I thought of his behavior when I saw a way to spike his plans. I gave him my assurance that you had left here without notice more than a month previously, and to convince him, rang for Mrs. Price to add her confirmation to mine."

"Oh, poor Mrs. Price. My name and title are written on the arc of the oval, too. Was she as taken aback as was Molly?"

"As pinched around the nostrils but not as white-faced, although Ellen dropped the sugar tongs in great style and accompanied the gesture with a rather audible gasp."

My sense of the farcical raised its head to join Damion's and I snorted. "And?"

"And Townley went on his way while I gave Elizabeth the bare bones of your history as I felt were owed, then removed myself to London to make dutiful brotherly appearances at Emma's Season."

I giggled. "As you did for Georgina?"

"I appeared three times."

"Twice." I laughed. "I was there for the whole."

"So..." He smiled. "With Byng and Amabelle, I attended every event of the Season, and between us, we set our own whispers loose on the Town."

"Of?"

"Of how desperate must have been the treatment of the daughter of an Earl that the only course left to her was to flee her home, with our nods and winks toward the innuendo surrounding Townley circulating in the Society columns of the newspaper. I do not believe you will find any but the starchiest of matrons disapproving of you now, although I cannot say the same for your mama. My own is furious, as are several of her contemporaries."

"I can say no other than I believe Mama loved me but had no reserve of character to withstand Townley, and as she will never again enter Society, she will never face its disapproval."

Damion topped up our glasses. "That is for the best, I think."

I sipped my wine. "So?"

"So, when Townley returned to London, it was to find himself in very bad odor. I wrangled an invitation to his club, forced an argument on him and called him out."

"Damion!" I spluttered into my glass. "You could have been killed!"

Damion wrinkled his nose and drank. "I knew he would not accept my challenge, and as I expected, he wriggled, blustered and hedged, so I informed him, with plenty of witnesses to hear me, that henceforth he was persona-non-grata from all my property and land, and that any disregard of my edict would be dealt with under the law of common trespass. I cannot promise he will abide by my instruction, but you, I or anyone else can shoot him if he sets foot on Ashton land now, with the full weight of the law behind us, and Society will only give a cheer if we do."

I nuzzled into Damion's neck. "And I do thank you for the doing of it. I am very glad to be back at Ashton. I missed you so much."

Damion kissed into my hair. "And I you. But miserable as we have been, the outcome is happy if we no longer have to deny our relationship. You do not have to hide in the laundry any longer..."

I lifted my head and nibbled his chin. "If you are about to offer me an allowance to be in your bed, I am going to bite you" — I nibbled again — "very hard."

"I wouldn't dare." He laughed. "But there is the little matter of my racing stable. I have not the time to manage it with the devotion required to produce a Derby winner."

"You wretch!" I snorted. "The very thing you knew I could not resist."

Damion smiled. "I have had several months to think on it. You can keep the prize money earned."

"Half the prize money," I offered.

"Half the prize money," he agreed.

My stomach grumbled, having not been filled since my last meal at the Dog and Duck the evening before, and Damion patted my rear. "To the kitchen with you, my wench. Your tummy is giving out the noisier message of what my own is telling me."

I slipped off his lap. Damion picked up our glasses with the wine bottle as he stood and led the way to the kitchen. A lamp sat on the table and I lit it with a match from the Vesta box at its side then turned the wick up higher against the early evening darkness. Two place settings were laid, and I breathed in a familiar savory smell.

"Rabbit covered in onion stuffing?"

"What else for a supper that can be left warming and not spoil for hours?"

I took the dish from the oven, placed it on the table and lifted the cloche covering the breadboard as Damion put the wine on the table and pulled back my chair for me to sit. He sat beside me and looked expectantly at his plate. The steaming dish in front of me could easily have served four, so I spooned two-thirds of it onto his plate and a third onto my own.

"That's not very much," he said as he looked at my portion.

I buttered several slices of bread. "I am not a small woman but only stand five inches over five, not however many inches you are above six."

"Three, the last time Nanny Prout measured me against the wall." Damion admitted and cut into his rabbit.

I quartered a slice of bread and dipped a piece into my gravy. "Has she returned from the Trinion's?"

"The month before Christmas and has been happily putting the village to rights ever since."

I smiled as I pictured it then asked. "And Emma's Season? It went well?"

Damion nodded. "She married the Duke of Bradbury at Christmas."

"The Duke? And he is not so very much over forty."

"He was her choice and the one she set her cap for. Emma has ever enjoyed the baubles of her station and has a wish to add a few more. Mama is rather triumphant."

"I should imagine so." I smiled. "A fine catch — and in her first Season, too."

Damion took a slice of buttered bread. "Tell me of the Dog and Duck? I presume from the extreme beauty of your dress that you secured a position out of public view."

I sipped my wine before I answered and decided to make light of my time working there, so as to leave Damion with no doubt that I had returned to Ashton from my wish to be with him and not in any part because of the misery of my winter.

"I did. And with the addition of a large, ugly mop cap, walked to and from the inn to make my bread without attracting the notice of anyone at all." I stuck my nose in the air. "I can bake you seventy loaves of bread, both white and coarse, in any one day now, I'll have you know."

Damion laughed. "I declare that your culinary skills have become very fine when I add your breadmaking to the wonderous mess that was presented to me as a trifle. Did you also cook meals for yourself on the little trivet I saw in your room at Mrs. Pratt's?"

"Unfortunately, I will have to admit to my failings there." I sighed. "My meals were provided as part of my salary and the only action my dear little saucepan saw was to heat water so I could wash myself in between my visits to the public baths of a Sunday."

"The public baths?" Damion snorted with a short bark of laughter. "No! Truly?"

"A very fine establishment, indeed," I declared. "Twenty tubs to the women's room with hot water on tap and we females bathe in our shifts or smalls at a penny for the towel and another for the soap—a bargain when you consider that the laundry for the week is also complete when you step out of the water."

"You nearly make it sound like an experience that should be sampled, although I believe I will forgo doing so myself." Damion laughed. "Who is the Mrs. Grey you asked Mrs. Pratt to pass your possessions on to? A friend, like Molly? Did she go with you on your soapy outings?"

I ate a little more of my dinner before I answered. "No. She is a widow not sufficiently provided for by her husband, with a son who he may have expected to support his mother from the business he inherited but has declined to do so. Mrs. Grey ventures no farther than the church of a Sunday and the corner shop on other days to spend the few shillings a week that are her lot."

Damion frowned. "I will send my charity commissioner to her. She should not have to rely on such a thing. It is not right. A decent widow's portion should have been guaranteed if the business was successful."

"That is good of you." I smiled. "I do not think the cost would be great. She is a quiet lady. A few more shillings to ease her way is all that would be needed."

"The unfairness of your situation called my attention, but I find the whole issue vexes me more, the more I hear of it." Damion frowned. "I took my seat in the House when Parliament reconvened at the end of the summer recess."

"You have discovered a desire to enter politics?"

"I have." He smiled. "The law regarding a wife's property rights needs amendment, although it will be an uphill struggle. Even the most good-natured of men hold the opinion that females are not capable of rational thought for anything other than domestic matters. Then there are those that will oppose any suggestion that goes against their own self-interest. But still, there are some like-minded men, and it will be up to us to change the viewpoint of the others."

I toasted him with my glass. "I will hope for your eventual success, even if it has to be on behalf of women not yet born."

Damion laid down his knife and fork. "It may take that long, I'm afraid."

I stacked the dirty dishes, took them to the sink and washed them to Damion's grin at my domesticity. I looked at him as I laid down the washcloth, lowered my gaze to his cock then back to his face. His irises darkened as he stood and scooped me up. I unbuttoned the front of my shift as he carried me up the stairs, shrugged out of it and my dress when he laid me on the bed, and my skin heated as I watched him undress. His thick cock sprang free and my mouth watered as I looked at him as he gazed at me. "You are very beautiful naked, my sweet."

I licked my lips. "As are you. Let me taste you?"

Damion straddled me at my chest and offered his cock to my lips. I filled my mouth with the head of his shaft and sucked. His eyes closed. I swirled my tongue over and around his cockhead then drew harder, to his soft moan.

I pulled away to say, "How I've dreamed of this." I squeezed my breasts against his balls. "And this?"

Damion moaned and slid down my body, pressed my breasts to his face and feasted on my nipples to my whimpers of pleasure. I roamed my hands over his broad back and down to the roundness of his rear. He moved his face to my sex and I writhed as he lapped, licked and sucked. He lay over me, his cock poised. "You cannot get any more with child this night than you are or are not, with my seed already inside you."

I parted my legs and wrapped them around his thighs as he plunged his cock into my sex to my moan of delight as he filled me. I bit his shoulder as he nibbled my neck and we both panted and rocked faster. He grasped my breast, pinched my nipple and thrust harder. I met his movement hip to hip and dug my fingertips into his back as the muscles in my sex tightened. Damion stiffened and groaned. I pumped my hips against his, took what I needed from his cock and cried out my final pleasure as muscles spasmed through my groin.

He eased out of me, rolled onto his back and took me with him, wrapped in his arms, then kissed into my hair. "Don't leave me again, my love. Take me with you? I'd rather be Mr. Brown with you than here on my own without you."

"I won't leave," I promised. "I found it so very hard to be without you, too."

"Share my rooms with me as Letty does with Elizabeth? You will not find Elizabeth anything other than happy that you have returned to Ashton."

I nuzzled into his neck and agreed. "Yes, but as Amelia Brown, not The Lady Henrietta."

He pressed me closer. "As anyone you wish to be."

I tucked in tight to his side, the room lit by the glowing embers of the fire, and fell asleep to his soft caresses over my shoulder and down my back. I stirred twice in the night to the pleasure of being held in his arms and the comfort of a mattress that didn't crunch beneath me and nuzzled against his warmth each time as my eyelids closed again.

I woke in the morning and yawned to Damion's, "You slept well, love?"

I stretched. "I did."

He kissed the top of my head. "Stay there. I will see what I can do with the fire and draw you a bath."

I looked at the end of the bed and cast my expert tweenie eye over the fire. "A little thin, dry kindling and a puff or two from the bellows should bring you sufficient flame for the fire to be rebuilt."

Damion swung his legs out of bed, replaced his trousers and soon had the fire burning to take the March chill from the room, then walked to the bathroom to fill the tub and heat the room by way of steaming hot water. I drowsed for a few minutes then followed him in and sat in the bath in the V of his legs. He washed me and I washed him before we heard movement downstairs.

"That will be Hubert with breakfast and a change of clothes," Damion said.

He stepped from the bath and secured a towel around his waist. "He will not come up the stairs. I will retrieve my portmanteau from him and take it to the bedroom."

"If you would also bring up my shawl? My comb and clean shift are in it."

Damion shut the door behind him and I stepped from the bath, rubbed my skin and hair dry then walked to the bedroom, wrapped in a towel, to see Damion take a clean shirt, socks and his riding wear from his travel bag then lift out a wrapped package, which he offered to me. "To replace your black dress?"

I eyed the expensive wrapping on the package and hesitated to Damion's smile. "Come. It will not bite you. If I am permitted to provide your maid's working dress, I must also be allowed to provide an outfit that is suitable for the stables."

I gave in, smiled, took it from him then laid it on the bed, plucked on a ribbon bow rather than string and parted stiffened lilac paper instead of plain brown to see ankle-length stockings, a cream camisole and a blouse of fine lawn sat atop a navy-blue skirt and jacket. I lifted the skirt and shook it out to find it was not only a skirt but a pair of wide-legged trousers with a separate skirt in the style of a full-length kilt to go over them. I looked at Damion and let my delight show with a wide grin. "You bought me *trousers*?"

"Of course." He laughed. "The over-skirt will fold without creasing, so you may tuck it beneath your pommel when riding astride and replace it on your dismount."

I walked to him, pulled his head to mine and kissed him. "It is wonderful, and I thank you for it."

He smiled and patted my rear. "Dress, wench. Hubert is preparing our breakfast, and after it, we can walk to the stables."

I combed and pinned my hair into a chignon on the nape of my neck, dressed in my new clothes and found everything, including the close-fitting tailored jacket, a perfect size. "You guessed my measurements very well."

"I cannot take the credit." Damion smiled and offered me his hand. "I took your blue skirt and bodice with me when I visited the tailor to order it."

I put my hand in his and we walked down the stairs to see Mr. Hubert standing at the range, tossing kidneys and bacon in a fry pan. He gave Damion his half-bow. "Good morning, My Lord. Amelia."

"Good morning, Mr. Hubert. That smells very good. I didn't realize you were also a cook," I said.

"I will make no claim as to that, but I can rustle up a snack or two if needed."

Damion pulled my chair back from the table. I sat, smelled the heady aroma of Above Stairs breakfast coffee and poured from the lidded jug into two cups as Damion took his place opposite me. Mr. Hubert put a sizzling platter in the center of the table between us and looked at me. "Lady Ashton wondered if you would care to join herself and Miss Leticia to take tea in their sitting room at four o'clock today?"

"That is kind of her. Please tell her I would be delighted to do so."

"My Lord, your further instruction?"

"If you would repack my portmanteau and add Amelia's shawl with its contents, barring the brown dress, which you will oblige me by feeding to the furnace."

Mr. Hubert bowed and I waited for him to leave the room before I laughed. "You have consigned my beautiful gown to the fiery flames?"

"It is the garment from hell. Its fate is just."

I giggled and spooned the hot food onto our plates then buttered bread. After we ate, I washed the dishes to leave the kitchen tidy then laced my boots at the garden door and threaded my arm through Damion's to walk to the stables. A flutter of excitement to see everyone Below Stairs tickled my stomach as we walked, accompanied by a just little nervousness as to how they would greet me now that they knew of my title.

We encountered no one on our way but saw the stable lads mucking out under Harry's supervision when we entered the yard. He looked in our direction and his eyes widened before his gaze slid away and he gave Damion his half-bow. His shoulders turned as if he were about to do the same to me, so I stopped him with a stamp of my foot. "Harry Burton, don't you dare!"

"But...um, you're titled now." He flushed.

I shook my head with a smile. "I always was and have as much want to be bowed and curtsied to now as then. Tell me instead how it goes for you and Daisy, for I have been months without news."

He glanced at Damion's face, found nothing on it but a look of polite inquiry and he relaxed. "We go on very well and would hope to go to church sometime next year."

"I wish you both to be very happy." I smiled. "And Molly?"

Harry finally returned my smile. "Is well, but lost another tooth at Christmas. She didn't eat the fudge to your design but rather several small pieces of it every day."

I laughed. "I should have encouraged her to eat her fill on the night of the cricket match. Do not tell her I am home when you sit to lunch? I will call at the laundry this afternoon."

Harry nodded and Damion said, "Bring the new mare out for Amelia, then saddle Prince, if you will."

Harry walked into the stable block and I looked at Damion. "A new mare? More suited to Prince than his harem?"

The gleam lit his eyes. "Of a very superior bloodline, I believe. You must give me your opinion."

I considered the gleam, but before I could question it, I heard her whinny and my hands shook to the frilly tremble that ran through me to my equally frilly squeal. "You've purchased her? You have my Star?"

Damion grinned and I threw my arms around his neck and kissed all over his face without caring that the stable lads were there to gawk, then let him go and ran to her as Harry led her through the stable door. Star put her head on my shoulder to greet me as I reached her. I pressed my cheek against hers, placed my hand on her neck to her gentle snickers of welcome and cooed, "Hello, my beautiful, girl. Did you wonder where I'd gone?" She rubbed her cheek on mine then raised her head and I gave her my kiss and blew over her nostrils.

"You know her, then?" Harry grinned and offered me her reins.

I took them close to her bit, noted the astride saddle and returned his smile. "She was mine once but sold from me."

Harry gave me a ghost of a wink then walked toward the stable to fetch Prince. I pulled on Star's reins and walked her to Damion. "Was she still at the Sherringhams'?"

He nodded. "I viewed the blood stock register at the Jockey Club and saw she had not been sold and that the price they had paid Townley for her was well below her value. Byng's second cousin Chuffy put in my bid for me to disguise my interest. I got her at a good profit to them but still below her market value."

"And you think she is a good match for Prince?"

Damion looked into my eyes. "Maybe she is or maybe she is here to plead my cause if I'd needed a little more persuasion to entice you home."

I stroked my fingertips along his jaw. "You never needed that—just for me to know that my presence here will not damage you and yours."

He took my hand to his lips, kissed and released it as Harry led Prince from the stables. Prince tossed his head and snorted his impatience for his ride. I looped Star's reins, released the two buttons that held my skirt in place, folded it and tucked it under the front of my saddle then walked her to the mounting block to the hint of a snigger from Stanley as he looked at my trousers.

I swung my leg over her back, settled onto the saddle, found my stirrups and nudged her on for Damion to use the block and mount. Harry offered me a crop as Damion threw his leg over Prince's back and we trotted out of the yard to the sound of Stanley's 'ow' as Harry cuffed him around his ear for his cheek.

"Will you give her head when she is warmed?" Damion asked. "I'm too heavy for her, so Harry's been riding her out and I have not asked him to do so."

"I'd like nothing better." I smiled. "I'll warm her with a couple of turns around the field."

I trotted Star on, her high-stepping, prancing gait in marked contrast to Prince's. I put my leg back and moved her into a canter after the first circuit then crouched over her back with shortened reins in racing stance and kicked her on with a swish of my crop on her rear flank. She stretched her legs and I body-lined over her neck, jumped the first hedge then let her have her head until we sped over the ground at her flat-out sprinting gallop.

Five fields later, I felt her begin to blow and slowed her to see Prince still near two fields behind us. I walked her around until Prince powered into the field, having barely broken a sweat.

"She is certainly fast," Damion said. "I don't believe I've seen any that could match her from a standing start. I'd like to time her over flat ground."

I patted her neck. "Even without jumps, a mile is her limit. The Thousand Guineas as a three-year-old may have suited her, but never the Derby."

"But a mix of her coupled with Prince's superior power and stamina?"

"May be a prospect," I agreed, "if nature should deign to design a foal in the proportion of each that would be needed. Have you viewed any other fillies to provide Prince's best chance of siring the winner?"

Damion looked into my eyes. "I've heard some American fillies may be worth a visit to those shores if you would like to do so?"

"A lucky guess or...?" I smiled.

"Or I may just have overhead Mr. Martyn make an inquiry of Molly on the subject when he noticed the new maid walking to the drying yard with her, rather than you."

I turned Star to walk beside Prince as we set off across the field back in the direction of Ashton. "I have an ambition to visit New York when I am of an age to be able to travel freely."

"We could travel incognito as Mr. and Mrs. Brown?"

"And conceal any hint of a title from potential sellers, so they do not up the price." I smiled.

Prince snorted his impatience at Star's delicate prance, so I shortened my reins and nudged her into a faster trot for his comfort, then a little faster to make the jump for the first hedge. Prince powered over it and I called to Damion, "I ran her to her length. I'll bring her back at a slow canter if Prince needs to stretch his legs." He nodded, kicked him on and I relaxed Star into an even pace and trotted into the stable yard to see Prince being rubbed down by Stanley while Damion waited at the standing post. I picked up my skirt, sprang from her back, looped and tied her reins and refastened it around my waist.

Damion offered me his arm and I threaded mine through his and said, as we walked to the Manor, "You have missed your luncheon. You should eat."

"And you?" He smiled.

"Have been rising at five and have breakfasted today much later than I normally would. I will go and gossip with Molly until it is time for tea."

Damion kissed my hand. "You will find me in the library after."

I left Damion at the portico to the front entrance, walked to the back of the house then through the yard and over to the laundry, while removing my jacket for it being a little too 'Above Stairs' smart. The door handle felt familiar in my hand as I twisted it open and walked inside to see a maid I did not recognize and Molly's back as she replaced a jar of dried lavender onto a shelf. The maid moved as if to bob. I shook my head to stop her, laid my jacket on the ironing table and waited until the jar was secure in its place before I said, "Molly."

She froze then turned, her face alight to match my grin as she squealed. "Am? Holy cow, I don't believe it! You did come back!"

I was glad to see her lost tooth was not missing from the front of her mouth, laughed and held out my hands. "Yes, I have. And I'm going to manage the Ashton racing stable, so I'm here to stay."

Molly danced forward and put her hands in mine. I squeezed and kissed her cheek as she kissed mine. I let her go, perched my rear on the ironing table and boosted myself upward to sit. Molly took her ease by sitting on the floor with her back resting against the wall then said. "He came like you said he would. I'm sorry, Am, but everybody knows who you are now."

I wrinkled my nose. "I know. I heard Ellen was in the room when he was here. I just hope it doesn't mean I'll get the cold shoulder from everybody now. Harry nearly bowed to me in the stable yard earlier until I stamped my foot and told him to pack it in."

"He did?" Molly grinned. "I would have thought he knew you better than to do that."

"As would I." I laughed.

The bright green gaze of the new maid looked back and forth between us and Molly said, "This is Natalie — or more usually, Natty."

I smiled at her. "Hello, Natty. I'm Amelia."

She looked at Molly. "That's the one what's really..."

"Yes, that one," Molly said. "Now, take the basket to the field and pick in the washing."

I waited for the door to shut behind her before I said, "I know there will be a difference now everyone knows who I am, but I hope that those who were my friends before they knew of it will not withdraw from me because of it."

"Those that did not know you very well when you were here before may," Molly said, "but I will not, no more will James. Then there's Harry, now you've put him straight—"

"Along with Mr. Hubert and, hopefully, Ellen, Fred and Bert," I added.

"Will you live Above Stairs now, Am?"

I nodded. "Sort of, but not as such. I have no wish to live the life of a Lady again. I didn't enjoy it when I did, and now that I've lived as not one, I know which I prefer. I will be sharing Damion's rooms, though, as Letty does Elizabeth's."

"It sounds very odd to hear you say their first names so informally," Molly said, "especially His Lordship's."

"My earliest memories of Damion are from when I was three and he was nine." I smiled. "Children are not interested in titles. I called him by his first name then as I do now that he's my lover."

"Except when he's William." Molly grinned.

"His second name along," I reminded her, "as my third name along is Amelia."

"I'm glad Amelia is one of your real names," Molly said. "How many more do you have?"

I shook my head and laughed. "Enough and none. They are gone now."

Natty opened the door and lugged in the basket of laundry to be ironed as the chimes of the church clock sounded four. "And now I believe I have an appointment to drink a cup of tea with Damion's wife."

Molly snorted. "Holy cow!"

I raised my eyes heavenward. "Ah, well, the things we do for love."

I left Molly still sniggering and replaced my jacket as I walked to the front of the house. James jumped from the hall chair as I walked through the front doors and tipped his head. I side-swiped his arm. "That's quite enough of that, I thank you. Or the next time I bowl at cricket practice, my ball will be heading straight for your middle wicket."

James' eyes lit up to his grin. "Molly will not like it if you do."

I laughed. "I've just come from the laundry. I've missed her so much while I've been away, as I have you and everyone at Ashton. I'm so happy to be back."

"As I am to see you," James said.

"Get your arse back on that chair then. I know my way up."

I walked up the carpeted stairs to the third floor, made my way along the familiar hallway, tapped on Elizabeth's sitting room door and walked in as her voice answered, "Enter." Fashionably and acceptably a few minutes late, I saw the tea tray had already been delivered as Elizabeth and Letty rose from their chairs to greet me.

"Lady Henrietta, you are most welcome," Elizabeth said.

Letty gave me her curtsey to the correct depth for my title and I joined in with the pointless etiquette and inclined my head to acknowledge her respects, then curtsied to Elizabeth as she did the same to me with my knees bending just a little more than hers in lieu of her superior married status, while I murmured, "How kind."

I straightened and looked at her. "I thank you for the acknowledgment of my title, but I believe we will go on more comfortably if we waive the niceties in the future?"

Elizabeth sat. "Yes. Tiresome, aren't they?" She picked up the teapot and poured. "Milk? Sugar?"

I perched on the chair opposite her while Letty sat at the end of the chaise lounge. I looked into the cup, saw the pale color of Earl Grey and replied. "Neither. I thank you."

She passed me my cup and saucer then Letty hers. "I am glad to see you back at Ashton. I am not so very well acquainted with my husband, as you know, but I would see him happy, which he was not while you were gone."

I sipped. "But you know the reason for it and for my being here in the first place?"

Elizabeth inclined her head. "I do. How do you mean to go on?"

"As I always have at Ashton—as Damion's lover and Amelia Brown, with just a little less secrecy than we had to employ previously. Lady Henrietta will still have to appear on occasions, but they will be as infrequent as I can manage."

"I respect your choice," Elizabeth said.

I placed my cup and saucer on the table. "I thank you for it. If we have any matter of import to discuss going forward, perhaps the invitation to take tea could be the signal for it?"

"Excellent," Elizabeth said and smiled.

I stood, left her sitting room and went to find Damion in the library.

Chapter Fourteen

Over the next few weeks I settled into my new way of life at Ashton, living Above Stairs but not part of it, with my refusal to be waited upon and by not entering any formal room apart from the private rooms I shared with Damion and the library. The majority of my day I spent at the stables, the rest, sitting at the desk compiling a register for myself of the pedigree and bloodlines of the winners of all major races for the last ten years. My breasts grew heavier and my nipples more sensitive with a continued absence of my flow. Damion began to glance hopefully at my belly, but neither of us said a word about the possibility of a child until the day Mr. Whistlethorpe's letter arrived.

Damion held it in his hand, a frown on his face as he entered the library in search of me. "Townley's coming north again, possibly on his way to the Kendell estate. A carriage bearing the Rockingham crest was spotted leaving London in the direction of the Great North Road yesterday."

I put my hand on my belly, as a need to protect that I didn't know I possessed coursed through me in sparkles of fizzing anger. "Then it is time to end the matter. The man has plagued my life for long enough. I refuse to be constantly looking over my shoulder for him going forward."

Damion looked at where my hand rested. "You are intending to hunt him down and make an end to him?"

"No," I snapped. "I am intending to entice him to set foot on your land, *then* I'm going to make an end to him. His influence has been the bane of my life for the last eleven years. It will not be the bane of any other's for even so much as a second."

I saw hope light Damion's eyes as he walked forward and took my hands. "Any other, my sweet? You believe we have made a child?"

I looked into his eyes. "I have missed my flow this week for the third time, my breasts are heavier than ever and my nipples tender for more than the reason of your mouth."

"Yes. They are, aren't they?" he agreed, his voice sounding a little smug.

I looked at the delight dawning on his face and laughed. "You look mightily pleased with yourself, My Lord."

"Don't I?" He grinned and scooped me up into his arms. "And that would be because I am."

Damion sat with me on his lap, put his lips on mine and I opened my mouth to his tongue as he deepened our kiss. I stroked along his jaw when we parted. "The baby will be born when I am still a month short of my majority. Townley can have it made a ward of the court under his guardianship during my pregnancy, whereas you cannot legitimize an unborn and have to wait until after the birth to make our child legally yours. I don't dare imagine the amount he would try to bleed you for to hand you the legal rights to your child."

Damion nodded. "And much as he has no knowledge of it, I would pay. So, how do we entice him?"

"He does not know I possess my pistols. If he believes I'm vulnerable and alone somewhere isolated on the very boundary of your land, I think he will risk a few steps onto it for the payoff he stands to gain. A witness who could just happen to be passing by to hear his threats and see my response to them would be ideal, if you can think of one."

"Not immediately, but I will. We have at least two days grace before he gets anywhere near York."

I gazed into the distance and pictured it. "We need two persons he is not familiar with to watch the Great North Road twenty miles or more out from York. When his carriage passes them, they will wait until it is not quite out of sight then fall in behind it—just fellow travelers on the same road. Townley will require a change of horses before York. They will pull up at a posting inn after him, and whether in the yard or the dining room, they will gossip within his hearing of the young Lady who ran away from home to find work as a maid but now exists in lonely, miserable poverty at…"

I looked at Damion.

"At the abandoned gamekeeper's shack to the side of the road just before you enter the Ashton Estate."

"Is there one?"

"No, but there will be as of tomorrow and it will stand just inside my land, not out of it. When he threatens you, I can step forward, remind him of my edict for the benefit of the witness and take care of him."

I shook my head. "No. If he decides to act on our misinformation, he will have his man Perry and groom Taylor with him. He is an underhanded bastard and they are his creatures. He may well confront me to engage my attention while sending one or both of them to circle around behind and take me from the rear. My aim is true. I can shoot what is in front of me, if you will protect my back?"

Damion kissed into my hair. "Our plan builds, and we have a little time to tidy the loose ends. Will you kill him?"

I nestled into his neck. "No. After eleven years of all he has done, I find I am not feeling that kind."

Damion put his hand on my belly. "A baby, though. Our child. I didn't mean for it to happen any more than you did, but since it has become a possibility, I have done nothing but hope."

I tucked in tighter. "I am glad."

* * * *

The next day, Mr. Hubert departed from Ashton in a plain, hired carriage with James alongside him on the box and Stanley following behind, mounted on Storm, to race back to Ashton and give us notice if Townley was intercepted. In the afternoon, Harry walked with Daisy to the vicarage to enquire of the Reverend that if he managed to obtain a little free time in the next day or two, would he walk out with them and impart his wisdom on the attributes for a happy married life, while Damion and I went about our normal business so as to give the rest of the house no reason to suspect

337

anything was amiss. I sought Mrs. Price that evening and took possession of the most decrepit dress in her cupboard with my excuse of a very dirty job at the stables in the morning.

Stanley cantered into the stable yard the following day just before the lunch bell rang and said, without the least inkling of the import of his message, "Mr. 'ubert says as they've stopped for a bite to eat and a change of 'orses."

Damion looked at me. "Shall we walk back to the house for luncheon?" I nodded my acceptance, turned alongside him and we sped up the pace as we entered the cover of the trees, the pistols in the pockets of my dress, banging against my thighs.

"It is a pity we can't travel mounted," he said.

I increased the pitch of my stride and walked faster. "We cannot have the sound of a neigh or a whinny give him pause."

We arrived at our hovel, newly created from weathered boards, and stepped inside it. Damion lit a dry nugget of fuel in a tin container to send smoke signals of it being occupied out through the flimsy roof, while I walked outside and strung a plaited cord between two branches and draped a bright red table covering over it. Then we looked out of the door and waited until a carriage appeared in the distance. Damion kissed my lips. "I will have you in full view."

He slipped around the back of the shack while I stepped out of it to gather pieces of kindling I did not need and patted my pocket as my heart raced when a crunch of bracken warned me of someone approaching.

I turned and stared into Townley's loathsome face then lifted my chin and gave him what I hoped was a look with all the disdain I felt for him showing on my face. "So, you have found me, for all the good it will do you. I will not marry Spittlemore and you can do nothing to force the words from my mouth."

His eyes glittered. "You will not diddle me out of your value. You will do so, or you will find yourself the centerpiece of my next entertainment for a group of Gentlemen who pay dearly to watch my punishment of a disobedient female. You will sob and beg as loudly as any of the others as I stripe your flesh with my crop, while my audience bid and out-bid each other for which of them will be the first to take you while the others look on and wait their turn."

My stomach roiled. I put my hand in my pocket and gripped a pistol. "What others?"

Townley curled his lip, his face a picture of crude enjoyment to further sicken my stomach. "The slums of the city are awash with spare daughters that may be bought for a few pounds from a father desperate to feed the rest of his family. I am kind, though. I give the girl a guinea in the morning and let her go, as I will *not* you. You will heal and I will use you over and over until I have my price."

My bile rose as I pictured his victims — innocent girls of poor families that in my head all looked like Molly. I pulled my pistol from my pocket and cocked it to the sound of bone hitting bone behind me.

Townley backed away. "Where did you get that? You will be hung for murder if you pull the trigger."

I took aim and spoke clearly for the benefit of any audience. "You are on Ashton land, when you have been informed that your doing so is a matter of willful trespass, Sir. You are as guilty of that as any common poacher."

Townley's face whitened and he gazed behind me. I hissed under my breath as I sent my first bullet into his shoulder. "If you are waiting for your groom to appear back there, he will not come." I put my second bullet into his valet's leg as he lurched forward and my third into the elbow of Townley's whip hand to the vicar's — for once — welcome voice behind me.

"Outrageous, Sir! I have never heard words of confession that disgusted me more!"

I stood over Townley and hissed again as he rolled on the ground and moaned out his pain. "My pistols were a present from Papa, given to me for dealing with scum such as you." I sighted his undamaged elbow and fired, then used my last bullet to shatter his knee. "And, henceforth, you will not be wielding your crop to abuse anyone's daughter."

The vicar harrumphed behind me as I replaced my pistol into my pocket. "Well said and well done. A fitting justice, indeed."

I turned and saw Harry had held Daisy at a distance while the vicar had hurried forward and I nodded in the direction of the Manor. He nodded his understanding and led Daisy away. Damion made his presence known, stepping out of the shadows, and walked forward to survey Townley writhing on the ground. His valet sat beside him, giving voice to his own pain and clutching his leg. "A vile creature and one I banned from my land."

"I couldn't agree more, My Lord," the vicar said.

Damion turned to him. "I would be obliged if you would return to your vicarage and prepare your written testimony of what you witnessed here today."

"I will," the vicar agreed. "Although it will disgust me as I remember his words in the writing of them."

"But still, it must be done," Damion said, "and preferably while they are still fresh in your mind."

The vicar acknowledged his dismissal. "Of course. Of course. I will set to it immediately, My Lord."

I waited for him to pass out of sight then walked over to Townley and surveyed my handiwork. "There is not sufficient blood for their wounds to be fatal. They will not bleed out, I think. Where is his groom?"

"It would serve them right if they did," Damion said. "I knocked out his groom and have left him behind the shack."

I nodded, took my second pistol out of my pocket and cocked it. Townley's valet's face drained of what little color it still possessed as I aimed and fired, first into his knee then into his shoulder. He screamed at the first shot and fainted at the second. I turned to Damion. "Did his valet think I might let him off with only a wound that may be recovered from and leave him able to come after me again with thoughts of revenge, do you suppose?"

"He is a fool if he did." Damion shrugged. "The first bullet you put in him should have been enough to tell him you are not squeamish."

I walked with Damion to the rear of the shack and used my last three bullets to mete out the same treatment to Townley's unconscious groom, already bleeding from his mouth, his jaw hanging at a very odd angle. I pocketed my pistol as Damion said, "It is over, my sweet. Let's find their carriage and send them on their way."

I put my hand in his and walked to the lane and down it until I saw the coach and four with my own crest on its doors and our Alain Coachman perched upon the box. Alain looked as I approached and his mouth fell open before his face creased with pain. "My Lady? What evil has that devil led me to now?"

My time Below Stairs provided my answer. "Nothing that has been done here today is due to you. The fault lies only with your employer. Follow along behind us with the carriage, if you please."

We walked back to the shack and I motioned Alain to halt, then opened the carriage door while Damion walked on and returned holding Townley by the scruff of his jacket and the seat of his pants and put him inside, to Alain's stare. Next, he fetched the valet then the groom and I slammed the door shut on them with my instruction to Alain.

"Return him to my mother at Gosmouth with my compliments and my advice to her to order him a wheeled bath-chair and make herself an appointment with a decent Land Agent to recover what she may for the estate, now that Townley will no longer be spending its revenue."

Damion tossed Alain a pouch of coins. "For the change of horses along the way."

Alain nodded without a word, cracked the whip and turned the carriage, but I caught the glimpse of a smile on his face as he drove past us. Damion put his arms around me and pressed me to his chest. "A fitting end to make of him, my love. Our child will be born with nothing to fear."

The tension drained from my shoulders as I relaxed in his hold. "In another month, the swell of my belly will be noticeable. Elizabeth must be told before then."

Damion smiled and offered me his hand. "We will tell her together."

I put my hand in his and we walked back to the Manor.

* * * *

The month passed, and as I had guessed, my belly swelled past being hidden, even by altering the position of the buttons on my over-skirt to accommodate it, so I invited Elizabeth to take tea. She made the telling of my pregnancy to her easy as she sat and I poured, by looking at my stomach with a smile and asking, "There is to be a child?"

I returned her smile. "Near Christmas, all being well."

I handed her her cup and saucer and she looked at Damion. "I am happy for you. You will put the paperwork in order to ensure the child may inherit?"

Damion nodded. "As soon as the babe is born."

"Then let us leave no room for opportunistic cousins to be able to question the matter in the future. Have the paperwork drawn up for me to legally adopt the child with you? Make the three of us an unbreakable triumvirate?"

Damion's eyes searched mine and I smiled, feeling nothing but happy for Elizabeth to be named alongside me as a mother of my child, to protect its inheritance, and said, "That is very generous of you."

The small bead of anxiety left Damion's eyes and he seconded my sentiment. "Very. And I thank you for it. I will have both sets of paperwork drawn up at the same time."

Elizabeth sipped her tea. "As I thank you. I had no expectation of being happy at Ashton when I visited at the time of our betrothal but have found happiness here such as I would have never dared to imagine at the time. I will always make your child's best interests mine."

Damion smiled. She placed her cup and saucer on the table and left us.

* * * *

My belly became obviously big with child as the year passed through autumn. November saw the re-establishment of Nanny Prout in the Manor to set up the nursery and December, the arrival of the midwife, Mrs. Goody. I became restless as Christmas appeared on the horizon with my stomach becoming so engorged as to make physical exercise nigh impossible and unspoken qualms settled over me of the size of the child to be birthed. My comfort and respite I found in Damion's arms each night as he held me, and we satisfied our need for each other using the only position still possible to us, him spooning into my back and easing into my sex from behind, until the morning before Christmas Eve when I swung my legs out of bed, put my feet to the floor and a flood of water—not of my making—ran down my legs.

I clutched the side of the bed as muscles tightened across my stomach without my asking them to and gasped at the ripple of pain crossing my abdomen. Damion woke and sat upright. "Amelia? The baby is coming?" I nodded. Damion put his feet to the floor. "I'll ring for Mrs. Goody."

The pain receded. I took a deep breath in. "No, it's gone now. But I think you should dress."

Damion walked into his dressing room and returned in no more than five minutes. He took one look at my whitened fingers grasping the bedcovers and pressed the call button of the bell set onto the wall beside the fireplace. "Come, love. Let me help you onto the bed."

I sat on the side of the bed, and with the support of his arm, moved nearer the center of the mattress then rested my back against the backboard as Damion lifted my legs. The pain and squeezing ceased and my breath came easier. I stroked my fingertips over the stubble on his jaw and took in his tie against the creases of yesterday's shirt that would still have had its collar attached. I opened my mouth to tease him about it when the contracting pain came and, instead, clenched my teeth against the squawk that would have taken the place of any words. I heard the tap on the door as the pain died away and clutched Damion's arm. "Don't leave me completely. Don't agree to it if she suggests your place is to wait downstairs."

"I won't leave you." Damion smiled. "I will remove to our sitting room and will be just on the other side of the door."

I clutched tighter. "Don't allow her to close it all the way. She's not to shut it tight. Leave it a little bit open so I can call to you if I need you."

Damion took my hand to his mouth and kissed. "They will not lock me out, sweeting. I promise."

I nodded and Damion called, "Come in."

Mrs. Goody opened the door and stepped into the room, the handles of her black bag over her arm and several copies of the newspaper tucked under it. She looked at the puddle on the floor beside the bed. "We are well on our way then, My Lady, as I can see." She looked expectantly at Damion then at the bedroom door. He kissed my cheek, stood and nodded at the sitting room door.

"You may close the bedroom door, Mrs. Goody. I am leaving through that one."

Damion opened it, stepped through and faded from Mrs. Goody's notice as I gritted my teeth against the next wave of pain. "They come then they stop."

Mrs. Goody walked to the bed. "As they should, My Lady...as they should." She waited for my face to relax then pulled a birthing sheet from her bag — and a spare. "If you would move to one side, My Lady?" I did so and she laid a thick layer of newsprint under where my rear had been then topped it with a sheet. "If you would move onto it, My Lady?"

I did so and made my own request. "May we dispense the 'My Lady'? I would prefer to hear your directions to me spoken plain and clear."

She patted my hand and relaxed into the earthy manner I had sensed when I had interviewed her and engaged her services. "Yes, dear. Now pop your shift up around your waist, I'll lay the courtesy sheet over your knees and we shall see how you do."

She waited for my next contraction to fade then made her investigation between my legs. "Very good, dear. All is as it should be. You must have slept through your early labor. You will not be more than an hour or two bringing this one forth, I believe."

I grunted my thanks as my next wave of agony caught me, and Mrs. Goody reached into her bag and offered me a leather birthing strap. "It is scraped first then boiled to fresh between every use." I took it, twisted the ends around each of my hands and bit my pain onto it as the tightenings of my stomach sped up and the intervals between the pain lessened until I could hardly catch my breath between the finish of one and the start of another. I ground my buttocks into the mattress as the pain altered and my stomach rose up without my permission to my wail. "It's coming out of my rear..."

Mrs. Goody patted my hand. "No, dear, it just feels like that." She peered beneath the courtesy sheet and I felt her hands at work as my stomach rose again. "That's it. Grind into the mattress and push downward, dear. The head is crowning."

Time melted with another pain, then another and another to Mrs. Goody's instruction. "Bear down...push, push, push. Breathe. Bear down...push, push, push. The head is out. A little more effort, if you please, and we shall see the babe."

I ground my rear into the mattress and felt relief between my parted legs as the pain suddenly stopped and Mrs. Goody said, "And here he is...a little Lord, safe and sound. I'll cut his cord."

She reached into her bag and pulled out a reel of thick black thread with a thin bladed silver knife as Damion's voice, full of barely restrained emotion, sounded through the gap in the door. "The baby is here? All is well? It is a boy? I have a son?"

"You do," I called with a smile as she wrapped Henry and offered him to my arms, but before I could take him, my stomach tightened again to my gasp of pain. Mrs. Goody stiffened. "The coming of the afterbirth should not hurt." I bit down on my leather strap. She opened the bottom drawer of the escritoire and laid Henry in it as I moaned with the renewing of my pain. She peered beneath the courtesy sheet and said, "He was the first of a pair."

I ground my rear into the mattress and shouted it out. "Damion! One night, one baby, you said."

"We are having more than one?" he said, his voice alive with more delight than I currently needed to hear.

The next pain caught me. "Damn it! Yes, and take that grin off your face. I can hear it, you know."

Mrs. Goody's hands worked to my stifled groans until she smiled. "A little Lady this time. There, there, dear. Take your ease now."

I relaxed against my pillow, took a deep breath in and Mrs. Goody cut Rose's cord and wrapped her. I took her into my arm as something slithered out of me without pain. Mrs. Goody peered then tugged and a second something passed between my legs. "Two afterbirths and both intact. Your travail is over and all is well."

I stroked my fingertip down my daughter's tiny face and resisted my urge to hold her to my breast and let her suckle. Mrs. Goody rolled blood and mess into the birthing sheet and newspapers then placed the bundle into her bag to take home and bury in her garden with a shovelful of lime. She folded the courtesy sheet then adjusted my shift over my thighs. "I will fetch your cleansing water."

I nodded. "If would you bring Henry to me first?"

She nodded. The door between the sitting room and bedroom opened and Damion stepped through to Mrs. Goody's startled, "You are a little premature, My Lord. Your Lady is not yet clean nor bound."

He walked to bed, sat on the edge of it beside me, looked into my eyes and stroked my wet and tangled hair. "She is beautiful, as always, and smells only of roses."

Mrs. Goody shook her head with a smile and brought Henry to us. Damion took Henry and I looked at the perfection of my babies' faces and the rise and fall of each tiny chest as they slept, with neither objecting to their entry into the world by crying.

Henry opened his eyes and gave his father a blue-eyed stare then closed them and returned to sleep while his mouth worked, suckling on nothing. Damion put the tip of his pinky finger on Henry's lips and Henry tried to draw it in. "Mrs. Goody, press the bell, if you please. My son appears in need of his supper."

A tap sounded on the bedroom door one second before it opened and Nanny Prout bustled in. Her eyes widened as she looked. "Master Damion! Two? You have been a very greedy boy, have you not?"

"Yes, Nanny, I have." Damion smirked.

Nanny stepped forward and plucked Henry from his arms. He smacked his lips as his mouth puckered in search of a nipple. Nanny looked at him and cooed. "Who's the hungry boy, then? Let's get you to Betty, little man."

She held out her other arm. I placed Rose into it and Nanny looked at Mrs. Goody.

"If you would come with me to open and close the doors?"

"My Lady is not yet refreshed," she replied.

"I will see to my Lady's comfort myself," Damion said. "You are excused to help Nanny, with our thanks for your skill."

Mrs. Goody's eyes goggled at the thought, but she refrained from comment, picked up her bag and followed Nanny out of the room. Damion swung his legs onto the bed. I moved under his arm and laid my cheek on his chest.

"You are tired, my love?" he asked.

"A little," I admitted. "And in need of a bath."

"I'll fill the tub and wash your hair while the bed is remade with fresh linen."

"Mmmm...yes. Shortly," I said and tucked tighter into his side as my eyelids fluttered.

"Two though, my love. When not long ago I didn't expect to ever be a father at all. They are perfect and beautiful, like their mama."

"Mmmm...yes. And as perfectly beautiful as their papa, too," I murmured as my eyes closed.

* * * *

Ten years later...

I sat at the desk in the library researching the bloodline of a stallion that interested me, but with less than half my attention on my task, as I listened for the sound of Damion's return from the Houses of Parliament while hoping for a good outcome when the members voted to pass into law, or not, the bill he had spent the last ten years campaigning for.

The door from the terrace opened and Henry walked in, so like his father at the same age as to fill me with proud wonder as I looked.

Rose, with no sign of her Papa's large frame but having features from both of us, walked in behind him, scolding. "Henry, you are supposed to hold the door open and allow me to enter the room before you."

"Yes," he said then shrugged, "but you put that frog in my boot for my feet to find this morning, so I didn't."

I could not hide my smile as I reproved them. "Manners, Henry. A Gentleman does not forget them, even in the face of an offensive frog. Rose, do not put frogs in your brother's boots. You will spoil the leather. Put them in his bed, instead."

"Mama!" Henry laughed.

Rose, wearing her newly fashionable cycling bloomers, stepped around him. "We pedaled to the village, Mama. Letty was placing fresh flowers on Mother Elizabeth's grave in the churchyard."

"We picked some poppies from the edge of the corn field and put them with Letty's lilies," Henry said then added, "even though we don't remember her being alive so very much."

"No, you wouldn't." I smiled. "You were only three years old at the time the influenza epidemic took her. But she was fond of you both and left her fortune to be shared between you. Letty will appreciate the kindness you have returned to her with the gift of your flowers."

I heard the crunch of wheels on the gravel of the drive at the same time as the children.

"Papa!" Rose squealed.

The smile on Henry's face widened and he walked to the library door and held it open. Rose rushed past her brother without a backward glance. I walked through it at a more sedate pace and inclined my head at the correct angle to acknowledge his courtesy. "I thank you, Henry. That is very kind."

"Yes. Yes, Mama, but hurry up, if you please," he huffed. "Papa will be in the hallway and I will still be holding this wretched door open."

Damion stepped in through the front door, handed his hat to Bert and received two armfuls of excited girl. He held her to him and kissed the top of her head as Henry walked forward with his hand outstretched. "Papa, I am very happy to see you home."

Damion caught my eye over the top of his head and I smiled with our knowing how much Henry would have liked the hug his sister had received, something no longer available to a big boy of ten. Damion shook

Henry's hand as manners dictated and replied, "As I am happy to be here, Henry," then ruffled his hair until it stood on end, to Henry's delighted grin.

The green door opened and Nanny Prout stepped through it. "There you are, you little tykes. To the nursery floor at once, if you please. Your papa does not require your noise after his long journey home, and there are currant buns awaiting toasting."

"Currant buns, Nanny?" Henry asked to Nanny's answering smile. "Oh, goody. Let us go up at once. I'm starving."

Nanny bustled away after the children. Damion looked at me and smiled, then looked at Bert. "Ask Bennett to put a bottle of champagne on ice, if you please? I will ring when I require it."

Bert gave his half-bow and I held my question back until Damion closed the library door behind us. "They voted in favor?"

He lifted me from my feet and swung me around. "At last. This time, yes. *The Married Woman's Property Act* passed into law on this day of eighteen-eighty-two. No longer will everything a woman owns become the property of her husband on the day they marry."

I laughed my delight. "After all these years? I can't quite believe it!"

Damion twirled again then sat on the sofa with me on his lap. I lifted my face for his kiss and he looked into my eyes as our lips parted. "So, is it enough? Will you finally make an honest man of me?"

I gazed back. "Well, I would...apart from there being that awkward little promise to *obey*."

The gleam lit his eyes. "Oh, and hiccup on the bey?"

I smiled. "I think maybe I will, then" — I urged his lips toward mine — "with perhaps just a little more persuasion."

Want to see more from this author? Here's a taster for you to enjoy!

The Girls' Club
Cassie O'Brien

Excerpt

The moon hid behind the trees to leave the path a dark trip hazard of exposed, misshapen tree roots for us to find. I grabbed Jules' hand to steady myself and giggled into the warm night air as I stumbled. Jules giggled beside me.

"Shouldn't 'ave had the last one, Ness."

"The B-52 or the pinta piña colada?"

Jules lurched against me as her shoe snagged and caught. I laughed and pushed her upright again.

"Both. Should'a got a taxi, though."

"Only gotta get through the par — "

Jules' chin hit her chest and her knees crumpled as the back of my head exploded with pain from a curled fist that I glimpsed out of the corner of my eye as my legs gave way. My butt hit the path and I joined my scream to Jules', kicked out with my foot and caught the thigh of the chunky male closing the gap between us with the high heel of my shoe.

"Fuck! You bitch!"

The man made a grab for my ankle. I brought my other leg up, kicked, caught his thigh again with the heel of my other shoe and screamed louder. Jules' shrill cry cut off with a crack of bone on bone.

"What the fuck you doin', man?"

"She's kicking me."

"Just shut 'er the fuck up!"

The man lurched forward and dropped his weight onto my legs, used it to stifle my struggles and cut off my voice with a hand clamped over my mouth and nose as I writhed beneath him. I fought for breath, aimed desperate fingernails at brown eyes beneath a knitted hat pulled down low and flashes of light swam before my eyes as a clenched hand connected with the side of my head.

"Get the fuck on with it! I've got the other one's jewelry and bag."

My arm was forced to my side and a heavy-heeled boot crunched down. My fingers were bent and twisted as my grandmother's eternity ring was yanked from my finger, my attempted high-pitched howl silent without air to give it sound. The chain of my necklace bit into my neck before it snapped. The flesh of my stomach caught fire as my belly bar was ripped from it without being undone. I curled into a fetal ball as feet ran away. I sucked air into my lungs in desperate gulps and my stomach heaved.

My butt hit the floor again and I woke, covered in sweat. I ran to my bathroom just in time to kneel and vomit into the toilet bowl. I kneeled straighter after my stomach emptied and my bedroom lit up over my shoulder.

"Ness? Another? So soon?" Jules asked from the bathroom door.

I nodded and flushed.

"I'll get you a water."

I ran the cold tap in the sink while Jules was gone, splashed my face and cleaned my teeth. Jules walked into my bedroom and handed me a bottle of mineral water as I straightened the duvet on top of my bed. I took the bottle and sat, legs out, my back against the headboard. Jules leaned back alongside me.

"So, walk me through your day."

I sighed and closed my eyes. Jules squeezed my hand.

"I know it sometimes seems pointless, babe, but it's got to be done. I'm sure there must be something that reminds you of the mugging and triggers a memory in your subconscious to make you dream about it, even if you don't recognize that something for what it is at the time."

I opened my eyes and drank a mouthful of water.

"It's been over three years since the attack, Jules. And still the dreams come and go for no particular reason that we can see. It does sometimes seem hopeless."

"Well, I'm not going for hopeless. Yes, the dreams appear randomly, none for three months then two this week, but that's the point. Something has got to be setting them off. So come on, girlie. Get on with it. Step me through your scintillating day in the back office of Belmond's of London."

I sat up straighter and squeezed Jules' hand.

"Thanks, Jules. I know it's tough on you, too, having to keep going backward. You were as badly hurt as I was."

"Yeah, but I don't get it all back in glorious technicolor when I'm asleep. So, yesterday, you got up, showered and walked to the bus stop. Take it from there."

I closed my eyes to concentrate and talked Jules through my very ordinary day. The queue at the bus stop, the passengers on the bus, a day at work in the office and we searched for a something—a pair of eyes that reminded me, a certain chunky body shape, beer on none-too-fresh breath, a piece of jewelry that looked similar to that taken from us—and came up with nothing, as usual. Jules put her arm around my shoulders when I finished.

"The trouble is that we've got so little to go on. It was so dark and once we were both down, we were in too much pain to take in the detail. But we're not giving up, Ness. We'll work it out one day."

I slipped my arm around my friend's waist.

"I hope so, because one thing I'm sure of is that I'm never going back on those tranquillizers the doctor gave me, even if I have to be like this until I'm old enough that I don't remember the bad stuff because my memory has leaked out through my ears."

Jules wrinkled her nose. "It was a bit like living with an automated puppet, babe. But the police have still got the DNA from under our fingernails. It'll make it better for both of us if they catch up with them one day."

I sniffed and rubbed my finger under my nose. "At least nobody will take us down like that again."

Jules sat up straighter. "Too right they won't. The Girls' Club has made sure of that. Anyone tries sneaking up on us like that and they're going to be the ones eating dirt, not us."

I let go of Jules' waist, picked up my phone and checked the time.

"It's nearly five. I'll try and get a couple more hours' sleep. If I go into work already yawning, I'll have nodded off at my desk even before the first coffee run at ten."

"Why don't you just tell the agency you'd prefer something else?"

I shook my head. "No, I'll have to see the rest of the six-month contract through at Belmond's. It'll look bad on my resume if I change jobs too quickly, although I could kill Liz at the agency. A challenging position in the finance department is what I asked for. A data entry payroll clerk is what I got."

Jules smiled and swung her legs off the bed.

"Yep, stunning use of your degree there, girlie. But you've nearly got the first month out of the way and at least you've got the Maisie, Annie, Jason thing to watch to stop you from falling asleep."

I slid down the bed and flicked my duvet over my legs.

"Well, Maisie was definitely the winner today by two coffees to one. And it's the big day tomorrow. The solid wall is coming down and the new half-glass one's going in."

I blew Jules a kiss as she turned my light out.

"Thanks, Jules."

"Night, Ness. See you in a couple of hours."

I slept and snoozed in fits and starts until the alarm on my phone trilled at seven and I arrived at work early enough to get a coffee from the machine in the corridor outside the office and take it to my desk. I nodded hello to Maisie and Annie, whose opposing workstations abutted mine then sat. They both lifted their faces and smiled when the main office door squeaked behind me.

"Hi, Jason," they chirped in unison.

"Morning, Annie, Maisie…Vanessa."

I watched their faces as Jason Peterson, my current boss, walked past my desk. Maisie and Annie turned their heads and gazed after him until he disappeared from their sight and shut his office door behind him. I waited. Maisie finally tore her eyes away and looked at me.

"The workmen will be in at ten."

I looked at the solid wall of Jason's office. Maisie followed my gaze and smiled.

"Vanessa, I think I'll take that workstation and you can have mine. We'll do it now before the office gets busy, if you don't mind."

"But, Maisie," Annie said. "What about me? We've always sat together."

Maisie dismissed Annie with a wave of her hand. "We'll still be opposite, but if I sit where Vanessa is, I'll be able see what Jason's up to without turning around. Don't worry. I'll keep you updated with what's going on."

I opened my workstation's drawer wider and took out the small store of stationery I'd accumulated during the first three weeks of my temporary contract while Maisie unloaded a rather larger accumulation from two years in a permanent position. I sat beside Annie, put my stationery away in less than a minute, picked up the cup tray that would allow me to hold multiple drinks and looked at Maisie arranging her pens and Post-it pads in her drawer.

"Is it too early for a coffee run? I could do with another dose of caffeine to wake me up this morning," I asked.

"No, that's fine. I'll have one, too." Maisie smiled.

I looked at Annie. She nodded.

"Okay. White without and white with one coming up."

I walked out of the office and into the corridor to where the drink machine stood in an alcove, tapped in the code for the first coffee and put the plastic cup in the drinks holder after the machine spat it out. The door from the office opened. Jason walked out and stood behind me. I looked over my shoulder and up quite a distance. Blond and at least six four, Jason towered over me, even with me in my heels.

I turned back to the machine and asked, "What code do you have?"

"Eleven. Just black, thanks."

I tapped in the code and offered Jason the cup when the machine finished filling it. Jason smiled his thanks as he took it and I turned to face the machine again.

"I see you've moved workstations."

I tapped in the same code as his for my own coffee and nodded.

"Yeah. I've swapped with Maisie."

Jason stepped alongside and looked sideways at me. "And that would have been your choice or...?"

I looked at Jason and saw from the half-smile tilting the corners of his lips that it was a question he already knew the answer to, so I gave him a reply he could take either way.

"Well, Maisie did say you've got a work crew in at ten. Perhaps she wants to face your office in case any eye candy appears along with your new windows."

Jason smiled. "Thought so. Never mind. It'll still be worth it to get out of the box."

"The box?"

"The office I worked in before this was open plan. I would have had the stud wall removed if I could, but our chairman, who still comes in and uses the office a couple of times a month, wouldn't have it, so we compromised on a half-way house."

"He does? But not this month then?"

"No. We're getting a month off for good behavior. He's away playing golf in Spain."

I picked up the coffees and turned in the direction of the office. Jason walked with me and opened the office door to let me walk in first. I thanked him over my shoulder and took the drinks over to Maisie and Annie, while Jason walked on and into his office for his last hour of not being on show.

I pulled my work tray forward and logged on to the payroll system. The workmen turned up at ten and Jason took his laptop into the meeting room next door to his office. The work was completed by lunchtime with the old stud partition coming down in sections and the new one going up the same way.

Maisie sighed as Jason walked into his new goldfish bowl. I spent the afternoon listening to a running commentary from Maisie to Annie every time he moved, only relieved by a short break to print three repetitions of hard copy of the data I'd input and leave them in the in-trays of other offices that might be interested in the figures. It was going to be a long week, I decided, when the following day I resorted to putting earbuds in and listening to music on my phone to escape the constant drone while Jason moved around the office, oblivious to the two sets of eyes that followed him everywhere. I bumped into him as he left the Human Resources office at four as I arrived there to drop off their hard copy.

"Are you okay? No problem, is there?" he asked.

I shook my head and showed Jason the report.

"No, no problem. HR just gets a printout of the figures I've input every day."

"They do?"

"And Facilities Management and Marketing. I've got no idea why. The same figures are available on the system."

"Thanks. I'll have a look at it. Let me know if you find anything else you're doing twice, will you?"

Two sets of eyes and one set of aching ears came to mind and I looked over my shoulder as I turned the handle on the HR office door.

"Two times everything where I sit in the office" — I slid my gaze down to Jason's tie. His gaze followed mine — "especially when you loosen that at lunchtime."

I opened the door, walked into the office and closed it behind me then put the timesheets in order for filing for the remaining hour of my working day. I spent the evening refreshing the playlist on my phone so I'd be ready to face another day of not listening to Maisie. When I went to bed, I said a quick prayer for no nightmares. Luck was on my side, because I awoke refreshed and ready to face Maisie and her antics once more.

Home of Erotic Romance

Sign up for our newsletter and find out about all our romance book releases, eBook sales and promotions, sneak peeks and FREE romance books!

About the Author

I love:
Being with family and friends.
Writing and having the freedom to do so now child four of four has passed her driving test and is off to uni later this year.

I like:
Any excuse to throw a party.
Any excuse to open a bottle of fizz.
Shoes in vast quantities — the higher the heel the better.
Ambitions:
To write many more books.
To own a pair of Louboutin's.
To never go near an iron or a hoover again.

Cassie loves to hear from readers. You can find her contact information, website details and author profile page at https://www.totallybound.com